When the steadfast Ruby Jane Whittaker drops out of sight, dogged ex-cop Skin Kadash sets out to discover what drove the woman he loves to leave her life behind so suddenly and without explanation.

The discovery of a dead man in Ruby Jane's apartment and an attack by a mysterious stalker send Skin from Portland to California—and into a charged encounter with her one-time love Peter McKrall.

As questions mount and answers grow increasingly out of reach, Skin and Peter cross the country on a desperate journey deep into Ruby Jane's haunted past—and toward an explosive confrontation which will decide their future.

Also by Bill Cameron
Lost Dog
Chasing Smoke
Day One

COUNTY LINE

COUNTY
LINE

BILL CAMERON

TYRUS
BOOKS

Published by
TYRUS BOOKS
1213 N. Sherman Ave. #306
Madison, WI 53704
www.tyrusbooks.com

Library of Congress Cataloging-In-Publication Data has been applied for.

12 11 10 09 08 1 2 3 4 5 6 7 8 9 10

9781935562351 (hardcover)
9781935562528 (paperback)

To K.D. James,
with thanks,
for Nash

And, always, to Jill

PART ONE

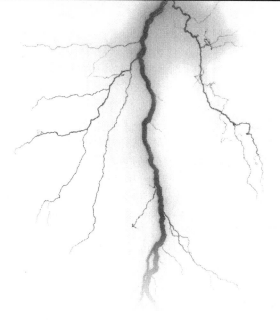

April 2008
Skin

1

No One Home

TO MY CREDIT, the first thing I don't do is go stand in the street outside her bedroom window, iPod in my pocket and portable speakers raised above my head. Not that she has a bedroom window—nothing so prosaic for Ruby Jane Whittaker. The point is I show uncharacteristic restraint and so—lucky me—miss out on the chance to watch a man die.

I've been away a month. Ruby Jane called it a retreat, a chance to get my head screwed on at last after a long winter brooding and recovering from a bloody confrontation which left three dead and me with a near-fatal gunshot wound. She's the one who found The Last Homely House, an out-of-the-way bed-and-breakfast near Manzanita esteemed for a breathtaking ocean view and the curative powers of its hot springs. When I asked if she'd chosen the spot because it sat in a cellular dead zone in a dale on Neahkahnie Mountain, she laughed and told me I'd have to hike into Manzanita if I wanted to call her. Doctor's orders were for lots of walking, but despite repeated marches down the mountain, I managed to reach her only a couple of times during my sojourn, the last a couple of weeks earlier. She hasn't picked up since.

. Too long for me, maybe not long enough for Ruby Jane. She dropped me off, and had planned to pick me up again. But as radio silence lengthened, I arranged for an overpriced rental car instead.

I dial her cell from Manzanita before getting on the highway. She doesn't pick up. During the drive to Portland—ninety-three-point-nine miles according to Google Maps—I keep my hand on my phone as though I can pull a signal from the air through the power of touch. By the time I'm negotiating the vehicular chop on Route 26 through Hillsboro and Beaverton, I've succumbed to the urge to redial at least twice as often as I've resisted. Doesn't matter anyway. Every attempt goes straight to voicemail.

Self-delusion was easier in the days before Caller ID and 24-hour digital accessibility.

I pull up in front of Uncommon Cup at Twelfth and Ash shortly before seven. Her apartment is a few blocks away, but I'm more likely to find her at one of her shops. Through the window I can see a guy mopping. He's mid-twenties, with dark flyaway hair and a five-day beard. As I watch, he spins and kicks one leg to the side. Fred Astaire with a mop handle. I don't recognize him—no surprise. Ruby Jane employs a couple dozen people now. A lone customer sits at a table next to the window, a fellow thick with layers. Thermal shirt under flannel under a half-zipped hoodie under a denim jacket. He holds a ceramic cup under his nose. There's no sign of Ruby Jane.

As I get out of the car, the guy in all the layers looks up, then checks his watch. He unwinds from his chair and is coming out as I reach the door. Tall and lean, baby-faced, with blue eyes peeking out from inside his hood. "Quitting time, man."

"I won't be settling in."

He slides past me out the door. Inside, I breathe warm air laced with the scents of coffee and bleach. The space is cast in dark wood, and sandblasted brick with mix-n-match tables and chairs from a half-dozen different diners. Barbra Streisand caterwauls from hidden speakers. The guy with the mop pauses mid-pirouette when he sees me.

"Sorry, man. We're closed."

"I'm looking for Ruby Jane."

He props himself up on the upright mop handle. His eyes gaze two different directions, neither at me. "Who?"

"Ruby Jane Whittaker? The owner?"

He sniffs. "Oh. Sure, Whittaker. I didn't make the connection." He looks around the shop as if he expects to catch her hiding under a table. "She's not here."

"So I see. Is she at one of the other shops?"

"How would I even know that, man?"

I don't like his tone, or maybe I don't like feeling so out of touch. "Who's the manager today?"

He turns his back. "Marcy's the only manager I know."

"Do you know where *she* is?"

"She took off at five. Something about seeing a band."

I take a breath and finger my cell phone. Ruby Jane's newest location, I haven't been to this shop more than a couple of times.

"Pal?" I look up. "I've got to finish up here, man."

Streisand gives way to Sinatra and I wonder what possessed this jackhole to tune in the Starbucks channel on the satellite radio. "Do you have Marcy's number?"

"Her phone number?"

"No, her social security number."

"I don't know you. I don't think she'd appreciate me giving out her number to a stranger."

"I'm Skin Kadash."

"Am I supposed to know who that is?"

My cheek twitches. "Who I am is a guy who has enough sway with the woman who signs your checks that you don't want to keep fucking with me." My fingertips run across a patch of red skin on my throat the color and texture of raw hamburger.

His eyes come into sudden alignment and he ducks his head. "It's just, well, I'm new here and I don't know you."

Now I'm the jackhole. I lower my chin and turn my hands over, conciliatory. "How about you call Marcy? Tell her Skin needs to talk to her. I'll be quick."

He considers that for a moment, eyes fixed on my hands. "Okay. Hang on a second." He props the mop handle against a table and goes back behind the counter. I wonder if I can convince him to sell me a bagel, closing time or not. I haven't eaten since morning. He checks a notebook from under the counter, dials a number.

"Hi, Marcy. It's Alvin … yeah, sorry, listen there's some guy here—" He looks up at me. "What did you say your name was?"

"Tell her it's Skin."

His face blanches a shade or two. "He calls himself, uh, Skin—"

He thrusts the phone my way. "Marcy, hey."

"Damn, Skin, where the hell you been? Been like a month since my last dose of bloodcurdling ugly."

"I was off scaring starfish and sandpipers."

"A month at the beach. Did you meet any nice lady sea monsters?"

"The surf was crawling." I clear my throat and change the subject. "Hey, you know what's up with RJ? I've been trying to get hold of her, no answer."

"Shit, man. You didn't know? She's gone."

"Gone? Gone where?"

"I'd have thought if anyone knew, it would be you."

"I don't understand."

"A couple of weeks ago, she asked me to manage the shops while she took care of personal business out of town."

"Did she say when she'd be back?"

"About two weeks, so she's due anytime." There's a slight pause, half a beat. "She didn't call you?"

I take a moment to respond. "Cell service was spotty where I was staying."

"She must not have been able to get through."

She could have left a voicemail, if nothing else. "You've no idea what's going on?"

"She said there was nothing to worry about, if that's what you're thinking."

"What do you think?"

"This is RJ we're talking about. I'm sure she's fine." I can almost hear her shrug through the phone. "Listen, I'm supposed to meet some people, but tell you what. I'll be working at Hollywood tomorrow. Why don't you come by? We'll catch up."

"Okay. Thanks, Marcy."

"Good to have you back, Skin."

Then she's gone. Alvin takes the phone, places it back on the charger behind the counter. "Find out what you need?"

"Uh, yeah." Ruby Jane, gone and out of touch, without explanation. Doesn't make sense. In all the time I've known her, she's taken only one vacation—a trip to Victoria with her one-time beau Peter and me. She fretted about the shop the whole time we were gone.

"You need anything else, man? Call you a cab maybe?"

Alvin's color is coming back, his expression growing impatient. I don't know if he senses my dismay or has recovered from the sight of my neck, but sudden heat rises in my chest. "Marcy told me to tell you to crack the register and sell me a bagel."

His lips form a line and a crease appears between his eyebrows. "Yeah. Sure. Fine."

"Sesame seed, with cream cheese. Toasted."

But when I reach for my wallet, my pocket is empty. Back straight, Alvin slices the bagel and drops it in the toaster.

"Hang on a second, I need my wallet." As I head for my car, I think about the guy in layers who brushed past me as I came in. I look up and down Twelfth. There's no sign of him. My wallet is in the gutter beside the rental car.

I sigh and head back inside.

Alvin is waiting for me. "Everything all right?"

"The guy who left as I came in, do you know who it was?"

He ponders. "Like I said, I'm—"

"New. Right. I got it."

"What's wrong?"

"Bastard picked my pocket. Took my cash and tossed my wallet in the gutter."

Alvin thinks for a moment, glances at my neck as he wraps the bagel. "I hope he left you your debit card."

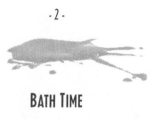

2

BATH TIME

I AWAKE FROM a dream in which unseen figures toss bloody bones wrapped in cloth into my backyard during a rainfall. Always count on my subconscious for a little melodrama. I lie disoriented in the dark, no memory of turning off the light. Rain taps at the bedroom window. After a moment, I feel around on the nightstand for my cell phone. The light from the display is a splash of acid in my eyes. No calls, no messages. It's not even eleven.

I throw my forearm over my eyes, but restlessness flits through my belly with reckless insistence. The air in the room is stale and my pillow smells like dust. After leaving Uncommon Cup, I'd stopped at Safeway for half-and-half and grape juice, an errand remarkable only for the woman snacking from an open bag of Purina Beggin' Strips in the checkout line. From there it was Hertz to drop off the rental car, then a ride from a taciturn cabbie whose only comment was, "Yar," when I told him my address. You can't prep too early for Talk Like A Pirate Day. Once home, I hadn't bothered to do much more than put away the groceries and check my email—opportunities to earn hundreds working from home or to get unlimited hits to my web site. Lacking either a web presence or a desire to work, I deleted it all. The fridge yielded a sound, if wrinkled, pear and some aged cheddar with a little fur on it. I slumped on the couch with my snack and a short Macallan, where the second half of *NCIS* failed to grab my attention. Before the credits rolled, I roused myself enough to switch off the TV and head to my room, there to fall on my own bed for the first time in a month. I don't remember stripping to my skivvies.

Outside, the rain continues to fall and the phone continues not to ring. I slide my feet to the edge of the bed and let gravity make my decision. A few minutes later I'm dressed and pulling a ring of keys off a magnetic hook on the refrigerator. I'd like to think Ruby Jane planned to be back before I'd know she was gone—the timetable she gave Marcy allows for the possibility. But how hard would it have been to drop me an email or leave a message on my cell? As I drive my car through the rain-slicked Portland streets, I ponder any number of reasons why she might drop out of sight without a word, none of which make what I'm about to do a good idea.

The original Uncommon Cup was in a building on a triangle block of Sandy south of Burnside. The Depression-era concrete block structure had been home to everything from small-scale manufacturing to warehouse-and-distribution to multiplex low-income housing. Ruby Jane had her own vision. She demoed the interior walls to create a large open apartment for herself in the rear, and remodeled the front for the café. A walnut bar salvaged from a long defunct tavern served as counter. Her first roaster, a refurbished cast iron beast from the prehistory of epicurean coffee, sat in a nook at one side.

As her small coffee empire grew, first with the addition of a location on Hawthorne not far from my house in the lee of Mount Tabor, then with a larger shop near the Hollywood Theatre, she began to feel the pinch of her original space. When the shop on

Twelfth and Ash became available, she saw it as an opportunity to decommission the mothership and create some distance between time on and time off. The new shop was close enough to allow her to retain her regulars, yet with a clientele of its own. Now the original space serves as home to a Probat five-kilo coffee roaster and her business office.

By the time I arrive, the rain has stopped. The air feels warm and heavy as I climb out of the car and look around. Only the teal awning over the entrance remains from the original shop. The windows and glass door now feature vertical blinds for privacy and a small sign reading UNCOMMON CUP—BUSINESS OFFICE. No light peeps out from around the closed blinds, meaningless at this time of night. If Ruby Jane is home she'll be in her apartment in the back.

A car passes on Sandy, muffler popping. I heft the ring of keys in my hand, a spare set RJ gave me months before. They jingle overloud in the misty night air. My footsteps rasp on the sidewalk as I circle the block. A few cars are parked on Tenth Avenue near her side door, none RJ's beater Toyota.

She lives close enough to St. Francis church, with its daily meal service, that it's not uncommon to see homeless men and women tucked under awnings or in doorways. Tonight, I see no one. The emptiness is unsettling. I round the block a second time. A row of dark windows runs between the roof line and the top of the door, too high to peep through even if the glass wasn't frosted. I rap on her apartment door, too gently to be heard by anyone who isn't alert for a knock. I take a breath and rap again, louder this time. No one comes. After compromising between a reasonable wait and eternity, I key open the door.

The first thing I notice is the silence. Nothing, not even the security system warning beep. I reach for the light switch I know is near the doorway. The bulb overhead flares and pops. My hand jerks back and a tremor runs through me. I give my eyes a moment to adjust to the darkness. In the faint light filtering in from outside, I make out the alarm control panel on the wall. Something doesn't look quite right. I ease my way into the foyer. The panel hangs off the wall by wires, many severed. I reach into my coat pocket for my phone. Someone has disabled the alarm.

I listen, my breath tight in my throat. After a moment I hear a plop, a single drop falling into pooled water.

Maybe I should be heading for my car and dialing 911, but my instincts tell me no one is home. The emptiness is too hollow, the air too still, the darkness too complete. I catch a dank, faintly noxious scent like spoiled milk. I don't like the idea of backing away without first knowing what I'm backing away from. If someone has busted into Ruby Jane's place, I want to know how much damage they've done.

I want to know what's causing the smell.

RJ's apartment is a single oversized room, the bare concrete floor covered by big braided rugs, the high ceiling an expanse of exposed girders and foam insulation. I can't see anything, not the bed on its platform at the far end of the room, not the regulation basketball hoop opposite the kitchen, not the bookcases or plush sofas. From where I stand, the passage leading up front is to my right through a door. The kitchenette is to the left, separated from the room by an island counter with a butcher block top. Past the refrigerator, I know a couple of doors open onto the bathroom, a closet and a small utility room. The main space is straight ahead, a looming cavern. I take a single, tentative step forward. The short hairs on the back of my neck stand up at the touch of open air.

A faint red light burns from the vicinity of the stove, an indicator of some type, providing no illumination. The dim glow shining through the high frosted windows on either side of the room is a little better. As my eyes adjust further, I make out the shape of RJ's four-poster bed, and the sitting area with its two sofas facing each other across the broad coffee table. A basketball rests on the floor below the hoop. I've seen RJ drain three-pointers from any spot in the room, nothing but net.

I take a few more jittery steps, wishing I'd brought a damn flashlight. An echoing droplet falls again—*plop*—into water. The sound comes from the center of the room. I see the claw-foot bath-tub I know is there less as an object than a formless shadow. Before Ruby Jane moved in, the tub had been a lone, modest luxury in what was an otherwise dreary studio apartment. Ruby Jane liked it so much she left it in place. I have no idea how often she uses it, though she's boasted of hot baths, candlelight, and loud music after a hard day's work. The tub has always been empty during my visits.

Not tonight.

As I ease closer, the tub takes shape, the pale porcelain catching what little illumination steals through the translucent glass. I make out a shadow next to the tub, a pile of clothes or maybe a blanket. Inside the tub, the water's surface is broken by a pair of dark humps at the midline and a round lump at the far end. *Plop.* Something is in the water, a figure, unmoving. I suck air through my nose and catch the stench of urine amidst the spoiled milk smell.

I turn and stumble toward the wall, emit an involuntary keen. The one unconsidered, intolerable reason for Ruby Jane's silence surges through my mind. The silence, the darkness, the still water in the tub all testify to my growing fear. I search for a light switch by touch, hands shaking—nothing—push along the cool wall until I pitch up against the refrigerator. Without thought I fling the door open. It crashes against the wall with a rattle of condiment bottles. A jar of pickles hits the floor and rolls to a stop against the island, trailing a thread of brine. The sudden light sears my retinas. I close my eyes and sag against the counter beside the fridge. I'm afraid to turn. Until I look, it's not real—isn't that how it works? As long as I hide behind Ruby Jane's butcher block, eyes closed, the form in the tub remains but a faint, visual echo of my own fear.

If I learned anything during my twenty-five years as a cop, it's that the body can't be wished away. Schrödinger's cat only lives and dies in the symbols of an equation. I push myself off the counter, flex my hands against a burning tingle in my palms. My heartbeat pounds in my ears. The fridge casts stark, leaping shadows as I edge toward the tub. Most of the room remains dark, but there's enough light to show me what I need to see. I draw a ragged breath and look down into the still water.

Plop.

The hair is a grey mat on the head, the body emaciated, the face a relief map of more years than my own five-plus decades. A man. It's an old man.

Relief floods through me like falling tears. I sag to the floor. It's not my Ruby Jane. But now I'm left with a new question to go with the one I came with. Where is she, and who's the old guy, naked and dead, in her bathtub?

- 3 -

SUSPICIOUS CIRCS

AFTER A MOMENT, old instincts take over. I get up off the cold, bare floor and scan the walls. At the end of the kitchen counter, there's a switch plate I skidded over moments before in the dark. I flick the switch and a cluster of emerald-shaded pendants cast a warm, yellow glow over the kitchen island. I put the pickle jar back and close the fridge, then cross the floor and turn on a couple standing floor lamps at either end of the couch.

I've seen a corpse or two in my time, but it's been a while since one gave me the squirrelies. I leave it for the moment and walk the grid. Nothing formal, it's not my job anymore. Just checking things out. I don't know who this old fellow is, but I assume he didn't come only for a bath. As I move through the room, I see signs he's been around for a while. Throw pillows on the floor and a old, ratty sleeping bag spread across one of the soft sofas. A squadron of empty soup cans and dirty spoons on the coffee table, a spilled tomato crust dried onto the cover of a volume of Sharon Doubiago poetry. A dead bag of blue corn tortilla chips on the floor among the pillows. Ruby Jane must have been out of salsa.

Nothing else appears to be out-of-place. Ruby Jane's not one for a lot of expensive gadgetry. The TV is a CRT model sitting atop a combo DVD/VHS player, both intact on their wooden stand. The small console stereo is on the sideboard. Books stand untouched in the pair of bookcases against the wall. Her microwave oven is still on the kitchen counter, her clock radio still on the bed stand. Behind the curtains of the four-poster, the bed is made. I wonder why the dead guy camped on the couch when he had a big comfortable queen-sized bed twenty feet away. Same reason he ate cold soup out of the can in sight of a stove maybe. The bathroom is a disaster, toilet seat up. He hadn't bothered to flush. If it's yellow let it mellow, maybe, but when it's brown, flush that bad boy down.

Plop.

The body remains. A voice in the back of my head tells me it's not my problem. I've been retired for nearly two years. Even if I wasn't, it would be verboten to investigate a death so close to home. But nobody's giving me orders anymore, no policy directives rule my life. I rub the bridge of my nose and turn my attention to the tub.

No one looks their best after they stop breathing, but I'm guessing the last time this guy looked good Carter was still president. His dark, mottled eyelids are at half-mast, but I can see that post-mortem corneal clouding competes with ante-mortem cataracts. His skin is blotchy and yellow, and livid lesions streak his chest. An old scar below his left nipple reminds me of my own healed gunshot wound. Even after an untold period soaking, he looks filthy, from his greasy, dandruff-flecked hair to his gnarled fingers and toes. I place his age in the upper sixties, though I won't be surprised if I've underestimated by a decade. The bath water seems to be cool, but I'm not dipping my hand in to find out for sure. His clothes heaped on the floor next to the tub emit the piss smell; the spoiled milk is all bathtub.

I don't touch anything. I've been Ruby Jane's guest often enough my prints could be anywhere. Doesn't mean I want them on some dead squatter's heap of shit. I turn away from the tub, swipe my arm across my forehead. There's more to see, but I don't feel like I can delay the call to 911 any longer. Just because I didn't see anyone on my way in doesn't mean no one saw me. Some witness turning up with a suggestion I spent a suspiciously long time alone in a house with a dead body is the last thing I need. I pull out my cell. I tell the dispatcher there's no rush.

Even if the cavalry charges, I've got a few minutes. I head into the old shop through a short corridor with a unisex bathroom on one side and a nook on the other, home to the dish sterilizer during the coffee house days. Both are dark and empty. Up front, industrial shelves stacked with beans and miscellaneous inventory. I got through the office door beyond the roaster.

Dust drifts in air tangy with the scent of raw coffee beans. The fluorescent light overhead hums. Ruby Jane's desktop is clear, a rare sight. The message light blinks on the office phone. Pens and pencils poke out of an old coffee mug. Her laptop is gone, but her cell phone is plugged into its charger next to the office phone. I move around behind the desk and slump into her squeaky old chair. A spring prods my ass. I pick up the cell phone, turn it over in my hands. Its presence troubles me more than anything else I've seen tonight, including the dead bastard in the tub. For reasons I can't fathom, she wants to be not merely out of touch, but out of reach. She could have avoided unwanted calls by not picking up. Leaving the phone behind suggests a more radical need.

I don't like the hollow anxiety tightening my chest, the sense of helplessness I feel. No note, no call. Nothing. I shake my head. The chair squeals as I stand up again. I pocket RJ's phone, then glance through the desk drawers, at the notes on the cork board behind the desk. Ordinary shop stuff, schedules, invoices, payroll. Nothing which tells me why Ruby Jane has vanished.

I turn off the lights, return to the apartment. The cops still haven't arrived, but they won't be long. I exit through the foyer and pull the door shut without latching it. The street is wet, but overhead I can see stars through shreds of cloud. The breeze smells fresh and clean after the stale, funky air inside. Across the street, a moving shadow catches my eye and I look up to see a figure moving away from me. Tallish, hoodie under a jacket. Familiar. I step off the curb as a patrol car rounds the corner from Sandy, light bar flashing. I turn back to the figure, but he's gone. The car rolls to a stop a foot from my knees and a uniformed cop pops out.

"You the one who called?" His hand rests on his weapon, a reflex gesture I hope. His expression is alert, without undue tension.

"Yeah. I'm Kadash. The body's inside." I wave a hand over my shoulder toward the door behind me.

"Anyone else in there?" A second unit pulls up behind the first and another uniform climbs out, cover for the first. He points a flashlight at the closed door.

"No one."

"You're sure?"

"Yeah, I cleared the place."

"Cleared." The covering uniform aims his light at my eyes.

"I'm an ex-cop, retired." You never lose the lingo. "Go through into the big room. You can't miss him."

"All right. Please wait out here."

Half an hour later, the street is crawling. There's more people than necessary for what I'm guessing will turn out to be a pretty routine D.B. I prop my ass against the hood of a patrol car, nannied by the first responders. They try to make small talk. I'm not feeling talkative, but they carry the conversation fine without me. One of them found some dope in his kid's room. The other wonders if he'll ever get another blow job. Maybe if you ask the chief real nice, I suggest. They laugh, but it's uneasy. As an ex-cop, they'll grant me permission to listen, but I'm not welcome to participate.

The only surprise, such as it is, is the appearance of Susan Mulvaney—my former partner, now lieutenant in charge of Person Crimes. Slender and self-possessed in jeans, t-shirt, and a tailored jacket, Susan looks like she stepped away from a casual brunch with friends. She nods to me, then stops in RJ's doorway to chat with the medical examiner as he rolls the gurney out. They talk quietly for a couple of minutes, then Susan approaches me.

"Skin, if you have a moment, we've got a few questions."

No *hello*, no *how are ya*. I'm not surprised. Under normal circumstances Susan wouldn't even get a phone call over a random stiff found in an empty apartment. She's here as a courtesy to me, as is pretty much everyone else, but that doesn't make it a social call. She guides me through the door and back into Ruby Jane's apartment. A couple of homicide dicks I knew back in the day are waiting next to the tub. Empty now. The spoilt scent lingers.

"What do you know, guys?"

Moose Davisson doesn't like me much and I guess the feeling is mutual, though the tension has never broken out into open hostilities. He glances at me from atop his mountainous frame then turns his attention to the girders and ductwork overhead. Frannie Stein, his partner, is less familiar, an up-and-comer as I was downward-spiraling. She regards me expressionlessly. Susan stops beside me. For a moment, no one answers her question, then Moose clears his throat.

"Not much to know, Loo."

"What are your thoughts? Any reason to think homicide?"

"Not yet, no. Probably not at all. The M.E. is leaning toward a natural manner of death, but we'll know more in a couple of days. He's not too backed up."

"Okay. Good." Susan turns to me. "Skin, what brought you here tonight?" There's a slight edge to her voice, and I wonder what the subtext is. If any. We haven't been on the best of terms for some time now. I could be detecting nothing more than generalized Skin antipathy.

"I was checking on the place for Ruby Jane."

"Bet the stiff was a surprise."

"I'd rather find a hundred dollar bill in my sock drawer."

"And you used your own key."

"We traded keys a while back."

"Where's Ruby Jane now?"

"She's away."

"How long has she been gone?"

A bolus of heat gathers in my belly. "What's the story here, Susan? Do you know who this guy is or what?"

She sniffs, then tilts her head toward Moose. He looks from Susan to Frannie, at last to me. I'm sure he's wondering what he's doing out in the middle of the night for this ticky-tack bullshit, and I can't say as I blame him. He fishes his notebook out of his jacket pocket.

"He had an expired Washington State driver's license in his wallet. Name, Chase Fairweather. Picture matches, but we'll confirm." He eyes me. "Name mean anything to you?"

I shake my head.

"There were a couple of bucks in his wallet, no credit cards. Sixty-two years old. No evidence of trauma. We found a bottle of baby aspirin and some insulin in his cargo pants pocket, no needles. Homeless, from the looks of him."

"You thinking he knew the place was empty and broke in to get out of the weather?"

"We'll check at St. Francis tomorrow, see if any one remembers him. But, yeah, I'd guess he broke in, fixed himself a warm bath, and died of shock at being clean for the first time since he grew pubes."

I blink, trying to shake the sudden image of the body in the water. "How'd he get in?"

"No obvious sign of forced entry, but you saw the security panel."

"Slick work, don't you think?"

"Not bad, no. Not like the system is state-of-the-art or anything, but he knew what he was about. There are scratches on the dead bolt too, though I can't tell if they're fresh or not."

"That old wreck was a lock-pick *and* an electronics wiz?"

"This ain't Fort Knox, Skin."

I chew on that for a moment, but I don't know what to make of it. Susan lifts her chin. "Do we have an estimated time-of-death, Moose?"

"The bath water confuses matters, but based on lividity and on-set of rigor, the M.E. guessed between six and eight this evening."

I almost came over about then. I wonder if I could have done anything for the old bastard if I'd stopped by. Or how I'd have re-acted if I found him in Ruby Jane's place still breathing. Not with warmth and hospitality, I don't imagine.

"In the end, nothing to see here."

"Old homeless guys die all the time. Not usually in someone's bath tub, but shit happens."

"How long do you think he was in here?"

"Hard to say. Not long enough to make off with the TV. Do you know if anything has been stolen?"

"Besides a half dozen cans of Progresso?" I suppose if she had a secret envelope stuffed with used, non-sequential hundreds, I wouldn't know if it was missing. "I didn't see her laptop."

"Wouldn't she have taken it with her?"

"Probably. Or, hell, it might be at one of the shops."

Susan studies me, her gaze pensive. "The cell phone charger in her office is empty. But she'd have that with her too." I can feel the pressure of the phone in my pocket. "You never did say where she is."

"It's a personal matter. She'll be back soon." I wonder if I manage to sound even remotely convincing.

"Do you know how to reach her? We'd like to talk to her."

Most likely the M.E. will come back in a day or two with a final report—natural death, no suspicious circs—and the file will close. No need to pursue the break-in, since they have the perpetrator dead to rights.

I look Susan in the eye. "Try her cell."

- 4 -

CARTOPIA

MOOSE AND FRANNIE are gone before Susan and I finish talking. She stands at the foot of the tub with her hands in her pockets,
casual and oblivious to the scent memory of Chase Fairweather's
passing. I lean against the butcher block. Ten foot buffer of dead air
between us, we exchange the kind of congenial chatter you share
with someone you've long since lost any significant link to. She asks
how I'm doing in a way which makes clear she expects bad news.
In the last two years, I've been brained with a flower pot, fought
cancer to a standstill, and survived a bullet in my belly. Susan can't
be the only one who wonders how I manage to remain vertical. I
assure her I'm as good as you might expect. She offers that her husband Eric is a law partner now, her daughter Leah anxious to finish
middle school. About the time she's ready to call it a night, I clear
my throat.

"I'll be seeing what I can find out about this guy."

The year before, she'd offered me a job reviewing open case
files. Not a sworn position, a stipend deal intended to take some

pressure off her cold case squad. I hadn't taken her up on it, but I knew she was still short of man hours.

"I figured you would."

Tomorrow or the next day, she'll glance over a memo, but far as Susan is concerned, the file on Ruby Jane's trespasser is already closed. She leaves me to lock up.

It's past midnight. I'm not tired. What I am is restless and dissatisfied. Anxiety has taken root in my chest. I'm not a night owl; my evenings may run late, but they tend to run close to home. Marcy, in contrast, is someone I've seen close Uncommon Cup one day, go clubbing, hit the bars and after hours joints, then skip sleep to open shop again the next morning. Work a long day and do it all over again. She'll be up.

I take a seat behind the wheel of my car and roll down the window, listen to the crackling hiss of tires on wet pavement as cars pass. Then I pull out Ruby Jane's cell phone. Unlike most every other electronic gizmo she owns, it isn't hanging by a thread over the pit of obsolescence. But it's nothing fancy either. I hit the power button.

Enter Phone Pass Code: _ _ _ _

The tiny screen is painfully bright in the dark car. I try four digits. Ruby Jane is too smart for my juvenile attempt: 7-3-8-3, the digits corresponding to P-E-T-E. She and Peter fizzled out over a year ago. I suppose I'm reassured his name doesn't work, but I'm left with ten thousand possibilities. Knowing her, the code is random, a sequence of numbers she chose for their lack of personal meaning. It won't be a play on Uncommon Cup, U-C-U-P, U-N-C-M, something like that. It won't be the last four of her social, her childhood street address—not that I know either one—or her birth year. It won't be S-K-I-N. As if to prove the point, I punch in 7-5-4-6.

The screen clears.

"Well. Hell."

A trill of pleasure runs through me, but I tell myself not to read too much into it. Probably thought she was being funny.

I pull up the Contacts list, scroll through to the entry for Marcy. She picks up after three rings. "RJ! Oh my god! You're back!"

"Sorry, Marcy. Not nearly so pretty."

"Skin? Is that you?"

"In the flesh." In the background I can hear voices and music, laughter.

"What are you doing with Ruby Jane's phone?"

"It's complicated. Listen, I need to talk to you. Do you have a minute?"

"I can't hear you."

"Something's happened at Ruby Jane's apartment."

"Something happened to Ruby Jane's apartment?"

"No." I hesitate, thinking. "Where are you? I could join you."

"I have an idea. Why don't you come down?"

From the sound of her, the smart choice might be to wait until morning. Except I'm in no mood for waiting. "Sure. Where are you?"

"Cartopia, man."

"The food carts?"

"You know, the food carts. Come get a pie, man."

Cartopia is at the corner of Hawthorne and Twelfth, a circle of trailers and panel trucks serving everything from authentic Mexican to crepes to southern barbecue and more. Before I got hurt last fall, Ruby Jane and I would grab dinner there after closing every week or two. RJ can't get her fill of poutine. I prefer fish tacos or a fried pie.

"I'll be right there."

"Careful where you park. The tow truck has been prowling all goddamn night."

She's at least half-drunk. I wonder if this will be a wasted trip. Still, I'm awake. Not like I have anything better to do.

I've never been to the carts this late. The after-midnight scene is nothing like I'm used to. A manic energy pervades the crowd gathered in the open space between the carts. Clouds roll overhead in long strips, the lingering threat of rain doing little to dampen spirits. There are a pair of large canopies, one twice the size of the other, with picnic tables underneath, but as many stand under sky as under cover. Competing scents of hickory, deep fryer fat, and cigarette smoke hang on the air.

As I weave through the crowd, the Whiffies girl recognizes me and beckons. My bagel is a fading memory, so I wander over and check the board.

"Hi, Summer. Busy night?"

"Picking up now that the weather's getting warmer. We ran out of brisket."

"I'll be throwing a tantrum now."

Gregg looks around from the back of the cart. "If we knew you were coming, we'd have saved you one."

"I keep forgetting to post my schedule online. Okay, start me a chicken pot pie, but don't rush. I'm looking for someone."

"You got it." Summer smiles and I hand her a five, then throw myself into the crowd.

Under the small canopy, someone has set up a portable karaoke machine. A tall lanky fellow belts out a striking rendition of "Total Eclipse of the Heart." Folks are clumped, not so dense I can't wend my way through. I see hoodies everywhere and for a moment I think about the fellow outside Ruby Jane's apartment. Portland is a city of layers, especially in the spring when we can go from rain to sun to wind storm over the course of a short walk to the coffee shop.

Hoodies over flannel over long-sleeve T's abound, many capped off with knit caps. For all I know, my wallet thief is right in front of me. I try to remember the sound of his voice as I scan for Marcy. "*Quitting time, man.*" Not much to go on.

I find her at a picnic table under the big canopy, a funnel of pomme frites in front of her. She's got a big red cup in her left hand, and a Marlboro sticks out from between two knuckles of her right. She uses it to point across the table at an Egyptian-eyed woman with teased and Dayglo'd hair. "If your idea of social media is to spam Twitter and Facebook with announcements of your skanky gallery openings, you're *doin' it wrong!*" Marcy's arms are a tracery of tattoos, green-leaved vines and orange trumpet flowers.

The other woman slaps the table top. "I only spam my skanky gallery openings on MySpace."

"MySpace is for douche bags."

"That's where I found you, bitch."

I assume they're friends. I drape an arm over Marcy's shoulder. She looks up at me and grins. "You're up late for an old puke." Her eyes are a little wild. I glance at the cigarette in her hand. "Don't tell Ruby Jane I'm smoking."

"As soon as I find her I'll make a point of not telling her."

She blinks, then laughs, the joke catching up with her on the back side.

"Whatcha up to, Skinster?"

"I came from RJ's apartment."

"Is she home?"

"No. I was snooping."

She raises her cup in a mock toast. I catch a whiff of lemonade fortified with tequila.

"There was a man there. He was dead."

Marcy blinks again. I'm beginning to see this was a mistake. "A dead man? Like, *dead-dead*?"

"Yeah. Dead-dead in the claw foot tub."

"That's fucked up." Her face loses a shade. "What's a dead guy doing in RJ's bath tub?"

"It looks like he'd been staying there. Did she say anything to you about that?"

She draws on her cigarette, releases smoke without inhaling. I lick my lips.

"A man was hanging around the day before she left."

"What man?"

"I don't know. She didn't introduce him. An old guy."

"How old?"

"Old. Older than you."

"Did he arrive in a coffin?"

"What?" She misses the joke. Maybe not so much a joke.

"Did she talk to him?"

"Yeah, for a bit. I think. She made him leave."

"Why? Was he causing a problem?"

"Not that I noticed." Suddenly she stands up and waves. Cigarette ash flutters over her bare arms, grey snowfall on entwined vines. "Fells! Hey, Fellsner! Over here!"

I draw an impatient breath. "Marcy?"

"Yeah?" She looks back at me as if seeing me for the first time.

"Can we go somewhere a little quieter? It won't take long, I promise."

She's still waving to Fellsner, I think, but then she stops and turns to the woman with the red hair. "I'm gonna go buy some crack from my friend here. When I get back, my spot better be waiting for me."

"In your dreams, ho."

Marcy unwinds from the seat, grabs her cup. Her cigarette vanishes, I hope not down the back of someone's shirt. She takes my arm and pulls me through the crowd. We head past Whiffies, where I see Summer waving to me from inside the cart.

"Skin! Your pie."

Marcy shifts direction without breaking stride. "Man's gotta eat." I take my pie and thank Summer. Marcy choo-choos us through the redolent aroma of deep-frying pies and past the chemical tang of the port-a-potties. She pulls up short on the sidewalk at Hawthorne.

I've known Marcy for a couple of years now. She was one of Ruby Jane's first hires, came aboard not long before RJ opened her second shop. She started as a part-time barista, but through a combination of native talent and a work ethic rivaled only by Ruby Jane's rose to become Uncommon Cup's first official store manager.

"What's going on with RJ, Marcy?"

"Seriously, man. I don't know."

"Not even a guess, maybe from something she said? How was she when she was getting ready to leave?"

She thinks for a moment. "Focused."

"She would be."

"I figured maybe she had a death in the family or something." Her thin eyebrows furrow for a moment. "I didn't think she'd leave him in her bath tub." Her eyes appear to vibrate and her voice drops. "Do you think it could have been her dad?"

"I don't know. She's never spoken of her parents."

"Her brother's still in San Francisco, right?"

"It wasn't him."

I met James when he visited Portland a couple of years back. I don't remember him well, but well enough to know he'd have had to come back in time from 2055 to be the fellow in the tub.

"You've been running the whole shebang while she's away?"

"Yeah. It's been a little hectic. I'm not used to taking care of three shops, but it's been good, you know?"

"And she hasn't checked in?"

"She said she probably wouldn't get the chance."

No matter the emergency, it's hard for me to believe she wouldn't be on the phone at least once a day. Uncommon Cup is her baby.

"Tell me about the old man."

"Not much to tell. He came in to Ash Street and they talked."

"Did you hear what they said?"

"Only a little. The old dude was wheedling her about something he lost and trying to get her buy his medicine. She hustled him outside and they sat at one of the tables outside for a while."

"And she said nothing about him."

"To be honest, I didn't think much of it. You know how she is. Trying to save the world one hobo at a time."

Ruby Jane will talk to anyone. She's generous with the homeless locals, donates ground coffee and cocoa packets to the St. Francis Dining Hall, provides hot water to people who show up at the shop with a tea bag and a cup. There on the street, I find myself inextricably on the verge of tears. In need of a distraction, I take a bite of my forgotten pie. It's good. They're always good. But even the buttery crunch of fried crust or the creamy chicken filling can't penetrate my anxiety. Marcy clasps her bare arms across her chest, cup hooked on one finger. I can feel the chill in the air now that we're away from the crowd. She tilts her head and looks sideways at me.

"What's up with you two anyway? You and RJ."

Her questions surprises me. "I'm worried about her. We're friends."

"Break-into-her-apartment friends?"

"I didn't break in. I used a key."

"So you snooped. Fucking stalker, that's what you are."

"Are you going to arrest me, Officer?"

"I think I'll let you off with a warning this time, kid." She lifts her cup, looks at me over the rim as she drinks. Her eyes are amber with flecks of glinting gold. "She told me you kissed her."

My face grows hot. Even in the scattered streetlight glow, I'm sure my cheeks flash as red as a baboon's ass. Crowd noise behind me seems to rise like a rushing wind.

Marcy smacks her lips and grins. "I can understand why you're in love with her."

"Who said I was in love with her?"

"No one has to, dipshit." Her grin morphs into a smirk. "You're not going to ask me how she feels about you?"

Jesus. I blink and look away, watch a tow truck cruise by. "She can tell me herself when I find her." My voice sounds thin and reedy in my ears. Ruby Jane had four months to tell me before she sent me on my retreat—she chose instead to busy herself expanding the Uncommon Cup empire. A fine mist gathers around us. Not quite rain, but thinking about it.

"Okay, think about this then. I'm twenty-three, turn twenty-four next month."

"Happy birthday."

"My mom is forty-five."

"When is her birthday?"

She gives me a look. "My dad turns seventy-seven the day after I turn twenty-four."

I notice the uneaten pie in my hand. Summer and Gregg will be disappointed. I've failed to give my Whiffies the attention it deserves. "You think I'm thirty-two years older than Ruby Jane?"

"God, I hope not. Gross."

"Marcy—"

She reaches up and pats me on the cheek. "Go get her, tiger."

"You assume she wants to get got."

LOT OF LAYERS

I DON'T FOLLOW Marcy back to her table. She's got trash-talking to do and I'd only cramp her style. She tosses the dregs of her drink into the street and leaves me with my cold pie in hand. The rain returns, a soft dribble from a sky less cloudy than star-filled. I hot-step it to my car, drop behind the wheel. According to the dashboard clock, it's after two. I'm awake again, cycling back to restiveness from troubled fatigue. A wriggling itch marches across my shoulders. At home, half a bottle of Macallan and what's left of the furry cheese and pear awaits me. Fuck that.

This time I park right next to Ruby Jane's side door. I don't expect to see anyone, so it's no surprise the night is empty of all but the rush of water over the edge of a clogged gutter down the street. Pockets of mist hang over the storm drains. In my trunk under a reusable New Seasons grocery bag I've never re-used I find a crushed and almost empty box of nitrile gloves, holdovers from my cop days. The click of Ruby Jane's deadbolt behind me is a thin reminder of its inadequate protection.

I cross the wide room to Fairweather's campsite. The only sound is the refrigerator's faint hum. I can smell his sleeping bag, a urea top note announcing a foundation of sweat and shit, finished by a basal fungal skank. The surest way to know someone is living on the street is to find yourself downwind from them. With no home to go to, your personal hygiene options are limited. Maybe you can take a shower at a shelter, assuming you can get into one. But a lot of street folks avoid the shelters, too often places to have their meager belongings stolen, to be beaten or raped. Chase Fairweather's bath in RJ's tub might have been his first in months, and this at the tail end of cold, damp weather when layers are the only protection. No telling how long he'd been marinating in his own secretions. In a way I'm lucky. His clothing will be worse than the sleeping bag, but they're the M.E.'s problem.

The cops left the rest of his detritus untouched. There isn't much. I circle the coffee table, review the evidence. The empty cans, a dried splash of either soup or vomit on the floor between the sofa and the coffee table. The cable remote pokes up from between the seat cushions. The TV stand is at the end of the coffee table. Fairweather could lie back in his nest and watch the tube while slurping unheated soup. I grab the remote and press the power button. The TV comes to life, midstream of a looping movie preview: half-glimpsed tits, shirtless men with goatees, nonsensical dialog. I bring up the menu and navigate to the account history screen. The bastard had been watching pay-per-view porn on Ruby Jane's dime for at least two days; he racked up over a hundred bucks in charges. I lift my gaze to the large framed print of Cézanne's *Bibemus Quarry* which hangs on the wall over the TV. One of Ruby Jane's favorites, purchased at the Museum Folkwang in Essen during a trip to Europe while she was in college. I wonder if Fairweather even noticed the painting's contrasting green and russet hues. Too busy pounding the pud on Ruby Jane's sofa. I shudder.

"At least now we know how long your guest was visiting, darling."

My voice sounds flat in the big space. I switch to the Weather channel and head for the utility room for cleaning supplies. The living room won't be too bad, but the bathroom is another matter. Fairweather was a poor aim from either barrel. I'm grateful he didn't spread out more. I snap on a pair of nitrile gloves and get to work.

Thirty minutes later I escape the bathroom, sweaty and smelling of bleach—a radical improvement.

The Weather Channel is running a scrolling list of forecasted highs and lows across the country to a backdrop of chirpy pseudo-jazz. I peel off my gloves to let my hands breathe. Los Angeles will be seventy-two and sunny, New York a cool fifty-one. Portland can expect the usual: sunny, rainy, cool, possibly warm. Wear fucking layers. I wonder if Ruby Jane's whereabouts are represented on the list.

A dark lump on the floor jammed under the end of Chase's sofa catches my eye, a battered backpack. "Dead Chase, you've been holding out on me." I pull on a fresh pair of nitrile gloves.

To my relief, the pack's contents aren't limited to overly-scrutinized porn rags. A small plastic box filled with half-smoked cigarettes, a wad of mismatched socks and underwear, a P-38 can opener. Another bottle of aspirin and a few empty insulin vials from a pharmacy in Anacortes, Washington. He never bothered to dispose of his disposable insulin syringes.

There's not much else, empty packages of peanut butter crackers and shreds of unidentifiable paper. At the bottom of the pack I find a large Ziploc bag with a photo album inside.

Jackpot. Maybe.

The album is snapshot-sized and half-full. Most of the pictures are impersonal location shots. A sunny street café with a chalk menu board in Spanish, a stand of tall trees with open ground between them. An empty beach, the water grey and washed-out. I see few people in any of the pictures, and none who appear to be the subject of the shot. They appear to be random passersby caught on film by mistake. A few pictures have locations written below in pencil—Norman, El Paso, Matehuala—but most are anonymous. From the looks of them, the prints pre-date digital.

The last photo differs from the rest. A boy and a girl sit together on a couch, a kidney-shaped table before them. An adult arm reaches from out of frame with a cigarette, captured in the act of flicking ash in an ashtray. The boy and girl sit hip to hip, the girl leaning away from the boy. His grin is exaggerated, the smile of a boy being told to say cheese. The girl isn't having any of it. Her arms are folded across her chest, her lips pursed in annoyance. She's maybe six or seven; I guess the boy at ten. Even though the color is faded, the focus soft, there's no mistaking a young Ruby Jane. Her features are more angular, less defined than in the woman she'll become. But it's her, rangy reddish hair and round eyes, a hint of dimples too deep to be obscured by her annoyance.

I return the album to the Ziploc bag. The picture of young Ruby Jane goes into my pocket. I stuff the rest of Fairweather's crap in the backpack. Ruby Jane can decide what to do with the photo album when she gets back. I might offer a suggestion on the matter, but in the end it strikes me as something she needs to see. I have no hypothesis about who Chase Fairweather is, not one which doesn't give me the willies, but he got that picture somewhere.

I toss the backpack onto the sleeping bag, add the soup cans and other trash, wrap it all up. Ruby Jane would expect me to separate the recyclables, but arm's length isn't far enough as I walk the stinking bundle out the side door. The rain has stopped. I head to the back of the building. The dumpster is locked. I don't know where the key is, maybe inside or maybe on RJ's key chain in her pocket. Clammy fog hangs off the exposed skin of my face and neck.

"I know your name."

The voice seems to come from all directions. I drop the bundle and spin. Soup cans clatter at my feet. A tall figure stands behind me. I fall, find myself pressed against the dumpster. All sound is magnified, from the scrape of the dumpster wheels to the man's breathing. The vague shape of a hooded face looms through the mist. My mind flashes to a moment the autumn before, when the bodies piled up on a rain-soaked hilltop at dusk and I put a bullet into a woman's head. A clean killing, saved the lives of a boy and his mother and my own as well. I came through it a different man. I'm not ashamed of the yelp, nor ashamed of the balled fist I drive forward from my hips. No one would look at me and think *he's a tough guy*, but in some ways I'm in better shape than I've been in two decades, dividend of giving up the smokes and adding miles of daily walking. The blow strikes the sweet spot below the man's sternum. Air whuffs from his mouth, a cloud of sour garlic. I push off the dumpster and almost fall as my feet tangle in Fairweather's sleeping bag. A hand grips my arm and I kick out, connect with something soft. We fall, but I catch myself on my hands and push off. And then I'm running. The echo of my slapping footsteps follow me to Ruby Jane's door. I skid to a stop and push through, slam the door behind me. Throw the bolt and wait. A different man, but not a fucking idiot. My heart pounds, my breath roars in my ears. The entry is dark around me.

For a moment, there's nothing. Then the doorknob shakes and I hear a scratching on the door. I step back, wish I still carried a gun. My shadow cast against the door by the lights over the butcher block is huge. For a moment I listen, my chest tight and head on fire. Half angry, half anxious. I picture the man on the other side of the door. Tall, indistinct face in the mist. God. Damn. Hoodie.

I smack my hand against the door. "I know who you are!" The scratching stops. "You stole my money, you piece of shit!" My voice sounds feckless and hollow.

But perhaps enough. Maybe I imagine the footsteps tapping away. Maybe he was gone before the echo of my shouts died away. I lean on the door, hanging there with my ear pressed against metal. All I hear is my own heartbeat.

I could call 911 again, but there's no point. Even if he's nearby, he'll fade long before the cops arrive. And then what do I say? *Some guy who picked my pocket is stalking me.* "Do you know who he is?" *He wears lots of layers.*

Sure.

I wait for another long minute, then two. Nothing. I'm still pulling in deep, ragged breaths. But they're slowing, slowing. I go to the kitchen sink, run water and splash my face. My hands are shaking. Behind me, the Weather Channel reports on a cyclone threatening Sri Lanka. I move to the sitting area, the long night catching up with me. Chase's campsite still smells of piss. I pull the cushions off the sofa and stack them near the entryway. Then I sit down, put my hand on the door. Tomorrow, maybe, I'll take the cushions out to get cleaned.

DIVIDEND TO STOCKHOLDER

I AWAKE SLUMPED against the door with my spine twisted into a contortionist's wet dream. A cell phone is ringing, an unfamiliar ringtone. I uncurl and pull Ruby Jane's phone out of my pocket. I have no business answering, especially given the likelihood Susan will try to reach RJ, but the call is from a 415 area code—San Francisco. I hit the TALK button.

"Hello."

All I hear is the anechoic sound of an open line.

"Hello? Any body there?"

Someone coughs, and then notices I'm here. "Yes, Ms. Whittaker, please."

It's a woman, her tone formal and a bit brusque. "She's not available. Can I help you?"

"Are you her representative?"

"Who is this?"

"My name is Joanne, from Pacific West Fidelity." She rattles off about twenty digits, though whether it's her phone number or latitude and longitude isn't clear. "When can I expect Ms. Whittaker's return call?"

"She's out of town."

"It's a matter of some urgency. When can I expect her return call?"

"Listen … Joanne?" She neither confirms nor denies. I take a breath. "She's away. I don't know when she'll be back. But perhaps if you could tell me—"

"It's a matter of some urgency."

"You're not too bright, are you?"

"Please have Ms. Whittaker return my call at her earliest convenience." She rattles off more numbers, too fast for me to note them. *Click.*

The clock on the phone display reads just before seven. Brain death and condescension alike know no schedule. The foyer is dim and cold, but daylight has invaded the main room beyond my feet. The piss stink from the stacked couch cushions assaults my nostrils.

I heave myself off the floor, unraveling the knots in my neck and cracking my ossified joints. In the bathroom, I dunk my face in cold water and brush my teeth with a toothbrush from the medicine cabinet. I didn't exactly sleep. Hell, I didn't even nap. I need coffee. Normally this would be the place to get some, but the only beans I've seen are still raw and Ruby Jane never trusted me with the roaster. At least Uncommon Cup is a few blocks away.

Marcy is farther, opening up Hollywood. It'll be busy there now, the morning rush. I sit on the clean couch, dial RJ's phone. Marcy picks up on the first ring, breathless.

"This still isn't Ruby Jane, is it?"

"I could fake it."

"And you'd pull it off too, because she totally sounds like a robot who swallowed a sheet of sand paper." She has to raise her voice over the chatter of customers and the whoosh of the espresso machine. "Whatcha need, Skin? I'm hopping."

"You ever hear of Pacific West Fidelity?"

"Sure. That's where James works."

"James Whittaker?"

"The very. Why?"

I describe the call from Joanne. "Any idea what it might be about?"

"Not really, no. I don't handle any financial stuff, except the daily deposits and reporting payroll to ADP."

"Okay. I'll let you get back to it. If you happen to hear from Ruby Jane—"

"You will first, man. Trust me. But if by some twist of fate it happens to be me, I'll tell her about Joanne."

"Thanks."

The Weather Channel is still murmuring, the business travelers report. The day will be nice everywhere, spring fully sprung. I take out the photo of Ruby Jane and the boy. Though there's a lot of years between the man I met in passing and the boy in this faded snapshot, I'm confident it's Jimmie. He shares with Ruby Jane his round cheeks and high forehead, if not the mischievous tilt of her head. The hand with the cigarette is pale and feminine, perhaps her mother. What I know of RJ's life pre-Uncommon Cup wouldn't fill a three-by-five note card. She grew up in Louisville, Kentucky, went to college in Ohio, then moved west in her twenties. Beyond that, she insists she's a full-blood Oregonian now—a contention certain genuine natives would take issue with. I'm a genuine native, but I've never been one to favor fortune over wits.

What else I know is she's not on the best of terms with her brother. He helped her get Uncommon Cup started by providing the seed capital. They've clashed ever since. The shops have been doing well, the expansions successful. "The greedy prat is making money—" she once said, "—the only thing he cares about." Ruby Jane bristles whenever Jimmie comes up in conversation.

Still, perhaps she spoke to him before she took off. If I can track him down, he might tell me what's going on. Or at least explain what the hell Joanne wants.

I scroll through her cell's contact list. No Jimmie. No James. No other Whittakers at all. All things considered, I'm only a little surprised. I head to Ruby Jane's office.

The desk phone has speed dial, but Jimmie isn't assigned a button. Marcy, me, the other shop managers, direct lines to each shop. She doesn't have an address book that I can find. It would be in her laptop anyway. There's no folder for James Whittaker in the filing cabinet among the Wells-Fargo statements, tax forms, and payroll records. After some digging I find record of a quarterly disbursement to a Pacific West Fidelity LLC memo'd DIVIDEND TO STOCKHOLDER. The address for Pacific West is in San Francisco, the phone number has a 415 area code. Saves me the hassle of repressed memory hypnosis to recover the endless string of digits Joanne threw at me.

I dial the number and spend ten minutes fighting a voice messaging system. No James Whittaker is available through the touch-tone directory. I leave a vague message on the general voicemail, certain no one will call me back. Places like that never call back, not unless you have something they want. Joanne may call for RJ, but even if she knows Jimmie she won't admit it. Likely as not, she'll be calling from Bangalore, ignore everything I say, and demand to speak to the woman who isn't here. A matter of some urgency.

There's nothing else. If RJ has Jimmie's phone number somewhere, it'll be in her laptop, or in her head.

For the hell of it, I call Information and request San Francisco, listing for James Whittaker. The operator asks me if it's Whittaker with one T or two. There are twenty possibilities if I include the

initial J, still more if I expand my search to include the full Bay
Area. I thank the operator and hang up. With so many options, a
computer search will be easier.

I lean back, Ruby Jane's desk chair squeaking beneath me.
Right now, home isn't where my heart is, but it is where my computer can be found. I think of another Jimmie I once knew, a man
who died on the deck in my backyard. I feel like I'd have more luck
finding him than Jimmie Whittaker. James. Ruby Jane once told
me he hates being called Jimmie. "My grandmother started it. 'Jimmie and Ruby, come to supper.' I ran around chanting it, *Jimmie
Jimmie Jimmie*. It made him so mad."

"Good thing you didn't let that stop you."

I imagine the morning ahead of me, running on fumes and
dialing number after number for various J. Whittakers and Whita-
kers—can't count on consistent spelling with online directories.
During the work day, I'm as likely as not to reach voicemail. I'll
leave the same message over and over: "My name is Thomas Kadash and I'm calling from Portland, Oregon. I am trying to reach
James Whittaker, brother of Ruby Jane Whittaker, also of Portland.
If you're the James I'm looking for, please get in touch with me ..."
Not all the calls will go unanswered, but odds are against anyone
fessing up to being RJ's errant sibling.

What I want is for Ruby Jane's phone to ring, for me to answer
and to hear her voice. "I knew you'd answer." *Of course I would,
darling.* I click navigation buttons at random. Missed call list, set-
tings menu, a game, *The Oregon Trail.* She'd taken the Trail in her
own way, I suppose, a hundred and fifty years after the original action, east to west, a journey with its perils even if times were very
different. That gives me a new thought. I take out my own cell
phone, bring up my own contacts. Scroll down the list, stop at a
number Ruby Jane has erased from her own phone.

I haven't talked to Peter McKrall for the better part of a year, though there was a time when I called him friend. The three of us met during the course of a murder investigation back when I was still working and partnered with Susan—a god awful mess thick with bodies, RJ and Pete nearly among them. In the aftermath, as she recovered from a gunshot wound and he recovered from a decade's worth of psychological fuckery, Pete and Ruby Jane found themselves an unlikely couple. The romance was born of tribulation, and twitchy from the beginning. Pete was never sure of who or what he wanted to be; Ruby Jane was as focused and assured as anyone I've ever known. That they were together at all is a mystery I'll never solve, but at his best he could be charming and thoughtful. I assumed they shared something on a more intimate level than either was willing to share with me.

Things deteriorated when Pete took a job in California, manager of a commercial plant nursery. The position was supposed to be temporary, a stepping stone to a better job at a larger nursery back in Oregon. The better job never materialized. The last time I saw him, Pete had come to town for a long weekend to see Ruby Jane—his final trip from Walnut Creek before the relationship went tits up once and for all. Not that the breakup was clear to anyone at the time. I didn't learn it was truly over until months later when I made a clumsy, semi-spontaneous pass at Ruby Jane. A day later, I was in intensive care—gunshot wound of my own—followed by months of difficult recovery. I never did find out what Pete thinks about me and Ruby Jane—or if she's even spoken to him about us. Far as it goes, I'm still not sure what Ruby Jane thinks about me and Ruby Jane.

I highlight his entry and hit TALK. He answers just as I'm sure it's going to voicemail.

"Hey, Pete, it's Skin. Long time."

I hear the faint sound of an engine. Maybe he's on the road.

"Pete? You there?"

Another pause, but then I hear a breath. "Yeah, I'm here."

"Did I catch you at a bad time?"

"I'm at work." There's no mistaking the tone in his voice. Terse.

"I won't keep you then—"

"Good." And he's gone. Call time: sixteen seconds.

I leave the small office, my mind a turbulent stew of confusion and exhaustion. Past the roaster, through the hallway, into the apartment. I come to a stop next to the forlorn claw foot. Chase Fairweather left a scum ring. All the cleaning I did, I forgot to scrub the tub. Or maybe I made an unconscious choice. Doesn't matter now. The atmosphere in the room is oppressive; a dense, still reminder of Ruby Jane's bewildering absence. I move quickly, turn off lights and television. I hesitate near the smelly couch cushions, decide to leave them for now. Maybe I'll come back for them, or maybe Ruby Jane will return first. I don't know. Someone will have to deal with the alarm panel too, but not now, not today. I open the side door. Stop short.

As I stare at the empty spot where my car used to be, I find myself imagining Ruby Jane in California. In Walnut Creek.

With Pete.

It would explain everything.

7

Every Exit an Opportunity

I'VE BEEN DRIVING past almond trees, celery fields, and straw-berries for the better part of an hour when my phone rings. A 503 number according to the display, but not one I recognize. Not Peter, not Ruby Jane.

"Sir, I'm calling to let you know we've recovered your car." It's a cop.

"Thank you. Where is it now?"

"We've brought it to Rivergate impound."

I wince; that'll cost me. If he'd called me first, I'd have asked him to make sure it was locked up and leave it parked until I return. "Okay. I'm out of town. I'll see if I can arrange for someone to come pick it up." Marcy might be willing, assuming I can get some cash to her. There's paperwork too, but maybe I can get Susan to grease that. She knows Marcy and can vouch for her.

But the cop isn't finished. "I'm afraid it will need to be towed, sir."

"What are you telling me?"

"It's in pretty bad shape."

"Stripped?"

"Not really. We pulled it out of Johnson Creek."

"You're kidding me."

"Someone drove it down the Springwater Corridor and dumped it in the water at Tideman Johnson Preserve. A cyclist reported it."

"Christ."

"You're gonna need some engine work and a professional cleaning."

A triple-trailer blasts past me on the right, whacking the car with its backwash and putting my own excessive speed to shame. "Shit. I'll have to work something out."

"There's a storage fee—"

"I know. I know ..."

I hang up. I've been on the road since eight, having delayed only long enough to report the car and arrange for my second rental car in as many days and hit the road.

By the time I passed Eugene, a giant coffee with a couple of add shots burning a hole in my stomach, I'd convinced myself I'm out of my fucking mind. The thought of Ruby Jane with Pete floods in and out of my thoughts as I drive, a bitter tide. South of Roseburg I pull into a rest area to piss and refill my coffee. Before I get out of the car, I tilt the mirror to look at my blotchy, weary face.

Accusation stares back.

"If she's with him, it's because she wants to be with him." In the bathroom, as I wash my hands, I glimpse my reflection again, this time warped by the scratched, stainless steel mirror over the sink. "If she didn't tell you, it's because she didn't want you to know." The Lions Club volunteer in the traveler's aid booth offers me an Oreo with my coffee. All I hear is my own voice inside my head. "Go home, Skin." Back in my car, I continue south. Every exit offers an opportunity to come to my senses, turn off, turn around, turn back. I ignore them all.

My tenuous logic rests on a foundation of rationalization. *She's there, she's not there.* If she's not there, Peter will be, and Peter can tell me how to find Jimmie. And then, hell, at that point, I might just as well drive the remaining, short distance to Jimmie's house, apartment, condo. Jimmie is wealthy. I picture him with a place on Russian Hill or Pacific Heights, an anchor building on a well-trod corner, three or four stories with a *chi-chi* café or bar on the ground floor. He's got the top two floors filled with art and antiques purchased as investments, leases out the rest of the building. In my mind, he's a shitty landlord. But, really, I know nothing about him except he's Ruby Jane's greatest source of irritation, a man to whom she paid quarterly dividends, to whom she owed some percentage of her dream.

As the flat Sacramento Valley opens up before me, six hours out, I've worked through my rationalizations so many times I no longer know what I believe. She's there, she's not there. Peter knows something, Peter knows nothing. I've imagined scenarios so absurd and impossible that when I stop for gas in Red Bluff I'm half ready to believe I'll find Ruby Jane, Pete, and Jimmie in the truck stop restaurant. Playing euchre, drinking Old Fashioneds, plotting the overthrow of Cuba. It all makes equal sense. In a moment of lucidity, standing over yet another anonymous urinal, I call Peter again, get no answer, and find it within myself to leave him a reasoned message explaining why I'd called in the first place. I imagine him stepping away from the euchre game with a knowing nod to his partners. "Jimmie, I'm going to call Skin back and give him your home address. Okay?" Ruby Jane tells him to hurry up, it's his deal, and besides, he's responsible for coordinating the air cover for the marine landing.

I feel like I'm coasting downhill when I reach the I-680 cut-off from I-80. I haven't been in California in years, and never in Walnut Creek. At one time, that would have meant forethought and planning with a Thomas Guide and a highlighter. But now I've got the rental company's GPS telling me where to go, my very own digital enabler with a soothing, synthetic voice. If it had my best interests in mind, it would tell me to go home, or to go to hell. Instead it directs me to Peter's nondescript apartment complex east of the interstate near what I presume is Walnut Creek's commercial core. Or maybe the whole town is commercial core. Ever since I left behind the broad, agricultural flats of the Central Valley I've felt like I was driving through an endless combination industrial park/strip mall characterized by the Lego School of architecture. I follow Miss Tom-Tom's directions from the exit, right at the fork, ahead two-tenths of a mile, right again, watch for road construction. I know I've reached my destination only because she tells me so. The complex, called Vista View, is a Spanish Mission/Cape Cod mash-up which looks out at two other complexes and a church parking lot, catty-corner from the back of a Target.

I park, traipse through hyper-manicured landscaping until I find the entryway leading to Peter's apartment. Second floor, in the back.

My plan, such as it is, is to ask him how he's doing, when he last heard from Ruby Jane. The tide is out. Ruby Jane, I'm now sure, is in some unknown, unguessed location. But when I knock, he opens the door on the second rap, as if he was standing there waiting for me. The suddenness of his appearance is like a wave crashing in.

"Where is she?"

He blinks at me, his mouth working as if he can't decide how to respond. Then his eyebrows lower. "How the hell should I know?"

I try to see past him into the apartment. The door opens onto a short, dark hallway, the cool glow of a compact fluorescent light bulb in the room beyond. I can hear the television. "She's in there."

"Skin, what the hell is wrong with you?"

"You're saying she's not here?"

He looks at me with a mixture of contempt and sadness. "You drove all this way because you think I'm hiding Ruby Jane?"

"Pete, damn it."

"She's not here." He steps out of my way. "Come in, check everywhere. She's not here."

"Jesus." I run my hand over my face. My skin is hot to the touch. "Pete …"

"What on earth were you thinking?"

"You hung up on me."

"Maybe I didn't feel like talking to you." He turns and heads back into the apartment. I follow, sheepish. "You drove six hundred miles because I hung up on you."

"I'm worried. No one knows where she is. When I talked to you …" I sigh, collapse onto a dinette chair. "It had been a long night."

"And an even longer day."

"I drove fast."

"I haven't talked to her in months, Skin."

"How many months?"

"You feeling jealous? You?"

"Christ. I'm an idiot."

"Join the club."

I wait for him to offer me something. I'm not hungry, too busy digesting my own organs all day, but my mouth is dry and my head pounding. He joins me at the table, eyes on his folded hands. The room is classic Pete, one wall nothing but fastidiously maintained plants, but everything else in vague disarray. Newspapers piled up on the floor next to the couch, empty glasses on the coffee table. The television is tuned to what looks like an infomercial. Whatever Pete had for dinner, it featured garlic.

"In your message, you asked about James. You think he knows something?"

"I don't know. I tried to get hold of him, but I got stiffed at his company. Directory assistance was a brick wall."

"So you figured I owe you a favor?"

"Pete, come on, it wasn't me got between you and Ruby Jane."

"No, I got between me and Ruby Jane all on my own."

I can't tell if he's being serious or not. "All I want is to make sure she's all right."

He drums his fingers on the table, then reaches up and pulls at his lower lip. I've seen that look before. Peter trying to make a decision. He stands up suddenly. "Stay here." He disappears into the hallway, returns before I can object. He offers me a folded piece of paper. "Here."

I open a printout from a computer address book: *James Whitacre*, with a San Francisco address and phone number.

"You had this printed out already. Were you expecting me?"

"When I got your message, I looked it up. I printed it out and stuck it in my coat pocket in case you called me again. Never expected to be handing it to you."

In other words, I'm the crazy one sitting at this table. I turn back to the paper, ungum my tongue from the roof of my mouth.

"Whit-*acre*. How the fuck was I supposed to find that?"

"RJ told me he changed it when he got into venture capital. He thinks it makes him sound like landed gentry rather than some backwoods hick."

"He *is* a backwoods hick."

"Aren't we all?"

I'm urban trash, but it's a minor distinction.

"He lives in Sunset."

"Where's that?"

"See if you can guess."

"Pete, last time I checked the sun sets on the whole damn state, the Governator's ad campaign notwithstanding."

He's back at his lip, working it like a piece of dough. From the television, I learn I can get two Slankets for the price of one if I order in the next ten minutes. "You'll have to use your own phone. It's long distance from here."

"Pete, Jesus. We used to be friends."

A few years earlier, I let Pete walk away from a house with a dead body in it, him and his sister both. It was the day after Ruby Jane got shot, and he was anxious to go to the hospital to see her. He'd done nothing except find himself in the wrong place at the wrong time, and no one needed to know he'd been there. Now, two-and-a-half years later, I wonder if the favor buys me the privilege of making a play for his ex-girlfriend.

His answer, based on the stiffness in his back and the shadow over his eyes, is no.

I let out a long, slow breath and pull out my phone. I've got plenty of minutes. Then I have an idea and put it away, get Ruby Jane's phone instead. It had rang a couple of times during the day, but the 923 exchange told me the call was from the Justice Center—Susan. I'd let those calls go to voice mail.

Now, I punch in the digits from Pete's print out. Jimmie won't recognize my number in Caller ID, but he may know RJ's—assuming it isn't saved in his Contacts list. I'm not sure if that means he'll be more likely to answer, or less.

His voice is sharp when he picks up. "It's a goddamn miracle. You remembered my fucking phone number."

"Is that any way to talk to your sister?"

I hear a sharp intake of breath. "Who is this?"

"Skin Kadash, Ruby Jane's friend."

" Figure that." He's quiet for a long moment. "The cop."

"Ex-cop. This is Jimmie, right?"

"James."

"Right. James."

"What are you doing with Ruby's phone?"

"She's out of town and left it behind. I haven't been able to reach her. I was hoping you might be able to help me out."

"What makes you think I know anything?"

"You're her brother?"

"Sorry. I got no idea." He hangs up.

Peter regards me from across the table. "He blew you off."

"He thought I was Ruby Jane. First thing he did was go off on her."

"He's always been a dick."

I could try calling him back, but I'm well aware of the definition of insanity. The light from the TV reflects off Peter's eyes, white impenetrable rectangles. I can't tell what he's thinking. His fingers pull at his lip. From way back, I remember Peter as being someone who spoke first, thought afterwards. But not now. The moment stretches.

"What's on your mind, Pete?"

"Wondering what you're gonna do."

If recent history is any indication, I'm going to do something irrational based on insufficient evidence with little chance of success. My hands are shaking. It's hard for me to believe it's been twenty-four hours since I learned Ruby Jane is gone. I've cleaned up after a corpse and transfused myself with coffee. Lost my cash, lost my car, and apparently lost my mind.

"I'm gonna find her. And I'm gonna make Jimmie help me whether he likes it or not."

He nods. "Okay. Come on then. I'll drive."

8

G-AND-T

"WHY ARE *YOU* driving anyway?"

At least we're in my rental car and not his manure-dusted pick-up, which means I can ditch him if necessary. He can make his way home on BART or by cab or however they do it around here. Assuming I can get the car keys away from him. He took them from me in the parking lot of his cartoonish apartment complex like he was taking the keys from a drunk.

"I'm used to driving in San Francisco."

"Are you kidding me?"

"It can get a little crazy."

"Pete, I've driven in Saigon. I've driven in Bangkok. I've driven in *Boston*, for chrissakes."

"I know where we're going."

So he says, but he's paying a lot of attention to Miss Tom-Tom. Maybe he likes having a woman talk to him again after so long on his own.

We're on the interstate heading toward the bay. Nothing to be gained from bitching now, except I'm in the mood to bitch. I lean my head against the glass, stare down at the shoulder zipping past. Traffic is no heavier than what I see on an average Portland evening, Sunset Highway over Sylvan or through the Terwilliger Curves on I-5, but I don't say anything. We're in that preternatural period between sundown and full darkness when the light plays tricks on you. Cars heading away look like they're veering toward you, shadows leap and dance at the roadside. The concrete barrier beyond the shoulder throws the traffic noise back like a wall of falling gravel. Beyond, I see the spiky heads of unfamiliar trees.

"You put in a different address than the one on the printout." I didn't intend to speak, and my voice sounds like I'm drunk. Exhausted, I guess.

"There's a joint where he hangs out, a sports bar."

"And you know this how, exactly?"

Through the floor of the car, the tires sound like a fingernail dragged along a comb. He pulls at his lip with one hand and steers with the other.

"You thought he could help you with Ruby Jane."

Half-shrug.

"She hates him."

"She doesn't hate him. They ... differ on certain matters."

"Yeah, he's a rich puke and he lives to fuck with her."

"It's not that simple."

I close my eyes, listen to the tires for a minute, two minutes. Miss Tom-Tom tells us we're approaching the Bay Bridge.

"I hope he paid for your drinks after you drove this far."

"He's not doing as well as everyone thinks."

We slow and Peter mutters something about a toll, but I don't open my eyes. "So did he help?"

"Who?"

"Christ, Pete. Jimmie. Did he help?"

"He doesn't understand her any better than anyone else."

Before yesterday, I never thought she was such a mystery.

Ruby Jane once told me she felt her relationship with Peter was like driving too fast on a mountain road, up one minute, down the next, twisting and turning at reckless velocity. Hanging on by a thin-skinned traction and the breathless weight of inertia. Who knows what Pete thought? One side of the story is never enough, but when it comes to affairs of the heart, two sides is often too many.

Peter takes us across the bridge and down into the city. The light changes, as does the sound of the tires. I was last in San Francisco shortly after I got out of the army. Twenty-five years and counting. I recognize nothing. Peter finds his way onto a one-way arterial heading west. Cars clump around us. We pass storefronts and apartments jammed shoulder to shoulder with Victorians, single-family conversions to multi-family walk ups. There are more colors than I'm used to. The trees at the street's edge have been shaped by wind. We skirt Golden Gate Park, and I think back to my last visit when I wandered the halls of the De Young Museum and sat on the grass in the early evening dark. Now, as then, I can't see the sky, just a formless grey shroud, brighter than night, less revealing than dusk. I blink, try to make out a sound like a voice murmuring at the back of my head. And then, we're not moving.

"Skin, wake up. We're here."

I stir, lift my head off the window. A stab of pain shoots down my neck. Cold spit coats my chin. Out on the sidewalk, a Latino boy is pointing at me and saying something to a woman with him. I can't make out his words through the glass, but I can guess. "Look at the ugly man, mama." She smacks his hand and pulls him away. He can't take his eyes off me, his head corkscrewing around as he gets farther away. In an earlier era, he could have paid a quarter to a carny for a glimpse.

"You coming?"

We're parked on a broad avenue, wide sidewalks and multiple lanes.

"Where are we?"

"The bar I told you about. James has a place a few blocks away, but this is home."

I feel like my bones have been replaced with dry twigs. Peter heads up the street. Somewhere nearby Cambodian pop music plays. It feels late, but I see people all around, in cars and on foot. The street signs don't tell me much. Thirty-Second and Noriega. The main drag trends to small business: produce market, pharmacy, a Chinese bakery, hole-in-the-wall restaurants and shops. Most of the signs are bi- and tri-lingual: English, Spanish, Chinese. Peter ignores it all, heads toward a door standing open under an arched black awning. I glance at my watch. It's been less than twenty-four hours since I found Chase Fairweather soaking in Ruby Jane's tub, twenty-eight since I came home to find RJ gone. Feels like much longer.

I follow Pete into a long room with a tall ceiling. There are pool tables at the back, balls clacking, and televisions on the walls, couple of big screens dominating. Most are showing SportsCenter. The place is three-quarters full and noisy, lots of shapeless hubbub with the occasional voice rising clear above the din in response to something on TV. The air smells of beer, fried cheese, spring rolls. My stomach lurches a bit, but my mouth is dry.

"Is he here?"

Peter points with a sharp nod. "At the bar. Always at the bar."

James Whittaker—Whitacre I suppose—is not what I remember. He's slumped on his stool, glass in front of him. Whatever he's drinking is clear, on the rocks, with a twist. When he visited Portland a couple of years back, he was tall and confident, tanned face and russet hair, with dimples to match Ruby Jane's. I saw his less than hers; he wasn't generous with his smile.

Now, his skin is sallow, his hair wiry and gone to grey. A fading bruise shades one cheek a sickly green. Only his shoes stand out compared to the rest of him—brown Esquivel wingtips—which I recognize because I knew a cop who bought a pair after a promotion to lieutenant—the asshole wouldn't shut the fuck up about them. Jimmie has nothing else to brag about. He's wearing a green and grey glen plaid suit which looks like it came off the rack at Macy's during the after Christmas clearance. White shirt, collar open, no tie. Can't say I've ever dressed better, but then I'm not a venture capital douchebag who shits gold nuggets and pisses silver filigree.

Jimmie recognizes Pete, waves with a kind of forced affability. His eyes don't quite go two directions as he takes us in, but almost. "McKrall. What'n hell you doing here? Long drive from Turdnut Creek." Whatever he's drinking, it's not his first. He points at me with his glass in hand. "No one could ever forget that neck."

Peter lets me take the stool next to him. Jimmie knocks off the last of his drink, eyes at half-mast. "You never told me you were an astronaut, Kadash."

I glance at Peter, eyebrows raised. "Just an ex-cop." I emphasize *cop*, not so much *ex-*. Not sure what good it'll do me, but there's an edge to his tone I hope will be dulled if he thinks I'm in a position to give him some shit.

But he doesn't care. "You fly your rocket ship down here, astro-cop?"

"I'm not following you, Jimmie."

"James."

"I'm not following you, James."

"You called me like an hour ago or something. How the hell you get here so fast?"

I turn to Pete. "Maybe we should let him sleep this off, try again in the morning."

But Jimmie grabs my forearm. "Fuck that. You flew your space shuttle all this way, might has well have a drink."

"I don't think—"

"Park it." He throws up his hand and leans across the bar. "Darryl, we're dying down here, man."

I presume Darryl is the bartender. He's at the far end of the bar drawing a couple of beers. He passes them off to a waitress, then slides our way. A small fellow, Chinese maybe, with black, slicked-back hair. When he speaks, it sounds like he grew up in Brooklyn.

"Hey, what can I get you fellas?"

Jimmie slaps the bar. "G-and-T's all around." But I shake my head.

"Big glass of water for me and a cup of coffee."

"Christ, Kadash, you flying again so soon?"

Darryl smiles, accustomed to Jimmie. "And you?" He nods at Pete.

"Something light, whatever you have on tap."

"You got it."

I lean toward Jimmie, but Pete pipes up before I can speak.

"Hey, James, I wonder if you can help us out."

Jimmie stares suspiciously into his glass. "I hope you aren't here to borrow money."

"Nothing like that."

He laughs and stirs his finger in the leftover ice of his dead drink. "What'd she do to you this time?"

"She didn't—"

"Fucked ya and dumped ya. That's something, you ask me. Good riddance. Bitch."

I shift on my stool. Darryl returns, takes Jimmie's glass and replaces it with a fresh one. Sets the coffee, water and beer in a tight little line.

Pete puts a hand on my forearm for an instant, then tries again. "Here's the thing, James. She has taken off and no one knows where." I can tell he's struggling to keep his voice steady.

Jimmie doesn't notice. "You buying?" He rolls his head until he's looking at me. "Is he?"

I close my eyes for a moment. When I open them, Jimmie is back to his drink.

"Seriously, you get Cap'n Crunch to buy my drinks, maybe I'll help you."

I take a sip of water and hold it in my dry mouth before swallowing. "I'd think you'd be worried about your sister."

"Fuck her. She takes care of herself."

I've interviewed more than a few belligerent suspects in my life, so Jimmie doesn't ruffle my feathers. A cop who lets his personal feelings get the better of him isn't much of a cop. But a cop, a real working cop, also has leverage I don't. The threat of arrest or criminal charges can do a lot to loosen reticent tongues. I raise my hand, wave Darryl down. "Something else?"

"When the time comes I'll be taking care of my friend's check."

"Okay, sure. No problem."

I fix Jimmie with a stare. "We good?"

"I'm good with anyone who buys me a rack of G-and-T's." He knocks back his drink like it's water and slams the glass on the bar. "One more, Darryl!" Then he grins. His teeth are straight and as white as eggs. "Okay. What?"

"You don't know where she is?"

"Not a clue."

"When did you last talk to her?"

He thinks for a moment. "A month, maybe."

"About?"

"What's that got to do with where she is?"

"You tell me."

"It wasn't anything."

"Then it shouldn't matter if you tell me."

Darryl delivers another drink. He shows no concern for how drunk Jimmie is.

"She was all up in my face about Pacific West demanding she buy them out."

"Buy them out of what? Uncommon Cup?"

"What else?"

"I thought you were her partner."

"It's complicated. You know, money shit."

"Right. A guy like me rarely gets to see actual money. Lucky for your bar tab, I brought my marble collection for tradesies."

He tries to indicate disdain with a raised eyebrow and fails. "I sold my interest to Pacific West when I left. Roo thought I should have given her a chance to finance the buyout herself, but I didn't have time for that. Not that it's any of your business."

I try to catch Pete's eyes, but he ignores me. His back is straight. I have an idea what Joanne was calling about, but I can't see what it would have to do with Ruby Jane's disappearance. "Why do they want out already?"

"Too small for them, probably. They were doing me a favor."

"What made you decide to sell?"

He slaps the bar, then just as quickly shrinks into himself. Darryl looks up at the noise, but when Jimmie sags he looks away again. No one else pays any attention.

"Jimmie?" He won't look at me. "What's the problem?"

"Fucking Biddy, or whatever he calls himself."

"Biddy who?"

His head is flopping on his shoulders now. "Dudn't matter." We've passed a threshold, one gin-and-tonic past ataxia. Another drink and I could lose him. I grab his shoulder, try to drag him back to me.

"James, here's the deal. Ruby Jane left suddenly, told no one anything. She didn't even take her cell phone."

"She's always been unpredictable. Isn't that right, Petey-boy?"

Ruby Jane is one of the most rock solid people I know. But it's obvious Jimmie doesn't see her that way, and somehow views Pete as his ally. I can't be sure where this is going, but before it can devolve into a litany of past wrongs I switch directions.

"Tell me about Biddy."

His face goes carefully blank. "You're drunk, man." It's taking all he has to keep his eyelids off the bar.

"Might Ruby Jane's disappearance have something to do with this Biddy character?"

It takes him a long time to answer. Pete is a stone beside me, useless. Or agitated. Maybe he's mad I blew off his attempt to control the conversation. I don't care. Some kernel of knowledge marinates inside Jimmie's gin-sodden brain. I just need to figure out how to coax it out of him before Darryl calls an ambulance.

He sits up abruptly, his head at a precarious angle. "I bet she went home."

"Trust me, if she was home, I'd know."

"Not Portland, idiot."

"Where then?"

"Long, long way." He drops his head between his shoulders, and his face droops. For a moment I wonder if he's going to start crying. He gazes into his gin-and-tonic like he's looking into a crystal ball. "All the way back."

"Where, Jimmie?"

He looks up, startled as if just now realizing I'm there. "Where who?"

"Where? *James.* Kentucky?"

But he's far away now, drifted off, perhaps, to wherever he imagines Ruby Jane to be. When he talks again, his voice is low, barely loud enough to be heard over the cheers and shouts and laughter all around us.

"When you find her, ask her about that night on Preble County Line Road."

"Preble County? In Kentucky?"

"Why do you keep talking about Kentucky?"

"She told me you guys grew up in Louisville."

That amuses Jimmie. "She would."

Pete hunches over his beer. "She told me that too—at first. But then we actually got to know each other."

Aggravation—or humiliation—flares in me. I don't know if Pete is trying to rile me on purpose, or reflecting on what he's lost. Either way, I ignore him. "What are you saying, James?"

"The seminal events of our young lives took place out in the sticks between West Alexandria and Farmersville, Ohio."

"Your young lives."

"Hers, mine. Others. Someone tries to tell you how bad high school was, take it from me, they don't know shit."

"What happened, Jimmie?"

He stands, brushes his hands together like he's shaking off dust. "You want a drink? I'm having a drink." He lifts his arm to signal Darryl.

"I think you've had enough."

"Going cheap on me now, astro-cop? C'mon. G-and-T? That's what I'm having."

"Jimmie, sit down."

Instead he backs away from the bar, bumps into a chair behind him. A girl spills her drink, turns to yell at him. He doesn't notice. I reach for his arm, but he jerks it away. "You know what? Fuck you guys." Then he's moving toward the door like a sailor who's lost his sea legs.

I start to follow, but Darryl materializes across the bar.

"Pete, stay with him." I fish for my wallet, lose track of them both. Darryl takes my credit card as I hear Pete shout Jimmie's name.

Pete hasn't reached the door yet. I glimpse a flash of Jimmie's cheap green suit as he collides with a woman getting out of a silver SUV, catches himself on the hood, and runs into the street. I lose sight of him as I follow Pete through the bar and out onto the sidewalk. The woman from the SUV screams, the sound drowned out by the shriek of tearing metal. There's a loud crunch, the sound of breaking glass, rubber on the road. Screams rise as the squealing tires fade. Pounding feet, shouts. Pete and I charge across the broad street, swept along by a crowd which seems to materialize out of the very walls of the buildings around us. I see the body on the far sidewalk in a pool of blood, head jammed against the dark green base of a city garbage bin.

"Oh god—"

"—pancaked him—"

"—gone. Just tore outta—"

A man leans over the body, checks him with the authority of someone who's done this before. I recognize Jimmie's shoes, one brown wingtip still on his foot, the other in the street a dozen feet away. As his blood drains into the gutter, following the straight-edge line of black tire rubber across the sidewalk, I have an odd thought: he might have jumped clear if only he'd been wearing sneakers.

9

Population: 937

THE AIR IS heavy in a way I haven't experienced since I mustered out of the Army at Fort Leonard Wood in 1975. It's not merely humidity; Saigon was hotter and soupier, much more of a steam bath. This is different, a muddy vapor which is less damp than dense. Every breath is like trying to suck a boiled egg through a window screen. I'm wearing a plain white t-shirt and a pair of jeans I picked up at the Target across from Peter's complex, but I feel crushed under the weight of fabric. I wonder if my boxers can pass as shorts.

I feel a little better once we get into the car, a rental hat trick which tests the breaking strain on my credit card. At the counter, there's some confusion. GPS is an add-on, and they tell me they're out. We're going to have to use a map.

"You navigate."

Peter grunts. "I printed some Google maps."

"We're saved."

"At your age, I'd think a paper map would be a comfort."

It's been a long coupla days.

He guides me to the interstate, and soon we've crossed the Ohio River and are heading north through Cincinnati, a city similar enough tox Portland that its differences make it truly alien. Billboards blare with unfamiliar local radio hosts alongside Hannity and O'Reilly. The highway is a lane too wide, the hills too soft and round. Absent are Doug firs and monkey puzzle trees, long-needled pines in their place among familiar elms, oaks and broadleaf maples. The woven highways close to the river make Portland's modest system look like a series of wagon trails. I see more rusted-out hulks on the road in ten minutes than I see in a year back home, the result, Pete tells me, of winter road salt.

"Must be great for everyone's blood pressure."

"They don't eat it, Skin."

"No, they breathe it."

"It's not such a bad town. My family used to drive up from Lexington for Reds games. Riverfest too. It was fun."

I struggle to imagine Pete's past life. My eyes feel like they're full of sand. I slept on the plane. But squeezed into a seat designed for an underfed ten-year-old is no way to get any rest.

The AC set to arctic struggles to combat the sweat on my neck. While I drive, Peter is on the phone, dialing numbers from a print-out.

"Hello. My name is Peter, and I'm looking for an old friend from high school. Ruby Jane Whittaker ... okay, sorry for bothering you."

According to the online directory, there are over seventy-five Whittakers in the area around Farmersville, four times what I found looking for Jimmie in the Bay Area—we didn't limit ourselves to the initial J. I'm not expecting much, but it gives him something to do.

"Hi, I'm looking for an old friend and wonder if you might be able to help. Her name is Ruby Jane Whit—"

— + —

The San Francisco cops had kept us for hours at the scene of Jimmie's demise. There were plenty of witnesses, but Darryl ensured Pete and I got the lion's share of the attention. My explanation for why I'd come to town and what we'd discussed with Jimmie didn't earn us any points with the pair of sunken-eyed homicide inspectors who had the misfortune of drawing the case. Eldridge and Deffeyes: one short, thick and bearded and the other short, thick and bearded. I couldn't tell them apart.

"Mister Whitacre was your girlfriend's brother?" They tag-teamed me in the street outside the bar's entrance, the flashing lightbars and the murmurs of rubberneckers giving me a headache. Pete waited with a uniformed officer on the opposite corner. I was the lucky one; he had a clear view of Jimmie's body.

"*His* girlfriend. Well, not anymore. I don't know, really."

"You don't know who's girlfriend she is."

"Friend. We're friends."

"Mister McKrall says she's your girlfriend."

"Friend."

"And where is she now?"

"We don't know. That's why we were talking to Jimmie."

"James Whitacre."

"Right."

"And what did he say?"

"He didn't know where she was either."

I knew the cops came off more oafish than they really were. Trying to trip me up, play the fool to see how my story changed as I tried to correct their pointed misunderstandings. But they didn't trip me up because I didn't try to hide anything. I shared my worry and confusion, my attempt to reach Jimmie from Portland, my decision to drive down. Obviously they thought I was nuts. After a thorough work-over, they stuck me in the back of a patrol car while they gave Pete the same treatment. The car smelled of urine, but at least it was dark and quiet. I closed my eyes and waited. Apparently Pete was no more useful, though at one point either Eldridge or Deffeyes stuck his beard in the car and told me he'd backed up my story.

Yay.

Eventually one of the beards let me out of the car.

"I called your lieutenant. She vouched for you and your girl-friend's boyfriend."

"She's not my lieutenant. I'm retired." I don't know why this point is so important to me. Maybe because it's so irrelevant to everyone else.

"No one is your anything, are they?"

That didn't deserve a response.

"I still don't understand why you couldn't talk to Mister Whitacre on the phone." The implication being if I'd called, maybe he wouldn't be lying in a puddle of his own blood outside a Chinese bakery.

"Like I said, I couldn't reach him."

"So you drove all this way on the off chance you'd run into him."

Given the circumstances, I'm not thrilled by his choice of words. "I have a lot of time on my hands, Inspector." In his shoes, I'd have questions too. Dead man, hit-and-run, last seen talking to two guys who can offer no explanation for why the victim ran into a busy street. The car involved, a blue Ford Focus, was found a dozen blocks away, the interior on fire. Stolen. All I have going for me is the fact I'm an ex-cop and I wasn't driving the Focus.

"One more question."

I don't *think* he could hear my teeth grind. "Sure."

"The name Biddy Denlinger mean anything to you?"

That caught me up for a moment. The mysterious Biddy has a last name. "He mentioned the name Biddy, but he didn't say who they were."

"Whitacre had a note in his Filofax. 'Biddy Denlinger, 8:00 p.m.' He'd scratched it out, but maybe this Biddy showed up anyway. Whitacre wasn't talking with anyone when you got here?"

"He was alone at the bar."

"The bartender doesn't remember anyone but you and your friend either."

"Pete and I didn't get here til ten."

"So I heard." He sighs. "I'd tell you not to leave town, but gone might be the best place for you."

"Maybe the San Francisco tourist bureau would think otherwise."

"You planning on spending a lot of money while you're here?"

My pension would say no. "Not feeling too welcome, to be honest."

"A lot of that going around."

Back in Walnut Creek, Pete offered me his couch. I was awake before sunrise, drinking Pete's coffee and working the Google on his computer under the cool glow of the grow lights on his wall of plants. By the time Pete woke, I'd found Farmersville, found Preble County Line Road. Found my long list of Whittakers. What I didn't find is Ruby Jane, except as the owner of record of a small chain of Portland coffee houses. Even the mighty Google has its blind spots.

Pete poured himself coffee and opened the vertical blinds over the sliding glass door. Watery light filtered in across his balcony. "What's the plan?

"I think I need to go to Ohio."

"Okay. I'll arrange some time off work."

"You're not coming with me."

"Try and stop me." He turned on his heel and left me alone in his living room before I could argue the point. I heard the shower start, and took the opportunity to slip out. When I returned an hour later with underwear and toiletries, jeans and a couple of t-shirts, all in a black nylon pack, he informed me he'd booked us on a red-eye out of Oakland with a change in Denver. We'd get into Cincinnati about seven the next morning.

"Pete, I don't need a goddamn sidekick."

"You're not the only one who cares about Ruby Jane."

"Moving to fucking Walnut Creek is an odd way of showing it."

"What are you complaining about? I'm out of *your* way, aren't I?"

"That's not the point."

"I don't have to justify myself to you. And I don't need your permission to go to Ohio."

I wanted to argue further, but what was the point? Were our positions reversed, I'd insist on coming.

Pete spent the day on his computer, making his print-outs and offering up obscure data points about Farmersville. Elevation: 879 feet. Population: 937, down by four percent since the 2000 census. Seat of Jackson Township in Montgomery County. Local high school: Valley View—home of the Spartans—halfway between Farmersville and nearby Germantown. One web site revealed there have been five documented ghost sightings in town.

Around midday, I called Susan. Her tone was that of a disappointed grandmother learning her little cherub has been skipping school. Eldridge and Deffeyes had said little, except they were getting nowhere on Biddy Denlinger; didn't even know if Biddy was male or female. I could tell she'd joined them in the *Skin is out of his mind* camp, but she admitted the growing body count raised a question or two. She even admitted to visiting Uncommon Cups for a chat with Marcy. When I told her we were going to Ohio she paused for a long, pregnant moment before suggesting we try to stay out of jail.

— + —

We leave I-75 at Franklin, make our way north and west. Urban gives way to rural, though small towns materialize every few miles. Trees alongside the road struggle to stand upright in the heavy air. I stare out the window, mystified by large brick planters shaped like baskets in the broad front yards we pass. The world feels compressed and sleepy to me, from the sluggish Miami River to the clapboard houses and eroding concrete silos along Carlisle Pike. I find myself wondering who lives in a place like this, and I guess I say so out loud without realizing it.

"The world doesn't fucking end east of Eighty-Second and south of Powell."

"Just saying."

"You act like you've never seen a barn. Christ, you're worse than a New Yorker."

Maybe it's me.

Beyond Germantown, the road dips and climbs through scrubby woodland and open fields, with occasional big houses on giant lots. "Look, Pete. A barn." We pass the high school and I'm tempted to stop. It's been on the order of twenty years, I estimate, but someone might remember Ruby Jane, or know if she still has family in the area. But I decide to continue on to Farmersville. A couple of miles later we climb a gentle rise and we're there.

"Now what, Detective? Gonna roust us some rubes?"

Good grief. "How many Whittakers do you have left to call?"

"About a hundred."

"There were only seventy-five to begin with."

"You know what I mean."

"Yeah."

"So what do we do?"

"We get some lunch."

"It's not even ten o'clock."

"Breakfast then."

"That's your plan? We fly three thousand miles and your big idea is breakfast."

"Sooner or later, someone who knows RJ is bound to go out to eat."

"If anyone around here even remembers her."

"You could have stayed in California."

Farmersville is a rubber stamp pastoral village slipping into senescence. Saltbox houses on small lots mix with two-story brick or lap-sided commercial. The sunlight is sharp and metallic, the air earthy. I criss-cross the village at a crawl; the core is roughly six blocks by four, a quiet grid with minimal activity. A couple of guys chat outside U.S. Bank, kids play during recess at the elementary school. Trucks kick up fermented dust as they leave the grain elevators on the west side of town. I find what I'm looking for on Center Street: a bakery and café dripping with folksy charm. If we're lucky, it's full of Chatty Cathys with long memories.

The café is cozy, a little overwarm. There are a few tables, and a glass case filled with baked goods. At one table, a man stirs a corner of toast in a puddle of egg yolk on his plate. At another table, a couple talks over muffins and coffee. In addition to breakfast, the bakery offers wedding cakes, catering, and baking workshops. Pete and I wait at the hostess podium until a young waitress with egg-shaped eyes and a big smile asks us if we'd like a table for two. I turn my head to hide my neck and let Pete confirm. She leads us to a spot in the front window, hands us menus, and offers us coffee while we're deciding.

I say yes to coffee and then add, "We're in town for the day looking for an old friend."

"A friend?" Her teeth are like sugar cubes.

"Do you know a Ruby Jane Whittaker?"

"No."

"How about any Whittakers in the area?"

The corners of her mouth turn down a little, but she doesn't hide her teeth. "None that I can think of."

"Okay. Thanks." I turn to my menu.

"Where you from?"

"We drove up from Cincinnati." Nothing to be gained from mentioning the redeye from California.

"You drove up from Cincinnati?"

I eye Pete across the table. He deflects by ordering scrambled eggs, bacon, and whole wheat toast. I ask for two eggs over medium and a blueberry muffin from the case. The waitress leaves us to sit in weary silence and contemplate the view out the window.

A few minutes later, another woman approaches with coffee. "Missy said you're looking for someone."

"Looking for breakfast first."

"You came to the right place."

She's tall, six feet and some, with straight hair the color of India ink pulled behind her ears by a stretchy hair band. Her face is shaped like a spear tip, her cheeks sharp, her lips thin. The end of her nose aims east into low earth orbit. I put her in her mid-thirties, which would make her about Ruby Jane's age.

"Maybe you can help us out. My name's Thomas Kadash. This is Pete." I stick my hand out.

A crease appears between her plucked eyebrows. "If I can." She switches the coffee pot to her left hand and shakes. Her fingers are long, her skin cold and dry. She doesn't offer her name.

"Do you remember a Ruby Jane Whittaker?"

Her thin lips tighten for a second. "Doesn't ring a bell, no."

"You sure? It's been a while. She went to high school here."

"When did she graduate?"

I don't know, but Pete does. "1990." Chock full of secret knowledge.

"That's when I graduated, but I don't remember anyone by that name. Why are you looking for her?"

"It's a family matter."

"Nothing serious, I hope." She waits, as if she expects me to elaborate. I smile and thank her.

When she's gone, Pete catches my eye. "She was lying."

"You think?"

"She knew who we're looking before she came over. Missy must have told her."

"You're assuming that toothsome dingbat could remember RJ's name all the way back to the kitchen."

"She was probably flustered by being interrogated by the Elephant Man."

"Now you've hurt my feelings."

"My point is that woman knew what we wanted, but played it cagey. Why?"

Maybe he's right. Or maybe it's guarded, small town curiosity. The Elephant Man and his brooding partner appear out of nowhere to ask questions, it's bound to raise an eyebrow. As far as I'm concerned, if we get people talking, maybe sooner or later word will get to someone who knows something. In a town of 937, odds are we'll stumble across them sooner or later.

- 10 -

COLD SHOULDER

AFTER WE EAT, Pete follows me onto the street where I stand for a moment, gasping for air. A woman in a pickup drives by, waves to us as if she knows us. We're a long way from home, and I feel out of my element in ways I never have before, not even as an MP in Vietnam. Pete is right about me. I do think the world ends at the edge of my usual stomping grounds, Powell to Alberta, Eighty-Second to the river. Even crossing the Willamette into downtown Portland feels like an adventure now. I've become a smug homer.

"Now what, Skin? Is there a plan?"

Our options are limited. We ought to be working our way through the remaining Whittakers. A long shot, but more likely to yield fruit than asking random strangers if they happen to remember a girl who lived here twenty years ago. Back when I was a cop, I spent countless hours on such cold calls. The prospect now fills me with dread.

"Skin—?"

I can feel the tension radiating off Peter like heat off blacktop. "Let's go for a walk."

85

"What are you talking about?"

I don't answer, head east. Pete hesitates, as if he doesn't think I'm serious, then trots after me. I'm not moving quickly. Not sure I can move quickly in the heat and dead air, but I'm half a step faster than Pete. We pass a barber shop which also offers tanning, a nondescript white clapboard building on the next corner.

"What the hell's going on?"

"Look." I point to a restaurant across the street. The sign features an odd little drawing of a wizard coyly tilting his head. "We can have pizza for lunch. Do you think it's any good?"

"How the hell should I know?"

"You're the one who gave me shit about being an elitist urban prick."

"So that means I have psychic knowledge of the quality at Village Inn Pizza."

"Hard to guess what you haven't bothered to share with me."

"Christ."

The next block has Foreman Hardware, a hair and nail salon, the post office. I wonder what gets sold off around here often enough to support the auction company across from the hardware store. As I recall from Pete's research into the minutiae of southwest Ohio demographics, per capita income is nothing to bust a nut over.

"Where are we going, Skin?"

"How did you know Jimmie wasn't doing well financially?"

"What?"

"Ruby Jane never said anything about it. She always talked like he was richer than God."

"What's this about?"

"It's time for you to stop holding out on me. So what's the story with Jimmie?"

"I don't know what to tell you."

"You hung out with him enough to know where he did his drinking."

"So?"

"So Ruby Jane vanishes, no word to anyone. In her absence, a stranger dies in her apartment. A day later, her brother is killed by a hit-and-run driver. What we know is Jimmie and RJ are tied together financially, but you say he's on the skids."

"You think Jimmie's death is connected to RJ's disappearance?"

"All I know is Jimmie was dodgy with us." We cross the street, turn left. More brassy sunlight, more bucolic village byway. I can still taste my blueberry muffin on the back of my tongue. "Who's Biddy Denlinger?"

"The first time I heard of Biddy Denlinger was when you did."

"Tell me about Jimmie."

It takes him a moment, but after some huffing and puffing, he spills. "We started getting together after RJ and I broke up. Just shooting the shit over beers and gin-and-tonics. He got laid off around the first of the year, something to do with real estate going sour. He had a little money of his own, but mostly what he had was his interest in Uncommon Cup."

"What else did you two talk about?"

He looks like he's chewing on the inside of his cheek.

"You met him. He's good at talking without saying anything."

Jimmie's not the only one. I continue along, pulling long deep breaths through my nose. A flock of starlings drops out of a maple tree and into the yard we're passing. They peck at the grass and shit on an accumulation of kids toys in the lawn. A woman steps out onto her porch and bangs on the bottom of a sauce pan with a spoon until the birds scatter.

"Remember the day Ruby Jane got shot?"

Pete doesn't say anything. Of course he remembers.

"Caught us all by surprise." I met Peter the first time at the crack of dawn, day after Christmas, when he reported a dead woman in the playground at Irving Park. Susan and I got the call-out. The next day, we followed up on an anonymous tip and found a coat soaked with a second victim's blood in Peter's garbage can. Ruby Jane was with him when we brought him in for questioning. Took us another day to realize Pete was being set up by a fucked-all-to-hell psycho who somehow resented him for discovering the dead body in the first place. We weren't quick enough on the uptake though, because the guy went after Ruby Jane. Almost killed her.

I got to break the news of her shooting to Pete. Leg and stomach. Nasty. She almost didn't make it. They'd met the morning before, but somehow the chemical reaction caught, exothermic from the start. Pete blamed himself even though, as I explained at the time, only one person was responsible. The bastard who pulled the trigger.

We stop outside a small brick and columns building in the middle of a trimmed lawn, a Masonic Temple. Back in Portland, the Masonic Temple on Hawthorne houses a pub and an annual holiday fair.

"I get it, Skin. You took me to the hospital that day. You covered for me when that piece of shit died in my house—"

"That's not—"

"No. Fuck this. He almost killed Ruby Jane, he almost killed me. But whatever. I appreciate you looking out for me. I always have. But just because you did me a favor a few years ago doesn't mean I have to put up with your mind games now."

"I'm not the one who ran away, Pete."

The starlings return, tumbling off the roof of the Masonic Temple in waves. I feel their high-pitched chittering in my teeth. Up the street, the woman with the sauce pan reappears. The birds fly toward her, but as she raises her pan they swoop en masse toward us. I lower my head, flinch as something strikes my shoulder. For a moment I think it's one of the birds, but then I see Peter's fingers poking the damp fabric of my t-shirt.

"Is there a point to this?"

I sigh. "There was a time a few years ago when you were a hair's breadth from jail time. A day later, you and I both walked out of Ruby Jane's shop minutes before that freak walked in and shot her. We both looked at him, for chrissakes. The point is you don't always see what's right in front of you."

The exasperation plays across his face. "I can't believe this." He turns away from me and starts down the street.

"Pete, where are you going?"

He doesn't turn around, but I can hear him anyway. "I'm going to look for Ruby Jane. You can do what you want."

I let him go. He won't get far on foot.

Neither will I, but I still have the car keys. I retrace our steps to the rental car. Missy is looking at me through a window of the café, the spear-faced woman taking an order. I don't know how long it will take Pete to cool off, but I figure I have a little while. I decide to visit the school. If nothing else, I might be able to confirm if Ruby Jane ever attended.

I don't need Pete's Google Maps. Valley View High School is a mile or so back the way we came this morning. The school is a long, two-story brick structure all but without windows. I park in a visitor spot, then run my fingers through my hair. In the rear view mirror, I see a guy who looks like he spent the night on a plane and the day in an atmosphere designed to enlarge every capillary. A few students are coming and going in cars from the student lot at the far end of the building, but no one is nearby. I pull off my sweaty t-shirt and put on a fresh one from my pack. There's not much I can do about my hair; I didn't think to buy a comb when I was shopping for clothes.

In the office, the woman behind the desk manages to smile despite my unkempt appearance. I tell her my name and give her my spiel. She considers for a moment before reaching for her phone.

"You'll have to speak with Mister Halstead."

Halstead turns out to be the vice principal. Ten years younger than me, mid-forties, but with less hair. His white dress shirt and tie are crisp, his face recently-shaved. My precise opposite.

"What is this about?"

I tell him the same thing I told the woman out front, but in addition to my name I add I'm a retired police detective. Halstead strikes me as the kind of guy who'll respond to a cop.

He frowns and nods. "And how can I help you?"

"There's been a death in the family."

"Sorry to hear that."

"My problem is I haven't been able to find Ruby Jane. My hope was I might track down family in the area."

"I'm not sure she has family in the area anymore."

"You remember her then."

"A bit, yes." He holds up a finger, then turns in his chair. He takes a tall, slender volume from the bottom shelf of the bookcase behind him. A yearbook. He leafs through the pages until he finds what he's looking for, then offers the book to me.

The image is small and grainy, but Ruby Jane's dimples stand out. I think of the snapshot I found in Chase Fairweather's backpack, reflect on the arc of Ruby Jane over the years. "That's her."

"This was my first year here. I taught history and government."

"Did you know her?"

"Not well. She was in one of my civics classes, but never said much. I knew her better as a basketball player." He pages through to the girls basketball team portrait. Ruby Jane stands in the back row, second from the right. Next to her, tallest on the team, is another face I recognize. Clarice Moody, according to the text.

"What year is this?" I look at the book cover and answer my own question. 1989.

"She was a junior."

"Pretty good ball player?"

"Yes, quite good from what I remember."

"Do you have any others? Senior year?"

"She didn't come back for her senior year. I believe she transferred."

"Do you know where?"

Halstead takes the yearbook from me and closes it on his desk, then folds his hands over the cover. "Mister Kadash, here's the thing. I don't know you. You could be anyone."

"I understand. You can check me out. The Portland Police—"

"It doesn't matter. What I've shown you is nothing you couldn't find out at the Germantown Public Library. But I can't share confidential information about former students with you."

"I need someone who might be able to help me find her."

"I'm sorry, but as I said, to my knowledge, she has no family in the area. That's the best I can do for you."

"Perhaps someone else—"

"Mister Kadash, I'm sorry I can't be more help."

Outside, the air feels even heavier than it did earlier.

When I pull out of the parking lot, I see the cop coming up behind me, lights spinning. As I slow down and stop, two wheels on the shoulder, I realize I've been waiting for this. He's got someone in the backseat, but I can't make out the face through the glare on the windshield. By the time he approaches, I have everything ready and the window down.

"May I see your license and registration, please?"

I hand him my driver's license and the rental car agreement. He inspects them, then me. A big man, heavy and muscular, but not fat. His is natural meat, not the kind of carved muscle you get from a lot of time with the iron. His face is long, with thick red lips and a bulbous nose. He's not wearing a hat on his shiny, shaved skull.

I don't bother to speak. He knows what he wants, and I figure he'll get around to it sooner or later.

"You here for business or pleasure, Mister Kadash?"

I'll be pleased if I find Ruby Jane. Hell knows I got no business here.

"Just visiting."

"Who you visiting?"

"What's the problem, officer?"

"Chief. Chief Nash, Jackson Township."

I wait him out. He leans down and looks in the car, his face expressionless.

"You didn't say who you were visiting."

"Still working it out."

"Asking questions."

"I'm looking for a friend."

"Your friend has been gone for a long time."

"You know Ruby Jane."

He stands up, tilts his head to the side until his neck cracks. Then he hands me my license and rental agreement.

"I've come a long way. If you could point me toward family or old friends of Ruby Jane's maybe …?" I let my voice trail off. If he doesn't like me asking questions, one way to stop me is to tell me what I want to know.

"I don't think she has family around here anymore."

"Anyone who might remember her, then."

"What's your interest?"

"I'm her friend."

"From Oregon."

"Yes."

"Didn't realize she'd moved to Oregon."

I shrug. "Chief, I'm a former cop myself. I understand what your concern might be. You can call the Portland Police Bureau and ask for Lieutenant Mulvaney, head of Person Crimes. She'll vouch for me."

"Him too?" He points a thumb back at his car. I turn for a better look, realize it's Pete in the back seat.

"What did he do?"

"Got up in Clarice Nielson's face at the café. Yelling at her and calling her a liar. Clarice ran out of there in tears."

"Are you going to charge him?"

"Disorderly conduct comes to mind. Criminal menacing if he doesn't shut the hell up."

Now that I know who it is, I can make out the scowl on Pete's face in the shaded back seat of the patrol car. I can't help but think it's at least partly my fault for leaving him on his own.

"Listen, Chief. Something has happened, something of a personal nature. I'm sorry he caused a problem. We need to find her." I don't mention Jimmie or Chase Fairweather. Dead bodies will only raise his suspicions. As far as it goes, I'd rather he not call Susan. She won't be happy getting two phone calls in two days from two different jurisdictions to check up on me, especially with the threat of charges hanging over Peter.

"How long were you a cop, Mister Kadash?"

"Over twenty-five years."

"There's nothing to be found here. Ruby Jane Whittaker has been gone almost as long as you were a cop. Her whole family has."

"I know. But we spoke with her brother—"

"James."

"Yes. James. And he suggested she might have come back home."

"I'm not sure she ever thought of this place as home."

"What can you tell me, Chief?"

"Wait here. I'll be back in a minute."

He returns to his car. First he opens the back door and lets Peter out. They exchange words and Peter nods, lips tight. He walks to the car and climbs in beside me. He doesn't speak and I don't push it. I've got my eyes on Chief Nash. I can't see what he's doing. After a moment he returns and hands me a slip of paper. He's written a name—Linda Parmelee—and a street address back in town.

"I called her, told her you would be coming by."

"She can help us find Ruby Jane?"

"If anyone around here can, it'll be Linda. When Ruby Jane was still at Valley View, Linda was the only teacher who could get through to her."

"And they stayed in touch."

"I wouldn't know."

"Okay. Thanks."

"One thing. Lock that one in the car. I won't even cite you if you leave the windows rolled up." I try to look grateful. Not sure what I'm grateful for anyway, that Peter isn't in jail or that I have an excuse to talk to the woman alone. "When you're done, I don't imagine there will be any reason for you to stick around."

"I suppose it depends on what we find out, but we're not looking for any more trouble. Just our friend."

He frowns, hands on his hips. He turns and gazes toward the high school. A couple of students are watching from the parking lot. Nash puffs out his cheeks and shakes his head slightly. There's a fine sheen of sweat on his forehead.

"I always liked Ruby Jane, more than she realized."

"So you did know her."

"Hell-raiser, that one. Great basketball player."

"What else, Chief?"

"Talk to Linda." With that, he leaves us.

11

BIBEMUS QUARRY

"CAN YOU BELIEVE that guy?"

"You're lucky you're not facing an arraignment."

"All I did was ask some questions."

"And send a woman fleeing in tears."

"He was being dramatic."

"Have you ever seen a movie? You do not want to piss off a small town cop."

I have no trouble finding the address on a quiet little Farmersville street named for a tree or a nut. I toss the keys to Pete, climb out.

"I'll come in with you."

I shake my head. "You had your chance."

"Like you're such a charmer."

I respond through my teeth. "Be back here in an hour."

"Where am I supposed to go?"

"The Germantown Library. It's on one of your Google Maps."

"Why?"

"Ask for the yearbooks, look up Valley View, 1989. Girls basketball team."

He's silent, maybe picturing the basketball hoop in her apartment. "Ruby Jane's a helluva shot."

"Going way back."

"So?"

"She had a teammate too."

"I don't need to go to the goddamn library for that."

"Pete."

"What?"

"You could have stayed in California."

"Fuck you, Skin."

He tears away before I reach the sidewalk. I hope the bastard doesn't wreck my goddamn rental. I didn't take the supplemental insurance.

The house is a well-kept two-story Federal, blue-grey paint with off-white shutters. A pair of old hickory trees grow in the narrow front yard, just breaking out in leaf. The grass is trimmed, the flower beds tended. There are two mailboxes and two doorbells next to the glass-paned door. Inside, I can see a foyer with a single door, and a stairway leading up. I press the button marked PARMELEE.

After a moment, the door inside the foyer opens and a woman looks out. When she sees me, she comes to the front door.

"May I help you?"

"Are you Mrs. Parmelee?"

"You must be the gentleman Chief Nash called about."

She's a handsome older woman dressed in sharp-pressed khaki slacks and a blue button-down blouse. I have to look up to meet her gaze. Her grey hair is bobbed, her skin lined but clear. I try a smile not too obsequious and tilt my head to de-emphasize my neck.

"I understand you were friends with Ruby Jane Whittaker."

Her eyes are dark and they narrow slightly. "I was her teacher a long time ago."

"Has she stayed in touch with you?"

"What's this about?"

I'm growing weary of repeating the same, sad spiel, hoping someone will show a little mercy. If I still carried a badge, or had ever bothered to get a private detective's license, I might flash credentials and intimidate my way to answers. But all I am is dipshit Skin, oddball on the doorstep asking impertinent questions of someone who probably hasn't seen Ruby Jane in twenty years. "She's been out of touch. We're worried about her." Even as the words spill from my mouth, I know I sound like an idiot.

"Who's 'we'? I don't understand what you expect from me."

"Folks from work, mostly." I repress a wince.

"You work with her?"

"I don't work for her myself at the moment. She owns a number of coffee shops in Portland, and after I retired I worked behind the counter for a while."

"You're a retired what, then?"

"I was with the Portland Police."

"Has Ruby done something wrong?"

"Not at all. We're friends. I'm worried about her, me and … several others."

"So you came all this way from Maine looking for her."

"Oregon, actually."

"I don't know what to tell you."

"I know she grew up here, so I came. But as far as I can tell, she no longer has family in the area. Chief Nash suggested I talk to you."

She purses her lips. "I'm not sure I can help you."

I've chased a wild goose across a continent and all I've gotten for my trouble is wet feet. I'm not ready to give up.

"What do you remember about her? Was there someone she was close to, someone who might still be in the area?"

She shook her head slowly. "Mister—?"

"Kadash."

A shadow passes over her eyes, as brief and fleeting as a wisp of cloud across the sun. It's enough, and she realizes I caught it. "Mister Kadash." She blinks and looks away, then sighs. "I suppose you should come in."

"I appreciate it."

"She won't be happy with me."

"You can tell her I broke you down through skillful interrogation techniques."

She frowns, quick and tight-lipped. "She said you were a smart ass." I follow her inside.

The living room is walled with books, the shelves interrupted by a pair of wide windows and a framed *Bibemus Quarry* print, the same one hanging on Ruby Jane's wall. Museum Folkwang, Essen. I wonder if Mrs. Parmelee is the source of her interest in the Impressionists.

Mrs. Parmelee gestures toward the couch. "I suppose you'd like some coffee."

"It's not necessary."

"Of course it is." She stops and closes her eyes for a moment. When she opens them again, she attempts a smile. "I'm sorry. I don't mean to be short."

"Don't worry about it."

"I'll make some coffee. Give me a moment."

She leaves me and I sit on the couch. The room doesn't appear to get much use, except for a leather chair in one corner with a brass floor lamp looking over its shoulder. There's a stack of newspapers on the floor on one side, and a small table on the other with a couple of books and a pair of reading glasses. I catch the faint scent of lemon furniture polish. A mantle clock ticks on one of the bookshelves.

After a few minutes, Mrs. Parmelee returns with two cups of coffee. She sets one on a coaster on the cherry coffee table. "Do you take cream? I can get some."

"Black is good."

I sit back, try the coffee. It's good. I wonder if she picked up a few tips from Ruby Jane.

She sits on the edge of the couch next to me, khaki-clad knees pointing my way. "So."

"So."

"This is a bit awkward for me."

"I'm sorry. I don't mean to make you feel uncomfortable. I'm worried about Ruby Jane." The ticking seems to grow very loud. "You've seen her?"

She studies her coffee cup. "She's gone now."

"But you talked. You know what's happening with her?"

"Her situation here was always … complicated."

I sip coffee and wait for her to continue. Despite what I said to Peter, I've never been a skilled interviewer. My manner is too brusque, and my presence too discomfiting. Susan was the one to ask the questions when we were partners. But one thing I learned over the years is sometimes the thing to do is sit back and shut the hell up. Most people ache to fill the silence.

But she turns it around on me.

"Mister Kadash, how much do you know about Ruby's life?"

"Pretty much nothing. She never talked about her past. Until a couple of days ago, I thought she was from Louisville."

"Did you ever wonder why?"

"Under normal circumstances, I don't like to pry." A reaction, perhaps, to a career spent prying.

"But now you think you've discovered less than normal circumstances."

"Honestly, I don't know. She left suddenly without telling anyone where she was going, or why. For all I know, I'm just a presumptuous ass sticking his nose in where it's not wanted."

"Yet you came anyway."

"Like I said, I'm worried about her. And … things have happened."

"Things which led you to believe you needed to stick your nose in, wanted or not."

"Something like that."

"I won't betray her trust."

"I'm not asking you to."

"What then?"

"Whatever you're willing to tell me. Hell, if you tell me you know she's safe and I should go home and stop worrying, I might even listen."

"Really. And why is that?"

I nod toward the print. "That's one of Ruby Jane's favorite paintings. She's got the same print in her apartment."

She sets her cup on its own coaster and folds her hands in her lap. Her eyes move to the print. I wonder what she's thinking.

"It's just a painting."

"I suppose. But it tells me something about who you are to her."

"You trust me because of an old print."

"Why not?"

She reaches for her coffee, then settles back in her chair again without it. When she looks up, she's made a decision. "Mister Kadash, Ruby wasn't close with many people after her father disappeared, and as far as it goes, she didn't stick around here herself. She graduated from Dixie High School."

"Where is that?"

"New Lebanon. Up the road a few miles."

"Why did she move?"

"I don't see anything to be gained bringing up old memories like this."

"Please. I'm looking for a line on where to find her. Anything."

"How long has she been gone?"

"A couple of weeks. No one knows where she went."

"I don't even know if I remember much after all this time."

"What was that about her father?"

She closed her eyes and sighed. "It's a long, sad story, but an all too common one. He ran off. Fathers do, even in this day and age."

"Ran off where? With another woman, or …"

"No one knows. He vanished one day and that was that. As far as I know, no one ever heard from him again."

"How did Ruby Jane feel about it?"

"I was her English teacher, not her confessor."

"What was she like?"

"You're not going to let up, are you?"

"It's not my style, no."

"I suppose I should tell you to go, and leave it at that."

"I'd rather you didn't."

Her eyes go back to the painting, then jump to the mantle clock, almost as if she's looking for help.

"She was a good student. Not a great student, but good. Most of her focus was on sports."

"She was an athlete?"

"Basketball. Quite good too. College scouts were interested."

"She has a hoop in her apartment, makes baskets from any-where in the room." Her field goal percentage is otherwordly. "But she never mentioned playing. I remember her saying she went to a small college."

"She left Valley View before her senior year. To my knowledge she never played again."

"Why? If she was that good?"

"It's complicated. Her father, … he left ruin in his wake. Her mother went so far as to suggest Ruby had something to do with his disappearance. Can you believe that? A mother accusing her own child?"

I was a cop long enough that nothing surprises me.

"Then there was James."

"I've met him." I don't mention he's lying in a drawer in the San Francisco medical examiner's office.

"When James left for college, her mother went off the deep end. There was a police investigation, which came to nothing of course. Men run off."

"That must have been hard on Ruby Jane."

"She coped through sports, I think. She played hard, but to her credit she worked in class too. She never tried to use her status as an athlete to curry favors from her teachers."

"Why did she quit?"

"There was another girl— Mister Kadash, you have to understand that even on the same team, athletes are very competitive. And girls have their own issues as well. This other girl, she wanted to be the team's focus. She didn't like the attention Ruby drew. It all came to a head one day in the wake of a tragedy which was particularly hard on Ruby. She hit the other girl and broke her nose."

I think of Clarice Moody, her nose pointing over the horizon.

"Naturally, discipline was swift and sure. Ruby was suspended for a week from school and for seven games the subsequent basketball season. A lot of people argued for leniency, including me. She'd never been in that kind of trouble before. I was worried about her scholarship prospects if she missed so many games, but Ruby said the punishment was fair. She withdrew into herself, spent a lot of time in the school library or out running. She did a lot of writing for me too. Thoughtful material, though impersonal. Then, at the end of the year she transferred to Dixie."

"And that's when you lost track of her."

Her hands are a tangle in her lap. "Her mother moved away after she graduated, but she didn't stay at home her senior year."

"Where did she live?"

"As I recall, her mother sold the house when she left. I don't even know who lives there now."

Not what I asked. I'm getting close to matters she doesn't want to share, and I wonder if Ruby Jane stayed here her senior year. Mrs. Parmelee looks at the clock again. "Am I keeping you from something?"

"No, of course not."

I finish my coffee. My hand has a slight tremble when I set the cup on the coaster. "How long ago did she leave?" My voice is almost a whisper.

"She left when Chief Nash called."

"Does he know she's here?"

"No one does, to my knowledge."

"Where'd she go?"

She sighs. "She won't be happy I told you, but we didn't know it was you the chief was sending over. She thought someone from the old days recognized her on the road or something. I was supposed to brush them off. But it turned out to be you. Skin Kadash."

Her lips press together as she glances at my neck, as if for the first time, then she lets out a breath. After all these years, I'm used to the reaction, my neck cuing up a standard response in connection with my name. But just once it might be nice if someone shrugged it off.

"You can call me Thomas if it makes you more comfortable. Or Mister Kadash is fine."

"No. I'm sorry. I'm feeling a little caught off guard, and let's face it. I'm an old retired teacher. I'm not used to subterfuge." She flashes a quick smile.

"Why did she come back here?"

"I don't know exactly. She showed up, asked if she could stay for a little while. She's told me a lot, but only of matters far away. All about her coffee shops, and her life in Portland." When she smiles again, it's more at ease. "She told me about you."

My face feels hot.

"She goes out every day alone. Running, she claims, but I think it's something more."

"Running?"

"Along her old routes. In high school, I was more likely to see her running than sitting still."

"And today?"

"Her medium run. Eleven miles."

"Yes, but where—"

"It is you. Right?"

"Me."

"Skin."

I don't know what she means, but I know what I hope she means. "I need to find her, Mrs. Parmelee. Please, tell me where."

She nods, still smiling. "I'll give you directions. She'll be on Preble County Line Road by now."

12

PREBLE COUNTY LINE ROAD

PETE IS WAITING outside. As I climb into the car, Ruby Jane's phone rings. According to caller ID, the number is restricted. I feel a strange certainty it's her. But when I answer, all I hear is a ticking quiet.

"Is someone there?"

"I know you." The voice whispers. I can't guess who it might be.

"Congratulations." I'm not feeling patient. "What's your next trick? Remembering your own name?"

"I won't let you interfere."

"Good for you."

"I'm not fucking around here."

I pull the phone away from my ear long enough to confirm the incoming number is restricted.

"I don't take orders from Captain Ambiguous."

The call ends.

I drop the phone in the center console. Peter looks at me sideways from behind the wheel. I can't read his expression, a circumstance I'm growing used to. "What was that about?"

"No idea." My tone has an edge. I press my lips together and face the windshield. The sunlight is bright and harsh, rimming the hickory leaves in front of Linda Parmelee's house with a lucid halo. The breeze carries the scent of mown grass through the windows. A kid drags a backpack down the sidewalk across the street. The scritch of the bag on concrete and the call of a bird I don't recognize are the only sounds.

"Where are we going?"

I don't answer.

"Skin—"

"Head north out of town."

"Any particular route?"

"Look around. How many routes do you think there are?"

"Fine."

There's no reason to let my apprehension boil over onto Pete, but it's not like he's been so easy on me the last few days. I suck in heavy air, let it out as he pulls a fast U-ey. He heads back through town, turns left and accelerates. Bucolic small town gives way to fields interrupted by narrow stands of trees almost immediately. We pass ranch houses set back from the road, big front yards with those oversized brick baskets. I don't see a single cow or horse. After half a mile or so we pass a biker in spandex who might have been tele- ported right off a Portland street.

"What am I looking for, Skin?"

"Turn left when you come to Chicken Bristle Road."

"Chicken Bristle?"

"Didn't you grow up out here? You should be used to this."

"Hell knows there isn't a single farm or stretch of open road in all of Oregon."

After a minute or so, he points two-fingered without taking his hands off the wheel. "Chicken Bristle." The new road is narrower and rougher, but straight as a rod. To the left are a couple of older houses on multi-acre lots, to the right, a broad field with row after row of young sprouts. Corn, soy beans, I haven't got a clue.

"What are we looking for, Skin?"

"Ruby Jane."

"Damn it, I know that—"

"Surely she told you all about her high school athletic activities back when you were actually getting to know each other."

His jawline goes rigid.

I sigh and rub my eyes, then describe Ruby Jane's medium run: out Farmersville-West Alexandria Road to Chicken Bristle, west to Preble County Line, then north and beyond. Eleven mile loop, modest hills, quiet roads. Good air in the spring and fall, if oppressive in summer and bone-chilling in winter. Fields, scrub woods, hundred-year-old farm houses, twenty-year-old McMansions.

Ask her about that night on Preble County Line Road. Neither one of us has to mention Jimmie's words in the bar minutes before he died.

What happened out here, RJ?

"She used to run this route in high school."

"And she's out here now?"

"She left shortly before you dropped me off."

"How long does it take her?"

"In high school, between eighty-four and ninety minutes. But I don't think she's gotten much running in since she opened Uncommon Cup."

"What else did that woman tell you?"

"A lot of things."

The road dips into a shallow, wooded depression and crosses a weed-choked stream over a culvert. To our right, the terrain climbs into trees, but south the land spreads out in a broad fan. Peter is going about thirty miles an hour. I don't know if he wants to make sure he doesn't come upon Ruby Jane so suddenly he startles her, or if he's afraid to find her at all. We pass a house here, a house there. White clapboard with hundred-year-old windbreaks, some with barns and outbuildings. I see bikes in front yards, a dog sleeping in grass, a woman in a white sun hat working in her garden. Within a couple miles, Chicken Bristle Road T's at a stop sign, still no sign of Ruby Jane.

"Preble County Line Road."

"Turn right."

"You sure she came this way."

"No."

He blows through his teeth, but he makes the turn. Out the window I hear a strange singing hum. Bugs, birds. I don't know. Everything looks normal enough to feel utterly exotic. The road climbs. Corn, I decide. Woods. Farmhouse. More corn. A mailbox shaped like an old red barn. The fields are edged with heaped stone, like walls which have eroded into formless debris. At the far edge of a field a tractor as big as my house chugs, green and gleaming in the sunlight. Beside me, Peter draws a sudden sharp breath and the car slows. Momentum throws me forward. I see a figure ahead at the side of the road. Auburn hair, long legs and running shoes.

My eyes go wet. She waits at the end of a driveway.

"What should I do?"

The question doesn't require an answer. He slows to a crawl, edges out to the center line. She doesn't react until Peter stops beside her. The quiet which descends when he shuts the engine off is almost too painful to bear. I listen for the hum, but all I hear is a distant popping like gun fire. Ruby Jane rubs her eyes, then looks into the car. Her face registers nothing, no surprise, no anger. No pleasure.

"RJ—"

She turns away. I can see the tension in her shoulders. Pete shifts beside me, makes a little sound in the back of his throat. He wants to talk. I want to talk too, but I'm not sure what to say after coming so far.

When Ruby Jane turns back, she looks from me to Peter and back to me again. I believe I catch the faintest hint of a smile in her eyes, a sad smile. I hope it's not wishful thinking on my part. "I understand why you're here."

"We were worried—"

"You don't have to say it. I understand."

She crosses her arms over her chest. I can see a sweat stain on the neck of her t-shirt, a thin film of perspiration on her upper lip. She blinks in the clear air, her eyes glinting sapphire. She's the most beautiful thing I've ever seen.

"Can we—?"

She shakes her head. "Tell Peter to stay in the car."

I turn and look at him. He opens his mouth to say something, then closes it again. His eyes get hard and his hands grip the steering wheel.

"Give it a minute, Pete."

His voice is so sharp it cracks. "Hey. I got nowhere else I need to be."

I climb out, don't close the car door. Now that we've reached this point, found who we are both looking for, the girl of our dreams, I don't have the heart to close Pete out. I can't pretend I'm not pleased to be the one she wants to talk to, even if I fear what she might say. I've tracked her across the country, ignorant of what brought her so far. The one thing that's clear is if she wanted me to know where she'd gone, she'd have left a message. As I look at her, my heart pounds in my chest. I think about Mrs. Parmelee, and wonder what it would have been like to know Ruby Jane when she was in high school.

She's half-turned away from me. I can smell the shoots of corn behind me, a scent green and airy. I don't know how long she's been here, if she was able to run all this way, so far, so many years from a time when this was routine. Her cheeks are flushed, her hair a wind-blown disarray.

"You've come a long way."

"So have you."

I swallow. "I spoke with Mrs. Parmelee."

"She's always been so kind to me."

"She seems very nice."

Ruby Jane shrugs, her eyes remote. "What did she tell you?"

"She said a lot of things. You had a hard time, she said. Your father—"

She throws a hand up, cutting me off.

"It was such a dark night. There were thunderstorms all around, but by the time I got out here they'd tapered off to a steady rain." She draws a shuddering breath. "It was right about here." I follow her gaze up off the road into an open stand of trees. There's a house at the end of a long gravel driveway. Two stories of faux colonial, brick and white shutters, broad porch and tall columns. A free-standing four-car garage is off to the side, flagstone patio between. In the gap between the house and garage I can make out the edge of an above ground pool in the backyard. Though the nearby trees are tall, the landscaping has an antiseptic perfection, the lawn a checkerboard of establishing sod, the bushes under the tall windows head-sized balls. The flowers in the beds are no bigger than the nursery pots they came from. This house wasn't here a year ago.

"We tried to bury him right about where the garage is, I think. It's been a while. Jimmie stopped digging. He ran away. He drove off and left me here."

Even now, despite the recent development, the location is remote. I can't imagine what it must have been like twenty years earlier on a dark night under rain.

"Jimmie your brother?"

"What other Jimmie is there?"

I'll have to tell her he's dead, but I can't bring myself to say anything about it now. I'm too busy trying to make sense her words ... *tried to bury him right about where the garage is ...*

She looks from me to Pete, runs her fingers through her hair. "Do you love me?"

She could be speaking to either of us. I can feel Peter at my back, burning, a dark flame. A thick gob gathers in my throat and conspires to cut off my voice—long enough for Pete to speak if he's going to. He doesn't.

I swallow. "Yes, I love you, Ruby Jane."

She looks down at her hands. Her fingers are winding themselves into knots. Off in the distance over the sound of wind through the trees I hear a car approaching, a low diesel rumble. But I keep my eyes on Ruby Jane. "I never thought I would have to come back to this. I hate being here."

"Then let us take you away. Come on." I reach out to her. The rumbling engine draws nearer. The throttle drops as the driver shifts. A truck, I think, but I can't take my eyes off of Ruby Jane. I feel as though I'm falling, but I don't care. I don't care about Peter seething behind me, I don't care about Chase Fairweather or James Whitacre or the strange and ordinary landscape, the high vault of the sky, the whispering leaves, the soil. I'm staring into her fathomless blue eyes when the truck rams the rental car from behind. I'm still looking into the blue abyss when the sky jumps at my feet and goes black.

PART TWO

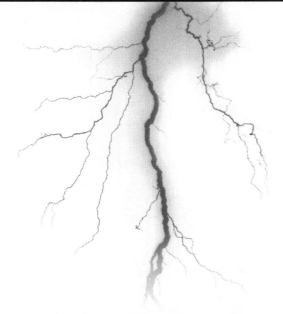

August 1988 – April 1989
Roo

13

Interview, April 1989

THEY CAME FOR her on Chicken Bristle Road, a quarter mile short of her second turn. Two police cars pulled off to the side in front of her, one a Farmersville vehicle and the other from the township. Werth Nash, the cop who did the DARE presentations at school, drove the Farmersville car. The chief sat next to him in the passenger's seat. Together they made up forty percent of the full time Farmersville police force. Lute Callan, a Jackson Township officer, drove the second car. She didn't know the man with him, or why it required so many cops to chase her down. So what if she broke Clarice's nose? It wasn't like she'd done anything wrong.

Ruby Jane glanced at her watch and checked her heart rate with two fingers on her neck. She was three miles into her run, a planned eleven at an eight-and-half minute pace. Easy, an unconscious pace. She doubted she'd get to finish.

Nash climbed out first. Callan and the stranger followed from the township car. The chief stayed behind. Heart rate: 105. Hardly worth the effort.

"Ruby? How you doing, darling?"

She eyed Nash for a long, uncomfortable moment, then turned her attention to the stranger. He wore a Farmersville patch on his shoulder and three stripes on his shirt. His face was pale, and a wattle hung below his chin. "Who are you?"

The men gaped at each other. Nash took another step.

"You know Officer Callan. This gentleman is Sergeant Grabel. He's new to the department."

He wore sunglasses, had prominent veins on his forehead and slicked-back hair the color of steel wool. Sweat gleamed on his cheeks despite the cool morning.

"A city boy."

Grabel's head popped up. Nash forced a quick laugh. "Sergeant Grabel did serve in Dayton before joining us." Nash shifted from one foot to the other, crunching gravel under his heel. "He needs to ask you some questions."

"How's he gonna manage that? He's obviously a mute."

Ruby Jane shook her head a fraction of an inch at the predictable shock on their faces, then turned to look across the cornfield beside the road. The cool morning air hung heavy above the green rows, new shoots barely ankle high. She could feel the policemen close by, seething with energy. Overhead, the power lines hummed.

Nash broke the silence. "Ruby, everyone knows you're a smart girl when you wanna be."

She took a breath thick with the scent of soil. "I want to see ID. For all I know, he's one of those perverts you hear about who can only get it up with teenage girls."

Grabel took a step toward her and thrust a finger at her chin. "That'll be enough out of you, missy."

"You *can* talk."

Nash's lips curved downward. He and Callan exchanged a look. Callan had taken the call the night of the Princeton game. "I told you she would be a pain in the ass."

Grabel scowled. "Then cuff her and let's get the hell out of here. It's too damn hot to be jawing with a smart-ass kid out in the boondocks."

"What are the charges, Detective Pervert?"

Grabel's wattle quaked in response and blotchy color rose on his neck. He opened his mouth but Nash took a step forward, both hands out. "Let's everybody calm down. Ruby, please. It's just a few questions."

"I got nothing to say."

"We'll see about that. Now come on."

"ID first."

"I can pick you up on my own authority, Ruby. You know that."

"This is township, not town."

"Ride with me, ride with Callan. Either way, you're coming in."

If anyone ought to be answering Turkey Neck's questions, it was Clarice. But that's not the way things worked in the treacherous ecosystem of Valley View High School. Clarice Moody sat atop the food chain. Everyone else was either her quarry or her confederate. What happened to Gabi Schilling wouldn't change that. The first two knuckles of Ruby Jane Whittaker's right hand couldn't change that either.

Sudden heat surged down her spine and into her legs, a sharp reminder of thoughts her run was meant to help her escape. She studied the heaped rock wall on the far side of the field, looked for gaps into the woods beyond. The muddy field would slow her down. She estimated twenty seconds to the trees, fifteen if the ground was firm. What could they do? Shoot her in the back, maybe. But they could never catch her on foot. Not Ruby Jane Whittaker, three miles into her run. She smiled, and then smiled wider as she realized her smile made them nervous. Nash bounced on the gravel, Callan's finger tapped his holster. Grabel breathed through his nose.

Try and catch me.

But she didn't run. She was a smart girl, like Nash said. They wouldn't shoot her, and they wouldn't chase her either. They'd get in their cars and catch her on Gratis Road or in the mobile home park at Lake of the Woods. Or wait her out. It's not like she had anywhere to go. The morning chill nibbled at her bare arms as if to drive home the point.

It was just a broken nose.

She folded her arms across her chest. The cops were getting impatient. She could feel it in the charged air between them, see it in their faces when she glanced sidelong at them. Even Grabel, his eyes hidden behind shades, wore his annoyance like a mask. She licked her lips.

"I'm not sorry I did it." She spoke to the corn, and for a moment wondered if they'd heard. "I'm not."

Grabel was the first to react, with surprise and a quick look flashed at Nash. *Easier than we thought,* the look said. "Why don't you tell us about it?"

"She deserved it, end of story."

Grabel was quiet for a moment. "Come again?"

"You heard me."

Nash was expressionless now, and Callan's mouth opened, not to speak—to catch flies, maybe. The scrape of Grabel's sudden footstep sounded absurdly loud. "Who we talking about, missy?"

A trill of fear ran through her. *Twenty seconds. Twenty seconds to the trees.* She swallowed, pulled her arms more tightly against herself. "Clarice Moody?"

One Grabel eyebrow appeared above the rim of his sunglasses. "Clarice Moody. Definitely." He smirked now, grim and satisfied. "Now get your ass in that car. We have matters to discuss."

Stormy Night, August 1988

STARTED LIKE ANY other Saturday night. They'd eaten, each on their own, left their dishes in the sink to await Ruby Jane's annoyance and impatience. It was always left up to her to clean up everyone else's messes. She felt restless, overheated, bored. School was still ten days off. Near, but not near enough to stoke that urgency the first week of September would bring. Bella had mixed her first pitcher of Old Fashioneds. She was in good spirits, singing to herself as she sipped from the sweating highball glass and listened to Stan Kenton. When Ruby Jane stuck her head around the corner and looked into the living room, her mother rushed her, Virginia Slim in one hand, drink in the other. "Dance with me, baby girl! *Dahhhnce.*" Ruby Jane recoiled. The burning tip of Bella's cigarette threw sparks off the hand Ruby Jane raised to deflect her mother's assault.

"Mother, watch out!"

Bella tried to snake her other arm around Ruby Jane's waist and pull her into a swing. "But we're dancing."

"What's *with* you?"

"It's a good day. Isn't that reason enough to dance, baby girl?"

Ruby Jane pushed her away. Bella spun across the floor, pausing to stab out the half-smoked butt in the overflowing ashtray on the kidney-shaped coffee table. She continued to the stereo and bumped the volume from blast to clamor. Ruby Jane fled to the kitchen, where Jimmie stared into the open refrigerator. Four chicken legs and a pound of potato salad from IGA hadn't been quite enough.

"What are you doing here?"

Jimmie was never home on Saturday night, not since graduation. At the beginning of summer he'd gone to work at the Wentz brothers farm out on Preble County Line Road. Long weeks for him, working, saving money for college. A lot of Friday nights he was too tired to do much except hog the remote. But Saturday night was drinking night with his wrestling buddies. The blockheads.

"Jimmie. Helloooo … talking here." Changes in routine made Ruby Jane nervous. Change led to trouble, and trouble meant a new mess for Ruby Jane to clean up.

"I could ask you the same thing."

"You're the one with the car."

"I'm going out later."

"Drop me at the Pizza Palace when you go?"

"I'm not going that way."

"What other way is there?"

Her father hadn't come home. No surprise. He'd been working overtime on a job in Brookville. Lots of Saturdays. He often went to the Eagles Lodge after work. Maybe he wouldn't come home until tomorrow morning. If then. Everyone was happy with Dale working overtime and drinking at the Eagles. Anything to keep him away from the house.

"Where are you going, Jimmie?"

"Don't call me Jimmie."

"Whatever. Where are you going?"

"None of your business."

"Are you going to Dayton? You could take 725 and drop me at the Pizza Palace."

"I'm going the completely opposite direction."

"Where? To West Alex? To Eaton? What the hell is there in Eaton?"

"There's plenty in Eaton."

"Is it a date? Did you actually find a girl in Eaton who would go out with you?"

"Fuck off, Roo." He stalked off, footsteps rattling the front windows as he stormed up the stairs. She heard the shower—had to be a date. Ruby Jane paced in the front hallway, eyes fixed on the bathroom door at the head of the stairs. What kind of girl would go out with Jimmie? Some watermelon-boobed dingbat—pretty, but dumb as a post, someone who thought Ronald Reagan defeated the Germans at Pearl Harbor with his bare hands.

Her mother interrupted her reverie. "Ruby, Jesus, do your homework if you've got nothing better to do."

"It's *summer*."

Bella wasn't listening. She flitted past, humming Kenton all the way up to her room. The stereo still blared, loud enough to loosen fillings. Ruby Jane lingered at the foot of the stairs, restless, annoyed by the music but unwilling to leave her post lest she miss the chance to harass Jimmie on his way out.

But when he left the bathroom he headed to their mother's room. Ruby Jane sidled up the stairs. Bella's door was shut. Ruby Jane went into her room and sat on the bed, took the book from her nightstand. *Watership Down*. Bunnies. She kept looking into the hall. When she finally forced her eyes onto the page she realized she was holding the book upside down. She tossed it aside and went to the door. Stan Kenton's horns drowned out any voices from behind Bella's door.

At least fifteen minutes passed before Jimmie appeared, dressed in navy sweats and a black concert t-shirt from when he and a bunch of blockheads went to Pink Floyd in Cleveland the year before. She followed him downstairs. He got one of their father's windbreakers from the hall closet and threw open the front door. She smelled approaching rain, heavy as cigarette smoke on the night air.

"Why on earth are you dressed like that?"

In answer, he slammed the front door behind him.

Had he called to confirm his date, only to learn his dimwitted girlfriend had found someone else? That wouldn't explain his visit to their mother's room. Ruby Jane and Jimmie never crossed that threshold except to retrieve the bundled sheets on Saturday morning or empty the ashtrays before Bella set the house on fire. Even Dale seldom slept there. Long and open, with good north light, it was not only her bedroom, but the place where Bella played at being an artist. Most of the space was given over to easels and shelves filled with paints and jars of brushes. The Studio, where gessoed masonite boards were stacked against the walls under the windows. Bella would watch Bob Ross on her portable TV, then paint happy little trees, happy little houses. The occasional murky watercolor found its way onto walls around the house. To Ruby Jane, *Twin Creek Railroad Bridge* was indistinguishable from *Deer on Diamond Mill Road*. They were all *Bella Vomits Out the Car Window*.

Bella came down, refreshed her drink, returned to the living room. The music changed. Rachmaninoff, a bad sign. The Russians made her mother moody. At least she lowered the volume; Ruby Jane could now hear the ice tinkling in her mother's glass. She needed something to do, somewhere to go. She needed to be gone before Rachmaninoff transitioned to Shostakovich.

But her phone calls were answered by machines or oblivious siblings. She considered biking to Germantown, but if the rain came she'd arrive looking like a drowned raccoon—with no guarantee she'd find anyone anyway. Instead she tore into the dishes. After a while, her mother came into the kitchen and looked out the window. Quiet Farmersville, the street dark and empty.

"What's up with Jimmie?"

"Who?"

"Your son? Jimmie?"

Bella stared out the window and pulled at her lip. Her cigarette had burned down to the filter.

"James Whittaker? You gave birth to him."

"He's out."

"I know that. I watched him leave." Ruby Jane inspected her mother's profile. Her earlier lightheartedness was gone, but whether it had been weighed down by the Russians or something else, RJ couldn't say. "What were you two talking about?"

"Who?"

"Your son. Jimmie." Bella's face remained blank. "*James*."

"We weren't talking."

"You stared at each other for all that time? Were you giving him a painting lesson?"

"When?"

"Before he left. He was in your room for like an hour."

"It wasn't an hour."

Ruby Jane groaned.

"It's none of your business."

"Is something wrong?"

"Nothing is wrong."

Bella fled to the living room without replenishing her drink. Ruby Jane followed.

"What's going on?"

"Nothing." Bella went to the stereo, hesitated, then she sank down on the couch and put her hand to her forehead. No Shostakovich, thank god.

"Why is Jimmie going to Eaton?"

"He's not going to Eaton."

"So you *know* where he's going."

"It's none of your business."

"He's too young to buy your liquor."

"Ruby Jane Whittaker, watch your mouth!"

Her mother rattled her glass, realized it held only ice cubes and maraschino cherry stems. She opened the video tape cabinet under the TV. A half-empty pint of Jim Beam was tucked among Jimmie's *Miami Vice* recordings. Bella splashed bourbon into her glass, sipped, added a little more. She held the glass to her forehead for a moment before returning to the couch.

"Why isn't Jimmie off partying with the blockheads?"

"Who says he isn't?"

"He went to Eaton."

"He didn't go to Eaton."

"Where did he go, then?"

Bella sipped her whiskey. "He's running an errand for me."

"Where?"

"Not Eaton."

"West Alex? There's nothing in West Alex."

The remnants of ice in her glass pinged as Bella's hands trembled. She refused to meet Ruby Jane's stare.

"What are you making him do?"

Bella had never been a pill-popper like Dale. Her father spent his days awash in Benzedrine, boozed after work to dull the edge, then chased sixteen hours of toxic soup with Seconal when he returned home at night. Perhaps Bella had sampled from Dale's stash and discovered an affinity for the speedball express. But would she send Jimmie to score for her?

With Bella, anything was possible.

"Don't you have friends, Ruby Jane?"

"Where's Jimmie?"

"You're boring. Go away."

Ruby Jane threw up her hands. "Fine. I'll go for a run."

"Where? Where are you going to run?"

"What do you care?"

Bella didn't answer right away. She swallowed bourbon, slouched into the couch as Rachmaninoff emoted. "It's too dark to go running on the country roads. Besides, it's going to rain."

"I'll wear my reflectors."

"I forbid it."

Ruby Jane ran in the dark half the year. Her mother had never shown the slightest concern in the past.

"Whatever. See ya later."

Her mother didn't move. Ruby Jane went upstairs and put on shorts and a singlet. After she changed, Ruby Jane looked through her bedroom window. Outside, the street was empty except for Jimmie's Vega parked in front of the house. How long had it been? Half an hour? She turned to the driveway, but her mother's rusted red Caprice was parked at an angle in front of the garage. She frowned. Maybe someone picked him up. As loud as the Stan Kenton had been, she wouldn't have heard a car unless it plowed through the front door.

Downstairs, the music stopped. A moment later, Bella stumbled against the telephone stand in the front hall, then climbed the stairs and continued down the hall. The Studio door clicked shut. Probably done for the night. At least she hadn't peered through Ruby Jane's door pretending to be someone's mother. *Sleep tight, baby girl. Don't let the bedbugs bite.* Ruby Jane went to her doorway and listened. From behind her mother's closed door, she heard a strange, foreign sound.

Crying.

Bella had never been one to waste tears on an empty room. Hers was a life lived on an imagined stage, Blanche Dubois yanked from a New Orleans terrace, Scarlett O'Hara airlifted against a matte-painted plantation backdrop and dropped in all her dramatic glory onto the streets of Farmersville. Bella Denlinger didn't cry behind closed doors.

Ruby Jane changed from shorts to jeans and pulled a hooded sweatshirt over her singlet. Erratic thoughts churned through her like muddy water down a sink hole. She ran down the stairs and out the front door, didn't pause for a jacket.

A dark shape hunched behind the Vega's wheel. "Jimmie!" He turned, his face a pale oval among shadows. She felt a flash of relief, but at the sight of her he scrabbled at the steering column. The starter clicked and screamed. She called his name again. The Vega's capricious engine roared to life. She was already turning back as he pulled away. Into the house, down the hallway. Fear hammered in her chest. She spilled the contents of her mother's purse across the kitchen counter and grabbed the car keys. Ruby Jane didn't have her license; she didn't care. She banged through the back door. From the house, her mother shouted. Ruby Jane lunged to the Caprice, cracked her forehead on the doorframe. Blinded by shattering light, she fell into the seat and found the ignition with her hands.

"Ruby! Don't you *dare*—!"

The rain began as she turned the key. She blinked tears from her eyes and dropped the shifter into reverse. The rear wheels threw gravel and the muffler shrieked across the curb. She threw the car into gear and stomped on the gas. Bella appeared in the street behind her, arms flailing. She stumbled and fell—Wyeth's Christina in the field. Moments later, Ruby Jane had looped through town and headed west on Gratis Road, following the bouncing red will-o'-the-wisp of Jimmie's taillights.

FIRST DAY OF SCHOOL, SEPTEMBER 1988

"YOU'D THINK YOUR brother could stop by on his way back."

It was six-thirty, a grey morning—the first day of school. Ten days after she chased Jimmie into a stormy night.

"He's got a lot to do. His classes start on Monday."

"He found time to drive to the Jersey shore with his no account friends."

Jimmie hadn't gone to New Jersey. That had been his excuse for leaving home early.

"I would have done his laundry. He must have brought lots of laundry back from the beach." Bella hadn't done laundry since Ruby Jane grew tall enough to reach the dials on the washing machine. "He stopped at your grandparents' house, but he couldn't be bothered with saying goodbye to me."

"Why did he do that?"

"How should I know? They were in London. Dorothy fixed him breakfast, and then he left."

Dorothy was the live-in cook. Ruby Jane didn't want to know why Jimmie visited their grandparents' house during his pretend trip to New Jersey, but if all he got was breakfast, maybe it didn't matter. "What do you want me to say?"

"Nothing. Why should you say anything? You always defend him. What chance do I stand against that?"

Ruby Jane took a bowl from the dish rack. Bella draped herself across the opposite counter, temple to Formica, arms stretched over her head. Her grey roots showed through the henna.

"I'm going back to my maiden name. Don't you think that's a good idea? Isabella Bidwell Denlinger, like the day I was born."

The sound of her mother's voice drew a tight line of tension across Ruby Jane's shoulder blades.

"You don't have an opinion? If anyone, I'd think you would have an opinion."

The sugar canister was empty. Only a crystalline crust coated the bottom of the sugar bowl. Ruby Jane rooted through the cupboards. Powdered sugar, brown sugar. No plain old white sugar. It was like living in the third world.

"I'm talking to you."

"I heard you."

"Nothing to say about my plan?"

"Whatever."

"Denlinger is a more refined name, don't you think? Perhaps you could be a Denlinger too. It would please your grandfather. Ruby Jane Denlinger."

"Nothing pleases Grandfather." Though that might change with Dale gone.

"You could change your first name too. Pick something more sophisticated than that white trash nonsense your father insisted on."

"I like my name."

"You might need another one. You never know who's going to come looking for you, baby girl." Bella laughed, a tittering falsetto, a little bit hysterical. "What say you to *that*?"

"I say it would be nice if we had some goddamn sugar."

"Language, young woman! Don't forget who you're talking to."

She took a bite of sugarless Cheerios. The milk was right on the edge. "As if I could forget."

"What was that? You mustn't speak with your mouth full."

"What kind of a person says 'mustn't'?"

Bella pulled herself off the counter and crossed the kitchen, opened the cupboard above the fridge. Ruby Jane had dumped all but a splash out of the Jim Beam bottle the night before. Bella swirled the thin line of liquor, puzzled. "I have no idea why you're like this. Where are you going with that cereal?"

"I have to get ready for school. The bus will be here in twenty minutes."

"There's no rush. That nice girl from your team called. Clarice? She said she would pick you up this morning."

Clarice Moody was nice the way a raccoon on a chicken bone is nice.

"Then I must hurry if I'm going to miss her, mustn't I?"

— + —

Clarice found her anyway. Off the bus thirty seconds and Clarice fronted her in the main entrance of Valley View High School. Home of the Spartans. Moira Mackenzie and Ashley Wourms attended her to either side. "Why weren't you home this morning?"

Ruby Jane adjusted her backpack on her shoulder. "I didn't know you were coming."

"Your mother said she told you."

She mimed tipping a glass to her lips. "My mother says a lot of things."

Clarice pinched her lips in a sharp little rose. Everything about her had an edge, from her chin to the straight cut of her black bangs. "I'll pick you up tomorrow then. Starters need to ride together. It's team building."

Ruby Jane didn't know if Clarice was offering her a compliment or bowing to the inevitable. Moira, nearly as tall but bulkier—Mothra to Clarice's Femzilla—was a natural forward, but her lack of a shot allowed opposing teams to ignore her when she had the ball. Her strength was defense, crashing the boards and intimidating shooters with her frightful eyebrows, perfect as a tattoo, and a joyless grin so taut her skin seemed on the verge of tearing. Ashley was more airy, a solid point guard with perpetually hurt feelings whose vanilla hair scattered individual photons. At the post, Clarice could count on Ashley for the pass, no matter how ill-considered; she led the team in both assists and turnovers the previous season. Together the two epitomized Clarice's concept of teammate: supporting cast to the one and only star.

"The bus is when I do my homework."

"We won't have homework for at least a week." Clarice and her minions turned in formation and weaved through the chattering throng. Ruby Jane dropped her pack on the floor and leaned against the cool cinder block wall across from the main entrance—office to her right, stairway and the door to Mrs. Arnold's math dungeon to her left. Last year her JV teammates would have joined her. As juniors they'd now gather in the upper class corridor between the cafeteria and the gym. Ruby Jane felt safer with the D&D boys who loitered near the trophy case and chattered about hit points and quantum mechanics. She ignored their furtive stares. She wasn't first tier in the social hierarchy—no Clarice Moody or Ashley Wourms—yet still something of a pretty girl, the girl who jumped from JV to varsity midway through her sophomore year because of her ability to sink the outside shot. Fifty-five percent from the field, forty-two from three point range. A lot of people said she'd start this year. But this year was separated from last by more than summer break.

Though the first team meeting was Thursday, formal practice wouldn't start for a few weeks. Coach liked to get the girls together right away. Gave him a chance to make his speech, the one about how everyone starts at zero, anyone can make the team. Frosh or senior, didn't matter—performance and teamwork win a place on the team. Nonsense, of course. Three or four girls were on the bubble, but the varsity core was set—a young team, with Moira the only senior likely to start. Ruby Jane figured she'd rotate in off the bench at first, get good minutes and score some points. But she'd start as soon as she demonstrated last year wasn't a fluke. The morning Jimmie fled, she'd gone to the court at Farmersville Elementary and shot for hours, counted her misses in single digits.

"Whittaker."

Sure enough. "Hi, Coach." She'd had him for health her freshman year. Tall and thin like his favorite players, he was a better coach than teacher. Ruby Jane was grateful she'd never have to face another term of *that* fourth period. "Take out your notes and copy this down." Every day, all semester long, the monotony interrupted by the weekly tests—open note. The only way to flunk his class was to have lousy handwriting.

"You know about the shoot-around during lunch period, right?"

"Sure."

Coach had brought an athletic renaissance to Valley View Girls Basketball, district runner-up three years earlier, in the regionals the next two years. Last season, Clarice had sprung up to six-one and gained the inside presence to control the key. Ruby Jane showed she could score from the perimeter. Shut down one, get eaten alive by the other.

But Ruby Jane wasn't sure she wanted to play anymore.

"You've missed work-outs the last week or so."

"Sorry, Coach. Things came up."

"I understand you've been shooting up at the school in Farmersville."

"Yeah."

"You found time for that." His tone was less accusatory than disappointed.

"I needed to stay near the house. In case ..." She didn't finish. She didn't have anything to add.

"Of course." Coach's voice softened a bit. "I'm sorry to hear about your father."

"Yeah."

Coach was silent for a moment. People were squealing and laughing in the hall. First day of school, welcome back. "I haven't seen you in *forever*." Forever defined as *since last weekend at Pizza Palace*.

"You haven't heard from him?"

The front doors opened and another pack of students came in, buses still arriving.

"I'm sure it's not easy, but people have been surviving broken homes for ages."

In other words, *buck up, trooper!*

"If you ever want to talk about it, I'm available."

"Thanks, Coach." Ruby Jane almost laughed to imagine that conversation. *My father knelt in the mud and begged for his life.* Should she find the nerve to make such a confession, Coach would only worry about how the experience affected her shot.

He headed off to find more team members to motivate. But Ruby Jane could see him look back over his shoulder, concerned.

"Without my outside threat," he was probably thinking, "Clarice will have to carry the offense." Ruby Jane knew what Coach knew, what Clarice Moody would never admit—she let the double team fluster her. Ruby Jane smiled as she remembered the story of Clarice falling apart in the regional semi last year. Two Femzillas from Piqua ate her alive. Ruby Jane hadn't been able to play: she'd had to drive a bleeding Jimmie to the emergency room—despite not having her license—after another fight with Dale.

Coach had fresh expectations for this year.

My father knelt in the mud—

Jimmie was smarter. He'd wrestled, a more individualistic sport in a school not known for its wrestling program. There'd been no Clarice Moody among the muscle-bound farm boys who made weight during the season by switching from beer to vodka. And now Jimmie had constructed a hell for Ruby Jane to share with her mother and fled, nine excruciating days before her own first day of school. With Bella's help, word got out fast. Dale Whittaker ran off and left those children and their mother. Bella was a master of working the crowd for sympathy. Ruby Jane saw the *tut-tut* chins at the store, at the doctor's office when she went in for her athletic physical. At home, she suffered through days and nights of her mother, moaning and intoxicated. "Where is your father? Ruby, why has your father left us?" As if Bella hadn't orchestrated the whole thing.

During the long, dead week after Jimmie escaped to Bowling Green, Ruby Jane could run only so far, could practice only so many shots on the playground court at Farmersville Elementary. Two hoops, no nets, one rim less crooked than the other. The start of the school year offered refuge. Classes, homework, practice, and, as always, roadwork. Basketball practice, even with Clarice Moody, beat the oppressive house on the Walnut Street, haunted by her pickled mother.

"Are you awake in there?"

"Mmm?"

"You. In there? Are you awake?"

Her mother had kept her up late, cataloguing Ruby Jane's character flaws. Ruby Jane hadn't gotten to bed until three. Six o'clock alarm. Bella's timing was impeccable as always. Ruby Jane blinked and looked into the eyes of a strange man with a razor nick on his chin and big, brown eyes. Crisp white shirt and a thin tie in Spartan blue.

"What?"

"The bell rang. First period?"

"Oh. Sure."

"Where are you supposed to be?"

She dug into her backpack and pulled out her schedule. "Halstead." She didn't know the name, someone new. "Constitutional Law."

He smiled. "That's me."

"You're late too."

"That was the warning bell. We still have about forty seconds. We can make it."

"You go ahead. I'll catch up."

"Is there a problem?"

The corridor was emptying as stragglers raced to their classrooms. "I need to make a stop."

"You should have thought of that sooner."

Among her frazzled thoughts, she found the one topic sure to drive him away: "I just hope I don't bleed all over my seat."

"Oh." He stepped back. "Of course. Well, be quick." He turned and trotted up the stairs.

Too easy.

She moved down the main hall toward the gym, her pace unhurried. She ran her fingers along the white wall, eyes stinging as

she passed through the lingering cloud of some freshman's Drakkar
Noir overdose. Soon, once the pep squad got to work, the bleak ex-
panses between classrooms would be adorned with butcher paper
banners, rallying cries in tempera paint. TAME THE WILDCATS!
… FELL THE LUMBERJACKS! … SPARTAN SPIRIT!!! For now,
it was bare cinderblock and speckled industrial tile. The cool ste-
rility suited her. When the Farmersville and Germantown school
districts consolidated back in the late 60s, this post modern catastrophe arose in the no-man's land between the two towns. Everyone hated it, except her. Ruby Jane liked to imagine herself running
two-ball speed dribble drills up and down the long hall, each smack
of leather against the floor like a gunshot.

"Ruby Whittaker! Where are you going?"

Mrs. Parmelee seemed to appear out of nowhere, tall and
imposing.

"Mister Halstead's."

"The stairs are behind you."

"I'm getting a pop. I didn't get much sleep last night."

"So? You forgot today was the first day of school?"

*No. But my mother was drunk and required an audience last
night.* But she only looked at the floor between her feet. Speckled
industrial tile. "Sorry."

Mrs. Parmelee put a hand on her forearm, a feathery touch.
"Be quick. And tomorrow, get your soft drink before the bell rings."

"I will."

"See you sixth period."

First Day of School, September 1988

THE POP MACHINE was empty, most likely by the football team during two-a-days. At least she didn't have to explain to Mister Halstead why she was bringing a Pepsi to class when she was supposed to be in the bathroom arranging to not bleed all over her seat.

He smiled nervously when she slipped through the door, sent her to an empty seat near the back. An unfamiliar girl had the spot next to her. Ruby Jane nodded a greeting as she sat down. Halstead was talking. "Welcome to the new year," and so on. She hadn't missed much. She dropped her backpack on the floor and looked at the textbook centered on the desktop. She'd never known a teacher to put the books out like that.

He droned on for a while: test schedule, homework policy, term project requirements—the usual rulesy syllabus hooey. She retrieved a pen and her notebook from her backpack and pretended to take notes. After a while, the girl next to her gave her a nudge.

She looked up.

"Your book."

The girl had her own book open. Ruby Jane saw everyone else did as well. Some people were writing their names inside the front cover.

"Oh."

"My name is Gabi."

"Hi. I'm Ruby." She wrote her name in the first slot in the Assignment Form printed inside the front cover. Halstead had noted its condition: Good. The book was brand new, but somehow Hardy Berman had managed to draw a cartoon of an erect penis on the flyleaf. She knew it was Hardy because the dimwit had signed his artwork.

"You're on the basketball team."

The girl was still talking to her. Gabi. "Yeah, I guess."

"You guess?"

"I haven't decided if I'm going out this year."

"Oh."

"Why?"

"Just wondering what the team is like."

"You play?"

"I did back in Cleveland. Bay Village, actually. No one's ever heard of it. I'm living with my grandparents this year."

"What position?"

"Guard."

"Point?"

"We rotated. Three-guard offense."

"We run a post-up."

"You have a good center?"

Ruby Jane hated to admit it. "Yeah." Clarice would probably be the dominant Femzilla in the league this year.

"Why aren't you going to play?"

"Maybe I don't want to." Gabi flinched at her sharp tone, and Ruby Jane blushed. "It's just … I haven't made up my mind."

"Sorry. None of my business."

Ruby Jane turned back to her book and pretended to be fascinated with a sidebar on Roman law. Halstead had moved from the syllabus to a grand speech about the history of jurisprudence. Hammurabi's Code. English common law. Some guy named Montesquieu. Fascinating. She found herself glancing at Gabi, who watched Halstead in a kind of rapt trance. She was a slight girl, ginger-haired and freckled, with long, ball-handler's fingers. She wore jeans and a boy's white t-shirt, red-trimmed Nike basketball shoes.

Gabi turned her head, noticed Ruby Jane staring at her. Ruby Jane made sure Halstead wasn't paying any attention to them. "You know about the team meeting Thursday after school, right?"

"Already?"

"No one told you?"

"They had me fill out an athletics form when I registered, but no one mentioned the first meeting. At Bay, we don't start until October first."

"It's Coach talking about heart and effort. Practices won't begin for a few weeks." Ruby Jane pointed at her feet. "Are those your shoes?"

"Why?"

"Coach will want you to have new ones by start of the season."

"Oh." Gabi looked at her shoes. Her face cycled from carrot to pomegranate. "Okay."

"They have to be Spartan blue and white. But don't worry. I know where to get the best discounts."

"Thanks."

Ruby Jane was quiet for the rest of class. Afterwards, in the corridor, she felt a hand on her shoulder.

"Ruby, hey."

It was Finn Nielson, one of the cirrhosis cases who hung out with Jimmie the last few years—a senior now. Ruby Jane stopped in the hall and folded her arms across her chest. "Hi, Huck." He answered to Huck only for her.

"What's up with James?"

"What's what with James?"

"He vanished. Never showed for the party a couple of weeks ago. No one has heard from him."

"He went to Bowling Green."

"Early?"

"Yeah."

"Why?"

"How should I know?"

"He didn't tell you?"

"I forgot to subscribe to his newsletter." Ruby Jane didn't bother mentioning the Jersey shore lie. If Jimmie checked in with any of the blockheads, who knows what he'd say.

"When's he coming back?"

"Thanksgiving, I guess." Or never.

"He missed the party."

She rolled her eyes. There was always a party.

"What are you doing this weekend?"

"Not going to some blockhead bash, that's for sure. You think with Jimmie gone you get to hit on me?"

"Jesus, just asking."

"I don't know. I'm busy."

"I'm not hitting on you."

"Whatever."

He pointed to the Con Law textbook tucked in her arm. "Aren't you supposed to take American History first?"

"I took it last year."

"What're you, some kinda super genius?"

"Not really. Impatient, maybe."

"You could help me out. Be my term project partner." She hadn't noticed him in class.

"I already have a partner."

"What are you talking about? We don't even pick til next week."

Had Halstead said that? Ruby Jane saw Gabi ahead of her in the hallway, looking lost. Valley View wasn't complicated. Two floors, two wings. U-shaped, and without a second floor on the south wing because of the gym. Maybe it wasn't her next class she was looking for though. Had to suck to move halfway through high school.

"I'm going to be Gabi's partner."

"Who?"

"New girl."

"Oh. What's she like?"

"You gonna hit on her too?"

"Fuck, Ruby, I'm just asking."

"She's quiet." Hopefully Gabi would agree about the project partner thing. Nothing wrong with Huck. She maybe even liked the attention. But the habit had been ingrained into her since her freshman year by her brother's overprotective interventions: don't fall for a blockhead.

And anyway, a boyfriend was not in the plan. She didn't know what the plan was, but a boyfriend would add unnecessary complications. She had to get through the next two years. Then escape. Like Jimmie.

The fucker.

INTERVIEW, APRIL 1989

A THRONG OF starlings heckled from the roof as Nash led her into the municipal building. He stuck her in a second floor conference room. Not a cell, and not one of those small, airless rooms with the two-way mirror and the shackles welded to the steel table. Nash offered a perfunctory reading of her rights, Grabel rubbing his thin hands together during the recitation. She asked if she was under arrest, but Nash only glared sidelong at Grabel. She assumed he didn't like being pushed around by a newcomer. Nash was local, raised in Germantown—a Valley View graduate five years earlier. He'd left the area for two years to get an associate's degree in criminology from Wright State before returning to join the Farmersville police department. She knew all this because he told his life story at the beginning of every DARE presentation, as if being a hometown boy lent credibility to his message. *Bad news, bucko. Nobody's listening.*

She sat at a long, veneered table and looked out the broad window, south into town and east over woods and open fields. The occasional car passed on Walnut Street. East Walnut, five blocks from her house on West Walnut. As if Farmersville was so big and complicated it needed to distinguish between cardinal points on the compass. Broadway crossed Walnut at the corner, a street named by a town with small man syndrome. The conference room was small as well, barely big enough for the table and chairs around it. She had to twist sideways to stand up. A sour tang hung in the air like spoiled cream. The worn carpet was the color of swamp water.

She watched the lights blink on a phone on the narrow credenza and wondered if she could make a call before anyone noticed. But Jimmie was in Bowling Green and had barely spoken to her in eight months. Huck would be at school. He wouldn't cut on a dare—even claimed he'd show up on Senior Skip Day. The rules may have changed after Saturday night—for a while anyway—but that wouldn't matter to Huck. He'd arrive on time, attend the memorial assembly and share shocked whispers in the corridors, sign up for a session with the grief counselor. He knew what he'd been doing when it happened, same as she did.

Through the closed door she could hear murmuring voices, too low to make out the words. Nash's was pitched higher than the others, the chief's a gravelly rumble, three decades of cigarettes doing the talking. Grabel spoke the most, quick and insistent. She went to the door, put her hand on the knob. Turned.

Click.

She eased the door open half an inch, peeked out at a cluster of desks and steel chairs behind the chest-high counter, all awash in sickly overhead light. No way to pass undetected. But she could listen.

"—lieve some skinny little girl is going to pull one over on me."

"You don't know her, Coby."

"I don't have to know her. They're all the same."

"You need to understand some things about her and her family."

"Background, sure. Background is good." She heard pages shuffle. "This stuff helps, definitely."

"Not just background."

"Are you suggesting she's some kind of wide-eyed innocent?"

"I'm saying you can't assume you got this all figured out. This isn't some East Dayton drug deal gone bad. Chief, help me out here."

"Werth, we brought Coby on because of his experience. I'm inclined to let him follow his instincts."

"Thank you, Chief. Now, come on, Werth. Time to watch and learn, my friend."

She moved back to her chair and sat down. When the door opened, she was looking out the window as if she'd been sitting there all along.

"When do I get my bathroom break, city boy?"

"The name is Sergeant Grabel, young lady."

She blinked innocently. "Bathroom?"

Grabel's lips compressed. "Later. We're going to talk first." He squeezed into a chair. Nash closed the door after the chief took a seat at the head of the table. Ruby Jane could smell the chief from where she sat, two places away. Coffee, Camels, and sweat. Nash wrinked his nose and pressed himself against the wall, arms folded. Grabel arranged items on the table in front of him: thick manila folder, legal pad and pen, cassette recorder.

"Where's Bella? You can't just interrogate a minor."

Grabel leafed through the folder. "We spoke to your mother. She gave us permission to ask you a few questions." He waved a sheet of paper, as if she could read the fluttering page from across the table.

"Was she sober?"

"There's no reason to be like this."

She fixed her gaze on Grabel's wattle. "I want a lawyer."

Capillaries lined his cheeks and nose, a road map etched by alcohol. Her mother's face carried the same red lace. Grabel put the sheet back in the folder and looked up. "Young lady, you listen here. If you want to make this difficult, you certainly can. You do have the right to an attorney, but we're just talking here. You get all legal-eagle on me, I may start to wonder what you have to hide." He turned his head, but didn't take his eyes off her. "You got any secrets in there, missy?"

"You tell me. This is your peep show."

"That lip is gonna sink you if you don't fucking watch it."

"Coby." The chief cleared his throat. "I think we need to clarify our position here before we go any further."

Nash shifted his weight from one foot to the other and stared into the empty chair between the chief and Ruby Jane. After a moment, Grabel grunted and leaned across the table. "Fine. We'll clarify things. Miss Whittaker, I need you to state for the record whether you are invoking your right to counsel."

"What happens if I do?"

Grabel balled his fists. The capillaries on his nose seemed to pulse. "We rain hell down around your ears, that's what."

"Coby."

"What?" His head snapped around.

"Let's do this right." The chief inhaled, a sound with a day's worth of exertion behind it. "Now, Ruby, what my sergeant is saying is if you invoke your right to counsel, we might get the idea there's more here than meets the eye. But you can call your lawyer if you insist." He looked at his fingernails. "Do you have a lawyer?"

"I'm in the eleventh grade."

"So you are. And your mother already signed a waiver giving us permission to talk to you ..." His voice trailed off.

Grabel's fingers drummed on the table top. Nash frowned into his folded arms as the chief wheezed.

If she demanded a lawyer, what would her mother do? Bella had never worked, near as RJ could tell, but that didn't mean a whole lot. She would vanish for hours with no account of her actions. For all Ruby Jane knew, Bella was sneaking off to Dayton to sell hand jobs on Wayne Avenue. Somehow she kept the roof over their heads, kept a semblance of food in the cupboards, kept the Jim Beam stocked. That didn't mean there was money for a lawyer. Ruby Jane might get stuck with a public defender, assuming one was even available to a kid whose mother had signed away her rights. How much could she trust someone willing to work for free?

Clarice Moody wasn't worth this much hassle. "Fine. Whatever."

The chief exhaled stagnant air. "See, Coby. Ruby's a reasonable girl. Aren't you?"

She wasn't promising anything, but they didn't have to know that.

Grabel went back to the folder, sorted pages until he found what he was looking for. He read for a moment, then looked up. "I hope you're right, Chief."

"All right then." The chief pushed away from the table. "You two think you can handle this?"

Grabel nodded sharply. "Of course I can." Nash frowned, but didn't say anything. It wasn't his ball game.

The chief grunted as he rose from his seat, a sound less affirmation than raw effort, and wheezed his way out the door.

Ruby Jane wasn't sure if the chief's absence made things better for her or worse, but at least she didn't have to smell him any longer. She looked at Grabel. "Now what?"

"Tell me about yourself. I'm anxious to learn what in fuck made you the way you are."

STORMY NIGHT, AUGUST 1988

"WHERE YOU GOING, Jimmie?"

The rain brought with it cool air and distant lightning, far enough off that Ruby Jane could sense the accompanying thunder in her bones. She drove with her headlights off, hands sweating on the steering wheel as she leaned forward to peer out the rain-washed windshield. The rushing wind through the half-open windows did little to cut the tobacco-and-mildew miasma rising from every surface of the car's interior. She steered by the white line at road's edge, a faint border between car and weed-choked ditch. Overhead, the sky hung low and gunmetal grey, threaded with tarnished copper.

"Where you going?" She breathed the words, repeating them in rhythm with the wipers. The two red pinpoints far ahead offered no answer.

Gratis Road was long and narrow, and for miles hardly went anywhere. Folks lived out this way, sure, people from school, even a few blockheads. But Jimmie didn't behave like he was hooking up with friends. "Where you going?" She licked her lips. The dank air tasted of ash. The heater fought to control the condensation on the windshield. Between refrains, she caught herself breathing through her mouth, short loud gasps which made her head spin. Ahead, Jimmie's car crept through the falling rain, too slow for mere caution. The road dipped before crossing a culvert over a noisy creek, then began climbing again. He stayed well below the speed limit. Whatever Bella had sent him to do, he was in no hurry.

They had been traveling fifteen minutes when the Vega's brake lights flashed. She eased off the gas and coasted to a stop fifty yards back. The glow of his headlights illuminated a crossroad signpost. She was too far away to make out the words on the sign, but it could only be Preble County Line.

"Where you going?"

All she heard was the idling Caprice engine and the *tip-tap* of rain on the roof. Jimmie didn't move. She wished she knew what was going through his mind. If he had a carload of blockheads with him, they'd be passing a bottle, or one of those fake-o leatherette wineskins filled with bottom shelf grain alcohol. But Jimmie, alone? He wasn't a thinker. He didn't sit and brood about his troubles. He wrestled and roughhoused, worked through conflict and stress with sweat and physical contact. She shared a measure of that physicality with him—tranquility realized through exercise and action. But for her, a long run was a chance to reflect. As her heart beat and her muscles strained, her mind would clear, her thoughts would re-order themselves. She could find answers in the slap of her feet against asphalt, in the whap of a basketball against a maple floor. But she could also spend hours beside an open window gazing across a gulf of air at a reflection of her deepest thoughts. The only time Jimmie sat still was when he was too drunk to stand.

She eased her foot off the brake and let the engine's idle carry the car forward. The seconds ticked off as she closed the distance—seconds like minutes, minutes like hours. As she neared

Jimmie's car, she felt a growing uncertainty. A sensation flooded through her like she'd awakened in an unknown house surrounded by strangers. What was he waiting for? Surely he'd see her, a looming shadow in his rear view mirror. But the Vega didn't move. She braked, close enough to see wisps of exhaust and the glitter of raindrops in the glow of his taillights. At that moment, Jimmie threw the Vega into gear. His wheels spun out and he fishtailed north onto Preble County Line Road. Reflexively, she hit the gas and followed. Doubt blossomed within her. Perhaps he'd seen the glow of her brake lights in the darkness, or caught the reflection of distant lightning on her windshield.

Whatever had happened, he'd reached a decision. At thirty, as fast as she was willing to go in the dark, she barely kept his shrinking taillights in sight. He passed Zack Wentz's house near Chicken Bristle Road, and Saul Wentz's place a quarter mile farther up. If he kept going, he'd reach Route 35 within a few miles. Then, if she intended to keep following, she wouldn't be able to hide in the dark.

- 19 -

PRE-SEASON, SEPTEMBER 1988

"RUBY, BRING ME some coffee. Have a cup yourself if you want."

"No, thanks."

"Try it. You'll like it."

"I have tried it."

"*I have tried it.*" Bella's mockery reached a pitch Ruby Jane couldn't achieve without helium. "So try it again."

"I don't like it."

"You say that now. Someday you won't be able to survive without it."

"Get your own coffee. I'm in a hurry." The Moody Shuttle would arrive any moment—nothing could put Clarice off. "We increase team unity by spending time together off the court." Clarice played the *team unity* card like a joker in a game where the rules could change on a whim. Ruby Jane didn't need unity to make a pass or see the open shot.

As if on cue, she spied a pair of eyebrows through her bedroom window, Moira marching up the front walk. Clarice waited in the driver's seat of her Rabbit, tapping her fingers on the roof through her open window. Ever impatient. Ashley sat in back, talking with her hands.

"Ruby, your ride is here!"

She grabbed her backpack. Moira was already knocking when she reached the first floor. Bella waited beside the telephone stand, coffee in hand.

"You couldn't get the door?"

"They're not my teammates, little miss."

Ruby Jane threw the door open. Bella loomed at her side, grinning like a lady's magazine cover model. She enjoyed pretending to be a parent when she had an audience. "Do your little friends know what you did to your father?"

Ruby Jane's shoulders jumped to her ears. She pushed past a dumbfounded Moira.

"Does she share her secrets with you, teammate girl?"

Ruby Jane trotted down the walk, backpack to her chest, and yanked open the passenger side door. Moira chased after her.

"That's my seat."

Ruby Jane pretended not to hear. She dropped her pack on the floor and climbed in. Moira squeezed in behind Clarice. "She took my seat."

Clarice was already starting the car. "She's quicker than you on the break too." Clarice showed her teeth to Ruby Jane. Her fakey grin emphasized the cracked concealer at the corners of her mouth. Camouflaged whiteheads cast soft shadows on her chin.

Ashley leaned forward between the seats. "So anyway, Junus said he would only ask me to homecoming if I put out. Right to my face. Can you believe that?"

"I can't believe his mother named him Junus."

"Clarice, are you even listening to me?"

"If you want Junus Malo to spend money on you, you have to let him cop a feel. Maybe jerk him off to be safe."

"That's disgusting."

"Wake up, sweetie, and smell the economics."

"I just don't think—"

"Stop acting like you've never touched a penis."

Ruby Jane looked out the window. The car's atmosphere was a cloying soup of White Shoulders and Estée Lauder—Moira and Ashley's dueling attempts to smell like adults. Clarice headed east on Gratis Road. The long way. Moira continued to sulk in the back seat, and now Ashley had joined her. Clarice drove, chin high, pleased with herself. Her conversations with Ashley never changed. Ashley sought an ally against whatever boy she'd set her sights on. Clarice responded as the pragmatic slut. Ashley pretended to be scandalized. And the cycle reset.

"Who has the cigarettes? Moira?"

"My folks are trying to quit."

"So go buy some. Christ."

"Where am I supposed to buy cigarettes?" No one in German-town or Farmersville would sell smokes to a member of Coach's basketball team.

"Drive up to New Lebanon."

"Why don't you drive to New Lebanon?"

"Because it's your job."

"Ruby should have to bring them. Her mother smokes."

Ruby Jane snorted. "Coach will have an aneurysm if he catches anyone smoking."

"It's not like we inhale."

"Now we know why you almost failed biology."

Clarice pressed her lips together. Silence hung in the car for the space of a dozen breaths. "Ruby Jane Whittaker, your attitude works against team unity."

In the back seat, Ashley squeaked. "Your middle name is Jane? My mother's name is Jane."

"Ashley, shut up."

"Why are you always such a pain, Clarice? I just asked Ruby a question."

Clarice hit the breaks. Ruby Jane looked over her shoulder. Ashley had her arms folded across her chest in the tight space behind the seat. Ruby Jane couldn't remember Ashley ever standing up to Clarice. She smiled. Moira caught the look and her lips retracted from her teeth.

"Ruby's mother said she did something to her dad."

Quick as a snake, Clarice turned on Ruby Jane. "What does that mean?"

"My mother is nuts."

"What did you do?"

"I didn't do anything."

Moira keyed on Clarice's sudden interest. "But your mother said, 'Do your little friends know what you did to your father?'" Her voice gained half an octave.

"Your mother calls us your *little friends*?"

"Can we go?"

"Not until you tell us what your mother meant."

"My mother's a drunk. You can't believe anything she says."

"Maybe you're the one we can't believe."

"Clarice, shut up."

"Did you tell me to shut up?"

"What? You forgot to clean Hardy Berman's cum out of your ears?"

The idling engine ticked, and vinyl squeaked as Ashley shifted in her seat. Clarice worked her jaw from side to side. Ruby Jane could almost hear the judge, prosecutor and jury hard at work behind Clarice's cold eyes.

"Get out of the car."

"Oh, for God's sake, Clarice—"

"Get out!"

Ruby Jane looked at Ashley for support, but she'd crossed Clarice as much as she ever would. "It's her car, Ruby." She sounded like a cartoon mouse. Moira was more emphatic. "You took my seat, bitch."

Ruby Jane grabbed her backpack. Clarice had the car in gear before Ruby Jane got clear of the door. She jumped back as Clarice tore away.

She checked her watch. First period in half an hour, three miles from school. An easy pace under other circumstances, but she didn't normally run with twenty pounds of books bouncing against her spine. All she could do was walk and take a tardy. Coach didn't like tardies or absences by his girls—a fact which no doubt played into Clarice's sentence.

Twenty minutes later, not even to the grain elevators at the west end of Farmersville, a car slowed beside her. She heard it before she saw it, guessed it was Clarice returning. Pretending to be magnanimous. Or maybe she'd gotten hold of some cigarettes and wanted to make sure Ruby Jane got dragged into her miscreance. She gazed into the ditch beside the road as though fascinated by empty pop cans and broken beer bottles in the trickling water.

"Hey, Ruby."

She turned. Finn Nielson leaned across the passenger seat of his car.

"What are you doing here?" He lived in Germantown, in the opposite direction from school.

"My dad's car's in the shop. I had to drive him to the dealer in Eaton."

"Oh."

"Out for a stroll?"

"It's a long story."

"How long does it take to say, 'Clarice was being a bitch again'?"

"Clarice was being a bitch again."

"You want a ride?"

"Obviously." She climbed in next to him, crossed her hands on her lap. "Thanks, Huck."

"No problem." He drove through town, turned down Farmersville Pike. "You hear from James?"

"I haven't talked to him."

"You got a date for homecoming?"

Her breath caught in her throat. "No."

"I wasn't going to ask."

"Yes, you were."

"Pretty sure of yourself."

"On some matters, yes."

"Wow."

"That's all you got? Wow?"

"What am I supposed to do?"

"Try harder."

"Would it matter?"

"No." But then she shrugged. "I don't know."

Used to be, all it took was an icy Jimmie stare to get Huck to stuff the blue back into his balls. But Jimmie was gone now. When he called—rarely—it was only to hang quiet on the phone, breathe through his nose, and finally insist she put Bella on. That's the way he said it. "Put Bella on." He never asked Ruby Jane the question which had to be chewing him up inside.

"What have you heard?"

Nothing, Jimmie.

Later, she'd ask Bella what he called about. "He's sad. He got a bad grade in math. Who the hell knows?" She complained, but she took Jimmie's calls.

"So you really haven't heard anything?"

"Nothing, Jimmie."

"What?" Huck was pulling in to the school.

"Nothing from Jimmie, I mean." She felt her face go hot, but then she fixed her gaze on Clarice, Moira and Ashley crossing the parking lot. "Please tell me Clarice is still fucking Hardy Berman."

Huck raised an eyebrow. "He seems to think she is."

A few minutes before the bell, Ruby Jane passed Clarice at her locker. Their eyes locked, but neither spoke. Clarice was too busy offering Ashley a cost-benefit analysis of sucking Junus Malo's cock.

20

PRE-SEASON, SEPTEMBER 1988

COACH CALLED THEM together at center court. The girls gathered in a clump on the dark blue Spartan emblem. Ruby Jane held back, waiting to see how everyone sorted themselves. Clarice Moody stood a head higher than the others, her long face and shiny black hair a gravitational draw. Gabi remained in the back too. She gave Ruby Jane a tentative smile when their eyes met.

"Welcome, girls. As of now, all twenty of you are in the mix. Ten will make the varsity squad. The rest will move to JV. But as of this moment, you're all equal. You all have the same chance."

Ruby Jane pursed her lips. Clarice could coast through fall workouts and still start. Moira would be Ruby Jane's most direct competition, but Coach would carry five or six forwards. She wasn't worried. No one else shot better from the outside.

"We've got some promising girls hoping to make a move from JV to varsity this year, plus a transfer from Bay Village. Schilling?"

Gabi looked up. "Yes, sir?"

"Front and center, please."

The girl moved to the front of the group. Ruby Jane took a good look at her for the first time. She was shorter than anyone else. Her bobbed, ginger hair swung along her jaw line as she ducked her head.

"You played—?"

"Guard, sir. Point and shooting in rotation."

"Starter, or off the bench?"

"Both. I averaged fourteen minutes a game last year."

"You're a senior, right?"

"A junior."

Coach nodded, his long face thoughtful. "In the past we ran a three-guard offense, perhaps similar to what you're used to. But last year we had the chance to build our offense around Moody at center. Two forwards, two guards. I may suit up only three guards on varsity this season."

"Yes, sir."

"You're going to need a bigger voice than that if you hope to run my offense."

"Yes, sir!" Ruby Jane saw Clarice smirk and whisper something to Moira. Coach glared at her, then turned his gaze to Ruby Jane.

"Whittaker."

"Yes, Coach!"

"You found your shot last year on JV."

"Yes, Coach."

"Forty-two percent from three point territory."

"Yes, Coach."

"Impressive. But this year, expect to pass. You'll need more assists than points."

"I shot fifty-five percent overall, Coach."

Ruby Jane wanted to add her field goal percentage was better from eighteen feet than Clarice's from eight. But though Coach had a rep for taking what he was given, he'd need to see her on the floor.

"It's a different game against the big girls."

"Have you seen my brother wrestle, sir?"

"Once or twice."

"I taught him everything he knows."

Coach tilted his head, and a faint smile played across his lips. "This team will win if we play as a team. You ready to do that?"

"Yes, Coach."

"Expect to pass." He nodded her back to the group. "All right then." Coach stepped back and looked them all over. After a moment, he launched into his boilerplate. Shoot-arounds at lunch until formal practice started. Nutrition and conditioning tips, and reminders to those who hadn't done so yet to get their athletic physicals before the start of practice. Gabi looked worried, so when practice broke up, Ruby Jane approached her. "Go see Doctor Hart in Farmersville. She does everyone's physicals."

"My grandparents may want me to go to their doctor."

"Hart knows what the school requires, and she'll fit you in right away. Just so you know."

"Thanks." Gabi hesitated. "You decided to play after all."

"I don't have anything else to do."

"The coach—"

"Don't worry about him. He'll give you a fair shot."

Across the gym, Ruby Jane spied Finn Nielson. He was dressed in sweats, looking her way. She supposed he was going to work out in the weight room and had stopped by the gym to ogle the cheerleaders practicing at the other end. Ruby Jane turned to Gabi.

"You're taking Con Law as a junior too, same as me."

"At Bay, I did some classes in summer school. My folks wanted to keep me busy. So I guess I'm a year ahead."

"You want to be my project partner?"

Gabi blushed, cheeks flaring to compete with her red hair. "If you want."

"We're sitting next to each other already, I figured …"

"Sure." Gabi's gaze moved past Ruby Jane's left shoulder.

"Whittaker, what was all that about?"

Clarice. Ruby Jane smiled fiercely at Gabi.

"I asked you a question."

She turned to face Clarice. "I'm supposed to be impressed?"

"I'm captain of this team."

"Not yet, you're not."

"Are you going to challenge me? They won't vote for you."

"You overrated bitch, you might be surprised by who people *won't* vote for."

Clarice thrust two rigid fingers at Ruby Jane's sternum, lips tight against her teeth, mouth partway open. Her breath smelled of licorice and a hint of lunchtime smoke. Ruby Jane stood her ground, arms at her side, weight centered over the balls of her feet.

"What's going on here?" Coach pushed his way into the circle. Neither Ruby Jane nor Clarice moved. "Whittaker, Moody, is there a problem?"

Moira spoke first. "Ruby called Clarice a bitch."

"Is that true, Whittaker?"

Ruby Jane refused to break eye contact with Clarice. "The truth hurts, Coach."

"That's enough. Back off, both of you."

Ruby Jane waited. After a moment, Clarice folded her arms and let her air out. The gym was quiet around them. Coach drew himself up.

"If we're going to be successful, we have to work together. I won't have my players at each other's throats."

"She—"

"I'm not done."

"Yes, Coach."

"Whittaker, I won't tolerate name calling or profanity. Two hours detention."

Clarice grinned, but Coach turned on her.

"I hope you don't think this is funny."

Ruby Jane could feel the heat radiating off of Clarice. The grin collapsed.

"Starting tomorrow and for one full week, you two will go to Barker Stadium. Each day, you'll run five laps around the field, including up and down each set of stairs on both bleachers. You'll run them together, and neither can leave until the other is finished. I don't care how long it takes."

Ruby Jane closed her eyes.

"Any questions?"

"Coach, I didn't do anything. She's the one who—"

"If you want to be captain of this team, Moody, you have to behave like a leader. Leaders don't bully. They don't throw their weight around. And they don't get into spats with their teammates."

"Yes, Coach."

"I may not select the team captain, but I do decide who's eligible to run. And neither one of you will stand for election if you don't get this nonsense under control. Am I understood?"

Ruby Jane nodded, and after a moment so did Clarice. Coach left them. Ruby Jane caught Clarice's eye again, but the fire was out now. Ruby Jane didn't mind running. She could run all day. Clarice would have to keep up.

21

Interview, April 1989

RUBY JANE LIVED in a saltbox on West Walnut, the Brubaker silos rising across the street. Two floors, living and dining rooms, kitchen and mudroom on the first. Three bedrooms and a full bath upstairs. Ruby Jane's room, a cramped cell barely big enough for her bed, dresser, and a small desk, looked out over the street and driveway. Jimmie's own airless cube across the hall shared a thin wall with the Studio.

From the time they'd moved in when she was eight years old, the house had felt small. Dale and Bella filled every room with their voices, loud when happy, louder when not. The issue was always the same: Dale's failure to rise above his working class roots.

"I don't even know why I stay with you."

"You and me both, fucklips."

Ruby Jane knew why. Habit. Inertia. Shared victimhood. Grandfather Denlinger's refusal to accept Dale lent strength to the tenuous thread which bound Bella and Dale's marriage together. Ruby Jane wondered if her grandfather realized the surest way to drive a wedge between his wayward daughter and her blue collar husband was to welcome Dale into the family. If that ever happened, Bella would drop Dale like an empty bourbon bottle.

Grabel seemed most interested in these details of Ruby Jane's home and history, trivialities which had no bearing on Clarice and Gabi. He put a tape in the cassette recorder, tested it, and recorded the date, location, the names of those present. Then he propped a pair of wire-rimmed reading glasses on the end of his nose and started in on the pointless questions. As he spoke, she kept her head tilted back against the window, eyes fixed on the acoustic ceiling tiles. She listened to the hiss of the recorder, to the soft whoosh of the air conditioning. The fluorescent lights hummed.

"You have a brother, right? James."

"Yes."

"He graduated last year?"

"Yes."

"Where is he now?"

"College."

"Where at?"

She wrinkled her nose at a salty tang rising from her singlet, faintly acrid like her basketball uniform after a loss. She didn't want to talk about Jimmie. Nash saved her the trouble. "James is up at Bowling Green, I believe."

Grabel ignored him. No doubt his folder had a notation of Jimmie's whereabouts. He turned a page, read for a moment. "I understand your grandmother Whittaker passed last year. Sorry to hear it."

"Why? Did you know her?"

"Never mind. Tell me about your mother's parents."

"I don't see them much."

"Why not?"

"Ask Bella." She stole a glance at Nash. For a moment, he met her gaze without expression, then he looked down as though he feared what his eyes might give away.

"You do see them from time to time though, right?"

Ruby Jane reached up to knead a sudden cramp in her trapezius. She probed with her fingertips, winced as she pressed into the ropy muscle. Grabel looked up.

"You do see them."

She dropped her hand into her lap. "Once a year or so."

"They live half an hour away."

"Takes longer when you have to hitchhike."

"How does that make you feel, that your grandparents aren't a part of your life?"

"Relieved."

"At least you got to see a lot of your grandmother Whittaker before she died."

The acrid scent grew stronger. She stared at the ceiling.

"Ruby?"

"I didn't give you permission to call me by my first name."

"Christ. Your teachers must love you."

She sniffed. Teachers were figures to be tolerated until class ended, then forgotten. Mrs. Parmelee was the only one who treated Ruby Jane like something more than an entry in a grade book.

"How about your old man's father? What can you tell me about him?"

"I never knew him."

"How come? Your grandparents split up?"

"Why would you assume that?"

"What happened then?"

"He died a long time ago."

"How did he die?"

"How should I know? It was centuries before I was born."

"No one ever told you?"

"Obviously not."

"Why didn't you ask?"

"If anyone thought it was my business, they'd have told me."

Grabel leafed through the folder. "His name was Norbert Fulton. He ran off when your daddy was a bump in your grandmother's skirt. They were never married."

Ruby Jane shifted uncomfortably. The backs of her legs stuck to the vinyl seat and an itch raced across her thighs.

"Out of snappy comebacks?"

"If you already know so much, why ask me?"

"I want to know what *you* know."

She rolled her neck, stretched her arms down to either side of the chair. "I know you're a jerk who won't let me use the bathroom."

The dry skin at the corners of Grabel's mouth and eyes creased into dozens of dendritic lines. His idea of a smile, maybe. "Why don't we cover territory closer to home. How did your parents meet?"

She shook her head. "I didn't realize we were going all the way back to the Mayflower landing."

"I didn't realize your parents were that old."

Nash cleared his throat, a sound she realized was his attempt to suppress a laugh. She refused to grant Grabel that much.

"It was some kind of high school sweetheart thing."

"Where did they go to school?"

"Bella went to Oakwood. Dale went to Dunbar."

"Interesting. Dunbar and Oakwood kids don't usually cross orbits."

"My mother was probably slumming."

Grabel lifted his head, gazed at her over the top of his reading glasses. His erosional smile remained, arid and thin. "Define slumming."

She didn't know what he wanted from her. Her only clues were an overheard snatch of cop talk and the looming presence of Clarice Moody's broken nose. Was he trying to drag an admission out of her, trying to get her on the record as an unrepentant thug who'd bust out on a fellow student without a second thought? Or was there something more behind all these questions?

"You're kidding, right?"

"What about you? Been slumming too? Like mother, like daughter?"

Sudden heat flooded her cheeks. She forced it down again with a blank smile to match his own. "You're the one who had to come all the way out to Farmersville to find yourself a high school girl to hit on."

"Finn Nielson must be the one who's slumming then."

At his post on the wall, Nash's arms tightened across his chest. Grabel, decaying scarecrow, showed his teeth, cracked and grey like old ceramic. "What the hell. Fuck Finn Nielson." He chortled, a sound in tune with his rippling wattle. "Oh, sorry. Poor choice of words."

Ruby Jane's heart jumped in her chest. She found herself pressed against glass, a wave of nausea churning through her gut. The rumor mill never rested. *Finn Nielson, Ruby Jane Whittaker*—she'd had no chance to make sense of it herself. Two mornings before she'd awakened on a far shore, and found her return journey interrupted by the world turning upside down.

Nash stirred. "Coby, can we step outside for a minute?" His voice was low, tentative.

"Not *now*." Grabel snapped his head around to glare at Nash. "Christ." He turned back to Ruby Jane and closed the folder, leaned forward. Ruby Jane found herself looking through a silvery lens, a wash of fluid in her eyes. Vague and out of focus, he was even more frightful to her, a figure less a man than a shadow of menace.

"You've diddle-dawdled long enough, chippie. It's time you tell me what happened to Dale Whittaker."

STORMY NIGHT, AUGUST 1988

A PAIR OF headlights appeared in the distance. The Vega's brake lights flared. Ruby Jane hit her own brakes, too hard. She skidded on the wet, oily pavement and came to a stop at an angle across the center line. In the darkness, she wasn't sure how far she and Jimmie had come, but she knew they were close to the isolated six-points where Farmersville-West Alex and Dechant Roads met at Preble County Line. The gun club was ahead, but little else until Route 35. To her left, one of the Wentz brother's fields stretched into the west. The nearest houses were south of her, an eighth of a mile or more, hidden in the trees on the east side of the road.

The oncoming car could be anyone, but if it was Lute Callan or Werth Nash, she was screwed. She didn't want to lose Jimmie; even less did she want to get hauled home in the back of a township cruiser. As Jimmie and the approaching headlights came abreast of each other she turned onto a dirt access track which led into the Wentz field. If anyone checked on the mystery car, she could duck behind the heap of stones piled at field's edge, boulders which came up each year during the spring plow.

She climbed out into drizzle. The late season corn on either side of the track reached higher than her head and blocked her view up County Line Road. The Caprice's engine ticked as it cooled. The leaves of the cornstalks whispered in the soft rain. Lightning flickered far to the north and west. She edged toward the road. Soft mud sucked at her shoes with each step. She paused next to a lone fence post, as if a six-inch circumference of half-rotted yellow pine could shield her.

Up the road, at least a hundred yards off, the two vehicles had stopped side-by-side. They were too far away for her to see much, but she could tell from the separation of the headlights and their height above the road's surface they belonged to something big. A pickup.

Neither car moved for some time. All she could hear was the wind in the corn and the runoff flowing through the ditch at her feet. A raindrop splashed down the back of her neck. She felt like an idiot, out in the dark and rain, watching her brother and some stranger yuck it up. Probably a wrestling buddy. *When's the next party, man? We oughta score a keg.* Two blockheads passing in the night. She shivered and chafed her upper arms against the chill.

The pickup began to move. Slow at first, though it was hard to be sure at this distance. She wiped rain from her eyes and leaned against the post. Jimmie matched the motion, reverse lights bouncing as he weaved down the road alongside the pickup. As they gained speed, the two vehicles veered toward each other, bumped, then caromed away again. Without thinking, she rushed into the road, arms over her head. Just as quickly the futile warning died on her lips. The headlights bobbed and, as if he had been waiting for his chance, Jimmie cut the Vega's rear end sharply across the path of oncoming truck. The pickup swerved into the opposite lane and slammed to a halt, one wheel in the ditch. Jimmie stopped beside it.

Ruby Jane's tongue felt heavy in the back of her throat. She took a few steps and paused. The rain pattered around her—soaked into her sweatshirt, plastered her hair to her head. Cool air clung to the ground, a turbulent inversion chest high. Up ahead, all was still and quiet. Then she saw a flash of light in the truck's cab as if the dome light had flicked on and off.

She waited. A breeze lifted the leaves of the trees across the road. The Vega's lights moved away from her and then winked out. She drew a long breath and then trudged up the road.

Dale, she thought, *drives a pickup.*

- 23 -

PRE-SEASON, OCTOBER 1988

"I SAW YOU."

"I knew I'd regret chucking the One Ring into the Cracks of Doom."

"Do you ever ease up on the wise guy act?"

"Do I look like a guy to you?"

"Not at all." Huck grinned at her, then shrugged and looked away. "I saw you running the bleachers down at the stadium. That's all I meant."

"You're kinda creepy."

"I run there too sometimes. Not as many laps as you do. Jesus, girl."

"I like to run."

"But not Clarice."

"Running the bleachers might damage her image as a perfectly formed celestial being brought to earth to amaze us with her post-up move."

"Why are you running with her then?"

"We're being punished."

"Right. Coach."

"He wants us to spend quality time suffering together."

"Ah. Growth through shared adversity."

"Exactly."

"But—"

"I like to run. It's hard, sure—"

"It's the kind of hard you like."

"Yes."

"But not Clarice."

"She's too accustomed to being a natural."

"I like to run too."

"I'm not looking for a boyfriend."

"I just thought we could run together some time."

"You think you can keep up with me?"

"I can try."

"I like my solitude."

"Well, if you change your mind."

"Maybe. I'm still not looking for a boyfriend."

"At this point I'd settle for project partner. I ended up with Hardy Berman. All term I'll get to hear how Clarice is a screamer."

"I wouldn't wish him on Gabi in a million years. Besides, you're tough. You can take it."

Huck left her, and she joined the others for the shoot-around. She'd avoided the gym during the week since the fight with Clarice. She knew she wasn't helping her case for making varsity, but the thought of running set-ups with the Monster Squad had no appeal. She'd relented when Gabi approached her in Con Law and pleaded. "No one talks to me."

Coach nodded when she entered the gym, then distributed balls and told everyone to warm up. After a stretch and a few short shots to get the feel of the ball, Ruby Jane went to the right corner, her favorite spot. Her first shot fell short and the second bounced long, but the third dropped through, followed by half a dozen more. Coach watched from half court as she netted ten, eleven, twelve in a row. Clarice was trying to put together a post-up drill, but Ashley pointed and lowered her hands. Beside her, Moira's eyebrows were still but she grinned her strange grin, as if trying to hold back some inner turbulence.

Gabi shagged balls and passed them in, crisp and from the chest. *Sixteen, seventeen, eighteen.* Aside from offering Gabi the occasional grateful smile, Ruby Jane ignored everyone. Gabi smiled back and kept the balls coming. *Twenty-seven, twenty-eight.* Coach folded his arms across his chest, whistle between the middle and ring finger of his right hand. She allowed herself a glance to see his expressionless face, his eyes moving to track the ball up and through the hoop. More often than not they touched only net. The rest kissed the rim before dropping through. *Forty-one, forty-two.* Around the gym, others stopped to watch, even members of the boys basketball team at the far hoop.

"How many is that?"

"I dunno."

"Fifty. Fifty-one." Ruby Jane accepted another pass, threw up the shot. *Fifty-two.*

Gabi took up the count, not loud, her voice a decibel higher than the gym chatter. "Fifty-five, fifty-six." Clarice moved to the sideline, Ashley and Moira two steps behind her. They sat on the bottom bleacher. Others started helping Gabi shag the balls, held them for her until Ruby Jane was ready. New voices joined the count. "Sixty-eight, sixty-nine, seventy." Nothing else mattered. Not Clarice, not Jimmie. Not Bella.

"Eighty-one, eighty-two!"

Only the ball mattered, the hoop. Only the arc of the shot, the heat in her biceps and chest, the sweat on her forehead. Gabi grinned, Clarice scowled. Everyone else watched. "Eighty-nine, ninety, ninety-one!" Balls clapped the gym floor, voices chanted. Her breath was a metronome. "Ninety-four, ninety-*five!*" She hadn't felt this relaxed, this calm, in she didn't know how long. Alive. "Ninety-*seven.*" She took another pass, raised her arms. "Ninety-*eight!*" Coach took a step. The air around her lifted her up.

"*Ninety-nine!*"

The whistle blew, a piercing trill which ripped the air. Number one hundred rimmed out.

For a moment, no one moved. Then, everyone in the gym exhaled at once, a protracted gasp. Gabi set up for another pass, but Ruby Jane held up her hand. Sweat drained into her eyes. She walked to the key. Coach approached and looked down at her.

"I'd say you made your point."

She drew a breath. "Just shooting, Coach."

"Indeed."

Then everyone started talking at once. Bodies pressed in around her, hands patted her on the back. The voices were deafening. She found herself shaking her head, throwing up her hands. "Just shooting, just …" She saw Gabi grinning, and she smiled back. Then she caught Clarice's eye. She couldn't make out her expression, so she moved toward her. The others parted to let her through. She stopped, looked down at Clarice as she sat on the bleacher.

"This year, when you're open in the key, you'll understand why."

"I already know you're a good shot."

"Now you feel it in your bones, don't you, bitch?"

In her eye, Ruby Jane saw doubt, but Clarice didn't respond. She looked away as Coach put his hand on Ruby Jane's shoulder. "I heard that, Whittaker."

24

PRE-SEASON, OCTOBER 1988

RUBY JANE WAS the first to arrive. Mrs. Parmelee sat at her desk, a stack of papers before her. She chewed on the end of a red pencil.

"Does it matter where I sit?"

Mrs. Parmelee pulled the pencil out of her mouth. "Anywhere you like. You're it today."

Ruby Jane signed her name on the first line of the detention attendance form, then dropped her backpack next to a desk halfway along the middle row. Not her usual spot. She slid into the seat and looked around. Mrs. Parmelee's room had one narrow window behind her desk. The chalkboard was bare except for the words NO TALKING in block letters. The Cézanne print, *Bibemus Quarry*, anchored the center of the bulletin board. She liked the colors. Ocher and tan, blue and forest green. She saw something clean and pure in it, nothing like the muddy pictures her mother produced. Out of the corner of her eye, she saw Mrs. Parmelee make a mark on one of the papers and set it aside, take the next off the stack.

"What am I supposed to do?"

"Homework. Or read quietly. There's no one to chat with, so no danger of that." Her eyebrows raised, a pair of sideways question marks. "This is a good chance to finish your persuasive essay."

"Okay."

Ruby Jane took out her English binder and her brother's Walkman. He'd left it behind when he fled. When Mrs. Parmelee saw it, she cocked her head. "No Walkmans in detention."

"What about Walkmen?"

Mrs. Parmelee set her pencil down.

"What brings you in today, Ruby?"

"You don't know?"

Mrs. Parmelee gave a little shrug. "It's not really my concern. It's my week to cover detention, that's all."

"So I don't have to tell you."

"No." She studied Ruby Jane. "I never expected to see you here. Since it's just the two of us …" She shrugged again, dropped her gaze to the paper on the desk. "You don't have to tell me."

"It's nothing. I don't respond well to pressure."

"But I've seen you on the basketball court."

Ruby Jane shook her head. "That's not pressure."

"What is, then?"

"I should work on my essay."

Mrs. Parmelee looked at her, an ephemeral smile playing on her lips. But her eyes showed something else, something Ruby Jane couldn't recognize. "Of course."

— + —

A month later, Ruby Jane was back. She stopped at Mrs. Parmelee's desk to sign in.

"One of these days you're going to learn to lay off Clarice."

"I thought you didn't care why people got detention."

"You know how to draw attention to yourself."

"She called me a cunt."

Mrs. Parmelee's lips compressed. "Then why isn't she here?"

"Coach didn't hear her."

"But he heard you."

"It was worth the look on her face when I told her it was this cunt whose outside shot would keep her from dying under the double team all season long."

Mrs. Parmelee rolled her eyes. "Take your seat, Ruby. And dial back the language, okay?"

Ruby Jane sat near the Cézanne print. She tried to work on Con Law, but had a hard time concentrating. *Name the rights guaranteed by the First Amendment to the Constitution. The Fifth Amendment protects against what?* The sounds of pens on paper, pages turning, and Hardy Berman wriggling in his seat formed an irritation of distractions. Every time someone cleared their throat, she turned to look. At one point she caught Mrs. Parmelee's eye, but she couldn't read her expression. Hardy shifted his weight to one side and loosed a fart. Everyone laughed.

"Mister Berman, come up here."

Ruby Jane closed her eyes and lowered her head to the desk. The cool finish felt good against her cheek. The latest dispute started when Clarice jumped Gabi about a flubbed pass during a drill— a rare lapse on Gabi's part, who'd shown remarkable instinct with the ball. Her passes were sharp and on target. She could no-look a defender out of her shoes. But during the drill, on maybe the twentieth rep, she rushed a pass. The ball bounced off Moira's knee and skittered out of bounds. Clarice spun, eyes ablaze.

"What's your problem, Gabi?"

Gabi's conditioning wasn't what it could be. She tended to run down before the others. Ruby Jane had offered to train with her, but Gabi could rarely find time outside of school and practice.

Even meetings to work on their Con Law project together were tough to arrange. Gabi's grandparents kept her on a short leash.

"Ease off, Clarice."

Clarice threw Ruby Jane a glare over her shoulder and lowered her voice. "On cue, Gabi's cunt appears to save the day."

Ruby Jane hadn't noticed Coach approach from behind. A half dozen detentions might have been worth it if she'd been as clever as she claimed to Mrs. Parmelee. Not even one detention was worth, "You're the cunt, Clarice."

"Time's up, Ruby. You can go."

She opened her eyes. The Bibemus Quarry was before her on the wall. A slick of saliva spread from her mouth across the desktop. She looked up at Mrs. Parmelee.

"Normally I'd have to extend your detention for sleeping, but if you promise to keep your eyes open tomorrow, I'll let this one go."

Ruby Jane blushed. The classroom was empty except for Mrs. Parmelee. "Sorry." She reached for her backpack.

"Wait."

"I should go."

"I told Coach you'd be a few minutes late."

She considered her hands and thought about how it felt to hold a basketball. Secure. Safe. In control. She didn't want to talk to Mrs. Parmelee.

"What's going on, Ruby?" Mrs. Parmelee sat at the desk beside her. "You look tired."

It was hard to sleep in a house where Bella might fire up the stereo any hour of the day or night, or bang on doors demanding Ruby Jane run the vacuum cleaner or fold laundry. Daylight or dark, it didn't matter—someone else's mess was always hers to clean up. But if she told Mrs. Parmelee about Bella, things might lead to Dale. She tried a weak smile.

"I don't play well with others."

"You do all right during games."

"Games are different."

"I know." Mrs. Parmelee rested her arms on the desktop. "Did you know I played high school basketball?"

"You're kidding." Yet Ruby Jane could believe it. Mrs. Parmelee possessed long fingers and an athlete's gait. She was as tall as Clarice.

"I almost played in college, but I hurt my knee and never got my quickness back."

"That's too bad."

She waved a hand, dismissive. "I'd never have been more than a role player." She studied Ruby Jane's face. "Have you thought about college?"

Ruby Jane looked away. "I guess. I don't know."

"You have a lot to learn, but with your shot, you could start for a lot of programs."

"That's a long way off." But Ruby Jane couldn't help but feel pleased. She tried not to smile.

"Scouts will be at the games this season. They'll come for Clarice, but they'll *see* you."

"Yeah, right."

"Trust me, they will—if you can get over this problem you have with her. You need to play like you're part of the team, not a rival. The women's game isn't like the men's game."

"It was a fight. No big deal."

"Why is it always Clarice?"

"Sometimes it's Moira."

Mrs. Parmelee didn't have to say anything. Moira was Clarice's proxy.

"I'm not good at the popularity contest the way Clarice is."

"Is she popular?"

"That's what everyone calls it."

"What do you call it?"

Ruby Jane sat back. Her cheek was cold. "I get it. We're doing therapy."

"It was your question."

"Fine." Ruby Jane thought for a moment. "It's more like … authority. I mean, hardly anyone likes the popular kids. But everyone defers to them."

"I think that's an insightful observation."

Ruby Jane felt like she was being played, but she didn't care. If Clarice was what Mrs. Parmelee wanted to talk about, Ruby Jane was happy to oblige. "My brother does this thing. You ask him a question and even if he doesn't know the answer, he'll blurt something out like it's holy writ."

"Male Answer Syndrome."

"Hah. But it's not just boys. Girls too. Talk like you're in charge and people act like what you say is true even if it's total bullshit."

"Ruby, you really need to watch your language."

"Like you don't swear."

"That's not the point."

She was quiet for a while. "It's bullshit, but we let them get away with it because they act like no one else knows better."

"It's not all BS."

"Sure it is."

"You don't think you're popular?"

"Not like that."

"Sweetie, it's tenuous for everyone. Trust me. You're not alone."

Ruby Jane didn't have an answer for that. "I need to go."

"Practice?"

If she hurried, she could still make the second hour. Speed drills. Lots of sweat. "Yeah, fucking practice."

"Language." But it didn't sound like her heart was in it. Ruby Jane gave her a quick, tight smile, grabbed her backpack, and fled.

25

INTERVIEW, APRIL 1989

THERE WERE DAYS when Ruby Jane felt if she looked through the most powerful telescope or burrowed deep into the interstices between atoms, her father would be there. Dale Whittaker, the scarred-knuckle brawler who clawed free of the morainal till and into a life he couldn't hope to sustain. Child of a woman who worked twelve-hour shifts at the tire plant until she collapsed on the line weeks shy of retirement and died not long after, Dale picked up where his imagined father left off: lingering in West Dayton taverns and after hours joints until starting time on the road crew each morning. His marriage to the rebellious rich girl was less surprising than its issue—two children spawned in the ashes of countless cigarettes and the dregs of untold bourbon bottles. Bella and Dale held out for two decades, an eon of late night screaming fits and broken furniture. But not long enough to get the one thing they most wanted: the rebellious rich girl written back into her father's will.

Gone eight months now, Dale Whittaker, a man who behaved like the whole world owed him a favor because he showed up for work every day, hungover or still drunk, but on the goddamn clock. Every morning when Ruby Jane awoke his was the first face she saw, gazing up out of a muddy hole in the woods. When Jimmie called from Bowling Green, early in the day while there was still a chance Bella would be sober, it was Dale Whittaker's voice on the line ignoring her questions and telling her to put her mother the fuck on the phone already. Eight months, almost long enough to give birth if only Ruby Jane had had the sense to make a completely different kind of mistake. She couldn't be rid of him.

"So what you're saying is you don't know where he is."

Hands under the edge of the table, she put her fingers to her wrist and checked her heart rate. Too fast. Grabel had been on this track for half an hour. He had her perched on a knife's edge now. If she fell to one side or the other her life would change forever, for better or worse. But the real danger was in slipping straight down.

More than anything, she hated that Grabel had caught her off guard, had left her feeling so turbulent and lost. He'd played her from the beginning, dancing past Clarice and rooting around in her family history as if it was an aside, when it was the set up all along. She'd allowed herself to fall into his trap, given in to wishful thinking. She couldn't let it happen again.

"That's what I'm saying." Her throat felt raspy and dry. "I don't know where he is."

"He just up and disappeared."

"I guess."

"You guess? You don't know?"

She shook her head.

"When did he disappear?"

She let the crown of her head fall against the window again. Her chair squeaked, the cassette recorder whirred. Chilled air flowed across her legs and arms.

"I have no idea." She slowed her breathing and concentrated on lowering her heart rate.

"I find that hard to believe."

"You never met my father."

"Why don't you tell me about him?"

"What's to tell?"

"Most children would know right away if their father didn't come home."

"I'm not most children."

"So I gather."

She pressed her tongue against the roof of her mouth. The window vibrated with passing traffic. Nash adjusted his stance. His expressionless gaze annoyed her. Did he know people called him the DARE Dork, usually right after a bong hit? The thought almost made her smile. Instead, she tilted her chair forward. "This is stupid. You want to know about this stuff, ask *him*." She gestured toward Nash.

His mouth dropped open and he popped off the wall. "What's that supposed—"

Grabel cut him off. "I'm asking you, missy."

"What's the point?"

He shrugged. "I told you. I want to know what *you* know."

"You're just trying to trip me up."

He shook his head sadly. "Ruby, all you're doing is dragging this out."

"Telling some has-been city cop my life history is what's dragging this out. Maybe you should get back to me when you're done reviewing the background." She fixed him with a cold stare. "Background is good. *Right?*"

Grabel's wattle flushed. He looked at Nash.

She squeezed her lips together to keep from smiling. Her turn. Now he'd have to wonder how much she'd overheard. He wouldn't know she'd already used up all her ammo. After a moment he licked his thin lips and sighed.

"Okay. Fine. What can you tell me, Officer Nash?"

Nash looked at Ruby Jane for a moment. She thought she caught the flicker of irritation in his eyes. "Well, you know, Dale wasn't the most reliable fellow."

"How so?"

"He could be a bit of a problem. Heavy drinker."

"Meaning what?"

"You have the reports. Some drunk-and-disorderlies, a couple of DWIs. We've been out to the house more than a few times." Ruby Jane noticed he didn't mention the last time they were out to the house, the previous spring. Drunk and disorderly was the least of the problem.

"None of that explains why Miss Whittaker here is so unconcerned about her own father."

She shook her head. Nash was useless. "Because it was when he was around that my father was the problem. Is that so hard to understand?"

"Why don't you explain it from your point of view?"

"Would it help if I use one syllable words?"

Grabel sat back. He looked up at Nash, though Ruby Jane couldn't tell if he was looking for support or someone to unload on. Nash threw his hands up.

"Ruby. Damn it. Just answer the man's question."

"You're not scaring me, you know."

Nash stared at her. She gazed back impassively. Grabel watched with obvious annoyance. "Christ." He pushed away from the table, but there wasn't enough room for him to get out of his chair without turning. She started to smile, but then he smacked the tabletop with both hands. She cringed as the sound of sudden blow cracked the air around her.

"Your belligerence has grown tiresome." Grabel's dead eyes gazed at her from the dry chasms above his cheeks. A tremor ran through her and she struggled to keep her tears in check. She didn't want to give him the satisfaction of thinking he'd regained the upper hand.

"Dale didn't come home a lot, and we liked it that way. Does that answer your question, asshole?"

"Watch your mouth."

"Or what? You'll arrest me? You'll question me? You'll *threaten* me?"

Nash patted the air in front of him, a futile calming gesture. "Ruby—"

"Screw off."

"You're not helping the situation."

"It's not *my* situation to help."

She thought back to that Sunday morning, eight months before. She'd awakened at first light, certain this moment was upon her, sure the police would be at the door. But all was quiet. She was alone. Jimmie had left during the night and hadn't returned.

Nash caught Ruby Jane's eye, his expression pained. That's when it hit her. They didn't know anything. They *were* trying to trip her up. Someone had said something, Clarice most likely, running her mouth in a juvenile attempt at revenge. Not information, not fact. A hint, a guess, conjecture built on a foundation of sand. Then when questioned, Bella went screwy and melodramatic and suddenly this ex-detective from Dayton thought he was on to something.

If they knew anything, there wouldn't be questions, there'd be charges.

"This room is a little close."

She shut her eyes, unaware of who spoke. Her pulse thudded at her temples and her chest labored to pump air. Outside, she heard birds, and a sharp voice shouting at a dog. When she opened her eyes, Grabel was staring at her. She flinched, decided just as quickly not to give him the chance to savor the moment.

"Do you really care about my deadbeat father? He's been gone since last summer. All of a sudden *now* you're interested?"

"We got a report—"

"From who?"

"Not relevant."

"I know it was Clarice."

They exchanged looks. "As a matter of fact, Clarice Moody did make a statement."

"And you listened to her."

"She's a credible source."

Nash didn't believe it. She could see it in his eyes.

"Not when it comes to me, she's not."

"Isn't Clarice your teammate?"

"Not anymore."

"No? I'm told you're quite the player. There may have been an incident, but surely you can work things out. You were one missed shot from taking state. Next year the Spartans could win it all."

A semifinal loss in the regionals was a long way from taking state. "You're trying to pretend you're my friend now?"

"I don't know what you mean."

"Give me a break. I've seen *Hill Street Blues*. I've seen *Miami Vice*. I know how this works."

"Police on television and police in real life aren't the same thing."

"No kidding. TV cops are better looking."

Grabel didn't take the bait this time. "Let me explain something to you, missy. You committed felony assault against Clarice. If she, or her parents, choose to prefer charges, you could find yourself in a heap of trouble."

He paused. Ruby Jane kept her face blank. What Grabel didn't realize is all she'd thought about the last twenty-four hours were the implications of her actions in the gym the day before.

"Due to my intervention, the Moodys have agreed to hold off on their decision. I suggested this situation was more important, and in any case, I believe discipline in such matters is better handled through the school than through the courts. Don't you agree?"

"Just so I understand: If I tell you something you imagine I know about my father, you will convince Clarice's parents to not press charges against the most well-deserved uppercut in the history of Valley View High School?"

"I don't think we're imagining anything. There is the matter of what you told Clarice on the night of December tenth of last year."

"I don't know what you're talking about."

He went back to the folder. After a moment, he found what he was looking for, a sheet torn from a notebook covered with a looping scrawl. "Yes, here. Quoting, 'She was a little drunk, but it's not like she was out of it or anything. She said if anyone ever found out what happened to her father she didn't know what she'd do. Go to jail, probably.'" Grabel set the page down. "What is your response to that?"

"Sounds like you think I was doing some underage drinking."

"You may find this hard to believe, but I'm not troubled by kids cutting loose on a Saturday night. You weren't driving, and my understanding is you had something to celebrate. A big win against a worthy rival."

"We won a lot of games. So what?"

"But it wasn't just any basketball game, was it?"

"It wasn't even a league game."

"No, it was against Princeton down in Sharonville, right? State 3-A champ two years ago, and a favorite this year. Valley View doesn't often play against the big schools. You're 2-A."

"It's called Division II now."

"The point is you won an away game against a powerhouse program, and you did it in a particularly dramatic way. So you came home and celebrated. Understandable. I have no problem with that."

Nash shifted uncomfortably. He had a problem with it. DARE Dork. But he kept quiet.

"I don't remember it that well. I have no idea what Clarice thinks I said, but whatever it was, I was drunk out of my skull. Blotto. Hammered. Did my mother proud, I'm sure."

STORMY NIGHT, AUGUST 1988

THE VEGA WAS nowhere to be seen. The pickup hung half in the ditch, headlights illuminating the scrubby growth on the east side of the road. The night was still, quiet except for the patter of rain. In light reflected off the wet pavement, Ruby Jane recognized the long scrape Bella put in the passenger side of her father's orange Dodge Ram. She stopped a dozen paces away. A thickness gathered in her throat.

"Dad? You in there?" Her voice was so feeble she barely heard herself speak. She listened to the responding silence. "Dale?"

A dark form took shape on the road. She took a step back, resisted the urge to bolt. Jimmie's lanky form was as distinctive to her as her own face in a mirror. He moved slowly, hesitantly. One hand hung at his side, weighed down by an uncertain yet familiar object, something black in the black night. He came to a halt between her and the truck.

"What's going on?"

She couldn't tell if he heard. The glow of the headlights scattered in the falling rain and threw Jimmie into stark silhouette. His hair clung to his head. She heard his breathing, shallow and quick. He lifted his arm away from his side and the object in his hand took shape.

It was their grandfather's gun.

She and Jimmie had long understood Grandfather Denlinger saw his own failure in them. "Isabella should have known better than to go whoring with Drexel trash," he'd say with little regard for who might hear, "What did she get? A mouth-breather for a husband and two heathen spawn indistinguishable from monkeys." The previous winter, during their once yearly visit to the house on Patterson Road in Oakwood, Jimmie had led her to a door at the top of the tower, a door they'd never known to be unlocked.

"I found a ring of keys hanging on a peg in the basement." He jingled them for her, skeleton keys as old as the mansion itself.

The door led into a small study, the dark wood desk flanked by a pair of matching ceiling-high bookcases. Faded wallpaper and a few forgotten cobwebs in the corners. Only the lack of dust and scent of furniture polish suggested the room was ever used. There was a worn spot on the Oriental carpet in front of a dictionary stand, the heavy tome open to the D's. Her eyes fell on the word *disgrace* and she looked away. The window offered a view of the tennis court. While Ruby Jane ran her fingers across the spines of old books, Jimmie went through the desk, then got down on his hands and knees. She heard him jingling the keys.

"You gotta see this, Roo. It's some kind of hidden compartment." He grunted and there came a loud click.

"We should go."

He stood and showed her the pistol, a small revolver.

"Put it away, Jimmie. If Grandfather catches us up here—"

"He'll send us home?"

He had a point. "You still shouldn't fool around with that thing."

"I'm just looking." He turned it over in his hands, enthralled. She could smell machine oil. "I think it's a twenty-two."

She didn't know how he could tell. The metal finish was dark, the barrel stubby and menacing. She didn't want to touch it.

"Put it away."

Instead, he rounded the desk and crashed into the dictionary stand. The big book went flying. The stand crashed against the bookcase. At that moment, they heard footsteps on the stairs.

"Jimmie, put it *away*."

"I dropped it."

"*Find* it."

Jimmie dropped to his knees to grope under the desk. She righted the stand. He pulled himself upright as she put the dictionary back in place, open to the D's. She turned. His hands were tucked under his arms. She didn't see the gun.

"Roo—" His voice cracked.

"Don't talk. I'll take care of this." Her stomach turned over as the footsteps reached the landing.

But it was Dorothy, not her grandfather, who opened the door. "What are you children doing here?"

"We wanted to see. The door was unlocked."

Dorothy looked from her to Jimmie and back again, her gaze more worried than angry. "You need to run along."

The cook locked the door behind them with her own key and followed them down the spiral staircase. When they were alone again, Jimmie promised to return the gun to the hidden compartment as soon as possible.

But now the gun was in his hand. A caustic reek clung to him.

Moments before, light had flashed in the cab of Dale's pickup.

"Jimmie—"

"I'm sorry." His voice cracked.

She looked over his shoulder at the truck. The driver's side door hung partway open. Headlights bright, cab dark. No dome light.

"What did you do?"

"I didn't mean it." He seemed to choke on his words.

She moved past him, her eyes burning.

"It was an accident."

Dale slumped in the front seat, mouth loose, eyes half-open. His pallor matched his grey Dickies work shirt. A moist blotch darkened the area below the left pocket. Ruby Jane backed away from the truck.

"Jimmie—"

"I didn't mean it. She made me—"

She turned and staggered toward the opposite ditch. A stream of vomit preceded her.

"I'm sorry." Jimmie was behind her, right behind her. She felt his presence like a shadow, like a breath of cold, stale air.

When he put a hand on her shoulder, she screamed.

27

GAME TIME, DECEMBER 1988

RUBY JANE'S EYES were fixed on a spot at the far end of the scorer's table, the patch of floor beneath the feet of the opposing center: six feet of hard-muscled Femzilla, the girl who'd been making Clarice's life miserable for the last twenty-nine-and-a-half minutes. Clarice hadn't sat all game, was playing like it was tournament time, not an early-season, non-league game no one expected them to win.

The wood beneath Femzilla's feet didn't buckle. The girl had held her ground in the paint like a granite obelisk all night. Ruby Jane wiped sweat out of her eyes. Down nine with ninety-three seconds to go.

"Whittaker, eyes in, please."

Coach was feeling it. Feeling the chance in the air like the hum of an electrical transformer. Princeton girls were Division I, two years off a state championship, and had no interest in being shown up by a pack of Division II farm girls.

"Ladies, we're finishing as if there's a twelve second clock, okay?" Coach didn't wait for an answer. "These big girls are getting tired. Our speed can beat them. So I want clean shots up by ten, okay?

Keep 'em off-balance." He drew himself, a field general tasting a change in the wind. "You know what to do, same thing you been doing all night. Bring it in."

Gabi inbounded to Ashley at half-court, who bounced to Ruby Jane on the outside. She held the ball half a tick, juked a move and pulled the Femzilla off Clarice with a dribble.

"You not going past me."

Ruby Jane met her eyes, tried to read her intent. The words meant nothing. In her periphery, she absorbed the motion of the players. Someone called out, *open, open*. Femzilla pawed at the ball. Ruby Jane adjusted, spun on the ball of her foot and dropped a bounce pass to Clarice under the basket. Easy lay-up.

"Try that again, bitch."

"Next time." Ruby Jane backpedalled up the court. Coach shouted as she passed. "Great pass, Whittaker!" She fell back into D. *Next time.*

But it wasn't next time. Gabi went vertical to pull in a long rebound and dished to Clarice on the break. Ruby Jane pushed up court as Clarice dribbled at the double-team. But then she pulled up and dropped a nine-footer over the defenders, and they were back again.

"Ain't no next time, bitch."

Ruby Jane didn't see Femzilla, not as a person. She was an impediment, a thing to get past. An empty voice in a cavern of sound. Cheers from the bleachers, Ashley calling the play. Whistles, the squeak of soles on polished wood. Her breath in her ears.

"Bitch, ain't no next time."

"Next time."

Another rebound, this time under the basket. Clarice flipped the ball to Moira, who lost it. Gabi twisted past her and snagged the loose ball before Femzilla could snatch it up. The Princeton girls were faster than Coach liked to think, but Gabi dribbled through a closing gap as Clarice charged up the court. Ruby Jane broke half a step behind her, the impediment on her arm, hanging on tight. No whistle. Clarice had been hitting jumpers all night from eight, nine feet. But Princeton was learning and set up before she reached the top of the key. No one else was scoring. Ruby Jane glimpsed the clock above the backboard, under a minute, down five. The double-team closed on Clarice and she pulled up too deep. Ruby Jane broke for the basket.

"Bitch, what—"

Clarice passed, first goddamn time ever. Ruby Jane caught the ball, two hands, dropped a quick dribble.

"—happened to your—" The defense rolled off Clarice, and the impediment stretched, a wall between her and the lay-up.

"—old man anyway?"

Ruby Jane didn't see red—she saw white, the white-hot darkness of a long night under the trees. The impediment grinned, long-toothed. RJ lowered her shoulder and knocked her on her ass, moved into the gap beneath the net. Femzilla twisted toward the ref, screaming for the charge. Ruby Jane ignored her, heard no whistle. Wouldn't have stopped if she had. She was already off her feet, feeling the air thrum. She slammed the ball through the hoop, caught the rim on her way down. Femzilla stared up at her, eyes like saucers. Ruby Jane dropped to the floor.

The ref grinned and shook his head in disbelief. She looked down at Femzilla. "What was the question?" Princeton called time out—up three, forty-seconds to go—but it was too late. Clarice knocked out a monster block on Princeton's next trip up, and then a fiercely grinning Gabi dished to a waiting Ruby Jane in the right corner. Nothing but net. Princeton never scored again.

— + —

On the bus afterwards, Clarice paused at Ruby Jane's seat. "Bet you think you're special now."

Ruby Jane stared through the dark window. There was only one way Femzilla could have known to ask that question. But she knew Clarice would have handled the hole in the woods no better than she handled the double team. "I've always been special."

Coach made a speech. No one listened. Too excited. He let them have their fun. They'd beat Princeton. Ruby Jane heard Clarice shout from the back seat. "Division-fucking-one!" Coach grinned. Plans were made for a party, but Ruby Jane didn't participate. She felt good, tired, aware of every muscle. Glad she wasn't part of the crowd. She looked forward to a long shower and sleep. Saturday night meant her mother wouldn't be home, not til late and maybe not at all. From the seat beside her, Gabi squeezed her hand. Ruby Jane saw her face in the gleam of an oncoming headlight and smiled.

A good night.

Once off the bus, Clarice insisted everyone meet at her house. "Even you, Ruby." No one was driving to Farmersville. Another time, she might have run home, but her legs were dead weights. Unable to resist, she climbed into Clarice's Rabbit for the first time since being dumped on Gratis Road two months before.

Gabi's grandmother picked her up at the school. She was allowed to play basketball only so long as she came home immediately after every game. At Clarice's house, Ruby Jane hovered at the margins, her head pounding from the music, the voices, the shrieking laughter. She found herself unable to avoid being dragged into group hugs and exuberant, congratulatory gropes from people who normally wouldn't spare two words for her.

Hardy Berman handed her a drink. "What is it?"

"Dunk Juice, baby. My own recipe. Drink up!"

She sipped the sweet and sour concoction, heavy on grapefruit and carbonation. The bubbles felt good on her throat, and her sore muscles craved the sugar. Soon she was onto another, and another. Ashley Wourms cornered her to insist, "I always thought you were the greatest, Ruby *Jane*." Even Clarice pretended to like her. There was talk, and Dunk Juice, and more talk. Moira Mackenzie insisted everyone feel her boobs, then got mad when Junus Malo took his turn. "You got no business feeling me up with Ashley right in the room, asshole." More Dunk Juice. Later, she'd barely remember when Officer Callan appeared at the door, Bella beside him. The argument which followed was a blur of volleyed accusation.

"You got some nerve bitching me out for drinking."

"I'm an adult. You're lucky Officer Callan doesn't arrest you."

She awoke Sunday wishing someone would saw her head off. Her mother was gone until nightfall, the only bright spot in a day made of shit.

Monday morning, when Ruby Jane went out to catch the bus, Clarice was waiting for her at the end of the front walk. Alone.

"Ruby, Ruby, Ruby. You said such interesting things about your father on Saturday night. I must hear all about it."

28

INTERVIEW, APRIL 1989

THE LAST THING she wanted to think about was the basketball team. Not the practices, not the games, not the season. Not the Dunk. In the long, empty days which followed that night in the woods, she found equilibrium in the swish of the ball through the hoop and the long road miles in the early mornings before the sultry air rose like steam above the fields. The team and the games—those barely registered. Win or lose, none of it mattered. Only motion, sweat, repeated effort. If Gabi hadn't appeared at a crucial moment, the forlorn girl far from home, Ruby Jane might have skipped the season. She could get everything she needed on an empty court, shooting threes from the corner for hours. She played for the Spartans only because she knew no other way to protect Gabi from Clarice.

Grabel pulled off his glasses and rubbed the bridge of his nose. After a long silence, the cassette recorder clicked off with a loud pop. Grabel flipped the tape over. Ninety minutes a side, TDK C180. Jimmie preferred Memorex, C90s. He said the tape on the C180s were too thin to hold a clean signal for mix tapes. She supposed they were fine for voice recordings. Grabel looked at his watch. "Ruby Jane Whittaker interview continues, April 18, 1989, Eleven hundred hours. Tape one, side two."

Eleven hundred hours. What a fraud.

She stretched her arms, fought back a yawn. "I have to use the bathroom."

He put his glasses back on. "It's time for you to be honest with me."

"I'm being honest about needing to use the bathroom."

"I can't help you if you won't tell me the truth."

"No one helps anyone but themselves."

"You don't really believe that."

"It's not a matter of belief. It's axiomatic."

"Big words for such a young girl."

"Even bigger for a dumb ass cop who couldn't hack it in the city."

"I'd love to get into a debate about who can hack what with the girl who tossed up a brick in the regional tournament when she had her center open under the basket."

"She's not my center."

"Of course not. She's just a girl you sent to the hospital yesterday."

She deserved to end up in the morgue. But Ruby Jane knew better than to give voice to such a thought. "You don't know shit about it."

He smiled and looked over at Nash. "When they start cursing you know you're making progress."

Nash had been at that game. Ruby Jane remembered seeing him in the crowd shortly after the buzzer as the girls from Massillon celebrated at center court, swarmed by hundreds of their fans. Coach had rested a consoling hand on her shoulder, but her focus was on Nash. He smiled sadly, like he understood what she must be feeling. Other Spartan boosters were more grim, their disappointment as raw as an exposed nerve. After a moment Nash gave her a little wave. Then he was gone and she was pushing through the crowd to the locker room. In the shower, alone and still dressed, she let hot water run over her until at last Gabi brought a towel, helped her strip down and dry off. She was on the bus before the others had a chance to dress. When the team filed aboard and found their seats, Coach stood up at the front.

"Tough night tonight, ladies." He sounded like he was talking under water. "You have nothing to be ashamed of here. Not one of you." Ruby Jane stole a glance around the bus, but no one was looking at her. "Massillon is a great team. We are a great team too, and we played a great game. But tonight, they were a little better than us. And that's okay." He exhaled slowly. "That's okay."

A couple of seats ahead, Clarice stirred and got to her feet. She looked around the bus, and for a moment her eyes lingered on Ruby Jane. She wore an uncertain expression, a mixture of anger and loss. "Coach is right." Clarice's voice was stronger than his, as if she was more sure of herself. "We played a great game, and whatever happened you know what we are? We're champions."

Others lifted their heads.

"First, we're league champions. The Lady Spartans are league champions."

Someone else found their voice, tentative at first. "Spartans!"

"Second, we're district champions. Am I right?"

"Lady Spartans!"

"In the whole state of Ohio, there are only sixteen district champs. Two hundred and seventy-one schools started this season, and we stand among the elite! Am I right?"

"*Lady Spartans!*"

"We came this far together, and we're going home together, as champions."

She sat down suddenly. Ruby Jane looked at Coach. Despite the dim light in the bus she could see the shine on his cheeks. He nodded, pride tempered by sorrow in his smile. "Thank you, Clarice. Thank you." He turned to the bus driver. "Let's go home."

As the bus pulled out, Ruby Jane leaned back in her seat. She was tired, and sore, and sad, but Clarice was right. For the first time in her life, she found herself agreeing with Clarice Moody, for feeling good because Clarice was her captain, the team's captain. Their Femzilla.

But as the bus turned on to the on ramp to I-75, Moira stuck her head over the seat back behind her. "Clarice can say what she wants. We all know who blew that shot."

— + —

Grabel wouldn't care about any of that. Background was good, but only when it served the narrative he'd already chosen: angry, self-involved girl lets her team down in the big game. She refuses to accept her failure, so she takes out her frustration on her teammates.

History of violence and irrational behavior, your honor.

"Let's get back to your father's disappearance."

"Do we have to call him that?"

Emotionally detached from family and friends.

He switched from the folder to a notebook taken from his shirt pocket. He flipped through the pages, tilting his head back to read through the lenses of his reading glasses. "Your mother told us you took her car the night your father went missing."

"I doubt she could recall something so specific. She can barely remember her own name when she's been drinking."

"Where did you go?"

Nash knew. One item on a long checklist of things Nash knew. Dale's rages, Bella's drunken manipulations. If he found his voice now—shared what he knew about that night and Bella's car—

"Ruby?"

Nash had his eyes fixed on the swamp green floor.

"I went out for a drive."

"You didn't have your license yet." She still didn't. Bella refused to take her to the BMV for her driver's test. "Was anyone with you?"

Her heart rate jumped. She gripped her wrist and felt her pulse race. Inhaled through her nose. Her mind jumped to the night on Preble County Line Road, the darkness, the rolling clouds and rain. Jimmie with the gun. She took another deep breath. If she could hold herself together then, Grabel should be a snap now. He looked at her over the top of his glasses.

"You have no clue what it's like in my house. Sometimes I have to get out of there, any way I can."

"And you didn't see your father that night?"

She didn't answer for a long time. "No one even knows he left that night. I hadn't seen him in days."

"But you remember the night I'm referring to."

She would never forget. "It's the only time I ever took my mother's car."

"She told us you took it yesterday."

"The only time before yesterday."

"Did you see your father that night?"

"I never even wanted to see him."

"That's not what I asked."

There was no easy answer. Anything she said might awaken Nash. *I saw you on the road not far from Dale's truck that night.* Nash knew enough—if little else—to make trouble for her. But he only brooded against the wall, mouth twisted and frowning.

"Let's set your father aside for a moment. Tell me about your brother."

She opened her mouth, closed it again.

"We haven't really talked about him. What can you tell me?"

"I don't know."

"Do you get along with him?"

"Sure."

"No sibling rivalry?"

"Not really. We're in to different things."

"You're both athletes."

"Wrestling and basketball aren't quite the same thing."

"No, of course not." Back to the goddamn folder. "When did you last see him?"

She shrugged.

"Not recently?"

Grabel's hands rested on the table. He waited. Overhead she heard a sudden scrabbling. A moment later, dozens of starlings descended past the window. Their strange, boiling motion and frantic screeching sent a trill of anxiety through her. Something about them was like Grabel, the ice in his voice, the liquid movement of the flesh hanging beneath his chin. His impenetrable indifference to anything except his own foreordained trajectory. She wanted to shout at him to read his fucking file, to listen to his own fucking officer.

Nash already told the dried-up fucker Jimmie was in Bowling Green.

Or was he?

The thought hit her like a brick.

Tell me about your family, grandmother, grandparents. How did you parents meet? A line of questions all leading to Dale, sure. She understood that. But then, just as they were getting to the heart of her father's disappearance, Grabel shifts to Jimmie. She sat up, tried to read Grabel's thoughts in the tracery of capillaries and crevices on his face.

Even now, Jimmie might be in a room nearby, awaiting his turn to tell Grabel the story of his life. Or perhaps Grabel had already taken a run at him, badgered him, tricked him, broken him down.

Jimmie wasn't as strong as she was. He'd crumble at the first hint of pressure. They wouldn't even have to play it heavy, simply insinuate she'd already given him up. Separate rooms, separate lies. Manipulate both until one confessed.

Jimmie may have watched all those cop shows, didn't mean he'd learned anything.

She was almost disappointed they hadn't tried the same stunt on her. *We've already talked to James. He said you did it.*

Did what, Detective Pervert?

That's where she had them. Jimmie didn't know.

Even if he was sitting next door, even if he was babbling and crying and laying bare his soul, it didn't matter. Because whatever he thought he knew was wrong.

"Nothing to say?"

All this effort, but break it down and what did anyone know? Clarice had a barrel of pissed off and some drunk talk. Bella could say only so much before she incriminated herself. And Jimmie, whatever he thought he remembered ended before the night was finished.

All she had to do was wait them out. She smiled at him.

But then he smiled back. "Fine. In that case, why don't you tell me about your grandmother's missing emerald ring?"

- 29 -

STORMY NIGHT, AUGUST 1988

THE RAIN SOAKED her clothes and her scream died in thunder rolling across the fields. A memory surfaced like a bubble of gas in an overgrown pond. September or October—burnished leaves still clung to the sugar maple in the backyard—a Saturday morning. The dishwasher had broken again, and the dishes had piled high enough she was forced to eat her Cheerios from the one-quart liquid measure. After she ate, she started washing, the only one who would. Whittaker tolerance for mushrooming disorder was legendary.

She stared out the window over the sink while she scrubbed, the peeling olive paint on the garage a reflection of her thoughts. She hummed tuneless renditions of Q-102's latest obsessions: Madonna, Gloria Estefan, "Man in the Mirror" so many times in involuntary repetition she wanted to shove Michael Jackson off a cliff. As the soapsuds died she tried to force her attention onto some-thing—*anything*—else. The cough of the fridge's dying compressor, the scent of lemon Joy, the advance of mildew along the baseboards. Bella on the phone.

It was a typical call: town gossip, her unappreciated art. Ruby Jane half-listened, grateful for something to combat pop ear-worms but otherwise disinterested in Bella's prattling. When she mentioned Jimmie, Ruby Jane's ears perked up. The phone cord stretched from its wall mount below the stairs to one end of the house or the other. Bella walked a circuit, phone tucked between jaw and shoulder as she gesticulated in unseen emphasis to her con-federate in gossip. Bella avoided the kitchen, but as Ruby Jane's hands pruned she picked up snippets of conversation on her moth-er's loop through the dining room.

"Tell me about it ... James, yes, both these goddamn kids, but especially James ..."

Ruby Jane rinsed a plate, scraped at the scummed surface of another with her fingernail.

"... you have to know ... exactly. You have to know what but-tons to push— ... right, exactly."

Bella's feet padded across the cracked and fading linoleum in the hall. Dale often talked about ripping out the linoleum and re-finishing the oak he was certain he'd find underneath.

"—what I'm saying is James is the weak one ... yes ... he thinks he's tough ..."

Ruby Jane dropped a glass, heard it crack against the stainless steel basin.

"... comes down to it, he's the one I can—"

Hidden by murky water, the broken glass sliced into her fin-ger. Bella insisted it was a scratch, but she rode her bike to the ur-gent care clinic in Germantown anyway. Five stitches and a tetanus booster.

But she thought back to Bella's unfinished conversation now as Jimmie stood trembling beside her. Hunched over, forearms on her knees, she could feel him in the dark, hear his quiet whimpers.

"Roo?"

The stink of vomit at her feet assaulted her nostrils. She wiped her mouth on her sweatshirt sleeve. Her eyes were adjusting to the darkness at last. She could see his face now. Darting eyes, mottled cheeks. His mouth hung open, as if he had no strength to lift his jaw. He looked like something found growing in a damp basement.

He reached for her. "What am I going to do?" His voice quaked.

"Keep that away—" But the gun remained at his side. His empty hand hung between them.

"You gotta fix this, Roo."

She shuddered and turned away, found herself facing Dale's truck. "What I gotta do is get help." Her stomach lurched again, but she bit back the rising bile and drew shaky breath.

"Roo, please—" He scooted around in front of her. "They'll put me in jail. I can't go to jail over him."

She listened to the murmuring rain. "Maybe he's okay." The words sounded hollow.

"He's not okay!" His reckless agitation buzzed in the night air. "Look at him. Aw, fuck, Roo. Look at him."

Ruby Jane didn't want to look at him. She could smell gunpowder in the air, a dark base note under the scent of rain and green corn.

"Jimmie ..." She fought back another wave of nausea.

"You weren't supposed to know. I was supposed to—" He shook his head, harder and harder.

"Jimmie—"

"You weren't supposed to be here. I didn't ..." He turned to her suddenly. "You gotta do *some*thing."

"What can I do?"

"You've always been smarter than me."

"No."

"It's true. Even Mom says so."

"Bella is full of shit." Then the realization struck her, bright and sudden as lightning.

James is the weak one.

Bella had been planning this for months.

Ruby Jane knew whatever passion or defiance brought her mother and father together had long since eroded into malice. Dale saw himself as tragic and unappreciated, a man who worked his ass off to provide for a pack of ingrates. In Bella's mind, Dale was resigned to a life at the margins, the needs and hopes of his family—of his *wife*—be damned. A theatrical demand for a divorce was long overdue.

Instead, Bella had drifted into darker territory. Perhaps, after so many years of rebellion, she worried her parents would not welcome her back into the Denlinger fold. Dead Dale might offer more certainty, especially if there was insurance. For the cost of a single bullet Bella could receive a substantial payout and solve the problem of Dale all at once, without the muss and bother of what would surely be a bitter split. Drop the fucker and cash the check.

And besides, grieving widow looked a hell of a lot better than booze-addled divorcée.

Jimmie's visit to Bella's room earlier that evening wouldn't have been his first. Even the pliable blockhead would need more than a single brainwashing session in The Studio to convince him to take a step so drastic. Ruby Jane pictured it unfolding over many months. Whispered confidences and assurances, promises of support no matter what happened.

"People have the right to protect themselves. The way your father treats you, ..." *Swoon.*

If anyone had cause to hate Dale, Jimmie did. Ruby Jane had iced no end of Jimmie's bruises, cleaned and bandaged no end of cuts—all by Dale's hand. But left to himself, his feelings would never amount to more than a brooding enmity.

"Roo…?"

Jimmie stared, dead-eyed and helpless. In a week, he was supposed to leave for college, free at last of the stultifying weight of life on West Walnut. He couldn't wait. Dorm living, frat parties, college girls—a new world. He planned to major in business, learn how to get rich. He even joked about taking care of Ruby Jane someday. Big brother looking out for his little sis. One more week and he'd be free.

While she was stuck here two more years.

Her eyes flooded. The big, dumb blockhead.

"Jimmie, I need you to think. What did Bella tell you to do?"

The question seemed to make no sense to him.

"What were you supposed to do after—" She shuddered. "After this."

"After—?" His breath smelled of Jim Beam.

"Damn it, *focus*. Did you have a plan? What did she tell you to do?"

"I don't know, Roo." He hung his head, as if more ashamed of having no answer than shooting Dale. "She never said anything about …" He swallowed. "… after."

An icy calm came over her. Bella had set Jimmie up. She expected him to get caught. Should Jimmie try to implicate her, assuming she hadn't already convinced him it was all his idea, Bella would feign shock and innocence. "I don't know what he's told you, but I would *never* suggest such a thing to my son." The drunken bitch was a master of deflection.

The rain picked up. Broad flashes of lightning on the horizon resolved into distinct bolts to the north. The worst of the storm would pass them by, and with that thought the solution came to her in a long roll of thunder.

"Give me the gun."

30

MID-SEASON, FEBRUARY 1989

"HOW MANY TIMES have you been here, Ruby?"

"I don't know." Her neck hurt. Her legs hurt. Her whole body ached during the season. She wasn't getting enough sleep, and not enough roadwork.

"I do. Your next offense means a one-day suspension."

"Just because I swear at Clarice."

"It's not only that."

It wasn't Mrs. Parmelee's week for detention duty, but she'd come to Mister Halstead's room and pulled Ruby Jane out. Apparently the higher powers had chosen Mrs. Parmelee as Ruby Jane's unofficial head shrinker. They went to Mrs. Parmelee's room, sat under the Cézanne print.

"Ruby, if you get a suspension you have to sit out a game."

"Shit happens."

"Ruby ..." The compressed lips.

"Sorry." But then she shook her head. "Is everyone afraid I'm going to miss a damn game? Is that why we're here?"

"No one's worried about that. Not even Coach."

"Now *that* I don't believe."

Mrs. Parmelee smiled, conceding the point. Ruby Jane almost laughed. But then Mrs. Parmelee's expression grew serious. "Honestly, I'm worried how you're holding up. I know things are tough at home—"

"That's not it."

She instantly regretted the interruption. Mrs. Parmelee sat back and scrutinized the print on the bulletin board. The air felt as thick as syrup. A hot constriction formed behind Ruby Jane's breastbone.

After a long, taut moment, Mrs. Parmelee stirred. "I've seen you looking at this. Do you like Cézanne?"

"I guess."

"It's from a difficult time in his life." Mrs. Parmelee gazed at the painting for a moment, then closed her eyes. "Not that he ever made things easy for himself." It felt like an accusation. She opened her eyes again. Ruby Jane looked away.

"I don't believe I ever mentioned my ex-husband. Walter Parmelee."

Ruby Jane couldn't imagine Mrs. Parmelee with a life outside of school—she was part of the Valley View infrastructure, had been for eons. Ex-husband? The notion didn't make sense. Ruby Jane shook her head.

"No, of course not. There would be no reason. One's personal life is not the sort of thing one discusses with students."

"I guess not."

"But we've become more than student and teacher, don't you think?"

Ruby Jane thought of her other detentions. "Sure, yeah."

"Walter wasn't a kind man. I shouldn't say was. It's not like he's dead. He lives in Boston with his new wife."

"You kept his name."

"A matter of professional convenience."

"What happened?"

"The specifics aren't important. What is important is that I suffered through ten years of a very bad marriage, one I entered into too young and for the wrong reasons. Walter was cold. He could become violent if things didn't go his way."

Mrs. Parmelee paused and swallowed, then attempted a quick smile. Ruby Jane saw a tremor in her hand when she brushed a stray hair off her forehead. Ruby Jane turned back to *Bibemus Quarry*. She was unaccustomed to seeing adults vulnerable, unless she counted drunk off their ass as vulnerable.

"My brother is a district attorney for Montgomery County. He explained to Walter how far a motivated prosecutor can go in cases of spousal abuse. Roger helped me break away before the situation grew too dangerous."

Ruby Jane looked at her. The skin around her eyes felt tight.

"What I'm trying to say is I know how difficult it is when someone who should love and protect you chooses to hurt you instead. Self-doubt and guilt overwhelm you. You blame yourself for the cruelty you suffer. You come to believe you deserve it. Why would they treat you so badly otherwise? I understand these feelings. And I understand not everyone has the choices I had. Sometimes you must take matters into your own hands."

"Mrs. Parmelee, I—"

"Please, don't tell me anything." She gripped Ruby Jane's forearm. "Don't tell anyone anything."

Ruby Jane wanted to pull free. To run, to hide. She imagined a shadowy crevice in Bibemus to which she could flee. She supposed Mrs. Parmelee was trying to comfort her, to let her know she wasn't alone. Perhaps even offer a measure of absolution. But Ruby Jane couldn't help but wonder how many others had made the same astute guess about what she had done to her father, and why.

31

INTERVIEW, APRIL 1989

HER EYELIDS HUNG at half-mast but Ruby Jane wasn't ready to sleep. Grammy Whittaker sat on Ruby Jane's bed and gazed at the dark window. Outside, colored lights glowed in the night, Jimmie's attempt to add a little holiday cheer to the house. A few of the thumb-sized bulbs were burned out, but Ruby Jane didn't mind. Left to Dale and Bella, the place would look like Scrooge's counting house.

Grammy stirred. "Ruby, I want to give you something."

"But it's not officially Christmas for another half hour."

Her grandmother stood up and patted Ruby Jane's folded hands. "This isn't a Christmas present." She crossed the room to her suitcase. When she returned to the bed and sat down, she offered Ruby Jane a small black box.

"What is it?"

"Open it."

The box was soft and worn, with rounded corners: a jewelry box. Ruby Jane lifted the lid. A gasp escaped her lips. Inside, nestled in velvet, was her grandmother's emerald ring. The large, square-cut green stone was surrounded by diamonds and set in gold. Her grandmother wore it on special occasions.

"This is ... you can't mean this for me."

"It's always been meant for you."

"But ... not now."

"No, not until I die. It's in my will."

"I don't want you to die."

"Oh, sweetie, don't fret about that. I just wanted to tell you about the ring. It's been in my family for a long time, passed down from mother to daughter. But I don't have a daughter and, well, you and me both know your mother barely puts up with me. Anyway, your daddy would probably sell it. So I'm passing it to you." She smiled. "Would you like to hold it?"

She'd never known Grammy to let anyone else touch the ring, legacy of better times for the Whittakers. Now only Grammy, and this lone heirloom, remained of what Ruby Jane had heard was once a large and wealthy clan. She reached out her hand. "Yes, please."

"Put it on."

"It's loose."

"My old, arthritic knuckles, that's why. You can get it resized when the time comes."

"It's beautiful."

"That it is, sweetie, even more beautiful on your hand."

The ring felt warm on Ruby Jane's finger.

"It's like it was made for you."

"I don't know what to say. Thank you."

"You don't need to say anything more than that. All I ask is that you pass it on to your own daughter."

Ruby Jane blushed. She'd never thought about having a daughter, let alone imagined herself part of a legacy. She knew nothing of her grandmother's past, but as green gem flashed on her hand, she felt the sudden weight of history stretching out behind her.

"Objects have memories, you know. This ring carries the memories of all those who have worn it, the good and the bad. I hope you give it lots of good memories."

"Me too, Grammy."

"Now come here and give me a kiss, and then go get some sleep. Early comes early, you know. And that brother of yours is all in a tizzy at the possibility there's a Walkman under the tree."

"Is there?"

"Oh, probably."

Ruby Jane returned the ring to her grandmother's hand. She kissed Grammy's cheek, then went downstairs to the couch. Under the glittering light of the Christmas tree Ruby Jane thought about the ring and all the Whittaker women who'd worn it. Soon she drifted off, never dreaming this would be her grandmother's last Christmas, or Grammy's plan for the ring would fail.

Or, more than a year later, Detective Pervert would give a rat's ass about it.

Grabel glanced out the window. Sunlight filtered by high clouds cast a pall across the landscape. "The day's getting away from us."

"You want to speed things up, be my guest."

His lips twisted. "The ring? Any thoughts?"

"No one knows what happened to the ring."

"It disappeared shortly before your grandmother died."

"How do you know that?"

"She filed a police report. Accused her son of taking it." Grabel dug through the folder and pulled out one of his ubiquitous sheets of paper, a fax, curly and smudged. She could make out WHIT-TAKER, MAE typed in a box near the top.

"I didn't know she reported it." Many times the previous spring, her father denied taking the ring, but everyone knew better. When Mae Whittaker died, the subject of the ring died with her. One more thing lost.

"You were close to your grandmother?"

"Sure."

He laced his hands under his chin, squashing his wattle into a patty between his thumbs. "You must be upset about the ring."

"I'm upset my grandmother is dead."

"And the missing ring."

He wasn't very subtle. "I'd take my grandmother over some dumb ring any day."

"Of course you would. But it was still a very nice ring."

Ruby Jane didn't know what else to say.

"You want to hear my theory?"

"Not even remotely."

"I think your father ran himself a little scam. When his mom got sick, he rooted around the old homestead. Got hold of her checkbook, wrote himself a few checks."

Ruby Jane couldn't imagine her father doing that. Not because he wasn't a thief, but because he was too much of a coward to try a stunt so easily discovered.

"Maybe he told himself he'd pay the bills while your grandmother was in the hospital. Help his old mom out. But, he didn't pay many bills. And she never noticed. Her illness didn't leave her with much energy for balancing her checkbook or reading her monthly bank statements."

Ruby Jane thought about her grandmother those last weeks. She'd kept her illness secret until she couldn't hide it any longer. By then, she was too weak for chemo, barely survived the surgeries which removed first a couple feet of bowel, and then half her stomach.

"We believe your father stripped his mother of her life savings because he discovered she left everything to you and your brother."

"There was nothing to leave to us. Her house was all she had, and it was worth less than the outstanding hospital bills."

"Medicare doesn't pay for everything, does it? Still, your grandmother didn't have to die poor."

"She lived poor."

"Maybe she didn't have a lot of luxuries, but she saved some money. You must not have known."

"My parents had to pay for her funeral."

"I've reviewed her bank statements. In December of 1987, she had over three hundred thousand dollars banked. From what I can tell, she'd saved steadily for forty years, a little bit each paycheck. It didn't make her rich, not by your Grandfather Denlinger's standards, but it was a nice piece of change. It was supposed to see her through her retirement, or go to you and your brother."

"Nothing was left."

"Where'd it go?"

"How am I supposed to know?"

"Tell me this then. What happened to your father?"

"I don't know."

He waggled his fingers and smiled. "First the ring, then the money. That might piss someone off."

"I didn't know about the money."

"But you knew about the ring."

"Grammy said it would come to me when she died. She told everyone."

"And instead your father took it."

"If you know that, why wasn't he arrested? You say Grammy made a report, but she died in April, months before he disappeared."

His fingers untangled from each other. The wattle swung like a flag in the breeze. More shuffling, more pages. "He was questioned on March tenth of last year."

"I'm shocked he didn't confess. Did you make the mistake of letting him pee?"

Another grim smile. "Without the ring itself, and with only your grandmother's word against his, we couldn't do much. An effort was made to canvas pawn shops in the Dayton area, but there are a lot of pawn shops. One emerald ring, even if it was worth a couple grand, didn't merit the kind of commitment necessary for a rigorous investigation."

"So now you're hassling me? I don't have it."

"I don't think you do."

"I have to use the bathroom."

"Not yet."

Nash put his hands on the table and tilted his head at Grabel. "Coby, maybe we ought to—"

Grabel's jaw flexed with restrained rage. "Christ, you people have no spines."

"I think we could all use a break."

Grabel hip-checked the table as he got to his feet. "Fine."

"Hey, what about me? Bathroom?"

"You keep your mouth shut, chippie." The door opened and slammed, and she was alone.

The clouds had broken outside. Clear blue skies stretched to the east. The leaves of the maple trees swayed in a gentle breeze. A gull landed on the top of a telephone pole. Ruby Jane checked her watch. Almost one o'clock. They'd been in the tight conference room for hours. She slipped out of her chair and moved to the door. She was afraid to risk opening it a second time, but she didn't have to. They were right outside.

"Coby, what the hell is going on in there?"

"I'm conducting an interview."

"You're all over the place."

"I'm keeping her off balance. If we let her settle into a rhythm, she won't tell us anything."

"The way things are going, nothing she says will be admissible."

"I wouldn't say that. For one thing, we have her mother's permission—"

"A drunk's permission is what you mean. It's a small miracle the state hasn't intervened in that household. Any defense attorney worth his salt is gonna have you for lunch."

"—and for another, I was going to add before you interrupted me, what do you think I'm after here anyway?"

Nash was quiet for a long time. She heard the rustle of paper changing hands. "Christ, Coby."

"Have a little faith."

"How about you have a little trust? This isn't the time for me to be finding this out."

"I'm used to working in a different environment. Where I come from, patrol officers observe."

"Where you are now is nothing *but* patrol officers. We work cases together."

"Fine, fine. Untwist your titty, Werth. We got work to do."

"I'm going to take her to the restroom."

"Hurry it up then."

She wore an expression of weary indifference when Nash entered. He led her across the office to a recess in the far wall, two doors tucked to either side of a water fountain.

"Be quick."

"After you made me wait half the day?"

He grunted as she pushed the door shut behind her.

The bathroom smelled of pine cleanser. Thank god for small favors. She peed from a crouch, unwilling to let her skin touch a surface which may have served as throne for Grabel or the chief. Then she washed her hands and splashed water on her cheeks. The face in the mirror bore only a faint resemblance to the girl she thought she was. Pale skin, sickly green shadows under her eyes.

"I look like I have leprosy."

Her voice sounded tinny in the small tiled room. She wanted to get away. Huck would take her in, but she wasn't sure she was ready to go down that path. Something twisted low in her stomach as she thought back to Saturday night and for a moment she feared she would throw up. She let the water run, wet her face again. Her nausea subsided. Someone knocked on the door, a tentative rap. Nash. Grabel would have kicked the door in. She dried her hands and went out.

"How are you holding up, Ruby?"

"I'm fine."

He studied her face, his eyes bouncing up and down, back and forth. "It's been a tough day."

"Don't bother. I won't fall for some kind of *secret friend* routine."

"That's not what I'm doing." A niggle of worry stirred in her stomach as she thought of the story he could tell Grabel about that night on County Line Road. *I passed his truck earlier, further up the road ... Dale do something to you?* Grabel would love to hear that tidbit. For reasons she couldn't guess, Nash had kept it to himself.

Yet she couldn't bring herself to acknowledge even this small gift. "Whatever." She tried to move past him toward the conference room door, but he stopped her.

"You ask me, Sergeant Grabel has taken this too far." His hand felt hot on her forearm, or perhaps that was the heat of her own skin reflected back against her. "I'll be talking to the chief about it, for what it's worth."

What was it worth? She didn't know. She didn't even know if she cared. She felt herself blinking back tears for the umpteenth time that day; she refused to let him see her cry. She bit the inside of her lip and drew air through her nose. Then she looked at Grabel, who sat in the chief's office with his back to the open door. He said something and the chief laughed.

"Don't we have an interrogation to get back to?" She spoke through her teeth.

"There's someone here to see you first."

"Who?" *Please don't let it be Huck.* She couldn't think of anyone else, except perhaps her mother, but that was so unlikely as to feel like a bad joke.

"In the conference room. You can go in. I'll bring you something to drink if you want. Some water, or a pop. What would you like?"

"Nothing."

"I'll bring you some water."

She didn't want to see anyone. But her desires couldn't be less relevant. She went to the door, pushed it open.

Mrs. Parmelee stood at the window. She turned when the door opened and for a moment she gazed across the room. "Oh, honey, are you all right?"

Ruby Jane couldn't hold back her tears any longer.

STORMY NIGHT, AUGUST 1988

JIMMIE LOOKED AT the weapon in his hand as if he couldn't believe something so small and blunt could undo so much.

"Give it to me, Jimmie."

He offered her the gun without hesitation. She jammed it into her sweatshirt pocket, then circled Dale's truck to the open door. *Don't think, don't look—just another mess to clean up.* The stench of gunpowder almost overwhelmed her, but the presence of his body left her indifferent. All she cared about now was the passage of time. Kids from school often snuck onto the gun club grounds at night to look for clay pigeons and spent shotgun shells while they knocked off pilfered six-packs. Idiots, but idiots who could put Jimmie in jail if they showed up now.

She gazed into the woods.

"Roo? What are you doing?"

"We have to bury him."

"We can't do that." He inched toward her. "Can we?"

"Do you want to go to jail?"

"Jesus, I'm not going to jail—I'm going to *fry.*"

233

"Not if you do what I tell you."

"But, Roo—"

"Goddammit, stop whining and help me. We have to get him out of the truck."

"And take him where?"

"There." She pointed into the thicket. "We'll bury him. Then we'll leave his truck in the Eagles parking lot. If anyone notices it, they'll think he left it because he was too drunk to drive."

"Roo, we'll never get away with this."

"Should we go ask Bella what she thinks?"

He shut up. Ruby Jane reached into the cab and unlatched the seat belt, then hooked her father under his arms. He stank of scorched metal, cigarettes, and beer. She wrestled the body onto the road beside the pickup. Jimmie let out a squawk when Dale's lolling head struck the pavement with a sound like a bat whacking a melon.

"How are you doing this?"

The rain lashed at her. Her patience was slipping. "Jimmie, *help me*."

"How the fuck are you doing this?"

"Get his feet." She tried to pull Dale off the road, but the rough pavement dragged at his clothes like Velcro. Jimmie didn't move to help.

"Jimmie!"

"*What?*"

"Grab … his … fucking … *feet*."

Somehow Jimmie complied. They hoisted Dale across the ditch and through the spindly viburnum at the edge of the thicket. Ten feet into the woods they dropped him in a narrow clearing. Ruby Jane leaned against a tree to catch her breath. She could feel Jimmie staring at her.

"Now what?"

She ignored him, returned to the truck. Jimmie followed, his breathing noisy and ragged. The stink inside the cab was already fading. She found a flashlight in the glove box. It flickered when she shined the light into Jimmie's face. He blinked and his pupils contracted to points. His pulse jumped in his neck. "Check the truck. We need a shovel, or something to dig with. See what he has."

"Where are you going?"

"To look for a place."

"Jesus."

"You want me to clean this up, you have to do what I say."

His Adam's apple wobbled, but he went to the bed of the pickup.

She crossed the ditch and pushed through the brush. The wood was a mix of black maple and horse chestnut, with an occasional shaggy hickory tree. As she made her way under the canopy, rain water dribbled over her. Leaves rustled in the wind. She picked her way through the viny undergrowth, certain each step landed her in poison ivy or raccoon shit. Thorns dragged at her jeans and ripped the exposed skin on the backs of her hands. The soft earth gave beneath her feet. After a dozen steps, the trees closed in, and in another fifty feet the guttering flashlight revealed a shallow depression bordered with swamp rose and filled with last year's leaves. A night bird loosed a shrill, vibrant cry. She switched off the flashlight. She couldn't see the lights of Dale's truck behind her.

This would have to do.

Back at the truck, Jimmie stood twisting the hem of his windbreaker into tight little spikes in his hands.

"What did you find?"

"His tool boxes are in the cab behind the seat."

"What about a shovel?"

"Yeah. In the back."

"Get it. Get it all."

She waited while Jimmie collected everything, then led him back through the trees to the depression. "Drop the tool boxes here."

"Is this where…?"

"Yes, Jimmie. This is where."

"I don't understand how you're doing this."

"You're the one who pulled the trigger."

For a moment she thought he would start crying. A shudder rose up through her, a dark wall of desperation. The rain battered her neck and shoulders, the cold seared her skin. She ran her numb hand over her face. "You need to deal with the truck."

"Why?"

"We can't leave it here."

"What am I supposed to do with it?"

"Drive toward the gun club. There's a turn-out a little ways up on the right. Park and turn the lights off." She had an odd thought. "Maybe we'll get lucky and someone will steal it."

"No one is going to steal it, Roo."

"Okay, yeah. Whatever. But if someone does check it out, we want it to look like he left it there on purpose. The turn-out is far enough up no one will notice us down here if they do stop."

Jimmie hesitated.

"What's the problem?"

"It's just—" His lips pulled back from his teeth. "What if I get blood on me?"

She looked at the stretch of pavement between them for the length of a breath. "Jimmie, I cannot tell you how little I care whether you get blood on you."

He flinched, but then he moved away through the brush. She followed him as far as Dale's body, listened as the truck door closed and the engine started. The wheels spun in the weeds before gaining traction. The headlights flashed through the leaves and then the truck moved away.

Part of her wished he'd keep driving, never come back. She leaned back against the bole of a maple tree. The only sound was the soft susurration of leaves. The earthy smell of the woods was overlain by a salty musk laced with wet twill. She slipped around the tree. Rough bark dug into her back. She found a knot with her shoulder blades and pressed into it. The sudden sharp pain provided her with a point of focus, something which wasn't Dale. She leaned her head against the trunk and closed her eyes. The inside of her eyelids were no darker than the woodland around her. Rain drops struck her forehead and cheeks. Her weight settled into the tree. She inhaled, held the breath, let it out. An owl called, the forlorn sound an echo of her own anxiety, followed by the grumble of a vehicle approaching on the road. Not Dale's pick-up. The engine sounded smoother, the rolling tires higher in pitch. A car. She sank down, indifferent to the cold muck soaking into her jeans. But the glow of the headlights flashed through the viburnum and grew dim. The grumbling engine died away, lost in the tapping of rain. A moment later, she heard a hiss in the darkness.

"Roo ... Where are you?" Jimmie staggered toward her through the brush. She flicked on the flashlight. "Someone came."

"Who?"

"A cop. Nash, I think." His face was white and his eyes looked ready to pop out of their sockets. "I did like you said. I'd just turned the lights off when I saw him turn off Dechant Road. I crawled across the seat and got out on the passenger side and ran into the woods."

"Did he see you?"

"I left the keys."

"Jimmie, did he *see* you?"

"I don't think so. He slowed down, but didn't stop."

"No problem then."

"We should go."

"We have to finish this."

"Roo—"

"Shut up."

He didn't speak during the grueling effort to drag Dale's body through the woods to the depression. Ruby Jane couldn't manage the flashlight and Dale's arms at the same time, so they worked in darkness, grunting and stumbling over exposed tree roots and through the thorny scrub. They finally dropped Dale at the edge of the depression near his toolboxes. Ruby Jane didn't take time to catch her breath. She picked up the shovel and flicked on the light. Jimmie leaned against a tree, hands on his knees. She nudged him with the shovel handle.

"Push the dead leaves to the side. We need to cover the hole with them again when we're done."

Jimmie shook his head. "I don't know how you're doing this." But he started moving the matted clot of leaves, first with his feet, then with his hands. If she were to give herself a moment to reflect, she probably wouldn't understand how she was doing this either. Their only hope was to bury the whole, sick mess. Hide the evidence and pretend it never happened. *He never came home from work. We don't know what happened to him.* Bella would escape justice, but there was no way to hold her accountable without dragging Jimmie down with her.

Once he'd cleared a spot as long as Dale and half again as wide, she tossed him the flashlight. "I'll start." The earth was soft and wet, laced with roots and gravel. She piled dirt at the edge of the clear area, dug until her arms hurt. When she traded the shovel for the flashlight, the grave's outline had been drawn; the hole was a foot deep. Jimmie took over without comment. The rain continued to fall. The shovel thunked into the soil, the trees whispered. After a while, Jimmie pulled himself out of the hole and gave her the shovel. His face was a mask of fear and pain.

"I'm thirsty."

"We're almost done."

But she closed her eyes and rested her forehead against the shovel handle. Every muscle ached. Her skin was a landscape of wriggling itches, her hands numb. When she opened her eyes again, she found herself looking at Dale, still as a rag in the shadows at the edge of the depression. Jimmie followed her gaze and sucked in air, as if he was noticing the body for the first time. He put his hand to his forehead, a gesture so profoundly Bella that for a moment Ruby Jane thought her mother had come to take his place.

"He stole Grammy's ring. Mom said he showed it to her."

A choking ache rose up in her. She'd grieved for her grand-mother, still grieved for her. Now she felt that pain again, magni-fied and made black. Not for the ring, a bauble, but for the legacy. Dale had stolen a link to her past, and for what? A few rounds at the Eagles? When she spoke, her voice was quiet. Defeated. "It was just a ring."

"But—"

"It doesn't matter. Toss his shit in the hole."

"Mom said to bring everything back."

"Fuck Bella."

"Roo—"

"Jimmie, we can't have anything that belongs to him. If the cops find us with the smallest object, his watch, his wallet, even a fuck-ing screwdriver, they can tie us back to this."

For a long time, he looked down into the hole. She couldn't guess what he was thinking. Didn't want to guess what he was thinking. She was too tired to plead with him any more. He shuf-fled his feet, collapsed against the hickory tree next to him. She almost didn't notice when he started banging his head against the coarse bark.

She dropped the shovel, stumbled over to him. "Jimmie, stop." She took his face in her hands and pulled him away from the tree. He resisted for a moment, then sagged. She felt a slick fluid on his skin. He was bleeding. She tried to find the cut, but he winced and pulled her hands down.

"I didn't know it would be like this."

"Jimmie, it's okay."

"It's not okay!" His eyes flooded with wild terror. He pushed away from her and disappeared into the darkness beyond the hickory tree. She listened to him crash through the undergrowth in a circle around the depression. "Not okay, ... not okay." His voice was broken by sobs, punctuated by the snap of twigs and branches.

She dropped to the ground next to the hole, back to the hickory tree, and pulled her knees up to her chest. Her eyelids drooped and she breathed into her muddy jeans. It took her a moment to realize Jimmie's footsteps were growing fainter.

"Jimmie!"

No answer.

The rain hissed through the leaves. Then, in the distance, a car started. She recognized the tell-tale grind of Jimmie's clutch. A screech split the night as he bottomed out on the edge of the road. A moment later, the engine faded to silence.

She dropped back against the tree, resisted the desire to sag into the muck and cry. She wanted to leave it all here. Let Jimmie suffer the consequences.

But she knew she couldn't. Because now she was part of it. She'd helped move the body, helped dig the hole. Accessory after the fact, they'd say. Maybe obstruction of justice. Phrases tossed around on the cop shows, but whose real meaning she'd learned in Mister Halstead's class.

There was nothing left to do but finish, and quickly. Dale's truck wouldn't bear much investigation, and an errant flashlight beam could reveal where she and Jimmie had dragged the body off the road.

She jumped down into the hole, stabbed the ground with the shovel. The earth was hard, more gravel than dirt. Good drainage. Deep enough. She wiped her face on the sleeve of her sweatshirt and climbed out of the hole, paused near Dale's motionless feet.

Something stirred. Through a gap in the trees Ruby Jane could see the clouds tearing apart in shreds. A three-quarters moon shone into the clearing. She heard a cough.

"Ruby? Is that you, baby girl?"

- 33 -

POST-SEASON, APRIL 1989

RUBY JANE INTENDED to skip the awards banquet. Bella went out early, billowy and brash in a red silk blouse and jeans applied with an airbrush after a day packing Dale's clothes and delivering them to the Salvation Army drop box at the Germantown IGA. When quiet descended over the house Ruby realized how much she craved a peaceful night at home. It had been too long.

She went to the grocery for a pint of Häagen-Dazs and a chicken breast. She was chopping onions, carrots and celery when a car pulled into the driveway, an unfamiliar white Oldsmobile station wagon with fake wood side panels. She almost cut her thumb off when Gabi climbed out. She wore a white country girl dress and Mary Janes. A flush of peach blossomed in her cheeks.

"Your grandparents let you drive?" The lip gloss was even more surprising.

Gabi was all grins. "They said I'd earned it. I have to be home by ten."

"You look ridiculously cute."

Gabi giggled, but the laughter tapered off when she noticed the chicken on the counter, ready to go into the pan heating on the stove.

"What are you doing?"

"Fixing supper."

"You're not coming?"

Ruby Jane turned away to rinse her hands.

"Ruby, why not?"

She patted her eyes with a dry paper towel. "Oh. You know." It had to be the onions.

"But, you *have* to."

Ruby Jane leaned back against the counter. "I'm tired, Gabi. I need a break."

"But you're why we got as far as we did."

"I'm the reason we came home early."

"It was one shot." Gabi's eyes filled with tears. Maybe the onions were getting to her too. "You deserve this as much as anyone. At least as much as Clarice."

From mousy walk-on to starter on a district championship team, Gabi saw the last year as success beyond her wildest dreams. She hadn't been around long enough to feel the weight of expectation which came with being a Lady Spartan under Coach's reign.

"No one blames you."

"Clarice does."

"Fuck Clarice!" Gabi put a hand over her mouth.

Ruby felt her eyes go wide. "Holy shit, girl."

Gabi looked away and blushed. "You have to come. I need you there. I need someone who doesn't act like … you know."

The oil in the pan started to burn. She pulled it off the burner, waved her hand to clear the smoke. "I was going to watch HBO and eat ice cream."

"Come to the banquet. Tomorrow we'll go to a movie. My treat."

Gabi's need was a bubble growing behind her eyes. Ruby Jane felt helpless, ready to pop. "Okay. Fine." She sighed. "We better hurry."

She wrapped the chicken and dumped the veggies into a Tupperware bowl. Everything went into the fridge. She left the pan. Bella wouldn't notice.

Gabi dug through her closet while Ruby Jane pulled a brush through her hair. "Don't you have anything besides jeans and boy's shirts?"

"I've got other things."

"What did you wear to last year's banquet?"

"I missed it." Another emergency room trip: Dale had dislocated Jimmie's shoulder.

Gabi blew through her teeth. Maybe she wasn't as girlish as others on the team, but Ruby Jane didn't think of herself as a tomboy. She ran, she played basketball, she wore comfortable shoes. Big deal. Gabi's growing exasperation with Ruby Jane's wardrobe was tempered by her excitement about the banquet. She settled on a straight black skirt and a white blouse with shoulder pads. Ruby Jane wanted to wear her denim jacket, but Gabi insisted on a dark blue poplin blazer—again with the shoulder pads—Ruby Jane had worn once, at Bella's insistence, to her Grandfather and Grandmother Denlinger's New Year's Day brunch.

"I feel like a linebacker." She hated shoulder pads.

Gabi didn't hear. "All I can find are running shoes. How do you survive without at least a pair of sandals?"

"I have Tevas."

"Naturally."

"There's a pair of flats in there somewhere."

"Don't you have anything with a heel?"

"What do I need with heels?"

"Flats it is." She found them in the back of the closet. "At least they're blue. They kinda match the jacket."

"Is that okay?"

"It'll have to do."

Gabi drove to Germantown like she was running a break. Color rose up her neck and set her face alight. Ruby Jane gripped the armrest and smiled to herself, glad to reach the middle school intact. The wide, high-ceilinged corridors smelled of floor wax and decades of mimeographs. As she walked into the cafeteria, she realized the last time she'd been happy was during her time here. Basketball was new, still more game than competition. Her classmates were a little crazier, but less targeted in their cruelty. The discovery she didn't have to spend her every waking moment in the house on West Walnut offered her first taste of a life free of Dale and Bella.

She sat with Gabi at one of the two starter tables. The centerpiece was a bowl made from half a basketball and filled with carnations dyed Spartan Blue. As Mr. Unger welcomed them from the podium, Ruby Jane saw Ashley and Moira empty two pint bottles of rum into the punch. She spent dinner sipping water. Most tables were mixed, players and their families, but Gabi and Ruby Jane had no one. She liked it that way. She could prod her desiccated chicken—a sorry substitute for the stir fry she'd planned—and chat with Gabi. She clapped at the proper moments, and smiled blankly when Coach brought up the Dunk during a vapid speech about effort and the will to win. Smirked when the boys coach, Mister Minnis, did the same—the boys finished fifth in the league. The punch bowl drained so quickly someone's mother complained she didn't get a glass. Everyone spoke of next year, Clarice at her peak. No one mentioned Ruby Jane's record three-point shooting.

Gabi never stopped grinning. She carried her letter and varsity pin like they were made of gold, and didn't care no one said more than five words to either of them all evening.

After dinner, while the others stood in noisy huddles, Gabi and Ruby Jane slipped into the corridor. Every fourth overhead fixture was lit, and as they walked toward the front hall, their shoes tapped out an echoey rhythm through the silver darkness. Ruby Jane took comfort in the timeless emptiness, as though the building wasn't quite anchored in the present. She felt its age wrap around her like a cloak.

"I don't know if I could have done it without you, Ruby."

"Don't be silly."

"I'm not. You've been a good friend."

They stopped in the front hall. The fulvous light shining through the tall windows failed to illuminate the color rising in Ruby Jane's face. She read the bulletin board on the wall outside the office. Field Day was coming. Permission slips for the Washington, D.C. trip were due. She hadn't been allowed to go when she was in eighth grade. Too expensive.

"I never told you why I'm living with my grandparents."

"It's none of my business."

She saw a glint on Gabi's teeth as she smiled. "That's you, isn't it? Everyone's secrets are sacred to you."

"What do you mean?" Gabi didn't seem to notice the defensive hitch in her voice. She hooked Ruby Jane's arm with her own. Together they moved to the window ledge.

"Just, you know. You never pry. And you never tell."

Ruby Jane turned her head and looked out the window. Daylight was failing. An orange pickup passed on Comstock Street and for a moment she thought it was Dale. A ghost. The truck went under a streetlight—a Ford, not a Dodge. She let out her breath.

"People keep things private for their own reasons. It's not up to me to decide for them."

"That's one of the things I like about you." She lowered her head onto Ruby Jane's shoulder. "You're safe."

Not so safe. An image from Preble County Line Road boiled through her mind and she suppressed a shudder.

"The thing is, I got into some trouble in Cleveland. I did something." She inhaled. "My parents said it was the city's influence."

Ruby Jane felt a rising panic strobe behind her eyes. "You don't have to tell me, Gabi."

"They made a huge deal out of it, but I didn't think it was anything. None of their business, really."

"Gabi—"

"It's not like it was illegal or anything." Ruby Jane felt her squirm. "It shouldn't be, anyway."

A thickness gathered on Ruby Jane's tongue.

"My grandparents came up with the big plan to get me away from the influence of those evil city girls—that's what my mother called them." She laughed, quiet and bitter. "Do you know what a miracle it was I even was allowed to play basketball this year?"

"I'm glad you did."

"Me too."

She was quiet. Was it her turn now, a secret for a secret? What could she say? *My father knelt in the mud—*

"You've never gone out with Finn, have you?"

"No, I guess I haven't."

"Why not?"

She didn't know. Jimmie had forfeited any right to make decisions for her. Still, she held back. Huck, she knew, was waiting for her to make up her mind.

"It's hard to say."

"You don't have to explain it."

Ruby Jane turned and Gabi leaned into her. Ruby Jane had a sudden awareness of the smooth curve of the skin on Gabi's neck. In the creamy twilight, the pale, downy hairs took on a sudden clarity. She drew a sharp breath as their lips met. Gabi pressed into her, one hand snaking up behind her head. Gabi's lips parted. Ruby Jane tasted punch.

In eighth grade she'd gone into the closet at Hardy Berman's house with Oliver Mackenzie. Spin the Bottle. He'd jammed his mouth against hers, lips tight as a drum, and reached for her breast. She punched him in the belly and ran out. Everyone laughed at him. When Jimmie found out, he busted Oliver's lip. Until now, that had been the extent of her love life.

Someone giggled. Ruby Jane jerked away from Gabi, backed up against the window. The Monster Squad stood a dozen paces away. Ashley had her fingers to her open mouth. Moira was the one giggling. Ruby Jane hadn't heard the approaching footsteps.

Clarice crossed the corridor, the others in her wake. A hollow formed in the pit of Ruby Jane's stomach, and her earlier panic returned like a clap of thunder. In the uncertain light, Clarice's teeth looked like jagged points. Moira stopped next to Clarice and put her hand on her hip, a pose derived from Alexis Carrington. Ashley, gleeful rubbernecker, looked on from behind.

"I have to admit, Ruby ..." Clarice gestured at Gabi as if pointing out a splash of vomit on the floor. "I never pegged you for a lesbo."

A swirl of sensations spilled through Ruby Jane. Fear, shame, despair. "I—we were talking."

Moira's eyebrows lifted, a jester's sneer. "Hard to tell what someone's saying when you have their tongue in your mouth."

Gabi wore the expression of a stray dog cornered by neighborhood toughs: wary, hopeful, and terrified underneath it all. Ruby Jane felt her tremble, but couldn't bring herself do more than wrap her arms around herself. The hallway felt hot, the windows seemed to go hazy with fog. Outside, other players and their families were heading to the parking lot. Ruby Jane saw the hugs, the wide eyes and mouths round with laughter, all remote and nebulous, like watching a silent movie through the rain. She bit the inside of her cheek and her mouth filled with the taste of blood.

Coach appeared behind Clarice and the others. Everyone turned toward him, startled. He stopped, clasped his hands before him. "Ladies."

"Hi, Coach."

Ruby Jane didn't know who'd spoken. A stillness hung in the air, a mounting potential like a sheet of ice on a roof's edge.

"I'm glad I caught up with you. I know you heard my speech already, but I wanted to say this to you five in particular. My starters." He looked past them out the windows, as though he needed something inanimate to focus on. "You did me proud this year. You did yourselves proud too, despite your differences. I know it wasn't easy for any of you." He smiled awkwardly. "Carry on." Before anyone could respond he moved toward the doors. Ruby Jane wondered what he'd overheard. She'd never seen him so off-kilter.

When the door shut behind him, someone let out a long breath. Then Ashley started laughing, a gibbering squeal Ruby Jane felt in her teeth. Clarice gave her a look, and drew herself to full height. "We were going to invite you to the party, but the thing is—no dykes."

"Clarice—" She struggled to find her voice. "—why do you have to be like this?"

"I'm not the one making out with her girlfriend."

"We weren't making out."

"What do lesbos call it?"

Ruby Jane's head spun. Gabi reached out to take her hand. "Ruby, let's go."

The sheet of ice broke loose. She shrank away from Gabi's touch, instantly struck by the ease with which she could compound a mistake.

"Gabi, it's not—"

It was too late. She refused to look at Ruby Jane. Her eyes in their dark hollows were fixed on the floor. "I need to go home."

"Wait—"

"I'm sorry if I made you uncomfortable."

Ruby Jane turned, but Gabi was already gone. The door clanged shut. Clarice put a hand on Ruby Jane's arm. "Let the little dyke go."

Ruby Jane wanted to follow Gabi, to talk to her, to find a way to make sense of what happened. She didn't know what was holding her back. A writhing weight in her belly held her in place, a strange and desperate need to be understood.

Moira smirked. "We still know what you are." Ashley continued to giggle, the sound a jangle of nerves.

"No." The open space surrounded Ruby Jane like a storm cloud. She drew in a breath heavy with uncertainty and looked at Clarice. The other two didn't matter. Yet she had nothing to say.

She fled.

Post-Season, April 1989

WARM AIR HEAVY with the scent of cheese and rising dough wafted through the open door. All the tables were full, as were the stools at the counter. Madonna sang from the jukebox, the tune and timbre of her voice recognizable even if the chatter drowned out the lyrics. Ruby Jane stood in the doorway, a hot ache at her core. A tremor passed through her hands. She closed her eyes, tried to reach that centered place she could always find on the court. An amped Femzilla at the post was less intimidating.

Huck sat in the corner, jammed among a half dozen boys around a four-top, two pizza trays half-empty on the table, the blockhead core. No one worried about weight in the off-season. She knew what was in store for the night ahead. Pizza Palace, then raid the most recently stocked liquor cabinet. The party might be at a house, or out on the man-made lake next to the trailer park, or in someone's barn. The details varied, but the general sequence was the same every weekend. Unless some outside force interrupted the routine.

Like her.

She crossed the room, the sounds of conversation parting before her like tall grass. The blockheads broke out laughing. Fart joke, she assumed. Huck looked up as she neared the table, his big grin softening.

"Huck?"

"Hey, Ruby." He straightened up a little in his chair.

"You got a minute?"

He looked at Malo, deferring to his captain. She refused to defer to Clarice. Malo grinned at Ruby Jane, his lip curling into a leer. "What's up, Dunks?"

"None of your goddamn business." The boys hooted, but she ignored them. "Huck, please?"

"Uh, yeah. Sure."

"Outside?"

Blockheads exchanged looks as they uncurled from around the four-top. She knew what they were thinking, but she didn't care. Huck got to his feet, and she took his hand, pulled him after her to the door.

"Ruby? Is everything all right?"

One of the blockheads loosed a piercing whistle from the corner.

"Outside."

The night was chilly after the crowded warmth of the Palace. She pulled him around the corner, out of view of the windows.

"What's going on, Ruby?"

"I wanted to see you."

"You wanted to see me?"

Blockhead. But instead of making a remark, she wrapped her arms around him and pressed her face into his neck. She inhaled Irish Spring and pizza sauce.

"Ruby—?"

She didn't want to talk. She didn't want to explain any of it. She didn't know how to explain any of it. *Gabi kissed*, and then *Clarice said*, and then *I wouldn't*—How could she make sense of it to him when she couldn't make sense of it to herself? All she knew was she felt sad and alone and scared, all for reasons she couldn't comprehend.

"It's been a weird year." She spoke into the fabric of his shirt, her voice muffled.

"Tell me about it."

"Take me home?"

He was quiet for a moment. "You need a ride?"

She hesitated, then pulled him tighter to herself as if she could squeeze courage out of him. "Not my home."

He took a long time to respond. "Are you sure?"

She felt unmoored, incapable of certainty about anything except her need to forget herself. She let him lead her to his car. They didn't speak during the short drive to his house on the edge of town. He parked behind the garage and said one word. "Ruby." She put a finger to his lips, shocked by the heat of his skin. She almost turned back. But, moments later, when he shut his bedroom door behind her, she closed her eyes and imagined a girl who could desire another without restraint.

I know why I'm here, she thought, unsurprised by how easy it was to deceive herself.

- 35 -

INTERVIEW, APRIL 1989

"HOW DID YOU know I was here?"

Mrs. Parmelee wore a pair of battered cross-trainers, old jeans, and a tatty, washed-out polo shirt. She'd pulled her hair off her forehead with a tortoiseshell band. Dark circles rimmed her eyes. An errant wisp of grey hair hung loose at her temple. A weight seemed to tug at the corners of her mouth, making her face longer than usual. Ruby Jane found herself unsettled, as though she'd come across her teacher at a graveside.

Mrs. Parmelee keyed on Ruby Jane's unease. "I came from home." She glanced down at herself, waved a hand dismissively. "It was a crazy day at school. If not for Mr. Unger, I think we'd have an outbreak of Lord of the Flies. He decided on an early release."

Nothing like a little blood and bedlam to bring out everyone's holiday spirit.

Ruby Jane sat in Grabel's spot, as if his seat could somehow confer power. Through the closed door at her back, a rabble of voices of argued, one louder than the others. She couldn't make out the words, but it wasn't hard to guess the subject. Nash had dared allow a visitor to see Grabel's prisoner. Detective Pervo wouldn't understand that in Nash's world, a few years out of Valley View, Mrs. Parmelee held greater authority than Grabel would ever know.

Mrs. Parmelee took the chair next to her. Ruby Jane stirred, then folded her hands and looked out the window. She imagined herself back at school, seated in Mrs. Parmelee's classroom. Another detention. Everything in its place, Mrs. Parmelee at her desk. If she closed her eyelids to narrow slits, she could imagine Cézanne's vision of the quarry in the unfocused haze through her lashes.

"I heard what happened." They were both quiet for a long moment. "Clarice is saying she had you arrested."

Ruby Jane rubbed the drying tears on her cheeks. "She wishes."

"Do you want to tell me what's going on?"

"It's complicated."

"I called your mother, but she had nothing to say."

"I'm surprised she was coherent enough to not tell you anything."

"It was … an interesting conversation."

"They always are."

"I wish there was something I could do for you there."

"You showed up here. That's a hell of a lot more than you can say about Bella."

Mrs. Parmelee took Ruby Jane's hand. "I'm sorry. I really am." Her skin was warm and smooth. Ruby Jane felt an unexpected sense of calm come over her. Through her eyelashes, sunlight climbed the quarry wall. Shadows melted like butter and flowed over the stone face. She blinked, squeezed her teacher's hand back.

"What can you tell me?"

"It's not about Clarice. She's a side show."

Behind her, the muffled voices continued their quarrel. Her eyes stung. She thought of Gabi and the onions in her kitchen. They should have skipped the banquet. Made that stir fry and watched a movie on HBO. Eaten ice cream.

Ruby Jane wanted to tell Mrs. Parmelee the whole sordid tale. But not here, not while she remained within Grabel's grasp. The cassette recorder was quiet and dead on the table, but anyone could be listening. For all she knew, the phone on the credenza functioned as an intercom. Grabel and the chief, even Nash, might be listening to everything from the next room, their squabbling a ruse.

"It's about your father, isn't it?"

She flinched. *Does everyone already know?* She opened her mouth to retort, but held her tongue. Even so, Mrs. Parmelee guessed her thought.

"Ours is a small community, honey. Word gets around."

"It's sick."

"I won't argue the point."

"It's worse than school."

"Some things never change."

"There's nothing I can tell them."

Mrs. Parmelee knew what she meant by that as well. "Ruby, let me tell you what I've learned. Okay?"

Ruby Jane frowned at the table top. She didn't want to know what Mrs. Parmelee had learned, afraid, perhaps, her discoveries might lie too close to the truth. She only wanted to escape. To pound the asphalt, to dribble, to shoot. To climb the fluid terracotta quarry walls. Rain threes from the corner. Feel the wind in her face, smell warm stone. But she knew they could keep her as long as they wanted.

"Sure."

"You've put yourself in a difficult position. It's not fair, but it's the way things are."

"What do you mean?"

"Clarice has a lot of pull around here. You can't say the same."

"Because of one missed shot in the tournament."

"Like I said, it's not fair."

"You're saying if I made that shot, she'd be sitting here?"

"No, but she is the one people believe in right now."

"And I broke her nose."

"Yes."

"She deserved it."

Mrs. Parmelee licked her lips. "What she deserved is beside the point. This isn't the Old West. No matter how valid your grievance against her, in the eyes of the law you committed assault. And though I hate to say it, I believe you're this close to getting charged." She held up her hand, finger and thumb half an inch apart. "Mr. Grabel thinks it will give him some leverage over you."

"So why not charge me?"

"You said it yourself. Clarice is a side show."

Outside, the starlings returned with a clatter. The birds poured off the roof like water from a clogged gutter, their calls shrill and disconcerting. Her vision of the quarry washed away with their passage. She sighed and dropped her face into her hands, elbows on the table's edge. She'd been in this cramped, sour room for far too long. Her tongue felt thick and dry. Nash had promised her something to drink.

"Ruby? What are you thinking?"

Clarice was a smart girl. Her parents were no dummies either. She could press charges, drag Ruby Jane into juvie court. But what would happen then? It had been a fraught, unsettling week. Ruby Jane had no history of legal trouble. Not like this. With all that had happened, the mitigating circumstances would work in her favor. An assault charge would go nowhere. Clarice surely knew it.

But something more serious, a missing father and a drunken admission late one night, now *that* might have legs. Ruby Jane could picture it: Clarice answering Grabel's questions. "Has anything like this ever happened before?" *No, ...* But then Clarice could offer a tentative, *well, maybe this is nothing, but ...* dropped at the right moment, Grabel wouldn't be able to resist Clarice's gold nugget of accusation.

If it led to a genuine crime, the result might be far worse than the wrist slap a girlfight would bring. And if not, interrogation by Detective Pervert offered a measure of vengeance Clarice would never see in juvenile court.

Ruby Jane pushed her fingers through her hair and sat back. "Clarice is screwing with me."

Mrs. Parmelee went around the table to the window and leaned against the glass. Her dark hair haloed her long face. "Honey, it's going to get worse."

"What do you mean?"

"Has Mr. Grabel mentioned Gabi yet?"

"No." Her voice struggled to rise from a hollow in her chest.

"There's talk about you and Gabi, and Clarice is doing most of the talking. You can assume Mr. Grabel has heard, and will try to use it against you if nothing else works."

Ruby Jane sagged. She could almost hear the whispers, could almost feel the Clarice's lies and insinuations bearing down on her.

You should have seen Ruby and Gabi after the banquet, their tongues were like snails wrestling—

It would be bad enough at school, the talk and the looks, the sudden lulls in conversation as she walked past. But if Detective Pervert started in on her—*"Fuck Gabi Schilling—oh, sorry. Poor choice of words."*

Gabi didn't deserve that.

Mrs. Parmelee moved away from the window and kneeled at Ruby Jane's side. "Do you remember the conversation in my classroom a couple of months ago?"

She would never forget. *Sometimes all you can do is take matters into your own hands.* Ruby Jane stared at her hands.

"I can help you."

"How?"

"Don't worry about that. But there's something I need to know."

"You want to know what they think I've done. If it's true."

Mrs. Parmelee shook her head. "I know you, honey, maybe better than you realize. All I need to know is if you want my help."

Ruby Jane opened her mouth to respond, just as quickly closed it again. She dropped her hands into her lap. The idea Mrs. Parmelee might put an end to this nightmare sent a trill of anticipation through her, followed by a shadow of doubt.

Do I deserve what she's offering me? Does Jimmie?

Ruby Jane thought back to that day in the classroom, the long awkward pauses during Mrs. Parmelee's unexpected revelation. The message then and the message now was clear: the facts were less important than the truth they hid.

Only she could answer her own troubling questions. Did she deserve to go free? Jimmie pulled the trigger. Ruby Jane dug the hole. Perhaps the time had come to let justice have its way.

Ruby Jane gazed out the window, unable to invoke the Bibemus Quarry again. She felt insubstantial, like the filmy clouds which hung loose and fluid in the thin grey sky. At her back loomed Grabel. Before her, Bella.

Jimmie is the weak one.

Bella—mother, dispossessed rich girl, perpetual drunk—had concocted the whole dark scheme.

You never know who's going to come looking for you, baby girl.

Something hardened within her. She didn't care if she lost. She only cared that Bella not win.

She met Mrs. Parmelee's gaze. "I'm ready to get out of here."

"Of course you are."

"What are you going to do?"

Now Mrs. Parmelee smiled. "I'm going to have a little talk with Mr. Grabel."

STORMY NIGHT, AUGUST 1988

RUBY? IS THAT *you, baby girl?*

She shivered at the sound of Dale's voice rising out of the shadows. The last time he referred to her as "baby girl," he was lying in a pool of his own blood. She'd returned from a run and entered a house throbbing with noise. Bella sat at the dining room table, head in her hands, sobbing. Ice melted in a glass between her elbows. Jimmie, somewhere upstairs, vomited a torrent of pungent obscenities. Dale's moans set the base line, a pathetic drone laced with slurred entreaties for help.

Ruby Jane stepped over a broken bourbon bottle on the kitchen floor, paused at the dining room door.

"What happened?" She'd run thirteen miles at marathon pace in the cold January air. Her quads felt like they'd been stabbed with needles. All she wanted was a banana, a bottle of Gatorade, and a hot shower. "Mother, I asked you what's going on."

Bella ignored her. Ruby Jane moved into the hallway and found Dale at the foot of the stairs, Jimmie on the landing above. Dale moaned and reached toward her with a bloody hand. A gash on his forehead drained into his eyes and down his cheek, puddled beneath his head. His legs were a tangle on the ground.

"He hit me, baby girl. He hit me with that goddamn club."

Ruby Jane looked up the stairway. Jimmie's useless arm, in a cast since the last fight, dangled at his side. With his good hand, he wrung at his hair. The light from the landing shone on his face. She made out the stark red shape of a fist, all five knuckles clear in the soft tissue below the cheek bone. Jimmie never started anything.

"What happened?" She directed her question up the stairwell, but Dale stirred at her feet. "I tol' you, baby—"

"Jimmie?"

He turned his broken hand over and grimaced. "Same as fucking always."

Dale's groping paw found her ankle and she sighed. She tugged free of his grip and went into the kitchen, soaked a dishtowel in cold water and tossed a dry towel over her shoulder. She returned to the hallway and set to washing the blood off Dale's face. He winced when she touched the ragged wound with the damp cloth. "How bad is it, baby girl?"

"I look like a doctor to you?"

She pressed the dry cloth to the wound, told him to hold it there. Looked up the stairs.

"Jimmie, help me get him to the car. He needs stitches. And we need to get your arm looked at."

"Let him bleed to death."

"You don't want that."

"You're next, Roo. Soon as I'm out of here, you're next."

"Jimmie—"

There was a knock at the door. From the dining room, Bella wheezed. "I called the police."

As soon as Officer Callan stepped through the door, Jimmie started shouting. Bella appeared from the dining room and shouted back, though whether she was defending Jimmie or Dale was impossible to tell. Callan tried to calm everyone down. At some point he looked at Ruby Jane and asked her if she knew what happened.

"Look around. Look at Jimmie's face. How many times you been here?"

"That's not helping—"

"You're useless."

She went out and started the Caprice. The temperature hovered in the teens. A light snow fell. Ruby Jane waited in the back seat. Drying sweat contracted the skin on her arms and legs. After a while, Callan left—no charges filed, again. Shortly after, Bella helped Dale to the car, then returned to the house. Jimmie, sober and licensed, would have to drive. Bella wouldn't be spending her evening in the emergency room.

Looking back, it would have been better if Dale had bled to death that night. At least Jimmie could have claimed self-defense.

Now, in the brush at the edge of the depression, Dale moved. Not much, enough to make a sapling or twig crack beneath him. She didn't know whether to be relieved or terrified.

"Ruby, baby. Where am I? Something's wrong."

Grunting, he hoisted himself onto his elbow. A silver flash of moonlight gleamed on his forehead. "Christ, my chest hurts." His eyes were caverns of darkness, but as his head pivoted left and right she felt the weight of his gaze.

"What were you—?" His roving head locked on the hole, a trapezoid of mud and darkness.

She felt the pressure of the gun in her sweatshirt pocket.

"You're gonna put me in that hole."

He lurched to his feet, wincing, his face pale and wet in the flashlight's uncertain glow. Bemused. "Christ, it's your grandmother, isn't it?"

"Don't—"

"You found out, didn't you?"

"Shut up!"

You're next, Roo. Soon as I'm out of here ...

He moved toward her. She groped for the gun, jerked it from her pocket. Dale went still when the stubby barrel rose out of shadow. A Denlinger gun, not a Whittaker gun. A Whittaker gun might refuse to fire. But a Denlinger gun in the hands of one of Dale Whittaker's ill-used spawn?

No problem.

"Baby girl, you don't want to do that."

"Shut. *Up.*"

"Your brother, I know what your brother did to me. I'll tell—"

"You'll tell *no one!*"

He raised his hands. His expression twisted from confusion into fear.

"Listen, I get it, little girl. You're pissed, your brother is pissed. Maybe I earned that. But this, *this* is too much."

"Or not enough."

"Ruby, ... Christ."

"Where is Grammy's ring?"

"You can't ..."

One choice. Hide the body. But how do you hide a body when it's standing on two feet, trying to talk you out of putting it in a hole? What was she supposed to do? Let him come back? The hole couldn't be undug. The gun couldn't be unshot. She could see the dark shine of blood on his shirt. How much longer could he stand there with a bullet in his chest? How much more could she take?

It needed to end. He needed to be in the hole.

"Get on your knees."

"Ruby, for God's sake."

"Get ... on ... your *knees.*"

He knelt. She let the gun track him to the ground, aimed at the center of his chest. His damp face pleaded. In that moment, she could imagine a time when he had been handsome. Long ago, when he and Bella were young and brash and eager to flick shit into the eyes of whoever dared disapprove. But young and handsome and strong had eroded into a broken addict—a thief—begging for his worthless life from the girl least likely to grant it to him.

"Don't do this, baby girl." His rasp echoed the rain. "What would your Grammy say?"

She squeezed the trigger.

- 37 -

POST-SEASON, APRIL 1989

A PAIN IN her stomach awoke her. The pale touch of daybreak filtered in around the window shade. Huck lay on his side, facing away from her. He had taken most of the covers. The corner of sheet covering her smelled of a faint must, a scent which stirred her unsettled bowels. She threw the sheet aside and for a moment lay frozen, sure someone was watching her. But all she heard was Huck's breathing and the ticking of the electric radiator under the window.

She ran her hands across her skin. Her flesh felt strange to her. She turned her head, gazed at Huck's tangled hair, at his muscled shoulder sticking out from beneath the blanket. The smell was him, and it was her. The skin of her breasts and stomach and thighs was her, and him. The recognition gathered in her chest and swelled, a strange and curious feeling of loss. In the dark, she found herself blinking back tears. She looked at Huck again.

"You're a good man." She whispered. "I'm not sorry it was you."

Her skirt and jacket were draped across a chair back, blouse folded on the seat. Shoes side by side on the floor. She hadn't let him watch her undress—down to her panties and bra at first. Those came off later, as she warmed to his touch. She slipped out of bed and dressed quickly. Then she hesitated. She didn't know what to do. She didn't want to give him a chance to ask her to stay. She felt confused and disjointed and sorrowful. She needed to be alone, to escape from the scent and the electric tremor of his touch. But she didn't want to leave without an acknowledgment of ... what?

She didn't know.

At last she leaned over and kissed his forehead, then fled before he stirred through the quiet house and out to the road.

She wanted to get home before Bella realized Ruby Jane had been out all night. Her only choice was to walk. These ridiculous shoes. Yet before she could raise a good blister, a car slowed beside her, a silver Escort.

Mrs. Parmelee was behind the wheel. "Forgot your running shoes?"

Ruby Jane blushed and lowered her gaze.

"Climb in. I'll give you a ride."

She expected an interrogation, but Mrs. Parmelee only asked where she lived, then muttered something about West Alex and breakfast with her parents. The drive lasted a few long, aching minutes, Ruby Jane's nerves tight as a drum head. When they stopped at the end of the driveway, Ruby Jane hesitated. The house was dark, the Caprice in the driveway. No other car with it—her mother hadn't brought a friend home. Not a friend who could drive anyway.

"Out later than you were supposed to be?"

Ruby Jane nodded, though she'd never had a curfew. Her thoughts were still on Huck, and Gabi, a tangle of thorns. She turned to Mrs. Parmelee.

"Is hate a good reason to want to do something?"

Her teacher smiled, whimsical and a little bit sad. "Ruby, you don't need me to answer a question like that."

"I guess not." She breathed in, breathed out. "Sometimes I think I dunked because I hate Clarice."

"You didn't enjoy it?"

"Yeah, sure."

"How can you take pleasure in something you do out of hate?"

"Maybe I'm Darth Vader. My hate makes me strong."

"When you dunked, you used the dark side of the Force?"

"You make it sound so ridiculous."

"But Yoda told us, 'Fear leads to anger. Anger leads to hate. Hate leads to suffering.'"

"Hate leads to dunking."

"I don't think you're being very serious."

"I guess not."

"What are you afraid of, Ruby Jane?"

"Of not being able to dunk."

Mrs. Parmelee rests a gentle hand on her arm. "What are you afraid of in that house?"

She felt tears gather. "I should go." She got out before Mrs. Parmelee could say anything more, waited in the driveway until she pulled away. Mrs. Parmelee waved, fingers curled with uncertainty. But then she was gone.

Ruby Jane went to the back door, put her key in the lock.

The door swung wide. Her mother glared at her through the opening, eyes bloody coals in her drawn face.

"Where the hell have you been?"

"I—"

Her mother swarmed onto the stoop. Ruby Jane cringed. Bella's hair was a snarl on her head, a Medusa tangle of henna and steel. Her mouth was open now, teeth bared. "I asked you a question."

"Clarice—"

"I know you weren't with Clarice, you lying bitch. You weren't with any of your basketball friends."

They're not my friends. But then she thought of Gabi. Gabi was her friend, and she'd betrayed her.

"Get in here."

Ruby Jane ducked her head and pushed through the doorway past her mother. Before she could dart through the kitchen, her mother grabbed her forearm and yanked her around.

"Answer my question, young lady."

Since Dale's disappearance, her mother had bagged a new boyfriend every month, sometimes every week. But Ruby Jane understood too well there were rules for Bella and rules for everyone else.

"I was with a friend."

"What friend?" Bella's breath was ripe with a fresh bourbon rinse. "A *boy*friend? Were you slutting around with some boy? Is that it?"

Ruby Jane twisted free and fled up the stairs. Bella followed, screaming, but Ruby Jane was faster. She ran into her room and slammed the door. Bella rattled the doorknob, beat the door with her fists. Screamed. *Whore.* Ruby Jane leaned back against the door. *Cocksucker.* She felt each blow in her scalp, bit her lip rather than cry out. After a while, her mother gave up —*special place in hell for sluts like you*— and faded away. Back to The Studio, or down to the cabinet over the refrigerator. Ruby Jane fell onto her bed and imagined she was a little girl again.

Later, hours later, the phone rang. Ruby Jane opened her door as Bella answered. "Are you the one she was whoring herself to last night? ... I don't care what you think, fellow. You're not to call here again." Ruby Jane slipped back into her room before her mother knew she was there. Later, her mother's door slammed, and a little while after Bella stomped down the stairs. The car started. Ruby Jane watched her mother drive down Walnut and disappear.

She ran to the phone, but hesitated before dialing. Gabi, or Huck? She decided to call Huck first. The conversation wouldn't take long. She didn't know what to say to him, and after his chat with Bella, he would understand if she couldn't talk. She wanted to apologize for her mother. Then she'd call Gabi and, hopefully, fix things. Try to fix things.

No one answered at Huck's—answering machine. She didn't leave a message, didn't want his whole family to hear her voice. She took a deep breath, and dialed Gabi.

It rang and rang and rang. No answer, no machine. She hung up, dialed again. Same result. Outside, she heard her mother's car in the drive, tires popping on gravel. She slipped up the stairs and into the bathroom. She locked the door, turned on the shower. Bella could shout at the door all she wanted. Ruby Jane didn't care. She would fix things with Gabi tomorrow.

38

POST-SEASON, APRIL 1989

SHE ENTERED FROM the student parking lot. Not her usual way, but then she didn't usually drive her mother's car without permission either. She'd overslept and missed the bus. Bella would be pissed when she discovered the car gone, but Ruby Jane figured if Bella didn't want her to take the car, she shouldn't have chased Valium with bourbon. She parked a minute before the first warning bell, ran through the double doors next to the locker room as it rang. Hoping she wouldn't see Huck. Hoping she would.

The hallway was jammed, students gathered in clumps at open lockers. The girls were dressed like a collision of Molly Ringwald and Lucy Ewing: bangles, shoulders, and asymmetrical hair. The boys looked like they couldn't decide which John Hughes character they wanted to be. She looked at her watch. Less than two minutes til first period, but no one was moving. The atmosphere in the corridor was suffused with electric whispers.

Ellie called me. We'd just got home from church.
I was at the Pizza Palace.

Mister Unger appeared at the far end the hallway. "Okay, every-one, time for class. Find your rooms please." His voice was sharp; it pierced the veil of conversation. He repeated himself again and again as he moved down the hallway. Groups scattered in his wake.

He pulled up short when he saw Ruby Jane. His eyes narrowed, then he put his hand on the shoulder of one of the boys walking past, said something to him. The boy trotted off. The corridor went suddenly quiet.

"What's going on?" She wasn't talking to anyone in particular, and no one responded.

She doesn't know.

"I don't know what?"

How could she not know?

Unger stopped in front of her, his face unreadable. "Ruby, could you come with me?"

"What's the matter?"

"Just come with me."

It couldn't be about her and Huck. On the list of Valley View's sexually active, she didn't rate a footnote. There wasn't even a scandal in the making. Huck wasn't going with anyone, she wasn't going with anyone. There'd be none of the drama associated with cheating and break-ups. Huck wasn't Hardy Berman, and she wasn't Clarice. Ruby Jane was notoriously unattached. A lay might throw off her lay-up.

"Where are we going?"

"To my office."

"Why?"

"Ruby, please ..."

His voice wasn't angry. Wasn't accusatory. It was ... anxious. His eyes were bloodshot and rimmed with red skin.

"What's happened?"

"We'll talk in my office."

The hallway had begun to empty. First period bell rang. She followed a step behind Unger to the school office. Mrs. Parmelee waited inside. She gave Ruby Jane a tight, nervous smile and followed Unger around the counter into his office. Mister Unger gestured, and Ruby Jane sat in one of the chairs in front of his desk. Mrs. Parmelee took the chair beside her. She nodded to Unger. "Give us a few minutes."

"I'll be right outside."

Where were you when you found out?

"What's going on?"

"Ruby, I have bad news."

"Jimmie—?"

"Gabi Schilling has died." A tear hung at the corner of Mrs. Parmelee's eye, a glistening sphere. "I'm so sorry."

"I don't understand." It was a stupid thing to say. She understood perfectly. Mrs. Parmelee couldn't have been more clear. Her words weren't a metaphor, weren't an equivocation. A simple statement of fact.

Gabi Schilling has died.

"It happened late Saturday night. Her grandparents were asleep. She committed … her wrists …"

Ruby Jane closed her eyes. She could hear a ticking like a clock in an old movie and muffled voices from the outer office. Someone laughed, but the sound abruptly cut off. Gabi cut her wrists. She went home from the banquet, rejected by her only friend. She waited until her stern Baptist grandparents were asleep, and then she bled her broken heart dry.

"Ruby, honey, I'm so sorry."

"It's my fault."

"No, Ruby. Don't say that."

"I killed her."

She felt Mrs. Parmelee's hand on her back. "Honey, no—"

"You don't understand." She opened her eyes, pulled away from Mrs. Parmelee's touch. "We were at the banquet. She wanted someone to love her. But I got scared, or freaked out, and then Clarice—" Her breath caught in her throat. "Gabi ran away. And instead of following her, I stayed behind with Clarice. God. Damn. Clarice. I abandoned Gabi when she really needed me. I went to the Pizza Palace and found Huck and he took me home and I had sex with him. My friend was alone and dying and I was fucking Finn Nielson because I didn't want anyone to think I was a dyke."

"Ruby, please. Listen to me. This isn't your fault."

"I'm her friend. That's supposed to mean something."

"Please, this is too hard as it is—"

"No. It's not nearly hard enough." Ruby Jane jumped to her feet. Mrs. Parmelee reached out and tried to stop her, but she threw off the hand and rushed through the door. Mister Unger stood next to the secretary's desk, the PA microphone in his hand. Announcements time. He wasn't announcing. He was looking at her, eyes wet, mouth round. "Ruby, wait." She didn't wait. She rounded the counter, almost plowed through a terrified frosh girl.

"Ruby—!"

In the corridor, she imagined the ball in her hands. Dribble, bounce pass drill, take the feed, shoot. Over and over. A few kids lingered, aware the day was a different kind of day, almost a holiday. It didn't matter if they'd ever known Gabi, if they'd ever spoken to her. All bets were off. "Why weren't you in class?" *Oh, you know. Dead girl.*

She found Clarice in the gym, an impromptu team meeting. Ashley, Moira, the others were gathered under the east basket. No sign of Coach. At her appearance, everyone grew quiet. Moira wore street shoes. She began tapping one heel, clicks echoing in the open space. Clarice turned, the corner of her lip tilted up.

"Poor, sad Ruby Jane Whittaker. Her girlfriend is dead—"

Ruby Jane was screaming when they pulled her off the bleeding Clarice and dragged her into the locker room.

An hour later, as she sat alone in the athletics office, Coach came in. He stood at parade rest, three paces from where Ruby Jane sat. His whistle hung suspended in the center of his chest.

"Whittaker, look at me."

Ruby Jane gazed at her hands instead. She hadn't washed. The gritty tack of Clarice's blood on her fingers calmed her.

"We've made our decision. You're suspended from school for one week. You are also suspended from the basketball team for a minimum of seven games, reinstatement contingent upon you making appropriate amends and demonstrating you are fit to be part of the team."

Even without her—and Gabi—they figured to go at least 4-3, and possibly 5-2 in the early season next year. She'd return in plenty of time to help the team make the tournament. As for her reinstatement, the only thing she'd have to demonstrate was a continued ability to drain threes and keep the double team off Clarice.

"How many games is Clarice suspended?"

"Clarice is not the one who struck her teammate—"

"No. She's the one who drove Gabi to open her wrists."

"That is way out of line, young lady."

"Gabi is dead. Clarice is a cancer. But somehow I'm the one who's out of line."

"I know you and Gabi were close, but that doesn't give you the right—"

"You know what, Coach? Fuck you."

"Ruby Jane Whittaker, if you expect to ever play basketball at this school again—"

"Are you kidding me? That vicious bitch made Gabi's life a living hell, and you looked the other way."

"You're trying to deflect the issue—"

Coach held his ground as Ruby Jane surged to her feet. "Clarice *is* the issue. But you've closed your eyes because she's your Femzilla and all you care about is the size of the fucking trophy in the case up front." Her fists shook at her sides. "She's all yours now. Because no way am I ever going to play for you again."

"Get out."

"Gabi's death is on you—"

"Get out!"

Ruby Jane got out. Her mother's car was gone. She walked home, imagining a day at the elementary school hoops, and miles of mindless roadwork ahead. No one offered her a ride. She passed the Caprice in the driveway. Her mother waited in the kitchen. "Slutting around *and* stealing my car? I ought to have you arrested."

Ruby Jane walked past her. "Jail would be an improvement over living with you."

39

INTERVIEW, APRIL 1989

MRS. PARMELEE THREW open the conference room door. Grabel and the chief stood at the counter. Nash sat at a desk. The three turned, surprised, as Mrs. Parmelee marched through the office. Ruby Jane moved to the doorway.

Mrs. Parmelee stopped a foot from Grabel's chest. He had to lift his head to look her in the eye. "About time. You have no business—"

"I know who you are."

He attempted a smirk. "My name is stitched above my shirt pocket."

"You're the cop who perjured himself over that botched Stop-n-Go robbery last year. You falsified the report in order to implicate an innocent teenager whose only crime was practicing skateboard tricks a block away when the robbery occurred. Then you conspired with your partner to lie to the grand jury."

Grabel's face went slack. "That unfortunate incident was misrepresented in the press."

"You took a shortcut because you couldn't be bothered with do-ing your job. Thank God for that young man the prosecutor no-ticed inconsistencies in your report."

"That's not—"

"Credit where credit is due, though. You dodged the grand jury long enough for your partner to break under pressure and put his gun in his mouth. All you had to do then was deflect blame onto him for the whole sad mess." She shook her head, *tut-tutted* through her teeth. "Too bad your supervisors at the Dayton P.D. weren't sold on your story. Perhaps they knew it wasn't an isolated incident."

"You don't know what you're talking about."

"I'm surprised the chief here hired you."

Grabel swallowed. The flesh on his throat grew taut. He looked to the chief, who frowned.

"So now what? A repeat performance in Farmersville? Reach a conclusion and then squeeze some poor girl until you achieve the outcome you've predetermined?"

Grabel backed up against the counter. When he spoke, his voice spluttered. "She committed assault—"

"She had a fight with a classmate. The school dealt with the incident."

"It's not that simple."

"Let me explain to you how simple it is." Mrs. Parmelee leaned into him, her lips twisted into a nasty smile. "These fellows know me as a high school English teacher. What they don't know is my brother is Roger Lockman."

It took a moment, but what color remained drained from his face. Ruby Jane remembered Mrs. Parmelee said her brother was a county prosecutor.

"I'm going to speak with Roger now. If I have to come back here, I'll bring him with me. He's often mentioned his desire to have another go at you."

Mrs. Parmelee glanced back at the conference room door, her eyes bright with triumph. Ruby Jane smiled gratefully. Mrs. Parmelee nodded as if to say *you've got this now, girl.* Ruby Jane wasn't so sure, but made no move as Mrs. Parmelee banged through the gate at the end of the counter and stomped down the stairs. Grabel sagged against the desk, ran his hand over his face. Shaken, apparently unaware Ruby Jane had witnessed the exchange. She returned to her chair at the window.

She didn't have to wait long. When Grabel and Nash returned, they brought the smell of old air with them. Grabel's face was still pale, but he'd regained some measure of his composure. He no longer carried the folder. He held a couple of curling fax pages. He didn't bother to sit down.

"You do much traveling?" His voice was a rasp.

"What do you think?"

"You ever find yourself out Missouri way?" He raised the fax. "Dale Whittaker sold his Dodge Ram pickup to a soldier at Fort Leonard Wood, Missouri last September. Title transfer went through in October."

The arms of the chair grabbed the table edge as she pushed to her feet. She staggered, caught herself with one hand on the window. She felt a sudden urge to keep pushing, to lift her palm and strike the glass. Watch it shatter and slice into her wrist. She imagined the pain would offer escape from the turmoil in her heart. But with that thought she drew a sharp breath and jerked away from the glass. She turned her hands over and traced the faint blue veins along her wrists. All Gabi wanted was to be loved, and to be free of derision for who she was. Deprived of both, could she be blamed for taking the only escape she believed left to her?

At least, in the end, Mrs. Parmelee frustrated any chance for Grabel to attack Gabi's memory and spirit. And now Ruby Jane—deservedly or not—was free.

She thrust past Nash to the door. Grabel was talking, his words like marbles rolling around in a jar. When she slammed the conference room door, the whole building trembled.

Stormy Night, August 1988

LATER, RUBY JANE would wonder if she missed on purpose, or because of her overwrought nerves. Dale knelt beside the hole and reached out to her, hands beseeching, a mewling in his throat. The smell of gunpowder hung on the air between them and stung the inside of her nose.

"Ruby—"

"Don't talk."

"But I need help, baby girl. It hurts."

She wanted him to hurt. She wanted him to cry and whimper and beg. His eyes fragmented in the flashlight's glimmer, two empty holes. He swallowed, and the brush crackled under his knees as he shifted side-to-side. He tilted his head, cringing. In that moment she saw a shade of Grammy Mae in his stricken face. She remembered her last visit to the hospital, the night the morphine lost all power to blunt the jagged edge of her grandmother's pain. Grammy had wept and looked at Ruby Jane and told her to be a good girl. To be a true girl. To grow past Dale and Bella and become a woman shaped by her own dreams and desires, not by the petty cruelty of her parents.

She drew a long, shuddering breath and squeezed her eyes shut. When she opened them again, Dale seemed somehow further away, his whining fainter.

"I need a doctor."

"Shut up."

"Ruby—"

"You're dead to me." Sweat gathered between her palm and the gun butt. "I'm offering you the chance to keep that a metaphor." The edge in her voice was sharper than the need in her chest.

"What am I supposed to do?"

"I don't care. Go away. Never come back."

"I need—"

She pointed the gun at the bridge of his nose and he got quiet. "Your truck is up the road. Go." After a moment, he struggled to his feet and backed out of the broken moonlight. His footsteps crunched away through the woods. Likely as not, he'd be home ahead of her, patched up and angry, his gunshot wound raising questions she wouldn't want to answer.

But at least she wouldn't be a killer.

The truck started. Dale drove north, away from her, away from home. For now. She was alone. All that remained was to clean up. First the toolboxes, then the gun went into the dark cavity. The rain returned while she shoveled, but she welcomed its cleansing caress. When the hole was filled, she scattered wet leaves around the depression. In the fading glow of the flashlight, she saw what looked like a shallow grave. Form followed function.

She slogged back out to Preble County Line Road, left the shovel in the rain-clogged ditch. The flashlight died during the walk to her mother's car. She threw it into the Wentz cornfield. Headlights appeared in the distance a few minutes later.

She knew it was a cop. For a moment she considered hopping the ditch and vanishing into the corn. But her arms hung at her sides, dead weights. Each step felt like she was climbing through sand. She drew a breath and waited.

The patrol car stopped beside her. Werth Nash lowered his window and hit her with the beam of his spotlight. She squinted and raised a muddy hand to block the glare.

"Ruby?" He bobbed his head side to side. "Ruby Whittaker? Is that you?"

"Can you get that light out of my eyes?"

He swiveled the beam toward the ground. "What are you doing all the way out here?"

She lowered her hand. "I'm walking."

"Walking?" He moved the beam around, as if expecting to find a crowd lurking in the dark. "You're five miles from town and covered in mud. You look like you've been fighting the raccoons."

"I tried a short cut."

"Didn't work out too well, did it?"

There was no answer to that.

"Well, climb in. I'll drive you home."

She didn't want to get into a police car. Not yet. Soon, she wouldn't have a choice.

"I'm fine."

"You are not fine. You're soaked through."

"I want to walk. I *need* to walk."

He narrowed his eyes. "What's going on, Ruby?"

"Nothing."

He looked her up and down again, indifferent to the searing effect of the light on her eyes as he passed the spotlight beam across her face.

"You look like hell."

"No one ever taught you how to talk to girls, did they?"

"You have a fight with your mom?"

Something in her face must have betrayed her anxiety.

"That's her Caprice back there, isn't it? You took off in it. Maybe realized you had no business driving without your license yet. Decided to walk it off, then realized how far out you were?"

Her lip trembled. Nash tried a gentle smile. He didn't know she regularly ran this far and more. Her eleven mile loop took her right up Preble County Line from Chicken Bristle.

"Ruby, listen to me. You think I don't remember being a teenager, but hell, it wasn't that long ago. I'm not looking to make trouble for you."

"Uh-huh."

He was quiet for a long time. Then he licked his lips. "Did Dale come after you?" Her face must have betrayed something. His smile dissolved into a wary concern. "Earlier, I passed his truck farther up the road, but I see he's gone now. Did he do something to you? Is that why you don't want to go home?"

"He's not there." She said it more as a desperate hope than a statement of fact. But as she spoke, her words seemed to take on substance. Her heart rate slowed.

Nash spotted the change. His grim smile softened. "How about this? You drive your mom's car back. I'll follow after you, make sure you're safe. You get it home and we'll let this go, okay?"

"Okay." She went to the turn-out, climbed into the Caprice before Nash could change his mind. Bella would be pissed by all the mud on the seat and carpet. Ruby Jane didn't care. She started the car, and backed out onto Preble County Line Road. Nash flashed his brights as she pulled away.

She drove well below the speed limit, expecting Nash's lights to flash any moment as the news of Dale came over the radio. But she got all the way home, parked in her mother's usual spot in the driveway, left plenty of room for Dale's truck. Nash waved goodbye as she climbed out. She stood beside the car for a moment, tried to catch her breath. Jimmie's car was parked on the street. The house was dark, quiet. No sign of her mother, but Jimmie waited in the kitchen, alone. The only light was from the single dim bulb over the stove.

"What happened? What did you do?" He'd freshened up with Jim Beam.

"I took care of it, you coward." She went to the sink to wash the mud off her hands. Her father's scent lingered in her nostrils, cigarettes and machine oil and wet earth.

"I'm sorry, Roo. I freaked out. I—" He ran his fingers through his damp hair. "I don't know how to thank you."

"Don't thank me yet. Someone will probably find the hole tomorrow." *If Dale doesn't send the cops after you first.* She watched him pace, increasingly agitated by the squeak of his sneakers on the linoleum and by the ridiculous stammer when he repeated, over and over, "What was I thinking? ... What was I thinking?" Her anger raw, she left him to fret.

After a shower, she lay on her bed in her robe, hair wrapped in a towel. Her intention was to get dressed and await the inevitable, but she awoke at first light to a still, silent house. No cops, and no Jimmie. He'd left a note on the kitchen counter. "Got a chance to stay with friends at the Jersey shore before classes start. Going straight to BG afterward." Bullshit.

She went for a run, shot threes at the elementary school.

As the days passed into weeks, Bella and the shade of Dale haunting her days and nights, she came to understand she would never tell Jimmie the truth. He'd left her alone to face the repercussions of his actions, first on Preble County Line Road, and then in the house with the woman who'd incited it all.

41

AFTER THE INTERVIEW, APRIL 1989

RUBY JANE PAUSED at the door at the foot of the stairs, hands on the crash bar.

She supposed she ought to feel relieved. Relieved Jimmie hadn't murdered their father. Relieved she hadn't buried him in the woods. Instead she felt guilty—not for her decision to cover up the crime—but because, faced with the same choice as her brother, she hadn't shot the old man herself.

What kind of person feels guilty she couldn't kill her own father?

"What's wrong with me?"

"What was that, Ruby?"

Nash. He'd followed her.

"Nothing."

"I heard what you said."

"Then why did you ask?"

"Ruby. Sergeant Grabel isn't here."

"Did you stop being a cop between here and the conference room?"

He sighed. Maybe he hoped she felt bad about the trouble she gave him and Grabel, but if he thought a sigh would penetrate her armor, she had news for him. She lived with Bella Denlinger, for Christ's sake.

She pushed through the door. Nash followed, undeterred by her antipathy.

"I don't suppose there's any need to take you to school now."

"They had an early release."

He didn't seem to hear. "It's been a long day for all of us." He zipped his jacket against a chill that wasn't there. Maybe against Ruby Jane herself. "You want a ride?"

"My house is six blocks away."

"I thought you might not be ready to go back right away. Your mother—"

"Yeah. My mother. You think she played hooky too?"

"She was very upset when we talked to her this morning." Nash must not know that her mother didn't have anything to play hooky from. She was either home necking with a bourbon bottle or making her determined way to the liquor store.

"Very drunk, you mean. But you took her at face value anyway, didn't you?"

She laced her fingers behind her back, right from above, left from below. She needed to stretch, needed to sweat, needed to breathe. She never got to finish her run.

"Ruby, I realize you didn't want to talk to Sergeant Grabel. But, seriously—"

"Seriously what? You think I have anything different to say to you?"

"I'm trying to help you."

"Help me into jail, you mean."

"Ruby—"

"You people are all looking to hang me."

"It's just, if you know where he is, we could clear all this up. Think about your grandmother's money."

"I don't care about my grandmother's money."

There was more. She heard the need in his agitated breathing. Maybe he wanted to prove he could do something Sergeant Grabel, late of the Dayton Police, couldn't. Or maybe he gave a genuine damn about Ruby Jane Whittaker. It didn't matter. Everyone had either turned on her or abandoned her, except Mrs. Parmelee.

Nash was too late to earn her trust now.

Bella rolled up to the curb in the Caprice and stopped, engine idling. Ruby Jane ignored her and headed west on foot. Bella threw the car into gear and followed along beside her. The passenger side window was down, and when Bella pulled even with Ruby Jane she called out through it.

"Ruby, honey, get in the car."

"Fuck off."

"Language, young lady. I'm still your mother."

"I don't know what you are."

One of the valves was sticking in the Caprice. Bella's fingers twitched on the steering wheel.

"You wanted me to go out there that night."

"I don't know what you're talking about."

"Sure you do. All that coy, 'He's not going to Eaton,' crap. Then, pretending like you were trying to stop me. Well played."

Bella looked through the windshield, straightened the wheel. "You're being ridiculous."

"That day on the phone, were you actually talking to someone? Or was it all some kind of weird performance so you could sneak that 'Jimmie's the weak one' line in on me?"

"Of course." She blew through her teeth. "I'm the master manipulator."

"It's the only thing you're any good at."

"Not good enough, apparently, if you're on to me."

"It's worse than you realize."

"I still don't know what you're talking about."

Ruby Jane stopped short. Bella rolled another ten feet before she managed to slam on the brakes. The front end of the Caprice bounced on creaky springs. Ruby Jane waited. After a moment, Bella threw the car into reverse and rolled back until she came even with Ruby Jane again. Her expression was annoyed, a little petulant.

"I don't know why you're being this way."

"You gave me up to the cops."

"They had questions—"

"You're supposed to be my mother. I'd have been better off raised by hyenas."

"What do you want from me? Do you want me to stop drinking? Is that it?"

"I want you to fall down a well."

"I gave birth to you. I love you. I don't know why you're so cruel."

Ruby Jane closed her eyes. Bella heard what she wanted to hear. But then Ruby Jane realized there was one piece of information which might pierce Bella's carefully cultured indifference.

"It didn't go off the way you intended."

Bella's face darkened and she blinked. "I don't know what you mean."

"You know exactly what I mean. One of these days, *this* mess is going to come back and bite you on the ass."

The uncertainty in Bella's eyes was unmistakable. Ruby Jane smiled.

"I never wanted you. Either one of you!"

"Now you tell me." But Bella was already driving away.

Ruby Jane didn't care if she ever saw her again. She had a run to finish. North out of town on Farmersville-West Alex, left at Chicken

Bristle. Three and a quarter miles. Then, what the fuck, right turn, north on County Line. Didn't matter. Nothing was there. A couple of boxes and a revolver rusting under a few feet of mud and till. Four and a half miles to the hole, call it thirty-six minutes.

The starlings chased her out of town.

PART THREE

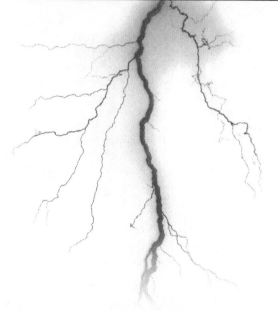

May 2008
Biddy

42

0.45% NaCl Solution for IV Injection

WHEN I OPEN my eyes I see Chief Nash staring at me from a chair at the foot of the gurney.

"You gonna die, Mister Kadash?"

"One can only hope."

My left arm is in a sling. A thin sheet covers me ankles to armpits. My feet, sockless, are exposed. The IV in the back of my right hand is attached to what I can only guess is liquid nitrogen.

"You do look a little worse for wear."

I wiggle my toes, and even manage to wiggle the fingers on my frozen hand. I ache all over, but everything seems to be in place. I'm in a tiny treatment room. Stark white light, plastic cabinets out of a catalog, wires and tubes and unrecognizable gear. I remember the ambulance, the emergency room. Talking to a nurse, maybe a doctor. It's all a little hazy.

"What happened, Chief?"

"Hit-and-run, though how anyone managed to drive away from that catastrophe I have no idea. You and your irritable friend got rolled over. Maybe turned a little bit inside out too."

"Is Peter okay?"

"More or less. They're putting about fifty stitches in him."

"Christ."

"A fair summation."

Outside the closed door, I hear muffled voices and movement, sounds I remember from my patrol days when I'd spend hours in the emergency room waiting to take a statement, or for a suspect to get patched up for transport. Nash is patient, a half-frown on his face. His hands are folded in his lap, and his shoulders sag. He looks tired. There are lines around his eyes I don't remember from our encounter outside the high school.

"Chief, what time—?"

"It's late."

I try to work it out. It had been early afternoon when we came upon Ruby Jane. I have no memory from the moment of the collision until I awoke in the ambulance. An hour later? Two? I have no way of knowing the response times out there. I recall slanted sunlight when they rolled me from the ambulance into the hospital.

I also remember lots of waiting. Waiting to be seen, waiting for my blood to be drawn. Waiting for x-rays. I remember a sensation like a knife blade in my shoulder, and lots of questions. "Does it hurt here?" *Fuck, yes.* Laughter. I guess an f-bomb counts for grand humor in acute trauma care.

A gurney rolls past the door. Maybe the dinner cart. I'm hungry enough to eat hospital food, which is either a good sign or a really bad one. My left shoulder pulses against the resistance of what I guess is acetaminophen and codeine. I vaguely recall swallowing a pill.

I wiggle my fingers again and draw a breath. "What can you tell me, Chief?"

"It looks like you were stopped, based on the skid marks and strike angle. The other vehicle rammed you off-center in the rear and pushed your car across the ditch. You seem to have been thrown clear. Both you and your friend were unconscious when Jackson Township EMS arrived at the scene."

"How'd they know to come?"

"Anonymous 911 call from an out-of-state cell phone."

I have Ruby Jane's phone, but she could have picked up a pre-paid cell anywhere.

"I don't suppose you have any idea of who hit you."

I shake my head, regret it immediately. A wave of nausea threatens me. I close my eyes, and picture Ruby Jane at the side of the road, the faraway look on her face, her fingers in knots. When I open my eyes, Nash is staring at me. "You haven't mentioned any-one aside from me and Peter."

"No one else was hurt." He pauses, then nods, more to himself than me. "You found Ruby out there."

"Yeah."

"A woman at the scene told EMS she came upon the wreck while she was out on a run. She left before I arrived."

I see the dark look on Nash's face. "I'm sure she had a good reason for leaving."

"I'm still going to have to talk to her." There's a strange note in his voice, doubt mixed with anticipation. He rubs his thumbs against his temples. "Not even Ruby Jane Whittaker gets to leave the scene of a hit-and-run."

Makes me wonder how well he knew her back in her Farm-ersville days. "She was standing at the side of the road. She wasn't involved."

"That's not your call to make, Mister Kadash."

He's right, but a slow burn forms in the back of my neck any-way. I fix on the bag of fluid dribbling into my arm. *0.45% NaCl Solution for IV Injection.* Rammed by a pickup and all I rate is half-normal saline. Maybe my blood pressure was high on admission. I feel it rising now.

"She's a witness at the very least."

"I get it."

"Why don't you tell me what you remember."

I opt for the *Readers Digest* version: we see Ruby Jane at the roadside and stop. An instant later we're upside down in a ditch.

Nash isn't satisfied. "Why do you think Ruby left?"

"I don't know why she was there in the first place."

"What did she say?"

"We'd barely gotten to 'long time, no see.'"

He regards me for a long moment, then shakes his head. "Christ, if you weren't so ugly, I'd think you two were twins." A wry smile dances on his lips, but then he finds his frown again. "You come across her again, try and stay conscious long enough to have her call me."

"She's her own boss, Chief."

"Tell me about it." He stands up. "I'll need your statement tomorrow." He sets a business card on the counter next to my gurney and walks out.

I'd like to get my clothes, or what's left of them, and find Pete. I'd also like to believe I'll find Ruby Jane at Mrs. Parmelee's. But a moment or an hour later, someone is saying my name. I open my eyes to see a woman standing next to the gurney. She's wearing pale blue scrubs, has my chart in her hand.

She offers me a quick smile. "I'm Doctor Lindoff. How are you feeling?"

"Like I've been in a car wreck."

"I understand it was a hit-and-run."

"It was definitely a hit."

"Are you able to sit up?"

My shoulder throbs, but I manage to get myself upright. She gives me the once-over, as impersonal as they always are. She listens to my chest, looks in my eyes and ears. I follow her fingers with my eyes, twitch when she taps my joints. She presses my belly, and draws a squawk out of me when she palpates the base of my neck above my collarbone.

"What's wrong with my shoulder?"

"Your clavicle is bruised. I'm more concerned about your head."

I raise my free hand to my forehead. "Where am I, doc?"

"You don't remember?" There's concern in her tone.

"I'm joking. In the hospital, obviously."

"Do you know which hospital?"

"It says Good Samaritan on your name tag, but that's all I got." The doctor watches me with wary eyes. "I'm not from around here. I flew in to Cincinnati yesterday, or the day before, depending on what time it is."

"You're in Dayton." She makes a note on the chart. "Where are you from?"

"Oregon." She looks up, her lips a line. "Listen, I'm a little beat up, but my noggin is fine."

"Perhaps. Your films are clear, but I've ordered a neuro consult. I'm admitting you for observation overnight. If everything checks out, you may be released in the morning."

I have no intention of staying overnight, but there's no point in getting into that argument. "What about my friend, Peter McKrall? He'd have come in with me."

"He's not my patient, but I'll see what I can find out."

I ease back against the pillow. "Thanks." Pete may want nothing to do with me after the scene out on Preble County Line Road, but I need to know he's okay.

She leaves the door open behind her. I can see the nurse's station, hear an incessant cough and a child crying quietly. A woman in a scrubs pauses to punch something into her Blackberry. My feet are cold. I blink, and when I focus on the doorway again, Ruby Jane is there.

"I don't know why you came, Skin."

My heart does a little flip-flop. She comes in and closes the door, takes a seat. Her eyes are far away. She offers me a quick smile, free of dimples.

"I was worried. No one knew what was going on."

"I'm fine."

"Are you really?"

"You're the one in the hospital bed."

"You know what I mean."

Ruby Jane leans back in the chair and stares at the ceiling above my head. I don't know if she's angry with me or thinking about something else. I resist the sudden urge to scratch.

"RJ, what's going on?"

"We have something in common." Her fingertips drum the tops of her thighs. "We've both been gut shot. How many couples can say that?"

"Are we a couple?"

"A couple of something."

"Tell me what's going on. Please."

"It's complicated."

"I can help."

"It's something I need to take care of on my own."

I draw a breath. The air tastes of chemicals. "Whoever was driving that pickup might have killed us."

She looks down at her hands. "It wasn't supposed to be like this." Another dimpleless smile. "I was supposed to be home before you got back from the beach."

"Sweetie, we're way past what was supposed to happen."

Whatever she set out to accomplish, dead bodies and hit-and-runs can't be part of it. I need to tell her about Chase Fairweather, and about Jimmie. But she looks so tired and vulnerable, nothing like the Ruby Jane I know, or think I know. She's crossed the country to find something, or to reconnect with her past. I don't know. I want her to let me help. But she's a woman encased in iron.

After a while, she glances at me. "They put your things in a plastic bag." She ducks her head, embarrassed. "I went through it earlier while you were asleep."

"That's okay."

She reaches into her jacket pocket, retrieves the photo of her and Jimmie as kids. "Where did you get this?"

I lick my lips, my tongue dry, and wish we were a thousand miles and years away. "That's complicated."

"I last saw this picture on my grandmother's bedroom mirror."

"Was it lost?"

"Stolen, I assume. Where did you find it?"

"There was a man in your apartment."

She looks away, unsurprised. "I told him to leave. He's not welcome there."

"He didn't listen."

Her chin rises. "Wait. Did you say *in* my apartment?"

"He broke in. He was eating your soup."

"Did you talk to him?"

I shake my head.

"Where is he now?"

I hesitate for so long she answers for me: "He's dead."

"You're not surprised."

"I'm not sure what I feel. I guess I'm supposed to be upset, but I don't know."

"He died in your bath tub."

"Oh. *That* upsets me."

. "Who is he, Ruby Jane?"

"Someone who wasn't supposed to ever come back."

I think of what Mrs. Parmelee told me in her living room under the Cézanne print. "Your father?"

The shadow in her eyes is answer enough. Too many people have died.

"There's something else."

"What?"

"Jimmie …" I can't finish the thought.

"What about Jimmie?"

I chase the right words, but I don't need them. She sees it in my troubled gaze.

"I'm lucky, I guess." Tears gather in her eyes. "I keep getting to not see people die."

"Ruby Jane, I'm sorry."

She stands and paces a short arc. She's struggling against her tears, a losing battle. "How'd it happen?"

"A hit-and-run."

"Just like you and Pete."

"Close enough, yeah."

"Why?"

"He was in trouble. Pete said he was almost broke. He sold his interest in Uncommon Cup."

"Jimmie was always hanging by a thread. Even when the money was pouring out of his ears, it was contingent on things beyond his control. But he took care of me. I wouldn't have been able to make Uncommon Cup happen without his help."

"Something funny was going on. Have you ever heard the name Biddy Denlinger?"

Her face goes blank. She hesitates a brief, indecisive moment, then reaches for the doorknob. I sit up, wince as a sharp pain stabs from shoulder to belly. "Ruby Jane, please. It's not safe."

"It'll be okay, Skin. Go home. I'll be there soon."

"Let me help you. Whatever's going on, you don't have to deal with it alone."

"This I do." Her words die in the empty doorway.

The plastic bag holding my pants and shoes is hanging on a hook next to the bed. They must have cut my shirt off in the ER. I'm stuck in a hospital gown printed with rainbows and unicorns. I yank out the IV, ignore the drop of blood welling up on the back of my hand. I manage to pull my pants on one-handed and slip into my shoes, the laces loose. I stuff the tail of my unicorn gown into my pants, but I can feel it billow behind me. My arm is killing me, my head swimming. Anyone who pays more than a second's attention will assume I broke out of a lunatic asylum. But no one notices as I hobble out of the room and down the broad corridor.

Outside, the night is cool. I have no sense of where I am, but the sounds and scents are urban. I follow signs to the parking garage, brick-faced recent construction with bright-colored metal scrollwork—some hospital architect's idea of warm and fuzzy. I trot along the sidewalk toward the street. A couple of unfamiliar cars go by on the hospital drive. Passing one of the exits I find myself bathed in headlights and turn. Ruby Jane, behind the wheel of her old beater Toyota, stops short. Her face reveals nothing and for a moment we stare at each other. Then she closes her eyes and her shoulders rise and fall. When she opens her eyes again, she looks exhausted. I move around to the passenger side but she shakes her head and pulls away. I run after her, gasping with pain, and reach the street in time to see her turn onto a major arterial. Salem Avenue.

An instant later, she's gone.

43

HERE'S TO HEALTH!

NO ONE IS happy I yanked out my IV. Doctor Lindoff suggests I might prefer the first aid aisle at Kroger's. I try a helpless shrug, made more ridiculous by rainbows-and-unicorns. Finally, after many dark looks and a condescending lecture, one of the nurses finds me a bed and sets a fresh IV. I'm in an open ward with polyester privacy supplied by wraparound curtains and my own miniature TV on an adjustable armature. The bed is wider and more comfortable than the gurney, but the ward is noisier than the treatment room. My arm remains a loaf of semi-thawed meat. My shoulder and head ache. Every time I doze off a nurse wakes me to check my vitals and shine a pen light in my eyes. Others nearby murmur and moan, cough and hack, or call for more pain meds. During each inspection tour, the nurse lifts my gown to examine the ribbons of bruising on my chest and punish me with her stethoscope. Her third or fourth time through, she clucks to herself. "Quite a scar there, mister."

"I got shot."

I don't think she realized I'm awake. "How did it happen?"

309

My thoughts are fluid and loose, and I almost unload the whole sordid tale. But when she adjusts my sling, a stab of pain in my shoulder provides a moment of clarity. "I used to be a cop." Unimpressed, she says she's sure the doctor will release me in the morning.

After that, she grants me some uninterrupted sleep. I dream I'm swimming against a cold current, my arms frozen and useless. At some point the quality of the light changes and I kick to the surface and awake. Pete stands at the curtain. His shirt and pants are spattered with blood. A bandage wraps his right forearm from elbow to wrist. Patches of gauze bloom all over him, like he fought his way out of a briar patch.

"Hey, Pete." He watches me through a pair of raccoon's eyes. "Did Ruby Jane ever tell you her mom or dad's names?"

"Good morning to you too, Skin."

"Sorry. Just wondering."

He thinks for a moment. "Dale and Bella."

"Was there a Dale or Bella on that list of Whittakers?"

"You're just thinking of this now?"

"Pete, dammit—"

"It was the first thing I checked. No Isabella either, assuming that's her given name."

It was a long shot anyway. "What did she tell you about them?"

"Barely their names. I don't think she has good memories of her childhood."

What had Mrs. Parmelee told me? Abandoned by her father and accused by her mother. No good memories indeed. I can't forget Ruby Jane's hints just before the accident. If I hadn't found Chase née Dale in her tub, I'd be ready to believe she'd buried her old man on Preble County Line Road.

"What are you going to do now, Skin?"

"Visit Mrs. Parmelee again."

"You don't believe she's still there, do you?"

I'd shrug if it didn't hurt so bad.

"We have to start somewhere."

"I suppose." He looks at his feet.

"What's on your mind, Pete?"

"Ruby Jane stopped by while I was getting my stitches last night …" He pauses, and if groping for words. After a moment, he shakes his head. "It doesn't matter. I just wanted to tell you I have a flight."

"A flight."

"Out of Dayton at noon. A cab is waiting for me."

No need to ask why. The last thing he'll remember from before the crash is me declaring my love for Ruby Jane.

"You were right. I shouldn't have come."

"I'm sorry, Pete."

I wonder what she said to him, but he doesn't enlighten me. He smiles, weary and scornful. "No, you're not." He doesn't say goodbye.

After he's gone, I press the call button, desperate to take a piss. A nurse throws the curtain wide so the whole goddamn world can watch me struggle to my feet and drag the IV on a wheeled pole to the john. When I return, Doctor Lindoff is making her rounds, her eyes caffeine bright and her manner ephedrine crisp. She checks me over and declares me fit for release. Shirtless, I'm allowed to keep my gown. I wonder how hard it will be to claim my meager belongings from the wrecked rental car.

A candy-striper younger than my last pair of shoes wheels me to the billing office, where I sign away what I presume are all my assets. When that's finished, I find myself in the lobby gazing out at too bright sunlight. My sense of regional geography is so uncertain I don't know if Farmersville is in cab range, or if I'll have to catch a stage coach. For a moment I consider following Pete to the airport, then wonder if they'll let a man dressed in a check-out-my-ass hospital gown through security.

I pull out Chief Nash's business card. My cell—and Ruby Jane's—is somewhere between Preble County Line and the rental company's tow lot; I have to use a pay phone. Collect. Nash accepts the charges and says he has something to show me.

"I'll send an officer to pick you up."

The least offensive t-shirt in the gift shop is a baby blue number with the words *Here's to Health!* in yellow puff ink across the chest. I buy an overpriced packet of Advil and find a restroom, where swapping gown for shirt and wrestling back into the sling is an exercise in agony. I wash down the ibuprofen with a too sweet vanilla latte from the cafeteria and return to the lobby as a Jackson Township patrol car pulls up in the traffic circle outside. Nash's officer, a youngster named Mackenzie, is so ramrod straight I get exhausted looking at him. He lets me sit up front.

"We're meeting the chief in West Alex."

I don't know where that is, but Mackenzie offers no clarification. We head west on Route 35, which passes through a number of fair-sized towns, then open countryside. He types on his computer and swerves through traffic. I squint against the high brassy glare outside, breathe conditioned air which smells of fried food and spilled coffee. After half an hour, we turn onto a narrow road lined with tract houses and steel pole barns. The road dead ends in a dirt lot. Behind a row of county maintenance trucks, Nash sits on the hood of his own patrol car, a Preble County Sheriff's car parked next to him. Nash is talking to the deputy. Beyond them, I see a pickup truck. The windows are broken out and the cab scorched black. When I open the car door, I smell the burn on the warm, heavy air. Beyond the lot, grass fields extend out to a line of trees. The air is filled with the sound of insects.

Nash eyes my t-shirt. "Nice get up."

"Be grateful I found the gift shop."

He points at the pickup, like I can't guess why we're here. "This the truck that hit you?"

The front grill is shattered, the bumper a broken memory. The metal flake gold paint has a vague familiarity to it, though I have no recollection of seeing the approaching vehicle. Ruby Jane's eyes were all I cared about.

"Probably. You check it for paint transfer?"

"Paint on the grill is a visual match to your rental. Got a tech coming out, but it'll be six months before I see any results. You know how it is."

"Yeah."

"But we're less than five miles from where you got nailed, and this truck was stolen from the short term lot at the Cincinnati airport yesterday morning."

My cheeks flush. "We were followed." Nash doesn't comment. We cross over to the truck, peer into the overcooked cab. The seats are nothing but springs and frame, the dashboard a vision out of Dali. I can smell kerosene and burned plastic.

"How often is this lot used?"

"Depends on the weather. It's been nice for a while."

My idea of nice doesn't include molten humidity. "So no one saw him."

"Preble County will canvas the houses up the road. Maybe we'll get lucky."

"We're a long walk from anywhere. One of the neighbors has to be missing a car."

"It's a fair bet." Nash folds his arms across his chest. "So, Mister Kadash, you ready to tell me what's going on?"

Sweat gathers in the small of my back. All I can offer is a weak shrug.

"This isn't some jerk who doesn't want to deal with insurance after a fender-bender. He tracked you from Cinci, and I'll wager he followed you from San Francisco before that."

I look at him sharply. "You've been busy."

His mouth is hard. "I tracked down that lieutenant you mentioned yesterday. She told me about James. I also talked to an Inspector Eldridge in San Francisco. Quite the trail of interstate mayhem behind you."

I wrap my free hand across my sling and stare at the burned-out pickup.

"I wish I had something to tell you, Chief."

"I bet you do." He gestures toward his car. "Come with me. Mackenzie will wait for the tech with the deputy."

"Where are we going?"

"I got more to show you, and then we're going for a visit."

"Mrs. Parmelee?"

"I already talked to her. Ruby left Mrs. Parmelee's house late yesterday afternoon. No one has seen her since." He regards me as we walk back to his car. "Or have they?"

I sigh. "I did try to stop her."

"Right." He shakes his head. "Well, to answer your next question, Linda doesn't know why Ruby came back either."

I'm not so sure. At his car, Nash pops his trunk and pulls out the cheap nylon pack I bought at the Target in Walnut Creek. "You'll need to do laundry."

The bag smells of radiator fluid. I find the two cell phones in the outer zipper pocket. Ruby Jane's display is cracked, and the phone won't power up. Mine is okay, but the battery is nearly dead. No calls, no messages. I open the passenger side door.

There's a folder on the seat. It's old, the edges furred and the surface scuffed. Maybe a quarter inch thick. I glance at Nash across the roof of the car. "What's this?"

"Take a look."

Nash returns to the state highway while I juggle the folder one-handed on my lap. Name on the file: WHITTAKER, DALE, followed by a case number and a string of names on the check-out log, Nash's last. The origination date is April 17, 1989.

"There was an investigation into his disappearance?"

"Read through it. Then we can talk."

The file starts with fading faxed copies of Dayton Police Department reports going back to March 1988. A Mae Whittaker reported a stolen emerald ring and accused Dale, her son, of taking it. There's a description of the ring and a handful of field contact reports—pawn shop visits mostly. The investigation went nowhere. Doesn't look like anyone tried too hard, but I doubt I would have either. Who's to say the ring wasn't simply lost? I don't believe that, based on the little I know of Dale Whittaker, but for a cop sitting on a stack of property crime files a foot thick, one missing ring wouldn't have rated much attention.

"Ruby Jane's dad was a thief. So what? I hear he was a lot of things."

"Keep reading." After the FCRs, there's a slew of financials: Mae Whittaker's bank statements. This kind of crap makes me cross-eyed, but I can't miss the series of large withdrawals during the early part of 1988. By the end, the account is zeroed out. A handwritten note mentions her death in April of the same year. On the same note, the words "Dale Whittaker scammed withdrawals?" is underlined three times. The note is dated April 17, 1989, signed by a Sergeant C. Grabel.

"Who's Grabel?"

Nash grunts. "He was a member of the Farmersville P.D. for a year or so back before the town contracted police services out to Jackson township."

"What was his interest in Dale Whittaker?"

No response.

Next is a handwritten statement in a round, curly script which at first seems to have nothing to do with Dale Whittaker. It's Clarice's description of a fight between her and Ruby Jane. I skim, until the second to last paragraph.

> *She was a little drunk, but it's not like she was*
> *out of it or anything. She said if anyone ever*
> *found out what happened to her father she didn't*
> *know what she'd do. Go to jail, probably.*

I have to concentrate not to tremble. Nash notices my reaction. "Keep reading, Mister Kadash."

"Christ. Where is this going?"

"Keep reading."

There's nothing more about the fight, no charging document or follow-up report. I see a DMV report, title transfer of a truck belonging to Dale, and handwritten notes of an interview with Bella Denlinger. According to the notes, Bella refused to state unequivocally that her daughter was not involved in her father's disappearance, saying, "Who can tell with that girl?" I can almost feel the ice in her words projected across the decades. But the real zinger follows: a single page summary interview report dated April 18, 1989. Officers present: Sergeant Coby Grabel and Officer Werth Nash.

Subject: Ruby Jane Whittaker.

"Jesus."

"Yep."

We're slowing, pulling up to the house where we found Ruby Jane the day before. A wide scar cuts across the ditch beside the road, the final resting place of my rental car. The fence is broken, and a set of dual tire tracks gouge the grass of the front lawn—from the tow truck, I assume. The house remains its pristine self, gleaming columns and brick, fresh off the assembly line. Nash pulls into the driveway. The gravel crunches under his tires, the sound heightening the tension in the chill air inside the car. He stops, but I'm still reading. The summary is thin, an acknowledgment the subject was picked up to respond to statements made in another report (reference: Moody) and questioned with the permission of her mother from 8:30 a.m. until 1:00 p.m. Nothing about the line of questioning itself, nothing about what was learned. After the summary, the file ends.

"You guys interviewed her for over five hours?"

"Thereabouts, yes."

"About the fight?"

"The fight was a way in for Grabel. He was on a fishing expedition. A lot of money went missing the year before and he thought she knew something—"

"That was a Dayton case, not Farmersville. If there even was a case to begin with."

"Grabel came to us from Dayton. I believe we were a retirement present to himself. Thought he'd get paid for easy duty in the sticks."

"And then he goes after Ruby Jane because some nitwit girl made a statement in what was probably an act of revenge? That makes no sense."

"You had to be there."

"Someone should have been there. What were you doing while all this was going on?"

"Doing my best to look out for her, as a matter of fact."

"Sure." Tension thrums through me like a vibrating wire. "Why aren't there any transcripts?"

"Mister Kadash, you're not the only one who felt the interview was an overreach. In the end, the chief shut the whole thing down and refused to sign a voucher to have the tapes transcribed. They were in storage with the file, but after all this time, the oxide is flaking off the tape surface."

A momentary sense of loss floods through me as I wonder what would it be like to hear Ruby Jane's voice, so many years past. Would I recognize the earlier incarnation of the woman I've come to love? Or would I find myself eavesdropping on a stranger? I put my hand over my eyes.

"She is more to you than just a friend, isn't she?"

"What difference does that make?"

"I'm trying to make sense of things here."

"The matter is in negotiations."

"Okay."

"Glad I have your permission, Chief."

Nash draws air through his nose. "Mister Kadash, you came to me. No one asked you and Ruby to drag your crap back here after all these years. We were doing just fine without you."

I put my elbow on the door frame, rest my forehead in my hand. My shoulder is pulsing and my mind is a confused jumble. Dank air seems to hang in the dead space behind my eyes. But I can sense something in Nash, a desire to help, perhaps to right a wrong he's carried with him for two decades. He didn't have to share this file with me. I take a moment, try to calm my racing heart, then turn back to him.

"I'm sorry, Chief."

He flexes his hands on the steering wheel. After a moment, he lets out a long breath.

"Ruby's home life was hell. Her mother was a fearsome mess, and after the fight with Clarice Nielson—"

"Clarice Moody?"

"Yeah, she was Moody then. After the fight, Ruby left town."

"And now you think she's returned because of …" I tap the file in my lap. "… this?"

He takes a moment to answer. "Here's the thing, Mister Kadash. I don't know all the specifics of what went on between Ruby and her folks. I know it was bad, and I know it was volatile. Dale was always hardest on Jimmie, but I do believe something serious happened between Ruby and her father. Something big."

"Why do you think that?"

"I'm working on old memories here, so bear with me. Right about the time Dale disappeared, I came across Ruby out here on Preble County Line Road."

"Here?"

"Close enough, yes. It was the middle of a rainy night, storms all evening throughout the area. I found her covered in mud, walking down the road. She was a wreck."

"What did you do about it?"

"We got a lot of calls to the Whittaker house. I figured she'd had a fight with her mom or dad. She'd taken her mother's car, she didn't have her license yet. I'd seen Dale's truck out this way earlier. So I got her home again, told her to call if anything happened."

"What about Children's Protective Services?"

"I was a young officer. Too young, maybe. I did my best."

He's been carrying this with him. I have a feeling he's been second guessing his choices for a long time.

"How did she do? ... in the interview."

Nash gets a look in his eye. The memory brings a rush of color to his cheeks. "Coby made a mistake a lot of people make when they come out here. He thought he'd got hold of some dumb country girl he could push around." He turns to me, his expression prideful. "She kicked his ass."

My Ruby Jane. No, not my Ruby Jane. No one have I ever known is so utterly her own person as Ruby Jane Whittaker. I feel suddenly a little less troubled.

"Now what, Chief?"

"We talk to Ray Malo." He points through the back window, and I twist, my shoulder complaining. A van is pulling into the driveway behind me. "He built this house. Yesterday afternoon, he talked to Ruby right here—not long before you showed up. Told me he showed her something he found during construction. He's going to show it to us now."

44

New Construction

MALO IS A big, rough-looking fellow, with the red skin and short, faded hair of a man who works outside. He shakes my hand, returns it bloodless and misshapen. Nash accepts Malo's grip like he's grabbing a cold beer on a hot day.

"Glad you could meet us, Ray."

"Lucky you caught me. I'm heading back to Columbus tonight."

"How much longer you working up there?"

"Long as they'll have me. You know how it is. Take what you can get these days."

"I hear ya."

Malo turns to me. "You must be the guy looking for that girl was out here yesterday."

"This is Mister Kadash, from Portland."

"She mentioned Portland."

"So you talked to her." My voice is pitched like a boy's anxious to find out what's under the Christmas tree.

"Sure. She said she tried to get my phone number, but all I have these days is my cell. Lucky for her I had to come back to meet with a realtor."

"You're selling the house?"

"Times change. My bridge loan is due, and work has gone south. If I can't sell, I'll lose everything I put into this joint."

"What do you do?"

"Construction. Residential and small commercial. But, shit, the whole damn market is falling apart. I haven't made my nut in over a year."

"You built this place?"

He takes a moment. When he speaks, his voice is wistful. "Yeah. Just in time to not be able to get a damn mortgage to pay for it. It's all drying up, and here I am living on a guy's couch a hundred and fifty miles from home so I can work at half wages doing demos on burn-and-turn remodels."

Nash claps him on the shoulder. "It'll come around, Ray." He tries to sound confident, but Malo shakes his head.

"Gonna get a whole lot worse before it gets better, Werth. You watch. Those Wall Street bastards done fucked the whole planet." Malo gazes up at the house, his expression both proud and melancholy. I look away, an uncomfortable witness to loss. A breeze rustles the trees next to the driveway, and when a breath of cooler air drops down among us the chief stirs. "You want to show us what you showed Ruby?"

Malo blinks. "Sure. Follow me." He leads us past the oversized garage along a flagstone path. The checkerboard sod is a month of good rain from being a showcase lawn. He and Nash move at a pace I struggle to keep up with. Malo talks as he walks. "She was waiting at the end of the driveway when I drove up yesterday. Must have been noon or thereabouts. Introduced herself. Said she used to live nearby, remembered the old woods." He gives a breathy laugh. "Not

the word I'd use for a bunch of rotted out hickories and black maples. I cleared the bulk of it when I bought the lot."

"How much?"

"Six and a half acres. There's a couple of places down the way,
built back in the 70s. They're on big lots too. We like our breathing room, I guess."

"When did you start construction?"

"Last summer. Dug the basement and laid in the foundation
last June."

"It's a nice looking place."

"Tell me about it."

Behind the house, the lawn dips toward a brook which runs
into the woods at the back of the property. Birds calling in the trees
punctuate the trickling water. A large brush pile is at the edge of
the trees, beside it a metal shed with firewood stacked on either side.
Wood chips surround the axe-scarred stump in front of the shed.

"Little by little I been reducing the brush to firewood. Got
about six cords laid up so far. Probably never use it. Werth, you
want some, let me know."

"Maybe things will still work out."

"Shit ain't gonna work out. You take it. I don't want some goddamn stock broker to have it."

He stalks over to the shed, unlocks the padlock on the door.
The hinges squeal when he throws wide the double doors. He has
to duck to step inside. Nash and I follow. I have plenty of head
room.

Shelves on the sides and back are loaded with tools, some I
recognize, many I don't: a pair of chainsaws, one bigger than the
other, and an axe. A group of splitting wedges, a maul and a couple
of sledge hammers.

"I never got around to moving this stuff into the garage. Not
much point now." It's like listening to a man talk about a dead lover.

He reaches up to a high shelf and pulls down a pair of metal toolboxes. Unlike everything else in the shed, the boxes are rusty and battered. I make out a patch of paint here and there, red on one, dark blue on the second. Malo carries the toolboxes outside into the sunlight and sets them on the chopping block.

"Here you go."

"This is what you showed her?

"Yeah. After she introduced herself, she asked what I knew about the construction. When I told her I'd built the damn place she asked if I'd found anything unusual. These turned up when we were digging the foundation for the garage."

Nash kneels down next to the stump to inspect the toolboxes more closely. "You say she knew what you found?"

"When I mentioned the toolboxes, she nodded like it was the most obvious thing in the world and asked if there was anything else."

"Was there?"

"Just a gun."

Nash and I both grow still. Malo looks at each of us in turn, then bursts out laughing, his first sign of mirth since he drove up.

"I knew that'd get ya."

"What kind of gun?"

He joins Nash and pries one of the boxes open. Inside is a rusty tray filled with corroding chrome wrenches. He lifts out the tray. On top of a pile of what appears to be scrap metal is an old pistol. A revolver. The surface is ruddy and cratered, the cylinder and hammer both fused to the frame. The trigger is gone, the trigger guard and grips all but rotted away.

I catch Nash's eye. We're both thinking the same thing. Ruby Jane, walking down the road on a rainy night, covered in mud. Nash is the first to speak.

"She wanted to see this?"

Malo nods. "Yep. She asked me to open each one, and she went through it all. Most of the tools are ruined, and you can see the condition the gun is in."

"I'm surprised you kept this around."

"I know. It's interesting, I guess. Couple of old tool boxes and a gun buried out here? Made me wonder."

"What did Ruby say?"

"She asked if there was anything else in the toolboxes."

"Was there?"

"What you see."

"Did she take anything with her?"

"Nope."

I pick up one of the wrenches. It's not in bad shape, not much worse than my own neglected set back home. The chromed-vana-dium steel held up better than the toolboxes themselves. I turn the wrench over in my hand. The letters DW are etched mid-handle. I show it to Nash. He nods.

"Weird shit, eh, boys?" Malo has cheered up a bit. Maybe con-templating a mystery is letting him put aside his own troubles for a moment.

I nod. "Weird shit."

Nash asks Malo to hang on to the toolboxes for a while, just in case. Just in case what, I dunno. They chat for a few minutes while Malo returns everything to the shed. I walk up toward the house, gazing into the trees to either side of the broad lot. I try to imagine what it must have been like twenty years before, the darkness, the rain. Ruby Jane out here alone and digging a hole to bury a couple of boxes of hand tools and a gun.

Back in the car, Nash drives toward town. "What are you thinking, Chief?"

"You gotta wonder what she hoped to find."

"Yes, you do."

"Something small enough to fit in an old toolbox."

I've got the old case file in my hand again. I raise it. "An emerald ring is small enough to fit in a toolbox."

"It wasn't there."

"You know Malo. I don't."

"It wasn't there. I guarantee you that."

"Okay."

"I know. You gotta ask."

"If it wasn't there yesterday, and it wasn't there when Malo dug it up last summer, it wasn't in there twenty years ago either."

"What changed to bring her back now?"

"Chase Fairweather."

"The dead guy?"

"Dale Whittaker."

He turns onto Chicken Bristle Road.

"That ID should be confirmed. Dale's prints will be in the system somewhere. He got arrested often enough."

"I'll call Mulvaney."

"No. I will. I'm the police officer here."

"I have an interest in this."

"Not saying you don't. Just saying you don't get to do my job."

With that, a shroud of gloom fills the car as we drive back toward Farmersville. Out there looking at those old toolboxes, it had been easy to forget the two dead men and the hit-and-run which almost killed two more. Ruby Jane was still in the wind. I scan the road, as if we'll pass her out for another run. Eleven miles, medium run, Tuesdays and Fridays. But she's moved on. I've lost track of the days, lost track of where I am. I feel blown off course, scattered by circumstance. Chase Fairweather's inconvenient corpse. Jimmie and Pete. Now Nash sits silent beside me. I suspect his thoughts reflect my own. What happened out here in the woods on that rainy night so long ago?

The lack of answers is an ache in my chest.

"You've done good work here, Chief."

"For a small town cop, even."

"I didn't mean—"

He waves a hand. "I know, I know." He takes a breath through his nose. "Just … you know."

"At a wall."

"And then some." I know how he feels. He leans forward, looks through the windshield, gestures side to side. "You should see some of the things we find in the fields around here. Dirtbags from Miami to Detroit think the countryside is their dumping ground. I've cleared drug murders which had their origins in Colombia."

He falls silent and the fields go by.

"You'll clear this one too, Chief."

"Thanks for the vote of confidence."

He's frustrated. I don't blame him. In a way, I'm lucky. I can keep chasing this wherever it leads. But he's limited to his jurisdiction. His hit-and-run could very well be solved in another time zone, if it's solved at all.

"When we get back to the station, you can write up your statement, call your rental car company. Whatever you need to do. Then Mackenzie or someone will drive you to the airport."

"I could stick around another day or so."

"Mister Kadash, you and me both know she's gone."

I wish I knew where to look next.

45

ROTTEN PEAR

I CATCH A flight to Dallas, then get bumped from my Portland connection to a redeye with a change in Los Angeles. Middle seat both legs. On top of the inflated, last minute fare, the sweatshirt I buy to blunt the edge of the hyper-chilled Terminal A atmosphere sets me back seventy-five bucks. I nurse a seven-dollar beer in a bar near the gate while I wait, then another when thunderstorms delay takeoff. It's just money. In LA, I have to sprint to make my connection. By the time I step out into the cool, rainy Portland morning—fifteen hours after Mackenzie left me at the Dayton airport—I'm glassy-eyed and adrift, too tired to do more than stumble to the taxi line. For a moment I forget my own address, which earns me a quizzical look from my Russian cab driver. He laughs at me when I try to give him directions, then drops me half a block from my house for reasons I can't comprehend. I drag my ass to the front door, grateful I still have my keys.

Inside, a fusty odor confronts me. A fog of fruit flies boils over the coffee table. The pear and a yellow scab of desiccated cheddar decays on the plate where I left it. I kick a week's worth of mail across the floor. Despite the clutter and the bugs, I take comfort in the pictures lined up on the mantle beneath the old mirror with the gilded frame, my mismatched furniture, the books in the built-ins. I drop my keys on the dining table and plug in my cell phone on the sideboard, then make my way to my bedroom. My big plan is to shower, eat, and then hunt for Bella Whittaker. Maybe see about my car if I'm feeling ambitious.

Planting my ass on the edge of my bed is as far as I get.

When I wake up, the light has changed and I'm being strangled by my sling. I glance at the clock. It's after eight—in the evening, I assume. Someone is banging on the front door.

"Christ, calm down." I don't suppose whoever it is can hear me muttering to myself. In my sleep, I must have kicked off my shoes. I stumble barefoot through the house and throw open the door. It's Susan.

"Hello, Skin. Got a minute?"

There's a film over my eyes. "I guess."

I let her pass. She's been smoking. The scent follows her to the couch where she turns. She doesn't smile, doesn't frown. Her only expression is a slight narrowing of her eyebrows, sign she's got something on her mind. Her cords and blue blazer fit her like a uniform. In contrast, I must look a sight. Wrinkled airport sweatshirt, twisted sling, stocking feet.

"What's going on?"

She regards me with her deep green eyes, then takes a seat on the couch. "You look like hell."

"I was up all night having an act of air travel committed against me."

"I hate flying."

Her eyes drift to the flies. I offer her a sheepish smile and grab the plate. "Give me a minute, okay?"

"Take your time."

I put the plate in the kitchen sink. In the bathroom, a splash of cold water washes some of the pallor from my flesh and a wet comb cuts through the bedraggle on my head. Fresh clothing is trickier. My shoulder has stiffened up. I groan as I wrestle free of the sweatshirt and *Here's To Health!* I want a shower, but settle for a clean t-shirt and jeans. Tying my Rockports is too much for me, but I find an old pair of slip-ons which have been in the closet for a decade.

I return through the kitchen for Advil and two glasses of water. Susan has turned on the lamp at the end of the couch. She looks tan and healthy in the dim yellow light. The skin of my hands appears jaundiced in comparison. In my absence, she gathered my mail into a tidy stack on the coffee table. She sets her glass on a coaster from a set Ruby Jane bought me.

"I talked with Chief Nash."

"He have anything new?"

"He still doesn't know who hit you." She studies me for a moment. "He asked me to check on you."

"I'm fine."

"How's your arm?"

I skipped the sling after dressing. My arm hangs awkwardly at my side. It hurts to shrug, so I sit in the chair across from her. "You didn't drive over here to check up on me for Chief Nash."

"I came over to tell you Chase Fairweather was murdered."

The news leaves me indifferent, but I don't know if it's because I've lost my capacity for surprise or because I somehow knew his death was not the inevitable end to a long period of declining health. Given everything else, Fairweather's passing has taken on the status of mere curiosity, a blip on a radar screen bright with worrisome and confusing tracks.

Susan takes a sip of water. "After James Whitacre and your hit-and-run, I asked the medical examiner to take another look at Fairweather. You remember Dan Halley?"

"Sure." A fellow with an excess of bluster—lousy poker player, but a competent medical examiner.

"Fairweather suffered from dangerously elevated blood sugar and dehydration. From there, without treatment, a number of negative outcomes follow."

"Dead would count as a negative outcome. What makes you think it was murder?"

"Dan examined Fairweather's belongings again. The low dose aspirin and insulin got his attention."

"Someone tampered with his meds?"

"My question exactly. Dan said Fairweather's insulin was fine, but the aspirin was another matter. There are dozens of store brands, all a little different."

"Let me guess. Sugar pills."

"The entire bottle."

I grunt. "Don't you take one a day? That can't be enough to kill a guy, no matter how sick he was."

"Hyperosmolar coma can develop over several days. Fairweather wasn't doing much to take care of himself and probably didn't recognize his symptoms. Dan suspects he was also using the aspirin for pain relief. If he took a handful before he got in the tub, his blood sugar could have spiked and pushed him into coma. Lying against hard porcelain for a while might have caused a blood clot to form in his leg. Next step: pulmonary embolism and death."

"Autopsy?"

"I've requested a full post-mortem."

For a case like this, having Halley do a second review of the evidence was already asking a lot. But Susan is the lieutenant. She'll probably get her autopsy.

"And that's why you say he was murdered."

"Someone switched his aspirin for sugar pills."

"Maybe he took them on purpose."

"Suicide? Why bother with sugar pills? They're not hard to get, but the sugar canister in Ruby Jane's cupboard was more convenient."

"What's your theory?"

She licks her lips and shrugs, drinks again. The clock on the VCR reads 8:44. Susan would have awoken with the birds. Long day. As a rule a lieutenant doesn't have a lot of time for follow-up visits with witnesses, even on a suspicious death. That's what detectives are for. She must be tired, but the only evidence is in the long silences between thoughts and the shadows under her eyes. I look at her sitting there on my couch, not smiling, not frowning, and it occurs to me I no longer miss being a cop. The grief, the rules, the endless reports. Detective Kadash would have been obligated to follow up with Marcy on her comment about how Chase Fairweather tried to get Ruby Jane to pay for his medicine. Skin Kadash the citizen can keep his goddamn mouth shut.

Susan meets my gaze. A fleeting shame runs through me, as though she can read my thoughts, but it passes the moment Susan looks away to set her glass on the table.

"I spoke with Inspector Eldridge. They're still looking for Biddy Denlinger."

I take a drink of my own water and wish I'd brushed my teeth when I washed my face. "And?"

"They assume Biddy is a nickname."

"One would hope."

"They've been through Jimmie's personal files and his computer. Aside from that one note in his Filofax, there's nothing else about Biddy." Susan folds her hands in her lap. The sun has set and out the windows on either side of the mantle twilight is fading. "Skin, what has Ruby Jane told you about Bella Denlinger?"

"Bella? Ruby Jane's mother Bella?"

"Denlinger is her maiden name. You didn't know?"

"No one knows."

"James was in touch with her, based on correspondence SFPD found."

"Who's Biddy, then? A relative?"

"Unknown."

I can still smell the rotten pear. I feel disoriented, and the cloying scent of lingering rot doesn't help. Susan rests her elbows on her knees.

"Were you aware James Whitacre was being blackmailed?"

My head swims. I stand, cringing, and move to the mantle. The glass of the mirror is darker than the room it reflects. I feel like I'm gazing into a reflection of my own mind. I don't like that this has suddenly become an interrogation.

"He had a lot of debt, and not much else. In the last month he sold what little equity he held, but his bank accounts are almost empty. Eldridge and Deffeyes believe he was paying someone off."

Ask her about that night on Preble County Line Road. "How much?"

"Not enough to keep him out of the morgue."

"Christ." But it makes sense, given how twitchy he was.

"Inspector Eldridge would like to talk to Ruby Jane about the financial arrangement she had with James."

I turn, my teeth bared. "That was completely above board. There's records—"

"Skin." She raises a hand. "You have to see this from their point of view."

"I don't have to see anything. She's a victim here too."

"Is she?"

"Susan. Jesus."

"Please, think like a cop for a moment."

Part of me knows Susan is right. There are too many incongruities. Jimmie's drained bank accounts are just one more troubling detail. I think of Mae Whittaker's financials in the folder Nash shared with me. Add the Denlinger factor, Biddy or Bella or both, and I can see why Susan is asking these questions. Doesn't mean I like it. I'm feeling bitter and unreasonable, anxious for Ruby Jane and desperate to know where I'll stand once I find her again. I'm not interested in thinking like a cop.

"What do you expect from me, Susan?"

She hears the distance in my voice. She lets out a breath. "At some point, she's going to need help. She'll call you, if she calls anyone."

That's what Marcy said, but I'm starting to wonder. If Ruby Jane wanted my help, she could have had it in Ohio.

"Please call me when she does."

I wait until I hear Susan's car pull away, then I go to my computer.

Google gives me over twelve thousand results for *Bella Denlinger*. There's a Salon Bella in Pennsylvania which must have shown up only because a competing hair salon called Denlinger's appears on the same business listing site. Lots of Denlinger links, lots of Bella links, none with both. I restrict the search to *+Bella +Denlinger*. The number of results drops to a dozen or so, most of them iffy internet operations offering background checks—for one easy payment of your life savings and credit limit if you're idiot enough to give them your name and credit card number. Something called *Isabella Farm* catches my eye. The link summary mentions Orcas Island, one of the San Juans—a mere two-hundred-and-fifty miles and a ferry ride north.

I click the link, then sprain my finger on the mute button when twee music starts playing. A picture of a long-necked creature dominates the home page under a florid logo. The background is a muddy-looking watercolor which might be trees, might be moss on rocks. A paragraph of purple prose describes the wonder and beauty of alpaca wool. A row of thumbnail images runs along the bottom of the window, one of which appears to be a woman standing next to one of the beasts. I click the thumbnail. The caption reads, "Bella with Ringo." She's a matronly woman, her face lined with capillaries, her hair grey. Her smile is what makes me copy the address and paste it into Google Maps.

I'd recognize Ruby Jane's dimples anywhere.

46

NEGATIVE SPACE

IT'S GETTING LATE. For now, my shoulder doesn't trouble me, but I make a mental note to put some Advil in my pocket. I print the Washington State Ferry schedule from Anacortes, plus the maps I'll need. Then I shower and shave, dress in layers, and skip the sling—hoping I don't regret it later. I pack a proper bag. Clean clothes for a few days, my phone and charger. A cab arrives to take me to Cartopia. The night is unseasonably warm, the air clear and fresh. Not the breathless soup I left behind in Ohio. I ride with the window down. Overhead, I can see stars.

I hear Marcy before I see her. "I know it's true because I read it on the internet, ass breath!" When our eyes meet she waves like she's flagging a ship at sea. I push through a crowd which smells of alcohol sweat and a half dozen food cart cuisines.

"Skin, you're back from— Wait. Did you go somewhere?"

"Still looking for Ruby Jane."

"Tell her to hurry up. I haven't had a day off in forever. There are bills I can't pay, and that Joanne keeps calling. She leaves a message at each of the shops every day."

"She'll be home soon." I don't know why I say that. I have no idea how much longer Ruby Jane will be gone, or if she'll ever come back. Marcy squeezes to the side to make room on the bench next to her. I pluck a Belgian fry from the cup in front of her.

"Marcy, listen. I have a favor to ask."

"Shoot."

"Any chance I could borrow your car for a couple of days?"

"Have you seen my car?"

"No."

"What's wrong with your ride?"

"Stolen, dumped in a creek."

"That sucks." She noshes a fry, then jostles a woman next to her. "Frieda, didn't your car get stolen?"

"My brother set it on fire playing with flares at Josh's party last weekend."

"That was such a great party." Marcy turns back to me. "Shit happens to cars, man."

I draw a breath. "I could rent a car, but it's the middle of the night."

She suddenly jumps up. Fries scatter across the table top. "Fellsner, you son of a bitch! Fuck you!" She laughs and flips a pair of birds toward someone in the crowd.

"Marcy."

"What?" She sits back down, her face flushed and excited. "Right. The car." Her eyes get thoughtful. "This will help you find Ruby Jane?"

"Yeah."

"When you want it?"

"Right now, if I can get it."

"Damn." She fishes in her pocket, pulls out a ring of keys. "My place is on Fifteenth about a half block south of Morrison. There aren't any other Gremlins anywhere around."

"Gremlin?"

"It's purple." She grins at my alarm. "Hey, you asked for it, man."

"I appreciate it, Marcy."

— + —

I can't remember the last time I saw a Gremlin in the wild. Must be three decades since they went out of production. There's rust on the hood and front quarter panels, broad patches of primer, and no evidence it ever had wheel covers. The interior smells like clove cigarettes. The vinyl seats are cracked, the carpet worn in patches to metal. I almost flood the carburetor, but the engine catches. I stop for gas before I get on the interstate, and cross the Columbia River ten minutes before midnight. The first morning ferry out of Anacortes to Orcas is at six o'clock. The Gremlin hits a wall at sixty-six miles per hour, fast enough as long as I don't have to pee more than once.

A full moon leads me north. The highway is empty and dark. Every now and then a semi-rig barrels past me. As the adrenalin buzz gives way to tedium, I roll down the window and let the rush of wind hold my eyelids up. I try not to think, try not to run through the possibilities ahead. Instead, I focus on the modest landmarks which serve as milestones on the trip north: Cougar, and the road to Mount St. Helens, the goofy right-wing billboard at Napaville, the capitol dome. Traffic picks up after Fort Lewis, but not enough to slow me down. Sixty-six, pedal to the Gremlin metal. Clouds gather over the Tacoma dome. The shadow of Mount Rainier forms a negative space on the horizon. Even though I slept all day, a shadow of exhaustion begins to overtake me. I feel as though I'm driving into a void. But as the miles pass and night lengthens, the shadow melts into stars. Words die on my lips, over and over. As my sight swims past Safeco Field and the Space Needle,

I imagine others with me. Sometimes it's Jimmie, his mouth forming hollow shapes in the darkness. Sometime it's Pete, or Chase Fairweather. Chase speaks in misspellings, Pete in accusation. Susan wants to know what I think I'm going to accomplish.

Whatever I can.

When Ruby Jane appears, she looks out the passenger side window, her shoulder curved away from me. She smells of apples in the darkness, stronger than clove cigarettes. I drive and drive and drive.

At Mount Vernon, ten miles from the landing, I fill the tank again. The chilly, marine air perks me up. It's four-thirty, time enough for a cup of coffee before I continue through Anacortes to the ferry. There's a line already, mostly early season tourists. At the ticket booth, I offer my debit card and hope it runs. I've lost track of how much money I've spent.

The card works, forty-four bucks. I take my ticket and find my lane, one of more than a dozen, some assigned to the inter-island ferry, some to the Friday Harbor express, some to Victoria B.C. The terminal building is at the far end of the holding area, next to the docks. There's a snack bar inside. The Gremlin wheezes and coughs when I shut off the engine. I hope it will start again. I climb out, stretch. A mist hangs over the water, the sky is clear overhead, a cold, deep blue splashed with faint stars. The moon has set. A radio plays in a nearby car, a voice arguing with itself in the still morning. Someone coughs. Others shuffle toward the terminal.

At the edge of the lot, the ground drops away quickly to the water, the bank overgrown with grass and twisted scrub. There's no real beach. Gentle waves lap the rocky flat. A figure walks across the rocks, a man hunched inside a dark jacket. He pokes his toe in the water, shakes it off. I pause.

He looks back toward me and stops, then turns and comes my way. I wait while he climbs the bank, his breath huffing and white.

He almost stumbles at the top of the bank, swings his arms for balance. I catch his hand, pull him up to the pavement.

"Long way from Walnut Creek."

Pete's expression is blank. I can't tell what he's thinking. "I had a chat with Eldridge and Deffeyes."

"What did they tell you?"

"Same thing Detective Mulvaney told you, I assume. Denlinger is Bella's maiden name."

"They told you where she is?"

"She wasn't hard to find."

"What's your plan?"

Mist scrapes along the rocks at water's edge, not quite fog. He rolls his eyes and starts toward the terminal. "Get some coffee and then go find out if Ruby Jane has been to see her mother. You coming?"

47

BIBEMUS-AUX-ORCAS

THE SAN JUANS are a cluster of islands north of the Puget Sound in the Strait of Juan de Fuca, all but a cork between the Washington state mainland and Vancouver Island. Hilly and forested, they're a popular destination for sea kayakers, campers, bikers, and whale watchers. Two years earlier, I visited Friday Harbor with Ruby Jane and Pete. Happier days for all of us, during the bright holiday before their relationship disintegrated under the weight of Peter's doubt and Ruby Jane's certainty. We never made it to Orcas Island, despite talk of climbing Mount Constitution. Victoria, across the strait, was a greater lure.

Pete hadn't been in a talkative mood in the terminal, so I left him to brood until departure. Once we're underway, I find him on the upper deck, outside at the bow. We look out across the water. The route will take us through narrow channels between the tightly clustered San Juans. It's easy to imagine a time when the islands formed a single landmass. Erosion and changing sea levels have conspired to separate them. The fresh, salty air clears my head. Gulls pace the vessel. Some land on the guard rail, alert for a dropped pastry or scrap of fried egg sandwich. Far ahead, a pelican dives, then lurches above the peaks of the waves, its pouch heavy. Around us, others gather in anticipation. Tourists, mostly. Families on a long weekend getaway. Men and women in biking gear, calves like carved stone. One guy raises a camera with a lens longer than my arm, points it at the shores ahead, but never takes a picture. Beside me, Pete is still. I wonder what he's thinking, if he's angry he found me, or surprised. Perhaps he hoped to find her before I would. Perhaps this was to be his chance to rekindle a love he let die.

He's the first to speak.

"I suppose we can drive up together."

"I printed a Google map."

He actually smiles. "I'm shocked."

"I didn't expect to run into you."

"No." The smile fades. "I don't imagine you did."

The ferry stops at Lopez Island, then Shaw. Shortly after, I hear the announcement for those debarking at Orcas to return to their vehicles. Pete and I agree to meet in the hotel parking area across from the ferry landing—I'll ride with him to Isabella Farm. It's early, not yet seven-thirty. Neither of us has the patience to wait for a decent hour. Inside the Gremlin, I smell apples and cloves. The ignition screeches, and moments later, I'm following others over the pier and onto the island. I quickly pull in to a narrow lot and leave the car under a "Hotel Parking Only" sign. Pete is waiting for me. He drove up from Walnut Creek in his miniature Japanese pickup, designed to get good mileage yet capable of hauling a load so long as it consists of a heap of feathers. I wish I had my rental with Miss Tom-Tom. The cab smells of compost.

Orcas is shaped like a pair of saddle bags. The ferry docks at the southern end of the western pouch. There's a small village at the dock: terminal building, a few shops and restaurants, plus the Orcas Hotel on a grassy rise overlooking the harbor. Killebrew Lake

Road runs past the hotel, then turns north and becomes Orcas
Road, the main route between the landing and Eastsound Village
at the island's northern hinge.

We won't be going that far. According to Google's cartogra-
phers, Isabella Farm is inland between Mount Woolard and Dolphin Bay on East Sound, the body of water which all but splits
the island south to north. We follow Orcas Road for several miles
through a forest of oak, lodgepole pine, and fir trees, and past small
farms and pastures. At intervals, tall aspens gleam against the darker trees of the forest. Soon we turn, and leave the tourist traffic behind. The road climbs and winds for a mile or two, and then we
turn again down a narrower road which curves back south. A vista
opens before us, a view of East Sound, sapphire blue and white-
capped beneath a clear sky. Across the sound, the green slopes of
Mount Constitution rise.

"I can understand why someone might want to live here."

Pete grunts. We make another turn and lose the view as we
drop through meadows glinting gold, white, and pink with wild-
flowers. At the bottom of a long slope, the trees return as the road
bends sharply west. A fenced field appears, and a sign. The painted
blue letters are weathered to almost the color of the silvered wood.
Isabella Farm. Pete stops the car.

The field rises toward the house, dotted with patches of phlox,
yellow lupine, and blue gilia. Swallows dart over the grass, snatch-
ing insects out of the air. A long-necked, shaggy creature grazes up
near the top of the field. Pete gestures.

"Alpaca?"

"According to the web site."

A lodgepole fence borders the field and extends past a low barn
to the left of the house. Fir trees and a broad oak shade the house,
none taller than the rocky escarpment which rises beyond the barn.

"It's like Bibemus."

"What's that?"

"The painting."

After a moment, I see the recognition in his eyes. He compresses his lips, as if he's angry I made the connection first. The resemblance to Cézanne's painting is fleeting. The Isabella Farm bluff is darker and draped with bushy ferns. Still, the grounds appear scooped out of the hillside.

"It must have been a quarry at one time."

The two-story, lap-sided farmhouse has a broad front porch, weathered grey, the roof is more moss than cedar shake. The front porch dips, reminiscent of my own. The flowerbeds are weedy and overgrown, but someone has mowed the patch of grass between the field and the driveway, which crosses in front of the porch.

Pete turns to me. "I don't see her car."

"The driveway goes around to the back."

"She won't be happy I came." He says it like the notion only that moment occurred to him.

"She may not be happy either of us came."

"Maybe we should have called the police."

"And tell them what?"

"They could check things out, at least."

"So can we."

"Cops have guns."

"Pete, relax."

Preble County Line Road must weigh on him. I feel a strange sympathy, or a pity. But there's no changing the fact Pete made his choice long ago. If Ruby Jane has moved on, to me—or to no one, as seems most likely—it's not because she didn't give him every chance in the world.

He parks at the foot of the front steps and kills the engine. The sudden quiet fills with the sound of wind in the firs and the bleat of the alpaca. Birds call from the trees on either side of the house.

The front door opens. A woman steps out onto the porch. Pete draws a quick breath, but relaxes just as quickly. She is too young, too pale, too tentative—one of those translucent redheads with paper-thin skin stretched tight over blue veins. Her face is dotted with freckles. She's wearing jeans and garden clogs, a yellow button-down shirt open to the waist over a white t-shirt, sleeves rolled up to mid-forearm. Pete and I get out of the car.

"May I help you?"

Pete lets me take point. "We're looking for Bella Denlinger. Did we come to the right place?"

She grabs her right elbow and looks off into the distance. "You're looking for Bella?"

"That's right."

"You've come to the right place, I suppose."

"Is something wrong?"

"You could say that." She rolls her head and hunches as though uncomfortable in her own skin.

I move to the foot of the steps. "We've come a long way. Perhaps you could tell us what's going on."

She thinks for a moment. Her eyes flick back and forth, as if she's watching the swallows in the field. "Oh, you know, Bella—" She gestures vaguely toward the house. "She's just not well, is all."

"What's wrong?"

"Had a stroke." She finally looks at me. Her eyes widen and I realize she's seen my neck. I tilt my head to de-emphasize the angry red flesh. Nothing I could do about the bruises which make me look like I came out on the wrong end of a roadhouse brawl. "You didn't know about it?"

Pete is frowning, still waiting beside the car. The woman draws a breath, blows it out. "I'm sorry. You caught me by surprise. Bella doesn't get visitors."

"Ever?"

"Not many. Last one was some old guy who used to work for her. That was a while ago, I think."

"Who are you?"

Another weak smile. "I'm the nurse."

"My name is Mister Kadash. This is Mister McKrall."

"I'm Taya."

"May we come up and ask you some questions?"

I don't give her the chance to answer. There are a couple of white wicker chairs on the porch. I gesture for Pete to follow and climb the steps. She backs up to the open door. "Okay. Sure."

"Maybe we could have a glass of water?"

"Oh." She reaches some kind of decision. "Sure. Or we have iced tea, if you like."

"Iced tea would be nice."

Pete crosses to the far chair and sits. "Yeah."

"Okay." She nods. "I need to check on Bella. She's asleep. I'll be right out."

I take up a post at the porch railing. Pete watches the open front door. "That girl doesn't seem like a nurse."

"No. She doesn't."

"So now what?"

"I ask questions."

Taya returns later with two glasses of tea. She hands one to me, and Pete the other, then sits in the empty chair, knees together and hands folded in her lap.

"How long you been a nurse, Taya?"

Her pale cheeks turn the color of butter. "Did I say that? I'm not a *nurse* nurse." I wait. "I have my CNA. Technically I'm an aid."

"How did you come to be here?"

"Well, it's a placement, you know. Through the state."

"And you're here full time?"

"For now." She looks up at me. "What do you want with Bella?"

"Nothing, specifically. We're looking for her daughter."

Taya is quiet for a long time. "I didn't know she had a daughter."

"She doesn't talk about her children?"

"She doesn't talk about anything. She can't manage but one word at a time."

"You said she was asleep?"

"She sleeps a lot."

"What's your responsibility?"

"Mostly I just look after her. I make sure she's clean and she eats—and can carry out the tasks of daily living."

Something is missing, but I'm not sure what. I think for a moment. Pete is looking out at the alpaca and ignoring his tea. She appears to notice, and in an effort to make her comfortable, I take a sip. It's watery. "This is good. Thank you."

"You're welcome."

"If Bella needs round the clock care, I'm surprised she's not in a facility."

She shrugs. "I don't know anything about that. I got assigned. Glad for the job."

"Of course." I follow her eyes out across the pasture. "This is a lovely spot."

"Yeah, it's nice."

"Did it used to be a quarry?"

"I don't know."

"It looks like it. Probably a long time ago."

"Over the ridge back there a ways is the Dolphin Bay Quarry."

"You must know the island pretty well."

"Sure. All the islands."

"How long have you been here?"

"At Bella's? Or in the islands?"

I turn a hand over. "Both."

"I came to look after Bella about a month ago."

"And how long have you lived on the island?"

"Oh, I don't live on Orcas. I mean except right now while this job lasts. I lived on Lopez as a kid, but me and my mom moved to Bellingham when my folks split. I came back two years ago to work for my uncle in Friday Harbor—he runs a whale watching charter. Because of my CNA, I can get jobs like this in the off season."

"Summer's coming."

"Yeah. It'll get busy soon. Uncle will want me to come back to Friday Harbor."

"What will happen to Bella?"

She looks through the front door, her face troubled. "I guess the state will send someone else." There isn't a lot of conviction in her voice, though perhaps she's weary. Caring for a sick old woman alone must be exhausting, no matter how gorgeous the view.

"Do you take care of the animals too?"

She waves. "Oh, there's just Ringo. I guess Bella sold off the rest. Ringo's so old, he's more a pet than anything."

"But you look after Ringo?"

"Just a little. Make sure he has food and water. He spends his days in the pasture."

"I see."

She gives me that weak smile. "It's not like Bella's any trouble. I get her to walk a couple of times a day, and then there's meals and bed and bath. Rest of the time she just watches TV or sleeps. I sit with her and read, or watch a movie. I work a helluva lot harder during whale season, let me tell you."

"Perhaps we could see her for a moment, ask her about her daughter."

She takes a long time to ponder the idea. Pete turns to look at her now, and she shrinks under the weight of his gaze. Finally she reaches out and takes Pete's tea from the table and drinks it half down, then looks up at me.

"I don't think that's a good idea. I wouldn't want to wake her up, and even if she was awake, she gets agitated. She couldn't answer any questions anyway."

"We're just worried about our friend. Ruby Jane. Does that name ring a bell? Maybe Bella mentioned it. Or, maybe she came by."

Taya's expression doesn't change. "I don't know anything about that."

I can't decide if I believe her, but I can see her gathering her determination. I don't want to push the issue. Not yet. There's a strong likelihood Ruby Jane hasn't reached the island. It's been less than three days since she left me at the hospital. I don't believe she could drive across the country alone so quickly, even if she took coffee intravenously. Our best hope may be to intercept her at the ferry. I'm not sure what's going on with this ephemeral young woman, but I know I'd much rather be along when Ruby Jane finally arrives.

I push to my feet. Pete looks at me, surprised, but he stands as well. I smile at Taya. "May I leave you my cell phone number? If by chance you hear from Bella's daughter, or if you talk to Bella and she's willing to talk to us, you can give me a call."

Taya shrugs, but nods. "I'll get a piece of paper." I look through the open door, but all I can see is a foyer, stairs to one side, and a pair of closed pocket doors to the other. At the end of the hall, there's a swinging door which must lead into the kitchen. Taya pops back through it as I watch, a bit startled to see me looking at her. She comes up the hall and hands me a note pad. I write down my name and number.

"I wouldn't expect much."

"I understand. Perhaps we'll stop back by if we don't hear from you."

She doesn't like the sound of that, which strikes me as a good note to leave on. I can see thunder building on Pete's brow. No doubt he expected more, or maybe he's confused. I don't want to talk in front of Taya, so I move down the steps.

Before I get into the car, I cross the driveway to the fence at the pasture's edge. The alpaca sees me, and approaches quickly. I hold out my hand and he nuzzles it. Looking for food, I suppose. I rub his neck. The wool is oily and gives off a strong musk, not unpleasant.

"You must be Ringo."

His eyes are deep and dark. After a moment, he loses interest in me and turns away. I watch him for a moment, then return to the car.

Pete looks at me like I've lost my mind. I shrug, then wave at Taya up on the porch. She offers a tentative wave in return. A moment later, we're heading down the driveway. Taya and Ringo vanish in a cloud of dust.

48

A Lesson in Stillness

PETE WAITS UNTIL we near the turn-off for the ferry holding lanes to state the obvious.

"She was lying."

"I'd say she was a girl following a script."

He finds a space in the public lot between the ferry lanes and the hotel. I'm glad to see Marcy's Gremlin hasn't been towed.

"Bella didn't have a stroke."

"Maybe, maybe not."

"Taya was hiding her."

"She was hiding something." A ferry is arriving. I can't tell if it's westbound or eastbound. I glance at my watch. Almost nine-thirty. Not too many cars are in line, but I have no sense of the rhythm of the islands. During our trip to Friday Harbor, we had to wait in line for a couple of hours for the ferry to go home. That had been summer, though, high season.

"So what do we do? Call the police?"

"And tell them what?"

"That something is going on."

I'm not interested in trying to explain to some crease-and-spit-shine deputy why we're here. At best we'd get the brush off. Or he might take one look at the desperation in our eyes and see trouble brewing. Who needs the headache? All I want is to find Ruby Jane before Biddy Denlinger tries to run her over in a stolen car.

"I say we let Eldridge and Deffeyes wrangle with local enforcement."

He makes an impatient sound in the back of his throat. "And we do what, then?"

"Watch the ferry. Taya is off, but she's also a distraction. We're a long way from Ohio, and I think Ruby Jane is still driving. Our best bet is to catch her here."

He chews on his lip for a moment. "You can stay here if you want. I'm gonna stake out that house."

"Pete—"

"Come with me if you want. Or get out of the car."

Even dimwitted Taya will get suspicious of Pete sitting in his car on the side of the road for hours on end. There's no obvious cover short of climbing the ridge in back and watching the house through binoculars. I try to explain this to Pete, but he shakes his head.

"Ruby Jane might have decided to fly back from Ohio." His voice almost squeaks with anxiety. "She could already be on the island."

The cars are starting to come off the ferry. I get out of the car and follow the path which winds past the hotel through azaleas and a grassy lawn to Killebrew Lake Road. A couple of dozen private vehicles debark, followed by a few commercial vans and trucks. The harbor air fills with the smell of exhaust. There's no sign of Ruby Jane.

When the outbound cars start to move toward the dock, I return to the parking lot. Pete is gone. Tourists stroll along the boardwalk and into the shop across from the hotel. Gulls dart among them, snapping up fallen popcorn. A line of cars waits for the next departure. I peel off my jacket and climb up to the front porch of the hotel, take in the view of the ferry dock and the harbor beyond. Across the water I see the shore of Shaw Island. A sailboat passes out beyond the ferry wake.

Inside, a handsome blond woman greets me from behind the desk in the small lobby. "Good morning, sir. Checking in?" Her face is tan, her eyes clear and blue. Her white, button-down shirt appears to be carefully wrinkled.

"I've arrived on short notice. Do you have any rooms available?"

"You're lucky. It's still early in the season. Plus it's mid-week."

"What's the damage?"

She offers me a pained smile. Maybe she sees it as a privilege to pay for one of her rooms. I suppose it is a nice place, all polished wood and Victorian details. But all I need is somewhere to camp in sight of the dock.

"The Killebrew Lake Room is available for one-seventy-six, plus tax. It has a lovely deck." The way I'm dropping green I'm going to have to rob a liquor store.

"Can you see the ferry landing from the deck?"

"The Starboard Harbor View room is one-forty-five." Another pained smile. "You'll have a lovely view of the boardwalk and the landing."

And lovely wafts of exhaust as the cars enter and exit the ferry. I give her my credit card.

"The room is available tonight and tomorrow night, but I'm afraid we're full for the weekend."

If Ruby Jane doesn't show by then, I'll need another plan anyway. I say that will be fine, and let her know I'm with a friend.

"Will you and your friend be okay sharing a bed, or do you need a rollaway?"

"We sleep in shifts."

She blinks.

"It will be fine." I look out through the double doors. "How often does the ferry arrive?"

"We have several a day. Would you like a schedule?"

I've got one in the car, but I let her give me another since she's anxious to please. When I write the make and model of my car on the registration form, she completes a pained smile hat trick. "We almost had you towed." I take the room key and go sit on a white wicker chair on the porch—much nicer than Bella's. Clouds break low over Shaw Island and sheets of rain obscure the distant trees, but overhead, the sky is blue. A fresh breeze blows into my face, carrying with it the scent of salt water and diesel. My shoulder is throbbing, and I wish I had the sling. All I can do is wait.

Ferries come and go. By the third or fourth I learn to recognize the approach of the eastbound ferries returning to Anacortes versus the westbound, those likely to bring Ruby Jane. Between ferries, I watch the gulls, watch the tourists. The adults are restless, the children frenetic. They screech as they run around the grass, or thunder across the boardwalk to the ice cream stand. The sound helps me stay awake. In the early afternoon, I cross the road for a bowl of chowder from a place called Mamie's. A crowd returns from a whale watching trip, chattering and excited about seeing a transient pod of orcas spyhopping the channel between Goose and Deadman Islands as the harbor porpoises darted among them. I imagine taking Ruby Jane on one of these tours when all this is over. She'll appreciate the grace of the whales in the water.

Another ferry lands, and fails to bring her to me. Back on the hotel porch, I dial Pete's cell.

"I'm fine."

"Just checking."

"I'm not at Bella's. I decided to drive around the island to look for Ruby Jane's car."

Not a half bad idea, if based on the notion Ruby Jane drove straight through from Ohio, twenty-five hundred miles, without sleeping. "I got us a room at the hotel."

"I'll see you when I see you."

He returns after dark. The last ferry of the day isn't due for another hour, and I suggest we get some supper while we wait.

"I'm going to bed."

He walks away from me.

"What if she comes?"

I have to call him back to give him the key.

He's asleep when I get to the room after the last, fruitless ferry. He's fully dressed except for his shoes, lying on top of the quilt on one side of the bed. I kick off my own shoes and slip under the quilt next to him, convinced I won't be able to sleep. The night sounds of the hotel—creaks and occasional footsteps, the distant quiet murmur of a television or radio—resound in my ears, unnaturally magnified. When I close my eyes, I see Ruby Jane looking back at me from behind the wheel of her car. Questions swirl through in my mind, questions and doubts. It's only a guess Ruby Jane will come here.

I awake to rain, the drops striking the roof like coins falling from a torn pocket. Somewhere far to the east the sun may be rising, but outside the Orcas Hotel, the sky is the color of slate.

Pete is asleep beside me, curled up like a disobedient child waiting for his father to come home. I prod his shoulder as the ferry horn sounds across the water.

"Fuck off."

"Come on, Pete. She could be on this one."

"She could be on a beach in Tahiti singing to turtles."

"Pete—?"

I poke him again, and this time he sits up. He twists toward me, but the room is dark and I'm not sure if he sees me. "I was dreaming."

"About turtles and Tahiti?"

"How'd you know?"

I stand up, knees popping. "Come on. The ferry's almost here."

"I need coffee."

"It's down on the beach with the turtles."

"What the hell are you talking about?"

I don't answer. While Pete ties his shoes, I wash my face and comb my hair. Downstairs, the cafe is open, and we both get cups to go. Pete tarts his up with soy milk and vanilla powder. The ferry is coming to rest against the dock bumpers as we cross Killebrew Lake Road. The falling rain chatters against my rain coat, but Pete's cotton jacket drinks it in like a towel. We take up a post next to the terminal building under a sign advertising sea kayak and bicycle rentals. He hunches his shoulders, one hand in his pocket, the other holding his coffee cup under his chin.

"Turtles, Pete? Tahiti?"

A voice sounds over a loudspeaker on the ferry, but I can't make out the words. Pete drinks coffee and frowns. "Just ready for a different life."

"Aren't we all."

"Mmmm."

Cars move off the ferry. I steal a glance at Pete, who looks pensive. He breathes into his cup as the first vehicles roll past us and turn up the road toward Eastsound.

"It's slipping away." His voice is quiet, as if he's sharing an afterthought. "It's all just slipping away."

"What, Pete?"

He shakes his head, likes he's still waking up. "Huh?"

"What's slipping away?"

He looks at the coffee cup in his hands, as if recognizing it for the first time. His exposed skin offers a roadmap of damage suffered on Preble County Line Road, his haunted eyes even more so. He smiles weakly. "The dream. The dream is slipping away."

When the last car passes, we return to the hotel. I wait in the cafe while Pete goes upstairs to change into dry clothes. Out on the patio, the rain tapers off to a drizzle. The ferry is loading a few people going to Friday Harbor. I snag a couple of scones, a banana and another coffee. Complimentary with the room. Pete returns, but says he isn't hungry. He refills his coffee and joins me at a table near the window. All we can do is wait.

"I almost spoke up out there."

I look at him over the rim of my coffee cup.

"I still love her. I almost said so when she asked. But I couldn't."

Grey mist filters out of a colorless sky.

"I know I'm the one who ruined everything. I know we'll never get back together. She's moved on. But that doesn't mean I don't want to help her."

"You don't owe me any explanations." I doubt Pete believes a word he said. I'm sure he hopes by coming so far he'll prove himself to Ruby Jane. It's a belief I understand, since I share it. *You left me in that hospital but I followed you anyway.* Pete and I may be two fools playing at being the hero. "I'm here to rescue you." The one thing we haven't considered is maybe Ruby Jane neither needs nor wants rescuing.

"I'm going back out."

He doesn't have my capacity for waiting. "Be careful, Pete."

"Yeah. Sure." The day has hardly started, but he already sounds defeated.

The clouds break as he drives away. I return to the porch, fresh coffee in hand. Time passes like sap melting. Ferries come, ferries go. I doze from time to time, awake with a start when cars bring noise and exhaust. At one point, one of the walk-on passengers, a woman in multi-colored Lycra leading a pack-laden bike, pauses at pier's edge in order to puke into the water. A similarly bedecked fellow puts his hand on her back. She slaps him. I look away, and spy an eagle perched on top of a Douglas fir on the headland beyond the landing. Every so often, a gull dives screaming toward it, pulls up short and flies off over the water. The eagle is a lesson in stillness. I watch him until the next ferry draws my attention. When the last of the debarking cars passes I look back at the fir tree. The eagle is gone.

My cell phone rings, a 937 area code. Familiar, but I can't place it. Ruby Jane could have picked up a pre-paid cell anywhere.

"Yes?"

"Is this Mister Kadash?"

Nash. I deflate. "What can I do for you, Chief?"

"I don't suppose you've found Ruby yet, have you?"

"Working on it."

"Your lieutenant told me she thought you went to see Bella."

Susan could always see two steps ahead of me. "You're working late, Chief." It's after eight where he is.

"I've learned a few things and I figured you want to hear." A pair of gulls lights near the eagle's perch. "You know how everyone always thought Ruby went up to Dixie to finish school after she left Valley View? Turns out she never attended Dixie. She got a GED instead."

"Okay."

"She could have finished anywhere. GED is an odd choice."

"Maybe she was sick of high school."

"Not like she didn't have cause."

"But that's not it, is it?"

He hesitates, long enough for me to wonder if I lost the call. "She had a baby."

I open my mouth, but my voice fails me. The cries of the gulls are muted, as though my ears are stuffed with cotton balls.

"A boy, born at Good Sam in January 1990. According to the birth certificate, his name is Bidwell Denlinger Whittaker."

A leaden shock plunges through me. "Holy fuck."

"Holy something."

"Biddy Denlinger is Ruby Jane's son."

"There's more."

"Christ. It gets worse?"

"I don't know about that. He was adopted three weeks after he was born. The adoption file is sealed, but I'm working on that. Be nice to find out where the boy ended up."

In the two-and-a-half years I've known her, Ruby Jane has never even hinted about a baby.

"Mister Kadash?"

"You're sure about all this, Chief?"

"They're the facts as I far as I can determine."

Facts can hide a lot. I look for the eagle, but all I see are the damned gulls. Out on the water, a flight of ducks crosses, wing tips skimming the waves. *Biddy Denlinger Whittaker.* He'd be eighteen or nineteen now—my mind can't quite work out the math. Is that old enough to cross the country committing assault and murder?

"You okay, Mister Kadash?"

"Not sure."

"I know what you mean." He whistles lightly. "I've informed the SFPD, just so you know, along with your lieutenant."

I thank him, my voice flat, and disconnect the call.

With a will of their own, my feet carry me through the village. Searching. I don't know for what. Nothing. A coffee ... a bourbon. I glance through shop windows, weave among children chasing each other as their ice cream cones melt over their hands. I find myself on the boardwalk, uncertain about how I came there. The ferry horn sounds. Cars start. I inhale exhaust, listen to the engines. My head starts to ache and I look toward the hotel. The Starboard Harbor View room might offer a moment's respite from the noise and dizzying air and anxious worry. Or come to feel like a prison.

I leave the boardwalk and screaming children behind. The cars have begun to move, slowly enough I can weave between them without incident. Across the ferry holding area, I find a narrow, empty road which rises gently through the trees. I climb, huffing and gasping, until the road levels out and curves past a dirt lot next to an electrical sub-station. The sun drops behind a cloud and a sudden chill descends, followed by a splash of misty rain. A moment later, the clouds clear again. I continue up the road. My injured arm is heavy at my side. My feet feel like stones. I keep moving.

Behind the sub-station I see a boxy, older sedan in familiar faded blue. A heaviness collects behind my heart. Ruby Jane's beater Corolla is from the last model year before they went bubbly and round in the early 90s. Water gathers in my eyes as I draw nearer, but I force myself forward.

It's empty.

49

No One Home

THE CAR IS much as I remember it, wearing its years in dings and scrapes. A walk-around reveals nothing. I find the spare key in the magnetic box hidden in the left rear wheel well. I've opened a few trunks over the years, and I know they're empty far more often than not, the evidence of film and TV notwithstanding. A breeze carries the scent of sea and evergreen, but odds and clean air do nothing to calm the tremor in my hand as I pop the trunk.

Inside, I find relief—and more questions.

There's a green holdall with some of Ruby Jane's clothes, and a cardboard carton with packs of dried fruit, Sun Chips, half-empty boxes of crackers. A small cooler holds a couple of bottles of Jones cola floating in dirty water. Cane sugar and caffeine for the long drive west—no way to know how often she could get a decent cup of coffee.

I can't tell if Ruby Jane parked the car and walked away, or if it was dumped by someone else. The spot is out of the way, un-likely to be noticed quickly, but close enough to the village landing that whoever left it could easily have made their way elsewhere, on island or off. After San Francisco and Preble County Line Road, I'll assume it was dumped until I prove otherwise.

I dial Pete on my cell phone. No answer. Fuck him. I don't bother to leave a message, dial 911 instead.

The dispatcher doesn't see the emergency. In her shoes, I'd have been skeptical too. I ask about Inspector Eldridge's request for an interview of Bella Denlinger, but there's no reason she'd know about that. At last, I get her to have a deputy meet me at Isabella Farm.

As I trot back to the village, I give Pete another try. Still brooding. The interior of the Gremlin feels like a sauna under the slanting sun. A ferry has begun to unload as I pull out, and I have to wait for a long line of cars to climb past to Orcas Road. My impatience vibrates through me on the drive north, the traffic ahead uncharacteristically committed to the speed limit. After a mile or two, a few vehicles turn west toward Deer Harbor, but the main parade continues north. Yet once I reach the turn off to Bella's, I go a little faster. The Gremlin strains to climb to the top of the ridge. In those rare moments when the road levels out, sharp curves slow me. I make better time after I get over the top, and all but coast the last mile or so to Isabella Farm.

A deputy named Rolf meets me at the end of the driveway.

"I'm the one who called."

He looks me over, and I wish I'd bothered to put on clean clothes this morning. His eyes linger on my neck. "I've already been up to the house, sir. No one is home."

"They must have taken her."

"Taken who?"

"My friend—Ruby Jane Whittaker. She's Bella Denlinger's daughter."

He studies me. "I did a walk-around. No evidence of trouble."

"What about Taya?"

"Taya who?"

"I don't know. She's Bella's aid or whatever. Since her stroke."

"I wasn't aware Miss Denlinger was sick."

"Do you know her?"

"To say hi at the farmer's market. I don't know anyone named Taya though." He shrugs. "We get lots of visitors to the island."

"She said she's local."

He shrugs again. "No one is home, sir."

"What about the car, my friend's Toyota? She never would have abandoned it."

"What do you think happened?"

I take a breath, try to explain things to him. I can sense his impatience, but after I run through the highlights—Chase Fairweather, two hit-and-runs—he makes a few notes. I describe Ruby Jane and her relationship to Bella Denlinger. I also give him Susan's name and number and suggest he call her. He nods. "Wait here." He goes to his car and gets behind the wheel. I can see him on a cell phone. After a few minutes, he returns.

"Where are you staying?"

"Did you talk to Lieutenant Mulvaney?"

"Someone will call her. Where are you staying?"

"The Orcas Hotel."

"Nice place, isn't it?"

I run my hands through my hair and resist the urge to scream. He frowns.

"I'll take a look at the car, but you need to understand that most likely your friend thought she found a handy spot to park. She shouldn't have left her car there though. It'll get towed."

"She didn't leave it there."

"Go back to the hotel. Someone will be in touch."

"That's it?"

He's getting annoyed. "Sir, we'll check this out. Relax. Go have a scone or something."

He waits until I get into the Gremlin, then follows me to Orcas Road. I turn left toward the ferry but he goes right, giving lie to his assurance he'd investigate Ruby Jane's car. As soon as he drives out of sight, I turn back.

I leave the car at the foot of the driveway. An eagle circles above the ridge against sapphire sky criss-crossed by pillowy contrails. I walk along the lodgepole fence. The wood is smooth and warm under my hand. There's no sign of Ringo. The pasture connects to the stable via a broad chute. A wide door in the near end of the structure stands open. Perhaps he's inside.

Swallows dart through the field as I approach the house. The curtains in every window are closed. The place exudes a quiet emptiness. I climb the steps. The two iced tea glasses remain on the wicker table where Pete and I left them. A dead yellow jacket floats in one. I look through leaded-glass panes in the front door, but all I can see is the darkened foyer.

I return to the driveway and head around the side of the house. The L-shaped stable stands in the far left corner of the deep yard. The driveway stops at a pair of garage doors in the short arm of the L at the rear. Beside the drive, a wide lawn stretches from the house to the trees below the bluff. Another outbuilding sits on the right side of the lawn: a small, cedar-sided shed with a bare-earthed pen on one side and a fallow garden on the other. Weeds and a few volunteers—tomatoes and stunted peas—push up through layers of composting straw covering the broad plot.

The back of the house is as dead as the front. The curtains hang motionless in the windows. I look through the glass door onto an enclosed back porch, but see nothing unusual. A row of rubber boots lined up beside the back door, rain gear on hooks above. A pair of binoculars rests on the sill of one of the porch windows near a round table and a pair of wooden chairs. I rattle the handle, but the door is latched. I decide to check the outbuildings before I resort to breaking-and-entering.

The grass is soft and mossy under my feet. Inside the shed, the concrete floor is swept, the air dry and stale. Double doors lead to the pen at the side. The walls are hung with shears and steel combs. There are wooden racks along the back, like newspaper racks at a library, and an old-fashioned spinning wheel next to a modern stenographer's chair. The space is tidy, but disused—a layer of dust coats every surface. I close the door and cross back to the stable.

The long arm of the barn red structure has a row of Dutch stall doors facing the driveway, all shut. I start with the short arm, raise the nearer of the two garage doors. It rattles and shrieks on its tracks. I expect the arrival of stormtroopers to investigate.

No one comes.

A battered Ford pickup with a fiberglass truck cap is parked next to a huge riding mower with a rototiller attachment. Rakes and shovels hang from the rear wall next to a work bench with a peg board above it. Hand tools and containers of screws, nails, nuts and bolts. Like the shed, everything is tidy and in its place—and long idle. For a moment I recall Ray Malo's perfect house, then pass behind the truck to the bulkhead wall which separates the garage from the stable.

A wide ladder climbs up to a hayloft, but I'm more interested in the shuffling sound I hear coming through a wide opening in the bulkhead. The opening is barred by a length of rope stretched about waist high. I stoop under the rope into a long room with stalls on the left and an open space on the right. Light streams in through the doorway at the far end and filters between the gaps in the Dutch stall doors. The rear walls, not visible from the house or driveway, are hinged in segments at the top and tilted open to form a kind of open breezeway, not unlike a carport. The lodgepole fence extends up from the pasture and continues behind the building and out of sight. The floor is gravel, not the concrete I expected.

About halfway up, Ringo noses around in one of the stalls. He raises his head, then clops toward me, a redolent aroma two steps ahead of him. I freeze, but his movement isn't threatening. He stops to nuzzle my outstretched hand. His lips feel like dry, prehensile leather. When he looks up, his eyes seem disappointed I have nothing to offer. He moves into the stall nearest me and noses the empty water trough. I watch until he lifts his head up and stares at me. There's a spigot at the end of the trough. I step into the stall, plug the trough drain with a rubber stopper suspended on a chain, and turn on the water.

He's drinking before the flow has barely covered the bottom of the trough, slurping like a clogged drain clearing. I leave the spigot open until the trough is nearly full. Ringo inhales water for another minute or so. When he lifts his head, the water streams off his cheeks and down the matted wool of his neck. I raise my hand and he nuzzles it again, then moves past me out of the stall. I follow, leaving the gate open so he can return for a drink later. He moves toward the doorway, pausing next to a stall further up. He peers through the gate for a long moment, then back my way before trotting out into the sunlight and out of view.

The space smells of hay and old dung, an earthy scent not altogether unpleasant. There's something else as well; a faint trace of underlying foulness stings my sinuses. Flies buzz between the light fixtures on the plank ceiling. I find myself holding my breath as I move toward the far end. Each stall bare, the troughs and hay boxes empty. Taya said Bella had sold most of her stock. Only Ringo remains. I wonder when he was last fed.

As I near the far end, the foul smell grows stronger, a sweet and sour rot. I hesitate, and put my hand into my pocket to grip my cell phone. There are only a couple of stalls left, but I already know the one Ringo paused near isn't empty. My feet scrape on gravel. The stall gate hangs partway open. At first, all I can see are flies contending over a shapeless lump on the floor. I stagger back as the lump snaps into focus and the full force of the rotten stench hits me.

A woman with long grey hair and arthritic claws for hands lies in a twisted heap on the gravel floor, a puppet dropped and forgotten. I see no obvious injury, though I'm not interested in a detailed forensic examination. She appears to have been dead a while, a week or more. I back away from the stall, stumble out the door into the open air.

Something hard slams into the crease between my neck and shoulder. Pain shoots down my spine. My legs crumple. I try to catch myself, but another blow lands between my shoulder blades, then a boot drives up into my belly. The twin barrels of a shotgun flash in the corner of my eye as vomit spurts from my mouth onto the dusty ground. A shadow passes over me.

"Soon as he's done puking, toss him in with the other one."

50

Shotgun Speaks Loud Enough

I'M NOT SURE who I feel worse for: the woman I assume was Bella Denlinger, or Ringo the friendly alpaca. In my experience, only humans and other scavengers will linger in the presence of death—except in most dire need. The poor beast must have been desperate for water. By the time I raise my head, Ringo is down at the bottom of the pasture nosing a cluster of blue-eyed Mary.

I feel empty, and not just because my stomach contents are soaking into the dry ground. I've been late from the start. Late returning from my so-called retreat, late reaching Jimmy Whitacre. Late finding Ruby Jane on Preble County Line Road. I was too slow to catch her when she ran from the hospital. I missed her coming off the ferry. Discovered her dead mother only in time to have my guts kicked out of me by the tall, lean figure I last saw in Portland. If he's here now, I'm too late to help Ruby Jane.

He's shed layers down to a denim shirt over a white tee, jeans and Doc Martens. His brown hair hangs in shaggy clumps, as if he went after his own scalp with a set of Bella's shears. I can't see a trace of his mother in his lean, boyish face, except perhaps in the blue of his eyes.

Taya stands nearby, holding her own shotgun, watching Ringo—she's only halfway here. The kid's lips pull back, revealing straight white teeth.

"You're Biddy Denlinger."

"It doesn't matter who I am."

"The police know I'm here." The words taste foolish in my mouth.

"We saw the deputy. I didn't get the idea he left with any reason to come back."

"You're lucky he didn't check the barn."

He rams the gun stock into the meat above my collarbone. As I gasp, he pulls the cell phone from my pocket. "You're lucky you're not with her."

Beside him, Taya flinches. He turns to her. "Take him up. I'll be right there." He gestures with the shotgun, then tucks the stock under his arm. It's a double-barrel side-by-side with external hammers. Old enough I wouldn't be surprised if it first saw use on a stagecoach a century earlier.

When I meet Taya's gaze, she turns away. "Come on." Her weapon is newer, a weighty single-barreled twenty-gauge. It may lack the punch of the twelve-gauge monster in Biddy's hands, but at this range, it's enough. She points toward the far end of the garage. I get to my feet and hobble across the driveway. Taya's footsteps behind me sound like the popping of small caliber arms fire.

Beyond the garage, the yard opens into a broad fan-shape with trees to either side and the bluff ahead. Thirty paces away at the edge of another fenced pasture, there's a weathered grey shack flanked by a pair of Norway maples. "Over there." The nose of Pete's baby pickup is visible from behind the shack. The air cools noticeably when we move into the shadow of the trees. I can smell vomit. The scent moves with me onto the low, plank porch of the shack.

"Could I have some water?"

Taya shakes her head and gestures with the gun barrel. The door barred by a two-by-four. As I lift it free of the brackets, I contemplate its concussive effect on Taya's forearm just above the wrist. Hard to fire a shotgun with a snapped radius and ulna. But when I turn, Biddy is approaching from around the garage. I prop the board against the wall and pull the door open.

The interior is dim and dusty. One room, with a pot belly stove and a plywood counter in the back. There's a deep basin sink in one end of the counter. The bare bulb hanging from the ceiling is off, as is the old lamp on the table under the lone window.

Pete lies on a cot against the side wall. He's not gagged, which surprises me until I realize he's unconscious. I move closer. His mouth is bruised, and threads of dried blood run from his split lip and nose. There's a red welt above his left eye. The orbit is swollen and bleeding. His hands and feet are bound with clothesline. Only the ragged sound of his breathing offers any reassurance.

"I guess you get the chair." Taya tilts her head. There's a coil of clothesline on the table.

"You going to tie me up by yourself?"

"Just sit down." She points the gun at me and I sit. Her voice is weak, almost too soft to hear. The shotgun speaks loud enough.

"Taya, you can stop this before it gets any worse. Nobody else has to get hurt."

She shakes her head. "Don't talk to me."

"Are you going to let us to rot out here like Bella in the stable?"

"He wouldn't let me move her."

"Not easy to face the body of a woman you've murdered."

"Nobody murdered anyone." Her eyes flare. "She just died out there. He said leave her, so I left her."

"You do everything he says?"

"You're not allowed to talk to me."

"Even if he didn't kill Bella, he killed her son in San Francisco. And he tried to kill me and my friend here." I have no way of knowing who is responsible for Bella Denlinger, if anyone, but I hope she'll take the lifeline I've offered and pin the death on her boyfriend.

But at that moment, he comes through the door. "I told you not to talk to them."

Taya fades back against the wall. "I didn't say anything. He was the one talking. All I did was tell him to stop."

He's clearly not convinced, but he turns his attention to me. "I don't know what the hell your story is, but I'm getting sick of you showing up all over the place. So how about you shut up before I shut you up for good."

"You might find it's a lot harder to shoot a man than to run one down in the street." The words are bolder than the man behind them. Biddy responds by dropping the shotgun and slamming his fist into my jaw.

My head snaps back and he hits me again, stomach and throat. The floor is worn smooth, a sudden, unsettling observation I make when my cheek slams against a grey plank. I scrabble for the shotgun, but Biddy picks me up by my shirt and throws me down again. I see the spatter of blood on my pants, on wood, on his furious knuckles. I have no power to stop the mewling rising from my throat.

"Please, stop." I think it's Taya's voice.

"Maybe he'll take me seriously now."

"It's too much."

"Shut up." But something changes; he stops hitting me. I hear footsteps. The floor vibrates against my face. When the door slams, the whole shack trembles.

It's a long time before I can do more than lie on the floor and try to breathe. A pocket of fear presses up into my lungs. Flies tick against the window and the shack creaks in the heat. My nose is clogged with snot and blood. I'm pretty sure I've bitten my tongue. My face has lost sensation, but the rest of my body feels like an open sore. I try to catch my breath, and manage to lift my right arm and wipe away some of the blood with my sleeve.

"They don't have her." Pete's voice is thick and muffled, as though his mouth is stuffed with cotton. I wonder when he came to. Or when I did.

I roll onto my side, then to my knees. "Are you sure?" He's barely able to open his eyes.

"They asked me about her." He takes a pained breath. "Well, he did. That girl just stood there."

"What do they want?"

"Money. He thinks there's some big stash somewhere."

I stumble to the basin. The pipe groans when I turn the spigot, but after a moment a thin stream of rusty water flows. I let it run until it's relatively clear, then wash the blood off my hands and face. There are no towels or rags, so I strip off my outer shirt and soak it with water. Pete winces and moans as I clean the blood from his face. Then I work at the clothesline. The knot is a problem at first, but with a little patience, I'm able to work it free. His arms fall onto the cot. I hear his tongue working inside his mouth. "Bastard loosened one of my teeth."

My eyes burn. I think of Nash's old police file. Mae Whittaker's bank account drained, Dale Whittaker gone, two old toolboxes and a revolver buried in the woods on Preble County Line Road. Is that what this is all about? Has Biddy Denlinger appeared, nearly twenty years later, to claim a long lost inheritance? Or did he wake up one day and decide it was time to take something back from the mother who gave him away?

I start on the cord binding Pete's feet. "Ruby Jane is on the island."Pete doesn't seem surprised. "When did she get here?"

"I don't know. I found her car, abandoned. The police wouldn't do anything. Biddy and Taya caught me sneaking around the barn."

He breathes noisily. "He yanked me out of my car. I was watching the house from the road, but never saw him coming."

"A couple of old pros."

We fall into an uneasy silence. I free Pete's legs, but he doesn't move from the cot. There's not much point. I can see Biddy and Taya through the window. They argue for a while, then Biddy heads off. Taya looks back toward the shack, doesn't appear to realize I'm watching her. I try the door, but they've barred it. The window is four panes in a hinged frame, nailed shut. If I broke out the glass, Taya would hear me. She doesn't look too comfortable with the shotgun, but I'm not ready to take the chance she won't pull the trigger.

I move the chair next to the cot and sit down. I put my hand on Pete's arm and look through the window. The house is framed against the deepening blue sky. The air grows hotter and stuffier even as the light fades. Pete's breathing sounds like a two-stroke engine. I catch myself imagining life in this shack, sleeping on the cot, cooking on the pot belly stove. One plate and one cup. A spartan existence, but in a different life perhaps not so bad. Ridiculous dreaming. But I've got nothing else, unless I want to spend the crawl toward nightfall trying to make sense of a sequence of events about which I know almost nothing. It's a swirling mess in my mind. Ruby Jane takes off without explanation. A man—her father—dies in her bathtub. Another man, her brother, dies outside a San Francisco sports bar. Pete and I almost join them both. We've criss-crossed the country, asking questions and getting answers which only lead to more questions. For all I've learned—about

Ruby Jane as a high school girl, about missing money and jewelry, about a child I never suspected—I'm missing the crucial piece.

"Pete, There's something you need to hear."

"Mmmm." I can't tell if he's awake, or lucid.

"Biddy Denlinger is Ruby Jane's son, born when she was in high school. She gave him up for adoption."

My breath catches in my throat. When Pete speaks at last, his voice remains muddy and indistinct, but I can hear the resignation. "I guess that figures."

She never told him either.

I close my eyes and a moment later the hairs in my nose twitch against the sharp scent of urine. Pete snuffles and as the sound increases, I realize he's crying. Shame floods through me. "Pete, I'm sorry." He doesn't respond. "I'm so sorry."

"He should have finished me."

"Don't say that, Pete." I lower myself down beside him. "Don't say that." I hold him until he stops trembling.

After a while, I open my eyes. Full dark now. I put my hand on Pete's chest and feel the thud of his heartbeat, the rise and fall of his breath. From outside, I hear voices. Biddy and Taya are arguing again, close enough now I can make out snatches of words.

"… don't like this …"

"As soon as we get the money, we're …"

I stand, cringe when a floor board creaks beneath my feet. Their silhouettes move outside the window. The sky is a carpet of stars, Bella's house a looming shadow beyond the garage.

"… about them?"

"Who cares about them?"

"We can't—"

A light comes on in the house and they fall silent. After a moment, I hear whispering, then the bar comes off the door. Taya steps through, the gun aimed at my chest.

"I need you to sit down on that chair."

I move back and sit. "What's going on, Taya?"

In answer, she edges along the wall until she reaches the table. Eyes still on me, she feels for the lamp. Ten years and a thorough beating earlier, I might have taken my chances and gone for the gun. As it is, all I can do is sit. Pete groans. She flips the lamp on, a pale light which does more to cast shadow than illuminate the shack's interior. "Skin, what's happening?" When I look away from her, Taya all but disappears. I take Pete's hand. He pulls on me, and I help him into a sitting position.

"Someone's here."

"Who?"

"Someone in the house."

"Ruby Jane?"

Taya gains substance in response to the name, but says nothing. We wait. Pete breathes heavily, as though the act of sitting upright takes all his energy. I look at Taya.

"He needs a hospital."

"Be quiet."

"Biddy hurt him bad. He needs help."

"There's nothing I can do."

"Call the police. You don't have to identify yourself. Tell them he's holding hostages. I'll say you helped us."

"You don't know him." She blinks, and for a moment I think something has changed, that she might help us. The translucent skin of her face stretches into a grimace, and a rim of tears forms in her eyes. But then a clatter of footsteps sounds at the door, and Ruby Jane stumbles into the shack. She catches herself on the end of the cot. There's a fresh cut on her cheek.

Biddy arrives two steps behind her, his face flush with excitement. "Look who I found going through Bella's dresser." He grins at Taya. "Pack up, baby. We're going for a ride."

I move to rise, but he points the shotgun at me and I freeze.

"What's happening? Ruby Jane—"

She seems no more surprised to see us than I am to see her. She's wearing a nylon pullover, olive hiking pants, worn athletic shoes. Her face is tan, her auburn hair pulled back, like she's spent a long day outdoors. Her brow furrows at sight of my face, a fright mask the best of times, but an extra special treat after Biddy's ministrations. When she turns to Pete, her lips fall open with shock. She raises a hand to her chin.

"You weren't supposed to be here, Skin. I'm sorry."

"You don't have to apologize to me, darling."

"But I do." She pulls herself up straight and takes a breath. When she looks at me again, I can't understand the lack of fear in her gaze. "I'm taking him to where my treasure is buried."

"Do you know who he is?"

"Does it matter?" Her voice shakes. "Just another mess to clean up."

51

BURIED TREASURE

IN APRIL 1989, right about the time Ruby Jane was breaking Clarice Moody's nose, a fellow I went through the academy with was found shot to death in his patrol car outside a strip club on Powell Boulevard. Officer Lee Ragland had made no report of trouble, hadn't requested cover. After roll call, I'd jawed with him over coffee before we headed out to patrol our districts. Four hours later, he was dead.

I was not yet a detective and over a decade away from Homicide. But I worked the case. When a cop dies on the job, no one rests until we find the killer. No discussion, no argument.

It's common practice to check tags on vehicles at strip clubs—something about jacking a car makes a lot of dipshits want to watch some titties jiggle. Our best theory was the shooter slipped up on Lee while he was writing down license plate numbers, a thief who didn't want to get caught or a gang banger bagging himself a trophy. But the evidence was thin. Small caliber slug from an untraceable gun. We heard no chatter, received no credible tips, turned up zero witnesses.

Months later, I ran into Lee's son at Coffee People, the one between MLK and Grand near the I-84 overpass. It's a Starbuck's now.

The kid—Lee Jr.—was drinking one of those twenty-four-ounce barrels of sugar, milk fat, and caffeine. He was a gangly kid, tall for his age, but still possessing the soft edges of childhood. I asked him how he was doing, and he shrugged, his eyes fixed on the traffic on Grand. His mind was somewhere else.

I couldn't fault him. His dad was dead, we had nothing to offer him. I got watery-eyed and felt myself contract under the weight of my guilt and failure. I offered stuttering explanations, made hollow excuses. *Following every lead, hammering every informant. Something will break, I promise.* I think I even apologized, as if I was somehow personally responsible for our institutional failure to find his father's killer.

"We won't give up, buddy."

He drank from his giant cup. I remember thinking he seemed so lost. Just a kid, thirteen years old. Heartbreaking.

"I shot him."

Around me, the cafe grew quiet. Lee Jr. looked up at me, and his eyes were like a well you look into expecting to see the reflection of the sunlight on the surface of the water below. But all you see is a void.

"I still have the gun. It was my birthday present. Do you want it?"

We later learned Lee had taken away his goddamn Nintendo. Bad grades.

Biddy shares with Lee Jr. that same emptiness. He has a story—we all do—a life history which might explain how he arrived at this moment with a shotgun in his hands and a mounting body count in his wake. Maybe it was abuse. If Chief Nash can track down his adoptive parents, we might discover a long, sad tale of neglect and beatings, affection withheld. I don't want to hear it. I want to ram that shotgun through Biddy's teeth and blow his spine out his back.

He walks two paces behind Pete, who is moving like a drunk. Taya is behind me, Ruby Jane between us both. The night has grown cold, and I can see our breath billow in the light shining from the house into the yard. Biddy leads us to the garage, has me open the door in front of the pickup.

There's some confusion about how to proceed. Two guns and three hostages don't add up to math Biddy likes. He and Taya discuss their options while the three of us cluster together at the bed of the truck.

I look at Ruby Jane, my eyes a question. She frowns and shakes her head. Pete's head sags, and his breathing sounds like a clogged drain. I pull him over to me. Ruby Jane's manner, remote and strangely calm, leaves me more unsettled than Biddy's shotgun. I'd like to think she has a plan. I'm all out of ideas myself.

In the end, Biddy has us climb into the truck bed and sit with our backs to the cab. He looks at Ruby Jane.

"Where to?"

"Do you know where Woodlawn Cemetery is?"

The idea of going to a cemetery fills him with glee. "Sick!" He tosses Taya a nod. "You drive. I'll ride in the back with the cargo."

"I'm not driving this piece of crap."

"Jesus. Fine. Whatever."

Ruby Jane points to the rack of tools hanging at the back of the garage. "You'll need a shovel."

That makes him laugh. Taya climbs aboard and rests her back against the tailgate. Through the scratched window, I see Biddy carry the shovel to the cab. As we pull out, Ringo comes to the fence to watch us pass. Biddy has to drive around a bike in the driveway and I realize why Ruby Jane left her car. She rented the bike, probably at the landing, so she could arrive in silence. I don't know if she meant to slip up on Bella unawares, or anticipated Biddy and the shotgun.

The ride takes forever. My head is swimming with diesel fumes. Pete sags against me. Taya stares at a spot on the roof of the fiberglass cap, shotgun across her lap. Only Ruby Jane seems alert. After the second or third turn, she leans forward and prods Taya's knee with her foot.

"Don't talk."

Ruby Jane has a sad smile on her face, and her eyes glitter in the dark. "You don't have to do this, Gabi." Her voice is soft.

"That's not my name."

"It doesn't matter."

"You need to be quiet now."

"You think when he has what he wants he'll take you with him?"

"Shut up!"

Ruby Jane settles back again. Even in daylight I'd have no clue where we're going. We pass dark forest and open pasture, the occasional house set back from the road. The truck springs protest every turn, and the engine whines when we climb. The full moon appears on the horizon as we turn off pavement onto gravel. The quality of darkness changes from slate to silver and I realize we're among gravestones and mown grass. The pickup stops.

No one moves until Biddy opens the tailgate. Taya slides out and stands beside him. He gestures for us to follow. Ruby Jane and I help Pete despite his protests.

"I'm fine."

He doesn't sound fine, but he keeps his feet. Biddy thrusts a flashlight into Ruby Jane's hands. "Lead the way, Mom." Taya goes tense beside me.

"First we need to come to an understanding."

"There's only one understanding. Show me the money."

"You have to let my friends go."

He doesn't like the sound of that, but I can see his mind working, trying to figure out a way to get what he wants while still addressing the problem posed by our very existence. If I was a stone killer, I wouldn't want to leave any witnesses either.

"How much are we talking about? The old lady said it was hundreds of thousands."

Ruby Jane is smart enough to know how this is likely to go down. But her face reveals nothing. "Do you want me to show you or not?"

"Get going." It doesn't sound like we've reached an agreement, but Ruby Jane moves ahead of us across the grass. She knows exactly where she's going. Biddy carries the shovel in one hand, the shotgun in the other. When I try to move alongside Biddy, Pete pushes between us. Taya puts an insubstantial hand on my arm and we move through the grass, spreading out. I'm not sure if this is by design or accident. Biddy doesn't strike me as one with a gift for tactical thinking.

The headlights of the pickup shine behind us, illuminating our path. We pass upright stones and flat markers. The cemetery isn't big, a few acres bordered on three sides by trees. I gaze up at the broad star field, struck by the thought I will soon be there. Then Ruby Jane points out a grave marker, flush with the grass.

Taya's shotgun barrel brushes my legs and I realize she's no longer holding it up. I turn, but all I see are shadows. Pete's head hangs down. His breathing is ragged and wet. In the uncertain illumination—truck headlights, flashlight, moon and stars—Ruby Jane's cheeks shine with a strange, electric energy. She holds the flashlight tight, like a club. Biddy seems to sense her intensity and keeps his distance, gun trained on Pete.

"Where?" His words are breathy with anticipation. "Show me."

She clicks the flashlight on and sweeps the beam across the grave marker. I see letters carved into the surface, but the beam doesn't hold still enough for me to make out the name.

"This is it? It's buried here?" His voice has gained half a semi-tone in his excitement. "Damn, you are one crazy lady." He jams the head of the shovel into the ground and moves closer, pushing Pete forward with his elbow. Then he stops. Ruby Jane fixes the beam on the marker. The angle of the light throws the letters into sharp contrast. Even from fifteen feet away, I can read the name.

BIDWELL DENLINGER WHITTAKER
"LITTLE HUCK"
JANUARY 14, 1990 – DECEMBER 11, 1990

"The original stone said Biddy Denlinger, but six or seven years ago, Jimmie bought a new one. He told Bella it had to include Whittaker, plus the name I'd intended for the baby." There's a calm, sing-song quality to her words, as if she's sharing a sadness with which she's long since come to terms. "She never knew how to care for a child." Her voice trails off until all I can hear is the faint whisper of a breeze through the trees at the edge of the cemetery. In the shimmering moonlight, Ruby Jane's face is like a portrait reflected in a dark mirror. She's looking at the grave marker, trace of a haunted smile on her lips. Her cheeks shine with reflected starlight.

A sharp, metallic crack splits the night—the sound of two hammers locking back.

"You fucking cunt."

Between the hit-and-run and the beating, my joints are like rusty gears filled with sand. Pete's no faster, but he's in better position. He deflects the gun barrel toward the ground with his hands. I push across the lawn, indifferent to Taya. I don't know if she's even there. She's a ghost to me. My only concern is for Biddy, and for the two barrels he fights to bring to bear on Ruby Jane.

The shotgun goes off. Double-ought buckshot shreds grass and soil. Pete drops to one knee and screams. He's ten feet from me, clutching at his legs. My shoulder protests as I reach out, lunging.

Whatever I hope to accomplish, I'm too slow.

But Ruby Jane rises out of shadow as if she was made for this moment, wielding the weapon Biddy brought at her request. She swings the shovel at his head, connects as he fires the second barrel. The sound hits me like I've slammed into a taut sheet of canvas. Pete stops screaming and falls.

For an instant as long as the night everything freezes: Pete on the ground, Biddy's shattered face, Ruby Jane with the shovel. Then, behind me, Taya materializes and fires. I don't know who she's targeting. Searing pain blossoms in my shoulder, but Biddy takes most of the blast, upper body and head. He drops without a sound, falling across Pete like a sack of potatoes. I'm there in an instant, toss him aside and kneel beside Pete. Ruby Jane flings the shovel at Taya, but she's already faded away. Then Ruby Jane is with me, with Pete. He makes a desolate, bubbling noise. I can't make out his face in the darkness, but I can feel his warm blood, so much warm blood. Ruby Jane cradles his head and whispers his name, over and over. "Pete, … Peter, …" The bubbling ends with a long, hollow rattle as the pickup starts behind us and tears away with a clatter of flying gravel.

I reach out and pull Ruby Jane close to me. She falls against my chest and sobs. I stroke her hair as my own tears flow, and she squeezes me tight and says my name. Soft, soothing sounds rise out of me as if someone else has taken charge of my voice. I'm not sure who's comforting whom.

That's how the San Juan County sheriff's deputy finds us, minutes or hours later.

52

GOING HOME

THEY KEEP US all night and all day. Deputies and techs come and go from the island by sheriff's department boat and by ferry. I don't pay much attention. My only interest is Ruby Jane as she tells me the long story of where she came from and how she grew to be the woman I love. All this time, so much I never knew, so much she tried to leave behind. I ache to hear it all: Bella Denlinger, Clarice Moody, a young girl named Gabi, a boy named Finn. A stolen emerald ring ... Jimmie Whittaker. A dark night on Preble County Line Road. A baby boy.

"She took him away from me. She called him Bidwell Denlinger, after the mother and father who'd disowned her. She thought she could win her inheritance with the empty gesture of a stolen child."

"What does that mean, she stole him?"

"It means I was a coward. I felt so alone. Jimmie wouldn't talk to me. I couldn't face people at school—not even Huck. My feelings for him were too tangled up with what happened to Gabi. I spent all my time out running, or shooting baskets at the elementary school. Or writing for Mrs. Parmelee—she was the only one I could trust. I wanted to run away, but then I found out I was pregnant and it was like the ground gave way beneath my feet." Her tears don't stop. "That's when Bella swooped in. I was too young to be a mother, she said. I told her she wasn't fit to raise a plague rat, let alone a child. But she threatened to turn me and Jimmie in for Dale's murder if I didn't do what she wanted."

"Dale was alive."

"I couldn't prove that. For all I knew, his body would turn up a county or a state away, dead from Jimmie's bullet. No one had seen him since that night. Besides, I'd watched enough cop shows to know just because there was no body in that hole didn't mean we'd be safe."

A body helps in a murder conviction, but it's not always critical. If enough evidence piles up, reasonable doubt erodes. Those toolboxes and the gun might have been enough to sink her. Certainly enough to make her life hell.

"What happened?"

"Her plan failed. Her parents saw right through her. So she found some new guy to leech off of and followed him out here with my baby. By that point, I think she was keeping him out of spite. But then she let him die. Viral encephalitis was the official cause, but I know the truth. She was a terrible mother." She draws a long, shuddering breath. "She wouldn't even let him have his own name."

"Huck."

An EMT checks us out. Ruby Jane is uninjured, but I've got a hole, front to back; Taya's #2 lead shot went through the trapezius muscle above my injured collar bone. He cleans and bandages the wound. "You need stitches." I don't argue, except to insist Ruby Jane and I not be separated. We ride together in the back of a patrol car to a clinic in Eastsound Village, where a doctor sews me up. He observes I appear to have a grudge against my shoulder. The bruises from Preble County Line Road haven't faded.

Another deputy takes us to a sub-station and sticks us in a conference room. We give our statements, mine in a weary monotone. Ruby Jane adds little. Then we find a couch and she falls asleep leaning against my good shoulder.

After a while, I slip away and spend some time tracking down Pete's sister, Abby, who lives in Seattle with her husband and daughter. She doesn't sound surprised he's dead. I tell her Ruby Jane wants to hold a memorial in Portland, but we both understand that as family, Abby's wishes come first. She's as peremptory as I remember from our last encounter, two-and-a-half years earlier. Says she'll get back to me and asks to speak to someone with actual authority. I'm grateful I used the sheriff's phone to make my call.

In the morning, a man in a suit identifies himself as a county attorney and takes me aside. If he offers a name, I don't hear it.

"You're the cop."

"Retired."

"Right. I spoke with your lieutenant."

She's not my lieutenant, but I don't see any point in clarifying the situation.

"What's the story?"

"We picked up Taya trying to board the morning ferry. She's going to cooperate."

"Let me guess. It was *all* the boyfriend."

He smiles wryly. He's a young man, not more than thirty, but with dark brown serious eyes. His manner is calm and confident, which is a comfort to me. "Robert Earl Perry. Someone she met while she was at school in Bellingham. After Bella's husband—her second husband, I guess—passed, Taya worked part time at the farm, went out twice a week to clean. Perry tagged along sometimes. Apparently he was there the day the county tax letter came. Bella was years behind and at risk of having her property seized. Her alpacas never paid."

"Do they ever?"

"Bella was out of her depth on her own."

"So what happened?"

"I guess she started raving about her husband Dale and a big wad of hidden money which could fix everything. The story is confused, but apparently she claimed her son murdered her husband and her daughter buried the body back in Ohio."

"Nobody has buried Dale Whittaker. He died a week ago in Portland. Probably still in the ME's cooler."

"Well, it didn't matter, because Bella stroked out. When she talked at all after that, it was only about some kid named Biddy, her grandchild, I understand. I'm not clear on the details, because Taya isn't, but it seems Perry dug through that old house and found enough to give him an idea of what might have happened. He went to San Francisco to take a run at James Whitacre, the alleged patricide, and left Taya behind to look after Bella."

"They never took Bella to a hospital, I suppose."

"Perry felt Taya was sufficient medical care."

"Jesus."

"I doubt Jesus had anything to do with it."

I look at my hands.

"SFPD tells me Perry posed as Biddy Denlinger and got a little cash out of Whitacre, but Bella's ravings had convinced him her ex-husband spirited away hundreds of thousands of dollars, that it had been missing ever since he died. She bounced between claiming it was buried in his grave, or her son had it, or her daughter knew where it was."

"There was no grave." Someone will tell this attorney about the toolboxes and rusted gun, I suppose—Nash, most likely. But none of them will ever learn what happened that night on Preble County Line Road. "So when things in San Francisco didn't work out—"

"Perry decided to go after Ruby Whittaker. But rather than getting suckered in a blackmail scheme, she slipped away. I guess she went looking for the money on her own."

"I don't think she cared about the money. I think she thought she would find a family heirloom, something her grandmother promised her and her father stole."

"Bet the money wouldn't hurt either."

I'm not going to try to explain Ruby Jane to a cynic.

"So then you got involved in the hunt after Miss Whittaker went back east. First down to San Fran, then to Ohio, finally up here."

"It got complicated."

"Evidently." The DA is quiet while he studies my face. I've washed up a bit, but I've barely slept in over a day. I've been beat up and shot. I'm sure I look a mess.

"Your lieutenant thinks Perry may have had a hand in a death in Portland. What can you tell me about that?"

"Ruby Jane's father. He showed up a few weeks ago after a twenty-year absence. He was still there when she left for Ohio."

"And he died of complications from diabetes."

"I'm not involved in law enforcement anymore. Susan will have more for you if you need it."

"But you're sure it's Bella's husband, Miss Whittaker's father?"

"Ruby Jane confirms it. She spoke to him."

"I wonder why Perry didn't go to him if he was supposed to have the money."

"May not have known who he was. He was going by the name Chase Fairweather."

He looks at me sharply. "Chase Fairweather?"

"You know him?"

His face is pensive. "Chase Fairweather has been kicking around the islands for the last few years. Never quite a vagrant, never quite making it either. He did odd jobs for people. I know he worked for Bella from time to time, back when she had more animals. Lived in the shack at the back of her property. We've had him before the court a few times. Public intoxication and disorderly conduct. Never anything serious."

"Bella had to know who he was."

"You would think, but then Bella was notoriously flaky and a heavy drinker." He shakes his head slowly. "I guess Perry connected with him in Portland somehow."

I could mention Biddy Denlinger was too blunt an instrument to pull off anything so subtle as sugar pills. But that would only raise questions of motive and opportunity, deflect attention from the real monster here. The day may come when Ruby Jane and I discuss Chase Fairweather's final hours, but that conversation will occur well out of earshot of prosecutors with dogmatic notions of law and order. As for Robert Earl Perry, well, some people are just wrong, and he was one of them.

"Just as well he's dead."

The attorney looks at me. "That how you see it?"

I think about Pete and Jimmie, nearly me. Nearly Ruby Jane. "The fucker would have racked up premier class frequent flyer miles traveling to all his trials. To hell with that. Let him rot."

"He will be doing that."

"Why Biddy Denlinger?"

"Taya says he thought it was funny—and a way to get noticed. Neither of them knew the real Biddy was dead."

He lets me return to Ruby Jane. There's more. Questions, questions. A deputy shows up with my cell phone, recovered when Taya was arrested. I call Susan, but there isn't much to say. She's pleased Ruby Jane is safe, which is all I care about myself. The district attorney wants to keep us another night, but I convince him we will make ourselves available as needed. We need to go home. Taya figures to plead out, so there won't be a trial. If I can arrange a deposition for the grand jury, San Juan County may not need us again.

We make the last ferry, 10:30 from Friday Harbor, and land in Anacortes just before midnight. I offer to find a motel, but Ruby Jane wants to keep going. On the way, she calls Marcy to let her know we're returning in Marcy's car—I'll fly back in a few days to fetch the Toyota.

Marcy is at the carts, her voice so loud I can hear her side of the conversation. She's damn glad to hear RJ is coming home.

"I'll need another day or two before I can get back on my feet."

"Just so long as I know you're back, honey, I'll be fine. But I want a week off."

"You can have two. Paid. And a raise. I owe you that much."

"Shut up, beotch."

Ruby Jane dozes. When she's awake, she rests one hand on my leg and gazes out the window. There's nothing to see except headlights and taillights and interstate chaff. I-5 between Seattle and Portland is about as boring a stretch of road as I've driven, but I have no problem staying awake. I'm going home with Ruby Jane.

Past Olympia, when the lights of the city are behind us and the night closes in, I hear her crying softly.

"Sweetie?" I squeeze her hand where it rests on my leg and she draws a breath. Then she starts talking.

"A few years after Biddy died, I ran into his father. I was working at a place in Cincinnati called the Highland Coffee House. I was just a barista in those days, barely holding my shit together. I'd never told him about the baby. I know that's not fair, but at the time, I could hardly admit it to myself. When Biddy died, it was like everything else. Something to put in a box and pretend never happened. Huck and I talked for a while. It was nice to see him, but awkward too. He tried to get me to take him home, back to my crap apartment in Walnut Hills." She shakes her head sadly. "I knew he couldn't take me to his place. He was already married to Clarice by then."

"What did you do?"

"I kissed him on the cheek and told him to go home to his wife. But something woke up in me that night. All these people who'd had such a profound affect on my life had moved on. Jimmie was in San Francisco, Bella was on that island. Huck and Clarice were making their own babies. I quit my job and moved in with Mrs. Parmelee. I went to Sinclair Community College for two years, then transferred to Wright State. After I graduated, I moved out to San Francisco to stay with Jimmie while I looked for work. It was a nightmare living with him. This shadow always hung over us. I should have told him about Dale, but the more time that passed, the more difficult it became. It was always going to be tomorrow. I'd visited Portland—all the west coast cities, but Portland felt the most comfortable—so when he offered the money to start Uncommon Cup, I took it and ran."

She thinks for a moment. "It's possible the money was my Grammy's. Jimmie's guilt money for killing Dale, my guilt money for never telling Jimmie what really happened. I was so angry he left me out there that night."

"But you made a life. You got past it."

"Yes. I did. I made a life. I quit making bad choices." She laughs a little. "Oh, maybe Pete was a bad choice. I don't know. I did love him, and I know he loved me."

"He wasn't a bad choice."

"You're right. I know you're right." She gazes out the car window at the stars. "Poor Pete. He saved us, and we couldn't help him."

"That bastard had already hurt him bad. Saving us might have been the last thing he was able to do."

She cries through Centralia and Longview. I drive. "Everything was going well. The shops, you ..." She shakes her head. "I missed you as soon as you left for the beach. I know it was me who made you go, and I'm glad you did. But I wanted you back immediately."

"Then Dale showed up."

"Yes. Dale showed up." Her voice transmits a shapeless dread, and her hand trembles under mine. She draws a deep breath, and when she lets it out the trembling stops. "He wanted to know what happened to his things that night—not that he came out and asked. He tried to be clever about it, pretending he was happy to see me and playing on my sympathy by complaining about his health." She shakes her head. "I always thought he sold Grammy's ring. It had never occurred to me to look inside those toolboxes." Unspoken is the fact Dale would have been thinking about the money too. As Chase, he must have realized Bella never got the money *or* the ring. And perhaps on some level she *did* recognize the long lost Dale—if only unconsciously—and saw the wreck he'd become, realized he never had the money either.

Not like we can ask either one of them now.

"So you went back to Farmersville to find the ring."

"I thought it would be a there-and-back trip. Drive out, visit Mrs. Parmelee, spend a few days digging in the woods. I didn't know that house had been built, didn't know no one would be home."

"The ring wasn't there."

"No. That's when I knew Bella must have somehow gotten it. Maybe it's in her house, or maybe she sold it twenty years ago." Her tears return. I have a feeling there will need to be a lot of tears. "That fucker had no right to do this to us." I don't know if she's referring to Dale Whittaker or Robert Earl Perry, but either way, she's right.

We pull onto my street as the first limb of sunlight peeks over the shoulder of Mount Hood. Ruby Jane doesn't want to go home yet. She wants to rest first, get her bearings. And I want to keep her with me. I park, and lead her into the house. We almost trip over three more days worth of mail. I collect it all and add it to the stack Susan created on the coffee table. Ruby Jane goes back to the bathroom and closes the door. I hear the shower. While I wait, I get a tall glass of water and a short one of Macallan, then sit on the couch. Most of the mail is bills, the rest bullshit. But one padded envelope gets my attention. Hand-addressed to only "Kadash," with no return address. A San Francisco postmark. I pull the zipper tab opening, allow a small, old-fashioned skeleton key and a half sheet of note paper to fall into my hand.

> *Kadash,*
> > *Roo will know what to do with this.*
> > > > —*James*

I have the note in one hand, the key in the other, when Ruby Jane joins me on the couch. She's wearing my bathrobe, and has wrapped her hair in a towel. She smells like Irish Spring and apples. Somehow, Ruby Jane always manages to smell of apples. She drapes an arm across my back, lowers her head gently onto my left shoulder.

"Does this hurt?"

It does, a little. "Not a bit."

She takes the note and studies it. Lets out a long, slow breath. "Oh, Jimmie."

"Do you know what it goes to?"

"I think so."

"Are we going back to Ohio?"

"You don't have to come."

"I want to."

"I'm glad." Outside, I can hear a wren claiming my front yard as his own. Another retorts from further away. The chattering voices, for all their challenge and response, bring a calm to me. Ruby

Jane lets out a long sigh and settles more firmly against my arm. My shoulder aches, but I wouldn't trade the sensation for anything. "Skin, I should have let you come with me from the beginning."

"Let's not worry about that. I'm with you now."

"Yes." Another sigh, contented and soft. "Yes, you are."

Notes and Acknowledgments

COUNTY LINE had many sources of inspiration, but I'd like to draw attention to one in particular. In May 2010 central Tennessee, including Nashville, experienced a flood of disastrous proportions. Homes and businesses were destroyed and many lost their lives. Damages reached $1.5 billion. In response to this disaster, three Nashville writers—Myra McEntire, Amanda Morgan, and Victoria Schwab—organized a benefit called *Do the Write Thing for Nashville*. They invited writers, editors, publishers, and literary agents to donate items and services for auction, with the proceeds of the sales going to Middle Tennessee flood relief. I had the privilege of offering a set of my books and naming rights to a character in *County Line*, then a work-in-progress. The response was both thrilling and humbling. The winner of my package, K.D. James, chose to honor the city of Nashville with the character she named. Hence, Chief Nash was born.

Myra, Amanda, and Victoria are amazing, inspirational women. You can learn more about *Do the Write Thing for Nashville* at:

http://dothewritethingfornashville.blogspot.com, and from there, you can find your way to their own web sites where you will learn they are amazing writers as well.

Many locations in this story are real. I attended Valley View High School in the late 70s and relied on both my memories and on family photos from the time in my descriptions of the school. I lived on Preble County Line Road not far from certain events in Ruby Jane's life.

Though I have many memories of the Farmersville/Germantown area—I ate pizza at both the Village Inn in Farmersville and the Pizza Palace in Germantown, and ran the bleachers at the stadium—those thirty-years-past recollections could take me only so far. Alas, a visit in person to re-acquaint myself with my former haunts turned out to be impractical. So I did the next best thing. I asked for help.

I owe thanks to Chief Jon Schade of the Jackson Township Police, who chatted with me both by phone and email. Chief Schade offered helpful details about law enforcement in the area. In 1979, I spent about an hour in the Farmersville police station waiting for my mom to pick me up after being caught in the act of trying the steal a Chicken Bristle Road sign. I didn't pay much attention to my surroundings, since I was too worried about what my step dad would do when he found out his screwdriver and wrench had been confiscated. As it happened, a friend's father—and teacher at Valley View—picked me up instead, the tools were returned, and no one else had to find out about this particular act of teen shenanigans. Since my memory of the police station is fleeting, the descriptions in these pages came from imagination. But hopefully my broader descriptions of Jackson Township and Farmersville law enforcement are a credit to Chief Schade.

I also want to thank Chris Brown, who provided on-site research and many helpful photos of contemporary Farmersville.

These images not only reinforced my memories, but showed how much the town has both changed and—in some ways—remained remarkably familiar. To the extent the Farmersville area in these pages fails to match reality, the blame lies with me. Chalk it up to author's license, author's impertinence or author's error. But wherever I got it right, it's thanks to Chief Schade and Chris.

Thanks go to Dr. Steven Seres, who provided valuable medical information, and to Jeff Auxier, who offered his insight into the game of basketball. If I made medical or basketball-related errors in these pages, they're all on me.

Courtney Summers, amazing author of young adult novels, read and commented on an early draft of Ruby Jane's story. Her books are brilliant, and her insight into the minds of young women was a great help.

Thanks as always go out to Janet Reid for her hard work on my behalf—I raise a shot, nay, a *bottle* of whisky in your honor. Thank you also to Tyrus Books publisher Ben LeRoy and editor Alison Janssen for continuing to believe in me and in the adventures of Skin and Ruby Jane. I remain humbled to be part of the of Tyrus family.

As always, Brett Battles, Rob Browne, Tasha Alexander, and Kelli Stanley—friends and fellow writers—are there to help me stay (relatively) sane. I don't know what I'd do without you.

I thank my good friends and fellow writers Candace Clark, Andy Fort, Corissa Neufeldt, and Theresa Snyder, who read *County Line* in progress and offered invaluable critiques.

And last, but not least, I thank my lovely wife Jill, who may make me sleep in the backyard when I kill off her favorite characters, but who loves me anyway.